THE
OUTLAW
FREDERIC BEAN

ZEBRA BOOKS
KENSINGTON PUBLISHING CORP.

To Giles Tippette, Master Storyteller
for the helping hand

ZEBRA BOOKS

are published by

Kensington Publishing Corp.
475 Park Avenue South
New York, NY 10016

Copyright © 1993 by Frederic Bean

All rights reserved. No part of this book may be reproduced in any form or by any means without the prior written consent of the Publisher, excepting brief quotes used in reviews.

Zebra and the Z logo are trademarks of Kensington Publishing Corp.

If you purchased this book without a cover you should be aware that this book is stolen property. It was reported as "unsold and destroyed" to the Publisher and neither the Author nor the Publisher has received any payment for this "stripped book."

First Printing: May, 1993

Printed in the United States of America

PART ONE

Chapter One

Gunsmoke hung in the still air like a blanket of early morning fog above Franklin, Tennessee. The rattle of muskets made such a din that only the occasional thunder of cannon fire gave it brief pause. Grapeshot had denuded every tree along the line of Confederate retreat, leaving only barren limbs reaching skeletonlike into the gray skies. Confederate General John Bell Hood had ordered wave after wave of his infantrymen toward Union lines, only to have them slaughtered and finally driven back. Hood, having only one leg and a useless left arm, rode back and forth in front of his dispirited men, urging them to fight. The Texan had to be lashed to his saddle every morning to lead the charge.

On the fifth day of bloody fighting, Hood's fierce Texas Brigade was decimated by Union cannon fire and reinforcements from the Grand Army of the Potomac. Outnumbered two to one, Hood's men started to retreat westward in spite of the brave general's pleas that one more charge would break through Union lines. But no one was listening. The earth beneath the Confederates' boots shook with the power of endless artillery barrages. Dead and wounded lay in grisly piles across the battlefield, and on the fifth day the stench of bloated corpses was overpowering. Disfigured men limped, sometimes crawled away from the grapeshot and musket balls. Wounded soldiers issued pleas for help from the places where they had fallen, begging for morphine or assistance to a place of safety. Litter bearers tried to keep up with the monumental chore, carrying wounded behind the Confederate lines, only the lines were constantly changing as the rebel army fell back in the face of Union fury. It was a task beyond comprehension. Wounded numbered in the thousands, and with each murderous volley from the east more men in gray were felled. Confederate ammunition was gone, and Bedford Forrest's reinforcements had not arrived. Defeat was certain now. Retreating soldiers hoped to escape annihilation.

Through the gunsmoke and confusion, came a cavalry squad from the south galloping lathered horses through the woods. General Hood saw them and wheeled his horse, riding out to meet them. The officer leading the squad halted his mount and gave Hood a hurried salute.

"We tried to outflank them, General," he said. He was interrupted by a barrage of cannon fire from the eastern hills. "We can't get around them. They've dug trenches for nearly four miles below Franklin."

Hood shook his head, staring across the battlefield after he heard the report. "They've whipped us, Captain Cross. Whipped us soundly," he said. "I'll give the order to pull back. It would appear the order won't be needed. There's the folly in a fight with undisciplined men, Captain. Look at them run. If I could have turned them back for only one more charge . . ."

"There's too many of them, General," the captain replied as a whistling load of grapeshot splattered through the trees behind them, shredding leaves like snowfall tumbling gently to the ground. "That artillery is chewing us up every time we make a move."

"Fall back," the general said in a tired voice. "We'll save as many lives as we can."

He reined his horse and rode away from Captain Cross with his shoulders rounded, a defeated man.

"Never saw him like that before," a soldier said. "Never thought I'd see it from him."

John Cross whirled around in his saddle. "Take a look out there!" he cried angrily. "There's more dead men in this valley than any man's conscience can tolerate!"

None of the men needed a second look. Since dawn they'd ridden through a maze of decomposing corpses, trying to flank the Union position, always greeted by a hail of Yankee gunfire from the tree-studded hills. John's company lost eleven men before noon. He was tired of counting empty, blood-spattered saddles.

"Let's ride," he said, swinging his sore-footed bay toward the line of retreat. The Confederate supply wagons had no more horseshoes, nor much of anything else. Food was so scarce that men were boiling acorns. The soggy, tasteless mash was keeping them alive.

Thus the forty-seven men remaining in Captain John Cross's company began their retreat from the battle for Franklin, riding starving, frightened horses away from the pounding cannons and rattling musket fire. In his heart, John knew the war couldn't last much longer. Lee was somewhere in Virginia, preparing to make a fight out of the Union advance toward the Confederate capitol in Richmond. Word had come that Sherman's Union army had advanced deep into Georgia, burning everything in its wake. It was only a matter of time before the war was lost. Then John and his men would be going home.

He closed his eyes to the horrible sights as he led his men through what was left of Hood's infantry, and tried to close his ears to the screams of wounded, dying men. Some were mere boys, cradling rifles as they hurried away from the battle. Many were limping, not from bat-

9

tle wounds but as a result of worn boots. Promised replacements never came, nor did the ammunition for their rifles. Hood had asked his army to fight without gunpowder or shoe leather. Or food. The battle to hold Franklin had been doomed right from the start.

They came upon rows of waiting ambulances in a grassy swale. Mules harnessed to the ambulances gnawed tree bark, for like the cavalry's horses they too were on the brink of starvation, eating anything they could find. Litter bearers trotted back and forth from the hospital tents with bandaged victims of the fight as preparations were made to begin the all-out retreat toward Memphis. John had witnessed a hundred scenes like this during four years of fighting, but there was something about the battle to hold Franklin that seemed final, as if there could be no more wars as terrible as this where the price had come so high.

Corporal Billy Cole urged his horse alongside John's. They were boyhood friends from McLennan County in middle Texas and now shared the war experience. Billy looked at his friend's face.

"Damned if we can keep this up much longer," he said. "There ain't gonna be none of us left. They shot us to pieces back in that valley. Tommy Joe said somebody counted six thousand dead wearin' gray."

Hearing someone's estimate of Confederate losses only added to the weight on John's shoulder. "We'll be goin' home before long, Billy," he sighed, watching a dazed infantryman stumble blindly into a tree trunk, then collapse on the ground staring blankly at the leaden sky. The soldier's face caught John's attention, a boy too young to need a razor, golden down growing from his pale, sunken cheeks. The infantryman's cap he wore spilled off his head, revealing a blood-soaked bandage. John halted his bay and swung down beside the boy.

10

"Can you hear me, son?" he asked, touching the soldier's shoulder.

His eyelids batted.

"You've got to get up," John whispered. "Can you walk?"

Blood seeped through the rag bandage around the boy's head.

"The Yanks are coming, son," John persisted. "You can't just lie here. General Hood sounded the retreat."

Glazed eyes stared past John. The boy couldn't hear him.

"Help me, Billy," John said. "I'll put him across my saddle until we find an empty ambulance."

"You're bein' a fool," Billy complained, stepping down to do as he was asked. "You can't help 'em all, Johnny boy. We've got to get the hell out of here afore them bluebellies come, or we'll wind up on the end of a bayonet ourselves."

Lifting gently, they draped the dazed boy over John's cavalry saddle, his arms dangling lifelessly below his head. John took the bay's reins and started forward again, moving down the line of ambulance wagons. Men were crowded inside every wagon, often lying atop each other, unconscious. Ashen-faced litter bearers hurried back toward the front lines carrying bloody canvas slings. Roaring artillery fire drowned out their voices when they spoke to each other about the dangers of making a return. Now and then a speeding cluster of grapeshot pattered into the tree limbs above the ambulances, then spent shot would fall across the tops of the wagons like lead rain, startling the mules. John moved past one wagon, then the next, searching for a spot to place the boy. But there were no vacant places inside and thus he hurried onward.

They passed groups of soldiers huddled beside tree trunks, some resting on their haunches, others leaning on empty rifles with their faces turned toward the battle sounds. Unaccountably, these men were no longer retreating.

"Fall back!" John shouted to one group, then another. "The order has been given! Fall back and form ranks!"

Yet none of the men seemed to hear him, as if some grim fascination with the battle held them to the spot to watch and listen, ignoring John's order. Many wore the same dazed expression he saw on the boy's face, and John supposed it was the shock of what they had seen on the battlefield this morning, and the four mornings before this final day of certain defeat.

All around them, as John led his men west, the trees seemed to be alive with moving bodies. Infantrymen staggered and stumbled through the forest, some clutching gaping wounds that left a trail of blood across the forest floor. November's colorful leaves lay like a carpet across the wooded hillsides where winter winds had driven them from the branches. And now retreating men slogged through the fallen leaves, their feet making a whispering noise that seemed curiously out of place against the background of booming cannons and crackling rifles. Amidst this odd cacophony came intermittent cries from the wounded who could go no farther without assistance. The sights and sounds became too much for John Cross on this particular day, though he'd seen similar carnage at Antietam and Bull Run and Manassas and dozens more. Now the casualties were almost exclusively Confederate ... six thousand of them, someone said. Suddenly the burdens of war, the bloated dead, the mangled bodies, made something recoil inside him. He wanted to get on his horse and run from what lay behind him, run all the way to Texas without ever looking back or firing another shot. He'd had enough of killing and watching other men die, had enough of following senseless orders and forced marches to find a spot where he would be ordered to kill again. He had enough blood on his hands to last the rest of his lifetime. For John Marshall Cross, the war was over on the thirtieth day of November, 1864.

Crossing a wooded hilltop, they encountered a line of supply wagons. The wagons were as empty as the promises Jefferson Davis made in the summer that new boots and uniforms and ample foodstuffs were on the way to the armies of Virginia and Texas. General Hood had read the dispatch aloud when it came in July, riding up and down his moving columns to the accompaniment of rousing cheers. Men who had marched barefooted for almost a year now cheered the good news from Richmond, that boots and clothing were on the way. The promise had been as false as their hopes for victory in the summer of 1864. McClellan and his Grand Army of the Potomac were already advancing toward the Confederate capitol with a force of one hundred thousand men.

John led the bay down the slope to the first supply wagon, where a white-faced quartermaster paced back and forth awaiting orders for his supply train.

"What the hell's happening back there?" the soldier asked. "How come everybody's runnin' the other way?"

John went to the tailgate of the wagon and let it down. "The order to retreat has been given, Sergeant," he said. "I'm placing this injured boy in your wagon. See to it that he gets to a doctor. We're pulling back, toward Nashville. Then I reckon we'll start for Memphis. Order your drivers to head west until they find the column. Now help me move this boy."

The sergeant aided John with the unconscious soldier to the back of the wagon. "Gen'l Hood ain't never retreated in his life," he said gravely, glancing over his shoulder toward the battle sounds. "Must've been one hell of a fight if Gen'l John Hood gave such an order.

13

Sweet Jesus! I never saw so many men runnin' the wrong way."

When the boy was properly fixed atop a blanket, John mounted his horse. "Make damn sure he gets to a doctor," John warned. "If I had to take a guess, I doubt that kid is more'n fifteen."

Before John reined away from the supply train, he noticed a subtle change in the noise coming from the east. Frowning, he puzzled over the difference, trying to identify the new sound.

"Mercy!" Billy whispered hoarsely. "It's them bluebellies yelling a battle cry. They're charging our lines now, Cap'n. I say we get our asses out of here quick as we can."

Tommy Joe Booker trotted his horse up beside John and Billy. Tommy Joe stood in his stirrups, facing east, and now the color had drained from his cheeks. "Let's go, Cap'n," he said. "I heard them Yank bastards yell like that once before. Means they're comin' for us hard as they can run."

John turned the bay west, noticing a knot in the pit of his stomach. "Move out!" he cried, waving a gloved hand over his shoulder. Forty-seven men in tattered Confederate cavalry tunics urged their horses to a trot behind him.

A moment later he thought about the boy he was leaving behind in the supply wagon, wondering if he had sentenced the young soldier to a certain death without medical attention. Then he took a deep breath and tried to put the boy out of his mind. Billy Cole was right. He couldn't save them all.

A mile deeper into the western woods they encountered a road where Hood's army had begun to assemble. Uneven lines of foot soldiers waited anxiously for the order to march. Remnants of other cavalry units formed between the infantry brigades. John counted eight men of the Seventh Cavalry from Texas, all that remained of the men from Fannin County. The eight survivors sat their horses with a look of utter despair, hardly seeming to notice when John led his men past them. A lieutenant had his eyes closed, enduring the pain of a severed right arm. The bloody bandage around the stump dribbled blood down his pants leg into his boot.

John found General Hood at the front of the column. Hood's eyes were glazed over, as if his thoughts were somewhere else.

"Awaiting orders, General," he said, snapping off a salute that went unnoticed.

"Scout the road to Nashville, Captain," he said in a faraway voice. "Lead us through. A Union force under Pap Thomas is said to be north of us, headed for Nashville. Keep a sharp eye out. If we can make Nashville ahead of him . . ."

John saluted again, needlessly. Hood's attention was elsewhere, perhaps back to the battlefield at Franklin where his reckless charges cost him a fourth of his army.

John heeled his crippled bay to a gallop down the Nashville road, riding toward a lowering sun at the front of less than fifty battle-weary soldiers. Among them, twenty-four had no gunpowder for their weapons. All were without rations, nor had they eaten for two days of fierce fighting. Captain Cross sensed that he was leading his men toward certain destruction, yet he led them as he always had, according to his orders.

At dusk he allowed the men to forage for badly needed food. Tommy Joe Booker begged seven chickens from a sympathetic farm wife. They were quickly boiled to make a meager soup. A private confessed to stealing three sacks of flour at gunpoint from a Methodist minister, though his gun would not have fired. He had no gunpowder, a fact that brought weak smiles to the faces of the starving men who ate the pan-fried bread doused in chicken fat along with their soup.

After just four hours of rest John ordered his men back in their saddles. Arriving in Nashville ahead of Union forces were his orders. He would follow them to the letter if he could.

Chapter Two

An icy rain had fallen on Nashville for two days, turning dirt roads into rivers of mud. By the fourth day of December most of Hood's army, now barely eighteen thousand strong, arrived in Nashville numbed by a cold march through the Tennessee hills. Most were starving. Hundreds of wounded were taken to a makeshift army hospital inside an abandoned cotton warehouse. Thousands of men roamed the city streets looting stores for food and warm clothing. Officers were ordered to restore discipline. Fortifications were needed to halt the advance of a huge Union force under General Pap Thomas. Most Confederate foot soldiers were too busy foraging for food to obey orders. Shivering men huddled around smoldering campfires trying to stay warm. Bootless men wrapped their feet in rags. Men without coats slogged about in the mud wrapped in thin blankets taken from the citizenry. Chaos prevailed throughout the shallow valley where Nashville sat, now squarely in the path of a Union army slowed down by more than a mile of heavy artillery. Captain Cross had been the one to bring General Hood the grim news, that Union artillery was a day away from Nashville, better than a mile of it. And behind it marched a swarm of blue-clad infantry that was certain to overrun the

17

poorly fortified Confederate positions in a matter of hours.

"An army fights on discipline, Captain," the general said as he hobbled back and forth on crude wooden crutches. His empty pants leg was pinned to his waist. Tears brimmed in his eyes and fell down his cheeks into his beard. John Hood wasn't the same man he was before his humbling defeat at Franklin. Like a man possessed by demons, he swept back and forth across his tent, struggling to remain both upright and mobile in spite of debilitating injuries, weeping bitterly. "Never before have I seen a Confederate army leave the battlefield in utter disarray. There's no discipline in them, Captain Cross. When Thomas arrives we'll hand him the key to the city."

"The men are hungry, sir," John replied. "Half of them are barefooted. All of them are freezing in this weather."

Hood stopped in the middle of his tent, staring coldly into John's eyes. "It's discipline they lack, Captain. Fighting men endure hardship without complaint."

John allowed an appropriate pause. The general did not want more bad news. "There's no gunpowder. No shot. The army we saw approaching Nashville is too large, sir. But we'll fight to the last man. Colonel Marsh is holding a regiment behind breastworks blocking the road. I've assembled my men and what's left of the Seventh. We'll try to flank them from the west. I've requested four crates of percussion caps from the quartermaster and three hundred pounds of lead. There aren't any shells for the Sharps carbines. All the .52 caliber ammunition was lost at Franklin when that supply wagon exploded."

The general let out a ragged breath. His shoulders seemed to droop in spite of the crutches. "Do the best you can," he sighed. Fresh tears rolled off his face to the

18

tent floor. "Try the hospital, Captain. Perhaps you'll find some men who are able to sit a horse. Mount every able-bodied man you can find and try to flank that bastard Thomas. Pap's a wily old fox. He'll be expecting you on his flanks."

John saluted smartly and wheeled out of the tent. Cold rain pattered down on his hat brim as he swung aboard the bay. Billy looked at him oddly when they prepared to leave the command tent.

"What the hell happened in there?" he asked. "You was gone a long time, Johnny."

"I told him exactly what we saw on the north road," John replied, buttoning his tattered coat about him. "Told him about the artillery. Everything. He wasn't happy to hear it. I think the fight at Franklin weighs heavy on his mind."

"It damn well oughta," Billy remarked, reining his horse away from the tent. "He damn near got all of us killed, orderin' them fool charges straight at Yank artillery."

They heeled their horses down a deeply rutted mud lane toward the field hospital. Groups of sullen-faced men watched them ride past, men crowded around smoky fires to keep warm. Sucking mud pulled at the horses' hooves, making a sound that drowned out muttered complaints from infantrymen when John and Billy rode abreast of their fires.

"Where are we headed?" Billy asked, puzzled by the direction.

"The hospital," John answered tiredly. "General Hood said to mount every able-bodied man we can find."

"Jesus," Billy whispered. "He wants us to fight that Union army with a handful of cripples. Next, he'll be tellin' us to arm the slaves and the women. I won't fight beside no darkies, Johnny. Not even if you give the order, I won't."

They dismounted in front of the old warehouse. John was dreading what they would find inside. Before he opened the door he caught the scent of chloroform, then he heard the pain-ridden cries and softer sobbing of wounded men. Steeling himself, he opened the door and clamped his teeth tightly together, knowing full well what sights awaited him.

Row upon row of blanket-covered bodies stretched across the warehouse floor. Harried doctors and nurses ministered to the wounded, rushing here and there with bedsheet bandages and pails of steaming water. At the back, beneath a cluster of lanterns, a table held a screaming soldier while a bone saw was at work. The unmistakable odor of gangrene hung heavy above the blanketed forms.

John halted a few feet from the doorway, certain that he would suffocate from the stench of decaying tissue. "I can't do it," he said softly, turning on his heel. "I can't take a man from this room and order him to sit a saddle. Damn those orders from General Hood! Damn them to hell, but I won't do it."

They abruptly left the hospital. On the steps John took a deep breath of clean air. "I've had enough of this war, Billy," he said. There was a trembling weakness in his knees. "I can't face another wounded man under my command, or even ask a soldier to risk his life for a lost cause. I've counted men's bodies until I'm sick of it. I'm done with this fight. Hood wants us to try to flank that Union column tomorrow, but I won't do it. I'd be leading my men to certain death."

He felt Billy's hand on his shoulder. "Let's go home then, Johnny boy. There's hundreds of men deserting this army every day. We'll have plenty of company on the ride back to Texas."

John sighed, rocking back on his bootheels with his thumbs hooked in his gunbelt, gazing across the rooftops of Nashville. Rain pelted his hat brim until a tiny spout of water ran in front of his eyes. "All this time I never disobeyed an order," he said quietly. "When the general told me to fight, I did. But now there ain't no sense to it, Billy. These men are hungry and cold. Most of 'em just want to head home like you and me. There ain't no fight left in this army. If we fight, most of them are gonna die tomorrow morning. I reckon you could say I found my conscience just now. Always had one, I suppose, but after what happened there at Franklin I keep hearin' this little voice inside my head that says it's time to go home. I've seen all the dyin' I ever care to see. Back there in that hospital, that little voice spoke real plain that I was finished with this war."

Billy stared thoughtfully at a puddle where raindrops made tiny circles on the surface. "You an' me never owned no slaves anyway, Johnny. No sense fightin' over somethin' that a man's too poor to own in the first place. Most I ever owned was a team of mules and a breaking plow. Forty acres of the sorriest land in the Brazos River bottom and a shack with two rooms. One old barn and a broke-down cotton wagon. Occurred to me lots of times that we was fightin' a rich man's war. If I'd owned a slave he woulda starved to death back in '59, when it didn't rain."

"Some claim we're fightin' over states' rights," John argued with little conviction. "Never was rightly sure what states' rights is. I went off to war like everybody else did, because folks claimed we had to, to keep what was ours. Whatever there is to states' rights, it wasn't worth six thousand dead boys at Franklin. Word is that Sherman's already burned down half of Georgia, and McClellan is headed into Richmond against General

Lee. It's just a matter of time now. Any fool can see this rebel army is whipped."

"What about the men?" Billy asked softly. "What'll you tell them afore we go?"

John shrugged, glancing up at the sky briefly. A cold wind had started from the north as they stood on the steps, sweeping sheets of wind-driven rain across the road. "I'll tell them this war is lost, which it damn sure is in my opinion. I'll tell them to head for home, same as we're about to do."

"When word gets to Gen'l Hood he'll charge us all with desertion," Billy remarked.

John shook his head. "He'll be too busy after tomorrow to worry about us. This army can't stop Thomas when he crosses that north ridge. If I'm any shakes as a guesser, I doubt those Yanks will even slow down when they take Nashville."

Billy nodded once. Behind them, a man screamed inside the hospital. Billy shuddered and said, "Let's go."

They mounted their water-soaked saddles and reined away from the steps. Bits of ice stung John's cheeks as they rode up a muddy lane toward the livery where John's men stabled their horses and slept on mounds of hay to stay out of the rain. Sleet rattled on rooftops, and on their hats as the storm worsened. The ice would only add to the misery of eighteen thousand Confederates waiting for the Union assault on Nashville to begin.

At the stable John assembled his men. When the order was given there was concern and fear on most of their faces. By the light from a single lantern hung from a rafter of the barn, John walked down the uneven row of troopers, preparing what he would say to them. Most of them had been with the company since the beginning of the war, like Tommy Joe Booker and perhaps two dozen more. John viewed them almost as kinsmen, and when eleven of their number were lost at Franklin it left a scar across his soul.

"I'm disbanding the company," he began, halting in front of a tough old fighter from Buffalo Gap named Wild Henry Roberts. Wild Henry would be the first to complain if he saw any reason to stay and fight. "I'm telling you to disobey orders. Our orders are to fight tomorrow morning. Straight from General Hood's mouth, he ordered me to lead you against the Union flank. But I won't do it. I'm resigning from this army and I'm going back to Texas. I won't lead you in another charge against Union soldiers. Most of you are out of ammunition. Some of you ain't got decent coats or boots and hardly a one of us isn't riding a sore-footed horse. This war is lost. I don't expect the Confederacy to win another battle and I damn sure won't ask you to risk your lives for a lost cause. Some of you have families back home. Ride back to your womenfolk and kids and forget about this war. It's over, and I'm headed home."

He could see the surprise and disbelief on their faces. Wild Henry shook his head, like he hadn't heard quite right. But Tommy Joe nodded, like he understood, and so did several more.

"I've took orders from you fer three years," Wild Henry grumbled after a minute of silence. "I've cussed you a time or two when your back was turned, but I ain't never accused you of bein' a yellow coward. If you say it's time to quit, then I reckon it is, Cap'n Cross. I'd say we was lucky to get clear of Franklin with our skins."

John's cheeks hardened. "Eleven of us didn't, and I won't have any more of you on my conscience. Load your gear on your horses when you're ready to leave. Best of luck to each one of you, boys. You've been a good outfit . . . some of the toughest men ever to wear Confederate gray. But it's over now. Ride back careful and don't travel together. If an officer stops you, you tell him you're the last of my command and I gave you orders to go back home to raise another company."

One by one they came to shake his hand. Some had tears in their eyes while others mumbled good luck wishes and thanks for the years of friendship.

"I'm goin' back with you," Wild Henry said after he took John's handshake.

"So am I," Tommy Joe added quickly. "It'll be just the four of us, when you count Billy."

John agreed silently. "See if you boys can rustle up enough balls and caps so we'll have loaded pistols," he said. "It's a hell of a long way across Tennessee, and Arkansas is liable to be plumb full of Yankees. Keep your carbines just in case we happen upon some .52 caliber somewhere along the way. Those little Sharps may come in handy if we find ourselves in a tight spot."

Tommy Joe hurried off with Wild Henry to find a supply wagon that might still hold a few handfuls of ammunition. Some of the men carried .36 caliber Navys, though John preferred his Dance .44, in part out of sympathy since it was made in Texas and his loyalty was to Texas things.

Billy watched the last soldier shake John's hand. "It'll be dark soon," he said. "I'll saddle your horse."

In twos and threes the men departed into the downpour, a sad sight in their faded and tattered uniforms atop rawboned horses too long without grain and rest. Sad too was the thought that it figured to be the last time he would see most of them, and he knew he would always wonder about their fate after the war ended. When the last soldier rode out of the barn John lowered his face to the ground, holding back a stream of tears. He hadn't cried since he was a small boy, but just then, alone in the dark livery, he wept silently. When he felt a tear on his cheek he fingered it away quickly, embarrassed by it, weeping for the men who rode away and the men who had fallen under his command. He would never have allowed himself the tears had there been any witnesses.

Moments later he heard Billy coming back to the stable leading their horses through the mud, and he quickly dried his eyes on his coatsleeve. It was time to start back toward Texas, leaving the tears he'd shed where they belonged. In Tennessee.

Chapter Three

Four men huddled inside woolen greatcoats urged their horses through the mud. All night they had ridden a twisting road through mountains and valleys in a driving rain that became swirling snow at dawn. The temperature was dropping. It was the fifth day of December and snow in eastern Tennessee was not unusual. The wind turned bitter cold, bringing frosty breath to the horses' nostrils as they labored up and down each mountain. Thick stands of trees helped to keep out the wind in places. All four men were shivering, tired, and hungry. Their horses had begun to slow, worn down by miles of travel on empty bellies and tender hooves.

John tilted his hat brim to keep the wind off his face. His legs had been numb for hours and now his cheeks had lost all feeling. He touched the tip of his nose with the back of his glove and felt a prickling sensation. They would have to stop soon to rest the horses and build a fire to prevent frostbite. Having something to eat would help matters. Hunting game with a cap and ball pistol required luck and perfect aim, although they'd seen no game along the way, only the tracks of other deserting soldiers heading west, both infantry and cavalry, and one or two wagons.

"Damn it's cold," Billy complained, rubbing his hands.

Billy's whiskers were loaded with ice. His ears and nose had turned bright red. A thin layer of powdery snow clung to his hat brim and shoulders, and across the rump of his horse.

"Never was so cold and hungry in all my life," Tommy Joe said weakly, slumped over the pommel of his saddle like a man with a pain in his belly. He was shivering.

"Let's stop an' boil some acorns," Wild Henry suggested, frost rolling from his lips. "My stomach's rubbin' against my backbone and I swear I'll freeze if we don't build a fire. I'd boil a pot of goddam grub worms if I could find 'em. My belly ain't near as particular as it used to be."

John tried to wiggle his toes inside his boots. There was no feeling below his knees thus he couldn't judge if the effort was successful. "We need something to eat mighty damn quick," he said. "Trouble is, the deserters ahead of us have picked this road clean. Maybe we'll find a farmhouse. These horses have got to have some grain or they won't carry us much farther."

They rode up a steep grade in silence, listening to the plop of horses' hooves and the whisper of snowfall on tree limbs. On a ridge north of the road, John saw the faint glow of a lantern-lit window through the snow.

"Up yonder," he said. "There's a cabin. Maybe they'll let us warm ourselves at their fire."

They encountered a dim pair of wagon ruts leading up the ridge to the cabin. In the swirling snow it was hard to see the cabin clearly. John led the way up the lane, working his hands to keep them from freezing stiff. All morning he'd been thinking about the soldiers at Nashville, wondering how the men were suffering in the bitter cold. Mud roads would turn to ice. Men with

27

rags around their feet would be experiencing hardship beyond anything they had ever seen, running to new firing positions across frozen mud. "Sure glad we aren't there," he mumbled under his breath. "We're cold, but we're still alive."

A log cabin sat in a clearing in tall oak and pine. A dog began to bark when they rode into the clearing, though John hardly noticed the dog, smelling woodsmoke from the chimney the way he was just then, thinking about the warmth of the flames. The cabin was a two-room affair with a dog-run porch. Before the horses halted in front of the cabin the door opened a crack, spilling golden lamplight across the snowy ground.

Then twin shotgun barrels appeared. John reined down and cupped his hands around his mouth to be heard above the wind sighing through the trees. "Hello the house!" he cried.

"Hello yourself," an angry voice answered. "Turn them goddamn horses around and get clear or I'll blow your heads plumb off'n your necks. Ain't no Confederate deserters welcome at this place. Got no food or comfort for a damn coward who won't fight."

"We're not deserters," John protested. "Goin' back to raise another company. Lost most of my men at Franklin. In case you ain't heard yet, we lost better than six thousand at Franklin. We're cold and hungry. If you call yourself a southern sympathizer you'll let us warm by that fire."

"I say you're a damn liar," the voice answered. "Been nothin' but deserters comin' by my place fer two days, beggin' food, tryin' to steal my chickens and hogs. Git clear of my house! All of you, before I fill your asses with buckshot!"

John saw Wild Henry reach for his pistol. John raised his hand to halt trouble before it started. "Let's go," he said. His teeth had begun to chatter. Reining away from the porch, he tried not to think about the warmth of the fire behind them.

"You shoulda let me kill him," Wild Henry groused. It was Wild Henry's brutal nature to take things he wanted. He had bearlike paws and a similar temperament when it came to men who opposed him.

"No sense gettin' ourselves in more trouble," John replied, guiding his horse through the deepening snow.

Wild Henry ran blunt fingers through his untrimmed beard. "I still say we hadn't oughta run from him," the big man complained. "We're near 'bout froze to death. The old bastard coulda shared his fire."

They swung back on the road. Snowdrifts had begun to pile up where stands of trees turned the wind. Billy's sorrel had trouble keeping up with the other horses, limping on a forefoot when they encountered steeper climbs. John could hear Tommy Joe's teeth chattering above the footfalls of the horses. His own teeth rattled violently when he relaxed his jaw.

Soon the snowfall became a blizzard and they were riding blind. John's bay stumbled when it came to deeper drifts. He could hear the gelding laboring for wind. "Can't go on like this much longer," he told himself, teeth chattering when he spoke.

Half a mile further on, his nose caught the scent of wood smoke on the wind. "There's a fire someplace," he said. "This time, we ain't gonna be so good-natured about being turned away."

The road bent sharply, dropping down into a wooded draw. At the bottom a fire flickered through clouds of billowing snowfall.

"Yonder it is!" Billy cried, urging his horse to a trot. The sorrel went a few yards, then stumbled and went down heavily on its chest, spilling Billy from the saddle into a snowdrift. The gelding scrambled to its feet and

29

shook itself. Billy came to his hands and knees, then he got up and dusted off a layer of snow from the front of his coat. "Horse can't go no farther," he said, taking the sorrel's reins. Leading the animal, Billy followed the other men toward the fire.

Seven men were huddled around a roaring blaze inside a small clearing in the trees beside the road. John glimpsed Confederate uniforms inside the blankets they wrapped themselves in. When the soldiers heard approaching horses some lifted their rifles toward the sounds. Three wore billed infantry caps, while the others had nothing to protect their heads from the storm except the blankets hooding their faces.

"Hold your fire!" John shouted.

Yet the rifles remained poised on John and his men. Unfriendly faces watched them from the fire.

"Keep movin', boys," someone said. "We ain't goin' back, so don't waste your breath on us. Just keep on riding."

John's shoulders slumped. He was too tired and cold to argue with the men even though he was staring into the muzzles of their rifles. "We're headed west," he said, pulling his frozen right leg across the bay's rump to step gingerly to the ground. "None of us will be tryin' to talk you into going anywhere. We're on our way back to Texas. Just need a few minutes at that fire."

A couple of the men exchanged doubtful looks, then one bearded soldier spoke to the others. "Hell, lower them guns. Cold as it is . . ."

John needed no further invitation. He approached the flames on leaden feet and pulled off his gloves. Billy came close to falling as he stumbled toward the circle of warmth. Then Tommy Joe and Wild Henry crowded in beside him.

"Damn that feels good," Wild Henry mumbled. His lips were a deep purple color. Ice hung from his beard.

30

"We're much obliged," Billy said, trembling, rubbing his hands together. "Where are you boys from?"

"Batesville," a soldier said hoarsely. "Our regiment got wiped out at Second Bull Run. Wasn't nothin' left of the First Arkansas Volunteers so Gen'l Lee sent us to Alabama to join up with Hood. Damn mistake was what it was. That Gen'l Hood is crazy as a sackful of loons. Sent us straight at them guns so damn many times there wasn't nothin' but dead bodies on them hills. It'll take 'em a month to bury all those dead, an' the stink is worse'n sin. Got no powder fer these damn muskets anyway, so we figured we'd head fer home. Figured maybe you men was sent after us to take us back. We've done decided we ain't never goin' back, not for nobody. Some'll call us deserters. But hell, a man can't fight no war without gunpowder."

A slender infantryman coughed wetly, shivering inside a damp blue blanket. John examined the soldier's face in the firelight as he spoke. "We're deserters too, I reckon. Hood's army is finished in this war. Men can't fight without food and ammunition. Nashville will fall and that'll be the end of it. A lot of good men will die on account of John Hood's stubborn nature, but it'll be the end of the fight for the Texas Brigades."

The young soldier's frame shook with a spasm of coughing and John recognized the sound. Hundreds of soldiers died in the damp caves above Vicksburg when the coughing sickness entered their lungs.

"That boy's sick," John said needlessly. Hardly a soldier escaped the winter without fits of coughing disease, especially the infantrymen waiting in cold, muddy trenches. At Antietam the coughing echoed from one end of the battlefield to the other at night. When the guns were silent.

"Got no medicine," another said, "nor no mustard to

make a plaster. We stopped to build this fire on account of the kid. Can't stay up with the rest of us like he is."

"You boys got anything to eat?" Wild Henry asked.

All seven shook their heads. "Boiled some acorns yesterday," one man replied. "Can't find no more now, 'cause of the snow."

Warmth and feeling had begun to return to John's limbs. His toes prickled like a thousand bee stings and his ears started to hurt. "We don't have any food ourselves," he said, stamping his feet in the snow.

"We aimed to hunt up a wild turkey or two," a soldier said, his face hidden inside his blanket, "but there ain't a single round of ammunition betwixt us. Doyle tried to beg a layin' hen from an old man down the road, so we could fix the kid some hot soup. Old man ran us off with a shotgun an' told us to freeze for all he cared."

Wild Henry grunted unhappily. "We met the ol' bastard too, maybe an hour ago. If the cap'n had let me I'd have killed the sumbitch for what he done."

The boy coughed again, bending over with pain. The man beside him held his shoulders until the fit of coughing stopped.

Tommy Joe's horse started gnawing bark from a tree trunk behind them. The sound drew the other horses to nearby trees. Soon all four starving animals were chewing oak bark, slobbering fallen bits and pieces onto the snow.

"Damn shame to mistreat an animal like this," Billy remarked sadly.

John shook his head, wondering how things could be much worse than they were now. "Don't appear we have much choice in the matter 'til we find something for them to eat besides trees."

Tommy Joe turned his back to the fire. "A man don't appreciate bein' warm until he's froze stiff. This is mighty cold country we're in and it looks to be gettin' worse. What'll we do, Cap'n? We can't just sit here 'til this storm breaks or we'll die from starvation first."

John turned his face to the west. The road climbing out of the draw was piled high with snowdrifts. "We keep pushing on," he said quietly, with a conviction he did not feel. "Can't be too far to the next town."

Half an hour later they mounted their horses. The weakening boy now lay beside the fire, shaking from head to toe, racked by worsening fits of wet coughing. John was certain the boy would die before morning. "We're obliged for the use of your fire," he said, gathering the bay's reins in one hand. "Good luck to you on the way to Arkansas."

"If we make it," a soldier replied weakly, waving to the departing riders.

John urged the bay up the grade through powdery drifts to the top of the climb, hunkered down inside his coat collar. A blast of wind greeted the men at the crest of the ridge, driving snowflakes into their faces as they moved steadily westward.

The little town was called Bakersville. A dozen log cabins were built around a false-fronted store on the banks of the Tennessee River. A hand-drawn log ferry sat at the end of the road, fastened to a pulley line crossing the muddy water. The river was on the rise after the recent rains and John wondered if the ferryman would take them across the current.

They rode down to the store an hour past dawn, after a night-long ride through snowy mountain passes, climbing steep grades to the next sharp descent aboard horses that were now slowed to a crawl.

"We'll buy something to eat," John said, his words almost indistinguishable from frozen lips. "I've got a couple of dollars in silver."

"Maybe some whiskey too," Wild Henry suggested, sounding like the croak of a bullfrog when he spoke. "I got a gold piece hid in my boot. May have to cut the boot off to get at the money on account of my foot's froze to the sole."

A split-rail corral behind the store held a snow-laden mound of hay where a team of brown mules grazed contentedly. John knew he must bargain for some of the hay for their horses or they'd be walking the rest of the way to Texas.

They dismounted in front of the store, each man eyeing a plume of blue woodsmoke lifting from a stovepipe at the back of the building.

"If that's a potbelly I'm gonna hug it like a grizzly," Billy said, wincing when he put his weight on frozen feet.

They tied off their horses to a hitchrail and climbed the steps to the front door. A rush of wonderfully warm air greeted them when they stepped inside.

An old man clad in a greasy apron looked over his spectacles when they came in, reaching for a shotgun on pegs behind him. Wild Henry was in no mood to face another shotgun and quickly drew his revolver, aiming it in the old man's face.

"Leave ol' Betsy right where she is," he warned, cocking his pistol. "We don't mean you no harm, ol' man, but you damn sure ain't gonna run us off with that scattergun. Folks in this neck of the woods ain't none too friendly, in my experience. But I'll teach the next gent who pulls a gun on me some manners."

"Just being careful," the storekeeper replied. "There've been hundreds of Reb deserters coming through this week. Some have tried to rob me. All are begging for something to eat and I can't feed the whole Rebel army." He put the shotgun back on its pegs.

"We've got a little money," Wild Henry explained,

lowering the pistol to his side. "If I can get this boot off I've got a five-dollar gold piece in it."

"Won't buy much," the storekeeper replied. "Prices are high these days, what with the war and all."

"It'll buy some beans an' whiskey," Wild Henry answered with heat in his voice, jutting out his bearded jaw.

"I've got a little more," John added, pulling off his glove to dig in his pocket for the coins.

Still glowering, Wild Henry sat on a stool to pull off his left boot, resting the Navy Colt in his lap. With some effort he got the boot off and shook a tiny gold piece into his palm. "There," he said with a note of satisfaction. "Now fetch us a jug of corn squeeze and we'll drink it back there by your stove."

The old man took a clay jug from a nearby shelf and pulled the stopper. He took a sniff and gave the jug to Wild Henry. "That's the cheap stuff," he said, taking the gold coin quickly.

John bought a wax-dipped round of cheese and box of soda crackers for a dollar and a dime. The big round of cheese would feed everyone. Billy and Tommy Joe added a handful of coins to the pile on the counter, enough to buy ten forkfuls of hay for the horses and a twist of chewing tobacco. The old man threw in a tin of sardines and welcomed them to benches at the back of the store to eat their meal beside the stove. As John walked toward the back he spied a box on a shelf behind the counter.

"How much is that box of .52 caliber cartridges?" he asked.

The storekeeper shrugged. "What'll you give? Been tryin' to sell it for six months around here. Nobody in these hills owns such a gun. Soldier traded it to me for a sack of sugar."

"I've only got a dollar left," John replied. He and his

men needed the cartridges desperately, to arm their breechloaders for the chance they might strike Union patrols, and for hunting game to fill a cooking pot.

"Done," the old man said, taking down the box of precious ammunition.

John felt better with the cartridges in his pocket. Now they could fight their way home if they had to.

Chapter Four

Candlelight flickered over Elizabeth's beautiful face and he was soon adrift in old memories. It had been thus since the beginning of the war. When he took the tintype from its hiding place at the bottom of his saddle-bags, then stared at it a few moments, his thoughts left the horrors of the battlefield to return home. Most often, he thought of a warm summer evening in July when they both drank too much mulberry wine on the veranda of her father's house. He was dressed in his new uniform. She wore a dress of green velvet that showed too much of her powdered bosom. He now kept the tintype wrapped in a piece of that same green velvet, and when his calloused fingers rubbed the little square of cloth he was quickly reminded of that dress. And of Elizabeth. And of one special summer evening before he went away to war.

A gust of wind howled through cracks in the shed, all but snuffing the candle, distracting him briefly. He glanced at his surroundings. Wild Henry snored in one corner. Billy and Tommy Joe slept on a mound of hay, wrapped tightly in blankets. What was left of the home-brewed whiskey sat beside him. He hoisted the jug and took a swallow, strangely unable to sleep in spite of two nights without rest. The old man had refused to run his ferry across the Tennessee, blaming the wind, granting John and his men the use of the mule shed until morning. And so it was that he found himself staring at Elizabeth's likeness again by the light of a fluttering candle, dreaming of happier days. And perhaps a wonderful homecoming. If he could only get there.

Palming the tintype's brass frame, he examined her face again. On a hundred moonlit nights, sometimes by firelight or in the golden glow of a coal oil lantern, he looked at her likeness and ran his fingers over the green velvet, remembering things. The color of her eyes, a deep emerald green. Golden locks of hair that fell across her milky shoulders, bouncing when she giggled or ran from the porch steps to greet him, smelling of lilac water. The feel of her tiny waist when he held her in his arms. And best of all, the soft press of her lips when she returned his kisses.

And then there was that night in July when her father was away on business. He had opened a bottle of Howard's mulberry wine, and then another. The evening had begun on the porch swing. It had ended beneath the canopy of Elizabeth's four-poster bed after the servants were asleep.

John closed his eyes, momentarily lost in a wonderful recollection of that night, retracing every footstep as he had a hundred times before this. Elizabeth's beautiful body, her soft cries of passion and promised love. In the years since, he kept the memory of that night alive in his mind by reciting every word that was spoken between them. One whispered line always echoed through his thoughts, Elizabeth's promise that she would wait for him until the war was over. "I'll be here for you when you come home, Johnny." He had carried that promise in his heart as dearly as he had the tintype among his belongings, dreaming of the day when he returned.

He opened his eyes to face a darker reality. Elizabeth's letters had stopped coming almost a year ago, the last making vague mention of another man. "Charlie Mongomery is having a hard time of it," her letter said. "His nigras keep running off and there is no one to pick his cotton. Daddy's slaves run off too, when word comes that we're losing this awful war."

John had written back, carefully penning half a dozen letters of reassurance to which no answer came. At first he blamed Elizabeth's silence on the faltering Confederacy. It seemed logical that letters couldn't get through when Hood's army was on the run. Plenty of other soldiers got letters when mail couriers finally found the Texas Brigades. But none came from Elizabeth, and gradually he was forced to face a black truth. Elizabeth wasn't waiting for him any longer.

He folded the cloth around her likeness and put it away to take more swallows of bitter whiskey. Outside the shed the snowstorm raged, but now John wasn't listening to the sounds or aware of the numbing cold. His mind was elsewhere, visiting the green lawns of Howard Lacy's plantation on a breezy summer night in July many years before. His heart was in Texas, embracing a beautiful young girl while his body remained in the snowy hills of middle Tennessee.

Later he slept a dreamless sleep, slumped against the wall of the shed.

A shaft of sunlight upon his face awakened him. He stirred, stretching stiff, cold muscles. The storm ended sometime during the night and now the rising sun shone through the trees on the eastern horizon. He noticed the clay jug near his feet and made a face, remembering his soft recollections of Elizabeth Lacy while he drank whiskey. In the harsh light of day he never thought about her, not since the letters stopped. He told himself that he should have known all along that the daughter of a wealthy cotton farmer would find too many pleasant diversions to wait steadfastly by the hearth for his return. Elizabeth's father would warn her that John Cross was the son of one of the poorest families in the Brazos River bottom, with nothing to offer her if he came back at all. Their romance had been doomed right from the start, for there was too great a difference in their backgrounds ... his desperately poor, hers one of uncommon wealth. Their fleeting love affair had been the result of a dashing gray uniform adorned with captain's bars and the momentum of a time when everyone was caught up in the idea of a noble war to preserve the South. Gallant men rode off on sleek horses to the cheers of an enraptured citizenry. Everyone believed that it was to be a short fight to win a just cause. Elizabeth told him she expected him home in time for Christmas.

Now, four years later, he understood why the letters had stopped coming. Even the most optimistic southerner knew the war would soon be over, handing the Confederacy a crushing defeat. The few men in gray who did return home were dressed in rags, telling stories of hardship and failure. The cheering crowds that bade them farewell were gone, for the dream of sweet victory and a glorious, swift return ended when newspaper headlines spoke the grim truth. The government in Richmond would soon topple. It was only a matter of time. Thus too would lovely Elizabeth abandon the dream they had shared of a joyful reunion to become the wife of Captain John Cross. Circumstance would lead her to make other plans. What woman of wealth wanted a poor husband with holes in the soles of his boots? A man who bore the shame of defeat?

Charlie Montgomery owned slaves. Elizabeth had undoubtedly found more common ground she shared with Charlie Montgomery.

He got up and wiped the loose hay from his coatsleeves, more determined than before to put Elizabeth from his mind forever. If he could. Clinging to her sweet memory had been solace through many lonely nights, but it was time to face harsh truth. Elizabeth wasn't waiting for him anymore.

Wild Henry opened one eye. "It stopped snowing," he said.

"Time for us to get moving," John replied. "Wake the others up. I'll see if I can beg the old storekeeper out of a handful of coffee beans."

His boots crunched through the fallen snow to the back of the store. A plume of smoke lifted from the stovepipe into the clear dawn sky. He knocked softly on the back door and waited, listening to the sound of scuffling feet.

"We're ready to go," John said, "if you'll ferry us across. Here's the forty-cent toll for us and the horses. We'd be mighty grateful for a few coffee beans."

The old man squinted toward the river. "River's mighty high, son, but I reckon we can make it. I've got coffee on the stove. Soon as you're saddled up you can have a cup." He glanced northward. "No more clouds. Storm's over. For a spell."

Warmed by tin cups of weak coffee, they led their horses down to the riverbank, then atop the ancient log ferry. Hand over hand, they pulled themselves across in gloomy silence. The old man had warned that Memphis was a week's hard ride to the west, and that the road was lately criss-crossed by Union patrols.

John halted the bay to stare at the bodies. It was just one more grisly sight to add to his memories of the war. Two Confederate soldiers dangled from an oak limb beside the road, swinging by their necks from hangman's

41

nooses. Pinned to the front of each man's tunic was a crudely written note. "Deserter," each note said, fluttering in a gentle breeze. The words had been scrawled in charcoal on pages of a schoolchild's tablet.

"Damned awful to look at, ain't it?" Billy observed.

"Poor bastards," Wild Henry added softly, gently.

John let out a whispering sigh. "It ain't enough to have Yanks tryin' to kill us," he said. "Now we've started killin' each other. Looks like we'll be dodgin' our own men as well as bluecoats."

The bodies twisted lazily in the wind. He forced himself to look at their faces. Sickened by what he saw, he was silently thankful the men weren't from his company, though he now worried more than ever about the fate of the soldiers he'd sent toward home. His kindness could wind up being a death sentence as certain as the one they had faced in Nashville. His stomach knotted. He and the three men who followed him homeward were risking the same form of execution if they ran across an eastbound Confederate detail.

John looked around to get his bearings, guessing they were a dozen miles or better west of the Tennessee River. Somewhere to the west was a settlement called Sugar Tree and he worried about the safety of riding toward it now. Perhaps fresh companies were being hurried east from Memphis toward Nashville, making the road they traveled too dangerous. Confederate forces had to be avoided because of what was being done to deserting men traveling in the wrong direction.

"I'm a captain," he said aloud, though his voice lacked much conviction. "I'll say we're headed west on orders from General Hood. Nobody'll doubt a captain's word."

He urged the bay forward again, inwardly thankful that he'd been one of the few recruits who was able to read. That simple distinction had been enough to earn him a captain's rank before they left McLennan County to join Hood in Nacogdoches. A man in command was expected to be able to read his orders. John Cross had been the only man in the newly formed company who could read the enlistment paper aloud on signing day.

After the road from Bakersville joined a fork from Murphy's Point, the ruts were heavy with recent tracks through the snow. Wagons and horses and men afoot had traveled the road both east and west, making it impossible to judge which tracks might pose a threat. Until they found the hanged deserters past the fork in the road they had been alone in the empty hills. But now, as the horses plodded west through melting snow they were entering more populated regions. With loaded rifles, their chances were better. Yet John still had an eerie sense that they were heading straight toward trouble.

He allowed himself a moment to think about what awaited him if Lady Luck prevailed to guide him safely home. He knew his father lay dead in a grave behind the barn, the result of a mule's kick in the spring of '62. His sister wrote to say that Hiram lingered many months before he died, how they tended to him faithfully until he finally went away in his sleep. How their mother had cried and grieved over it and didn't seem the same any longer, mostly just sitting in her rocking chair staring off at nothing. Then Mary closed her letter with the news that she had taken a job in town, to help them get by in Hiram's absence, needing the money. Mary had written only once since, to say that their mother was doing poorly and the farm had gone to sunflowers because they sold the mules and the plow, what with no one left to work the land. John had written Mary and his mother many times after that, promising that he would be coming home to work the farm as soon as the war was over. His letters went unanswered, leaving him to wonder what things were like on the eighty acres belonging to the survivors of Hiram Cross. He knew the sunflowers would be high. They always were, even in a dry year. Cotton and corn withered quickly without rain, but not sunflowers. He had been hoeing them since he was five, in good years and bad, and they always grew, no matter what.

It was pure chance that he saw them first, perhaps the goodness of Lady Luck's intentions. Crossing a ridge on the far side of a winding valley rode a column of Union cavalry. John pulled the bay to a sudden halt and pointed. "Yanks!" he cried, reining his horse toward trees beside the road. He had counted better than twenty blue-clad riders in the distance, moving eastward at a steady trot. The road disappeared when it left the ridge and had he not seen the column when he did, they would have ridden headlong into the Union patrol somewhere in the wooded valley.

They drew their pistols and headed deeper into the oak forest, leaving tracks that a blind man could follow across the melting snow.

Chapter Five

They could hear the rattle of curb chains now, and the click of iron horseshoes upon rocks buried in the drifts. John halted his men in a thicket and waited, scanning the hills behind them. If the Union patrol found their tracks leading into the woods, they could expect swift and relentless pursuit. Their horses stood no chance of outdistancing fresher mounts. Thus it would come down to a fight somewhere in the trees. Finding the best possible defensive position might lengthen the odds of their survival. He was wasting precious time.

Seeking higher ground, he swung the bay and hurried up a tree-studded slope. Firing down at the enemy offered many advantages if they could find the right firing position, a lesson Jubal Early taught other Confederate commanders during the fierce fighting up and down the Shiloh valley in '63. Had John Hood only heeded Early's example, the battle to hold Franklin might have had a different result. Hood's frontal assault upon artillery batteries firing down into the valley seemed a senseless maneuver even to the lowliest infantrymen. And it had cost the Confederates dearly.

He heard men shouting behind them. His stomach muscles knotted, sure of what the voices meant. The Yanks found their tracks too easily. Men were being dispatched to follow them, perhaps the entire company. "Damn the luck," he whispered, heeling his horse. No matter where they went, the horses left tracks in the snow. There would be no escape.

They crossed a ridge to a deep pine forest, forcing footsore animals to hold a steady trot. Beyond the pines lay more oaks, barren of leaves in winter, making the men easier prey for pursuing riflemen, away from the cover of leafy limbs. Following a switchback up the side of a mountain, John kept to the pines wherever he could, hiding their progress from the soldiers following their hoofprints.

"Up yonder, Cap'n," Wild Henry said, pointing to a rocky crag in the slope. "We can make 'em pay in blood if they rush that slice in the rock."

Heeling their mounts to an all-out run, they galloped up the slope and rode into the niche single file. Squeezing through, they entered a tiny basin thick with brush.

"Tie the horses!" John cried, swinging down from the bay with his Sharps. Each man had a dozen cartridges for his rifle. It would be a short fight with so little ammunition. "Make every shot count," he said, hurrying back down the narrow passageway. He was gasping for air by the time he reached the entrance.

Soon Tommy Joe and Billy were beside him, peering down the snowy slope.

"There they are," Billy whispered.

A column of blue-clad cavalry trotted along their tracks. They would have to climb two hundred yards of open ground to reach the mouth of the passage. Waiting for the right range, John and his men could pick them off. Until their ammunition ran out.

"Find cover," John said quietly, calculating the distance they would need for the Sharps. "Make damn sure of your target, men. These ain't the best odds we ever had."

46

He heard Wild Henry scrambling up the rockface above them, his boots sending little avalanches of snow into the passageway. Billy knelt behind a rock and spread his precious cartridges on the snow within easy reach. Tommy Joe disappeared to find a firing position higher up, climbing tiny footholds to a ledge sheltered by scrub pines.

John focused his attention on the first riders. Clouds of frosty breath rolled from their horses' muzzles. Without taking his eyes from the Union assault, he fitted a cartridge into the rifle breech and held his breath, sighting down the twenty-one-inch barrel until his aim came to rest on a soldier's chest.

He made note of a surprising fact when he examined the line of soldiers. They weren't expecting trouble . . . their rifles were booted beside their saddles and their sidearms were holstered as they came up the mountain. Men at the front were intent upon the tracks they followed. No one was looking for an ambush at the niche where John and his men were hidden.

Soon the horses were scrambling across open ground, leaving the trees. The soldiers were talking to each other, the sounds of their voices floating from the column above the clatter of armament and horseshoes. One soldier laughed.

A young captain rode at the front of his men, the soldier John meant to kill with his first shot. Bushy blond sideburns adorned the captain's sunburned cheeks. John found himself wishing with all his heart that this battle might have been avoided. Killing the boyish Union captain from ambush was the last thing on earth he wanted to do. Gritting his teeth, he forced himself to remember that he was still at war. If he could only make it home he could lay down his guns and stop fighting. . . .

The first gunshot was fired by Wild Henry, and when the sound echoed from the trees, John flinched. Then

Billy's rifle exploded with a roar that rocked Billy back on his haunches.

A wounded man screamed. Frightened horses whickered, bolting away from the thunder of rifles. Men shouted and cursed, fighting the reins on their terrified mounts. A soldier toppled off the rump of his horse, landing disjointedly in the snow. Tommy Joe's rifle barked from the ledge and still John held his finger on the trigger without firing.

Pistol shots popped from the slope and a lead ball whacked into the rocks above John's head. As if in a daze, John held his fire, watching the scene below across his rifle sights. He saw a bullet strike a soldier's chest, puckering the blue tunic before the man fell. Lunging horses wheeled away from the shots when Wild Henry and Tommy Joe fired again. A soldier dropped his pistol to grab his stomach, slipping sideways out of his saddle.

Billy's Sharps thundered. Three cavalrymen were charging up the mountain, bending low over their horses' necks. Billy's shot struck one of the soldiers in the face . . . there was a garbled yell as the soldier was torn from his saddle, blood spraying from his cheek as he rolled, ball-like, off the rump of his running mount.

Awakened from his trance, John swung his sights to one of the cavalrymen and gently squeezed the trigger. The .52 caliber slammed into his shoulder, rocking him back on his bootheels, and suddenly his ears were ringing with the sound of exploding gunpowder. He blinked, working the breech mechanically to eject the spent casing without taking his eyes from his target. He watched the bullet's impact . . . it happened with a syrupy slowness as if in a dream, and he wondered what had gone wrong with his senses. The soldier was lifted from the back of his horse, his eyes rounding with pain and surprise. For a fleeting moment the man seemed suspended

48

in the air, then he fell heavily on his chest in the snow with a little fountain of blood spouting from a hole in his back.

John thumbed a cartridge into the breech. Tommy Joe's rifle cracked and the last charging rider slumped over his horse's withers. Blood splattered down the sorrel's shoulders as the gelding swerved, toppling the rider from its back.

Men were galloping their mounts down the slope at full speed away from the ambush. Wild Henry fired again and knocked a man down. Billy triggered off a shot, catching a fleeing soldier between his shoulder blades. The man sounded an eerie cry and flew from his saddle. The Union troops rode into the trees before John found another target. He could see soldiers jumping from their saddles to take up firing positions behind tree trunks.

He was still puzzling over his own inaction when the first rifle pounded from the bottom of the slope, the deep sound of a heavy bore gun followed by the whine of speeding lead off the ledge where Tommy Joe was hidden. Then more rifles joined the first in a steady stream of gunfire. Bullets ricocheted off rocks all around them, some whacking dully to a halt against the rockface. It was senseless to answer the Union fire at this range. John's men had enough fighting experience to understand and their guns fell momentarily silent.

There was movement in the snow that caught John's attention, and when he saw the source of it, he was sickened beyond words. A wounded soldier struggled to his hands and knees with a stream of blood pouring from his belly. He tried to rise, limbs trembling with effort, then he collapsed on his face and started to crawl. Blinded by pain, the Yankee crawled toward the enemy position leaving a red smear across the snow behind him. They could hear the soldier sobbing, groaning when his legs pushed him higher up the slope. Bloody hands clawed for purchase as he advanced slowly toward John and Billy.

"Damn," Billy whispered, turning his face away.

"He won't make it all the way," John answered in a hoarse voice that sounded strangely like someone else's.

Gunfire from the trees died down to an occasional shot. Men shouted to each other across the Union line. Loose horses galloped farther down the mountain, trailing their reins. And the wounded Yankee continued his crawl toward John and Billy. His sobbing grew louder as the rifles fell silent, and now John could see his face clearly. Eyes tightly closed with pain, the soldier inched through the snow, groaning. John ground his teeth together and tried to shut out the sound.

"He's still comin'," Billy said, glancing down the mountain. "Poor bastard's headed the wrong direction and don't know it. I hate to shoot him again, Cap'n. He's bleedin' like a stuck hog."

John thought about the war's strange contradictions, watching the wounded man struggle upward. For four years he'd been ordered to kill his own countrymen who happen to live north of something called the Mason-Dixon line. And kill them he did, until he lost count of their number, for no better reason than the different color of their uniforms. When he saw a fallen enemy up close for the first time, it struck him how similar they were to the men in his own outfit. The navy blue tunics and some indefinable thing called states' rights was the only difference, for not a single man in his company owned any slaves. It had been a senseless war and now he understood it. He wanted to escape it, if only he could, without killing another Yankee.

"Cover me," John whispered. "Tell Wild Henry and Tommy Joe to hold their fire."

He was off in a running crouch before Billy could

protest, racing across the snow toward the crawling soldier. He knew it was a foolish thing . . . the man would die from his wound without medical attention, and yet somehow John had been unable to ignore the dying man's cries. Something inside him demanded that he go after this helpless enemy, a move he knew might easily cost him his own life when shots were fired from the Union line.

A rifle popped in the distance and a slug kicked up a puff of snow near his feet. Dodging back and forth to make himself a more difficult target, he ran to the injured Yankee and seized his coat collar.

"Hold your fire!" someone shouted from the trees below, yet one more explosion came, the shot high and wide, and then there was silence.

With all his might John pulled, dragging the soldier behind him. The coppery scent of blood filled his nostrils . . . he could not look back, for he knew the soldier's blood painted the snow behind them. Struggling to take each upward step, John leaned forward and forced his feet to run faster. The wounded man gave a soft cry, bouncing lifelessly in John's grip.

He made the crevice and fell to the ground, exhausted, panting. Billy came over to help with the Yankee, lifting his shoulders to pull him out of the line of fire. John came to his hands and knees to help Billy roll the soldier over on his back. Then he saw the bullet wound and grimaced. The Yankee was gutshot, facing a slow and painful death.

"He ain't gonna make it, Cap'n," Billy said needlessly. "That was a fool thing to do for a dyin' man."

Tommy Joe peered over the ledge. "How come you done that, Cap'n?" he asked, bewildered by John's actions.

"I couldn't leave him there," John explained.

"Couldn't watch him crawl another inch. He was headed straight towards us and didn't know he was aimed the wrong way. I just plain couldn't stand to see him suffer."

Tommy Joe shook his head. "Hell, Cap'n, he's a goddamn Yank and in case you've forgot, we're havin' a war with them."

"He's still a man," John sighed, staring down at the young soldier's face. The Yankee's cheeks were the same color as the snow and his eyes were glazed over. "If that'd been you out there you'd have wanted some help. I don't figure this boy cares what color my uniform is right about now."

Billy nodded silently as he pulled off his coat. "I don't figure he cares about much of anything, Johnny, 'cept maybe having the hurting stop."

Billy covered the soldier with his coat. There were no sounds from the Union line, and they could hear the man take ragged breaths in the silence.

"Fetch Wild Henry's whiskey jug," John ordered. "There's a little bit of it left and I reckon this boy needs it worse'n we do."

Billy got up and walked to the horses. John knelt beside the soldier, wondering why the boy's plight had touched him so deeply that he'd been willing to risk his own life. He had killed Yankees and watched them die for four long years without feeling any real emotion. And now, something about it had changed.

Billy returned with the jug and helped lift the soldier's head. The boy groaned and batted his eyelids.

"Drink some of this," John whispered. "It'll help with the pain."

Pain-glazed eyes tried to focus on John's face. "Thanks . . . for what you did," he croaked. "Why . . . ?"

Billy put the mouth of the jug to the soldier's lips.

The boy swallowed and made a face. "Burns," he said, closing his eyes.

"They're movin' down there," Wild Henry called out from his hiding place in the rocks. "Best we git ready fer another charge."

John placed the boy's head gently on the snow. Then he picked up his rifle and went back to the entrance to get ready for the next Union advance.

He was greeted by an unexpected sight. A lone Yankee rode out of the trees with a white handkerchief tied to a stick, aiming for the Confederate position. "Hold your fire, men," John said carefully, worrying that the flag of truce might be a trick. "We'll let them have their say. We'll listen, but keep an eye on our flanks in case some of them are comin' around."

John walked out in plain sight, cradling his rifle in the crook of his arm. The Union soldier continued up the slope. There was no sign of movement in the trees behind him.

The young blond captain approached the niche. He had somehow escaped the first volley of Confederate fire when the ambush had begun. Ten yards away, the captain halted his horse and lowered his white flag.

"Requesting a word about the prisoner you took, Captain," the Yankee said. His voice was tight when he spoke. "Corporal Spencer is my cousin. I saw you run down and I thought you meant to kill him. That was a brave thing you did. I suppose I'll always wonder why you did it. I could tell by the blood on the snow that his injuries are serious."

John shook his head once. "He's gutshot. I reckon you know what that means. We made him as comfortable as we could. Covered him so he'll stay warm and gave him a little whiskey."

He saw tears in the young captain's eyes. "I'd like to take him back with us, Captain, so he'll have a proper burial. My family and I would appreciate any consideration." Then the captain glanced around him, perhaps to see who was listening. "I know we're supposed to be fighting each other. But I saw what you did and I took a chance that you might understand my feelings. You risked your life to pull David to those rocks. It proves you're more than an ordinary soldier."

"How about us?" John asked, aiming a thumb over his shoulder toward his men. "What happens after we give you your cousin?"

The captain rested his hands on the pommel of his saddle and then took a deep breath, lowering his voice when he spoke. "I'll order my men to pull back, Captain. My report will say that we engaged a Confederate force deeply entrenched on a mountainside and our position was indefensible. We've taken eight casualties and three more of my men are wounded. No more shots will be fired, if that's agreeable to you."

John sighed and nodded his head. "It's damn sure agreeable with us," he said.

"We'll pick up our dead when the horses are rounded up," the Yankee captain explained. "I'll order my men to leave their weapons in the trees until the bodies are loaded. And now, if you'll take me to Corporal Spencer as quickly as possible. I'd like to be with him before he . . ."

"I understand," John replied in a quiet voice. "Follow me."

He led the way up the slope to the crevice, where the Yankee captain stepped down from his horse. Billy and Tommy Joe were watching the Union officer with caution on their faces as John took him to the dying boy.

"I'll help you lift him on your horse," John said, taking Billy's coat from the soldier's chest.

The captain shook his head and knelt beside his cousin. Fresh tears streamed down his face. "Can you

54

hear me, David?" he asked softly, choking with emotion. "Everything's going to be okay now. They're letting me take you back with us. I'll get you to a doctor as quickly as I can."

Without waiting for John's help, the captain picked up the wounded soldier and carried him to the horse. The boy groaned when he was placed across the saddle. Then the captain turned around, extending his hand to John. "Thank you, Captain, for your understanding of my situation. And thank you for what you did for David. We'll pick up our dead and be on our way."

They shook hands, and John felt oddly comfortable shaking the hand of an enemy.

John and his men stood in the niche to watch the Union detail lash the bodies of their dead to their horses. Wild Henry stood beside John, and when the Yankee captain waved a lazy salute as his men departed, Wild Henry shook his head from side to side.

"To my way of thinkin', it ain't a good idea to make friends with the men a soldier is supposed to fight," he said. "It's a hell of a lot easier to shoot a man when you don't know what he looks like up close. That bluebelly captain seems like a nice feller. I'd hate like hell to have to kill him."

Chapter Six

On the nineteenth day of December, traveling back roads to avoid both Confederate and Union patrols, they happened upon an overloaded wagon bearing a family fleeing the fall of Nashville. When John heard the account of the battle from a grim-faced storekeeper and his wife, he knew just how right he had been to disband the company and send his men homeward.

"Was the awfulest thing I ever seen," the woman said. Her husband nodded silently. "Soldiers was runnin' every which direction and the noise was somethin' terrible. Those Yankees came swarmin' down on us and took everything. Didn't leave us a thing 'cept these two old mules and what furniture we could put in the wagon."

"Looted my store to the bare walls," the storekeeper added, staring vacantly across the backs of his mules. "They kilt every Reb they could find . . . Even the ones who tried to give themselves up when their guns was empty. Shot 'em down right where they stood. Hands was raised up to surrender and they got kilt the same as them that tried to fight. Never saw such an awful thing in all my born'd days."

John listened to the story with a fist-sized knot in the pit of his stomach. The fate of Hood's army would have

56

been his fate had he stayed to obey his orders. He'd been wrestling with his decision since they left Nashville, battling his conscience over the choice he made to abandon the Confederate cause. It had not been easy. In more bloody battles than he cared to count he had risked his life for the uniform he wore, and a vague sense that what he was fighting for was just and proper.

"What happened to General Hood and the rest of his army?" he asked, fearing the answer.

"Scattered like quail," the woman replied, nodding her head when she gave her answer. "Most of 'em jus' dropped their guns and took off. Wasn't much else they could do."

"There was one outfit," the storekeeper said, remembering out loud, "that put up one hell of a fight. They was trapped in this old house at the edge of town, and when them Yanks came, it was a sight to see. Hardly a dozen rebs inside that house . . . belonged to Widow Murphy, the house did, and them rebs fought off every charge 'til they was out of ammunition. Then they used their guns like clubs. Fought them Yanks 'til there wasn't none of 'em left standing. Bodies all over the place. In the widow's yard there was bodies, and on her porch. We saw it from our front window while we was tryin' to load the wagon. Hell of a fight, it was. Shame it didn't amount to nothing. Too many Yankees. That's what it was. Too many Yankees."

John noticed the woman piercing him with a look.

"You boys deserters?" she asked, slitting her eyes.

"Goin' back home," was all he said, lifting his reins. "You folks keep your eyes open. These woods are crawling with Yanks."

He urged the bay past the wagon, down a lane winding through wooded hills, smarting from the woman's accusation. It was hard truth that they were deserting from Hood's splintered army, a desertion he felt was

57

justified. But when the woman questioned him he was haunted by doubts about the right and the wrong of what he had done. He tried to console himself with visions of the fighting at Nashville which the woman and her husband had described. The battle had gone as he predicted it might, a senseless bloodletting costing the lives of too many Confederates.

Thus he fought his conscience in a moody silence as he led his followers across empty Tennessee hills. The men were tired and hungry, their horses little more than gaunt skeletons barely able to carry the weight of a rider. But they were alive, and headed for Texas, albeit at a snail's pace. He reasoned that they were in better shape than the rest of the survivors of Hood's army after the fall of Nashville, putting distance between themselves and the invading Union troops. Fleeing Confederates would be hunted down by the victorious Yankees until all were killed or captured. Being cold and hungry was far better than being shipped off to a Union prison. Or resting in a shallow grave.

The crack of a gunshot caught him completely by surprise as he dozed fitfully in the saddle. In the same instant he felt a jolt of white-hot pain above his knee. The bay reared and lunged to one side, spooked by the sudden explosion. John was off balance and before he could right himself, the bay jumped again. He felt himself falling and was powerless to stop his fall, his hands clawing empty air where the pommel of his saddle should have been. He was dimly aware that men were shouting to him ... he heard Billy's voice and couldn't understand the words. Suddenly his right shoulder struck the ground, then his head slammed against something hard. Tiny pinpoints of light blurred his vision. He heard another gunshot above the clatter of horses' hooves. Someone called his name and he did not recognize the voice as he struggled to push himself off the ground with his hands.

He sat up, blinking furiously to clear the fog away that now blanketed his surroundings. Flashing lights rendered him momentarily blind.

"Billy!" he cried, reaching for his pistol, fumbling for the weapon with a numbed hand. At the same time he rolled over to scramble to his feet, until the movement of his right leg sent such a wave of pain through him that he fell back to the ground with an involuntary scream caught in his throat.

Nothing in his experience was like the pain flashing through him now, leaving him too weak to lift his head. He fought to remain conscious.

Gunshots thundered above him, from his left and right, a staccato of echoing blasts. Summoning every ounce of strength he had, he raised his head to get his bearings. In spite of the winter cold a clammy sweat came to his skin that sent a chill shuddering down his arms.

"I'll die right here unless I get to some cover," he groaned.

Wincing, he pushed himself up on his elbows, trying desperately to clear his thoughts. Renewed pain shot through his leg and he glimpsed the bloodstain above his knee, spreading from a dark round hole in his pants leg. Then he saw movement down the road from where he lay, galloping horses amidst clouds of blue gunsmoke coming from the trees on both sides of the lane. "An ambush," he whispered. He shivered again, now keenly aware of his dire circumstances. Unless he could somehow escape into the woods he would be killed, or taken prisoner.

He clamped his teeth together and rolled over. Cords of muscle stood out in his neck as he fought blinding pain to gather his good leg underneath him, stifling the cry welling in his chest while trying to remain conscious. Through his pain, he felt shattered bone grinding inside his thigh. His arms shook so badly that he couldn't keep his balance. He fell forward on his face, crying out in pain and frustration. The leg was throbbing now. Waves of nausea threatened to empty his stomach, and he wondered if he might be dying.

"Not here!" he hissed between clenched teeth, pressing his palms to the earth again. "I ain't gonna die here!"

He pushed upward, trembling violently, then he heard voices behind him and noticed that the gunfire had ceased.

"Got one of the reb bastards over there," the voice said. "The rest of them got away. I saw one take a bullet in the arm."

He heard boots crunching toward him. Dulled by the realization that he could not escape, he collapsed on his chest, panting.

"What'll we do with this one, Colonel?" another voice asked. "He's still alive. Looks like he took a ball in his leg."

John's thoughts were swimming toward a black fog when he saw cavalry boots around him. He was too weak to lift his head to see the men who had ambushed him. He knew the men were Yankees by their voices, and he wondered how he could have fallen so easily into their ambush.

"It'll be a pain in the ass to have to care for a wounded man all the way to the river," someone said.

"He's wearing a captain's bars, whoever he is," another observed quietly.

"I vote we shoot the son of a bitch and be done with him."

A soldier laughed. "These Rebels look like common

beggars, if you ask me. Look at his uniform. I've given away better clothing to the poor."

"I say we kill him. Nobody'll ever know the difference."

A silence lingered.

"If we leave him here, he'll probably bleed to death anyway. His horse ran off when the shooting started and we don't have any way to carry him. I damn sure won't carry him across my saddle. I'd bet a month's pay he's got lice all over him, filthy as he is. I'll be scratching lice for a month. I say we kill him. After all, there's a war going on. . . ."

John's addled brain tried to sort through what the soldiers were saying. Were they talking about killing him?

"I'll do it," a deep voice said.

John heard someone cocking a gun. He knew his life depended on taking some sort of action . . . he opened his mouth to speak and pushed his hands against the ground to rise.

He felt a dull thud against his back and heard a muffled explosion. It was as if someone cracked his ribs with a hammer, although strangely, there was no pain.

He was drifting off, surrounded by hazy darkness when he heard someone speak.

"Let's get after the rest of those rebs. Bring the horses."

He was in a swirling gray mist. And he was cold. A voice spoke, yet the words made no sense. Was it a woman's voice?

He became aware of a damp sensation on his skin. Then a dull pain he couldn't identify. The voice, a woman's voice, came from far away, somewhere deep in the foggy mist. "Who's there?" he heard himself say.

No one answered. And suddenly, he was afraid.

Afraid of the fog, and afraid of being alone. He wondered where he was, where the strange fog had come from, and why he was alone in it now.

"Help me!" he cried. The sound of his voice was hollow.

Very slowly, he slipped back toward sleep, puzzled by the foggy place where he had awakened. "Where am I?" he wondered. Then slumber overtook him and he let go of his fear of the fog.

Again, he saw a faint gray light around him. A hazy shape appeared before his eyes. Was it a face? Then he heard a woman's voice, and the sound was much closer than before.

"Who are you?" he asked. He couldn't make out the face above him, yet he knew it was a face.

"Is that you, Elizabeth? How did you find me?"

He felt something touch his lips, then there was liquid in his mouth and he swallowed it. And still his vision would not clear so he might see the woman's face. He wondered why she would not answer him.

More liquid entered his mouth and it was wonderfully warm, driving off the cold chill from the mist around him. He swallowed again and tried to thank the woman. His words sounded garbled and he tried to thank her a second time.

"Go to sleep," someone whispered. Was it the woman? And was the woman his beloved Elizabeth? How had she found him in Tennessee? He remembered only bits and pieces of things . . . riding his horse through Tennessee, bound for Texas with three men from his company. Then the gunshots. And then nothing, only the blanket of fog and no memory of how he got there. Where was this foggy place? He was still wondering as he went to sleep.

*　*　*

A cool rag passed over his face . . . he was sure of it. He opened his eyes, and saw a woman. The woman smiled, revealing perfect white teeth. Soft brown hair framed her lovely, oval face. A scattering of light freckles appeared on her cheeks and beside her nose.

"Where am I?" he asked. His voice was hoarse and dry.

"You're at the Parsons' place," she replied gently, wiping his forehead with the cloth again. "I'm Sallie Mae. You've been a mighty sick soldier, mister. For a spell we didn't think you'd pull through."

He let his eyes roam around the room. He was lying on a bed in a room made from mud-chinked logs. Animal skins decorated the walls. Deer antlers also adorned some of the logs with rusted animal traps dangling from them. "I got shot in the leg," he said, when his examination of his surroundings was finished. "I remember that much. . . ."

The girl's face darkened. "Your leg's broke. My paw made you some splints, but it weren't your leg that nearly killed you. Somebody shot you in the back, and the ball's stuck somewhere inside. Paw took the mule over to Waynesboro to fetch the doctor. Paw says that ball has to come out or you'll die sure as snuff makes spit. Glad to see you're feelin' better, mister. Mind if I know'd your name?"

"John. John Cross. How long have I been here?"

Before she answered he heard rain against a windowpane near his bed.

"You was out cold for better'n five days. Yesterday you woke up once. You was mumblin' somethin' about Elizabeth. Is she your wife?"

He shook his head. A dull throbbing had begun in his

right leg and in his chest. "I aimed to marry her when I got back from the war."

"Too bad," the girl replied, wearing a playful smile. "You're a handsome man, Mr. John Cross. I shaved your whiskers off while you was asleep, so I could see what you looked like. If you wasn't already planning on marrying somebody else . . ."

He returned her smile weakly. "You're a pretty girl, Sallie Mae. I reckon I owe you my life. How did you find me?"

"Paw found you on the Waynesboro road. No tellin' how long you'd been layin' there. Paw said you'd lost a lot of blood and when he first spied you, he figured you was dead. Brung you back to the house when he seen you was still breathin', only you was breathin' mighty shallow. I made you some soup, only you wouldn't wake up to swallow none of it. Keepin' you warm was about all we could do 'til you decided to wake up. You came down with the fever real bad, when your wounds got festered. I've been pourin' paw's liniment in your wounds and keepin' them clean, best I could. Paw said you had to have a doctor or you'd never get well. Said that ball had to come out or you'd die."

He touched the bandage around his chest, then he ran his fingers over the splints down his leg. "I appreciate what you and your paw have done for me. Soon as I'm able I'll get back on the road to Memphis. I don't have any money, so I can't pay for the trouble. But I'm obliged for what you've done."

She bent over him to wipe his cheeks with the cloth. "You won't be going no place for a spell, weak as you are. Paw found your horse in the woods. It's down at the shed, for when you're able to travel. Don't fret none about the money. . . ."

"What about the doctor's fee? I can't pay him."

Sallie Mae shook her head. "Paw'll trade Doc Sims

some corn whiskey for takin' that ball out. My paw makes the best corn squeeze this side of the Mississippi, in case you didn't know. Doc Sims buys it from us all the time, to make his elixir. When you get to feelin' better I'll give you some. It'll soften the pains you've got."

The girl got up and smoothed her dress. John noticed the swell of her breasts beneath the thin layer of sackcloth, and the rounding of her hips below her slender waist. At first, he had guessed her to be much younger. But when she stood up, he couldn't help but admire the woman's body poorly hidden inside her shapeless garment. Then he looked at her face again and saw pretty blue eyes. Something stirred inside him, the almost forgotten memories of what it was like to hold a woman in his arms.

Chapter Seven

He examined his face in the shard of mirror above the washbasin, leaning on the wooden crutch to keep weight off his injured leg. John saw a face that was much older than he remembered, with deep lines etched around his eyes and the corners of his mouth. He was twenty-six. He guessed it was the war that had aged him so quickly. He barely recognized himself now. Coal black hair hung to his shoulders. Dark beard stubble mottled his chin and cheeks. Obsidian eyes stared back at him without the boyish good humor that was once there. He wondered what had happened, what had changed his looks, for now his reflection reminded him of his father. Hiram Cross had grown old long before his time and he'd blamed it on farming.

He splashed his face with water from the basin, wincing when he moved his left arm. The doctor from Waynesboro had said it would take time before the swelling went down, before the red streaks of blood poisoning went away. When Dr. Sims dug the lead ball from his chest, he'd said how lucky John was that the slug had missed vital organs. A broken rib perhaps deflected the bullet's entry just enough to save his life, but the healing would be slow. And painful. He hobbled back toward the bed, always mindful of the leg, though he'd grown accustomed to the constant pain. Sallie Mae took his crutch and helped him down to the mattress.

"You're doin' better, John," she said, patting his shoulder gently.

Gritting his teeth, he lowered himself with an elbow, then he gave her a grin. "It still hurts like hell. Why don't you pour me another cup of that whiskey."

She placed the feather pillow under his head, pushing a stray lock of hair from his forehead with a flick of her fingers. "If you promise to behave yourself," she replied. "Yesterday you got half drunk on the stuff an' darn near fell off the bed."

He laughed. Then he looked at Sallie Mae and the smile left his face, for there was something about her that awakened sleeping desires within him. When her father was away from the cabin he found himself staring at her, when her back was turned. Sallie Mae had a different kind of beauty that set her apart from most women. Clad only in dresses she made from cotton flour sacking, she was prettier than any of the young maidens Elizabeth invited to her summer parties, even prettier than Elizabeth herself in many ways. Without red lip paint or rouge, Sallie Mae's face seemed to glow with her own natural color, her cheeks pinked by the sun. Even her freckles were pretty.

"You're a beautiful young woman," he said, watching her pour whiskey into a tin cup.

Sallie Mae blushed. "You're just sayin' that."

She came over to the bed. He raised himself on an elbow, secretly admiring the curve of her thighs where her dress clung too tightly below her waist. The dress was a size too small and faded from too many washings.

"Don't drink it too fast," she scolded, handing him the cup. Then she sat on the edge of the bed, gazing down at him while he took the first sip of whiskey.

"Thanks," he said softly, after the fiery liquid burned down his throat. "Where's your paw today?"

"Gone to town with the wagon. It's the first of the month an' that's when we buy supplies. He won't be back 'til dark."

John drank more whiskey, watching Sallie Mae over the rim of his cup. "You never mention what happened to your maw."

The girl shrugged. "Not much to tell. She died when I was born."

"Sorry. Didn't mean to pry."

"It don't matter. I never knew her. Paw told me about her, that she was the prettiest woman in these hills when he married her. Paw took it awful hard when she passed away."

He drank again, and now the whiskey had begun its work. The pain in his leg and chest began to subside. "I feel better," he said. "Your paw makes the best medicine I ever drank."

She giggled. "It ain't medicine. It'll wring every drop of sense out of your skull if'n you drink too much. Soon as you're finished I'll shave your whiskers again, and give you a bath whilst I wash your clothes. I can mend them bulletholes too, after your shirt and britches dry above the stove. Time I changed your bandages. Soon as that splint comes off I'll sew up your pants leg where Doc sliced it open."

Without waiting for his answer she got up, first adding wood to the firebox inside the cookstove, then filling a cast iron kettle with water to boil. He wondered if she understood that it was improper for a woman to bathe a man, even a man in his condition. He watched her go about her preparations on the far side of the room, sharpening her father's razor, working shaving soap to a lather, ignoring him for the moment.

She crossed the room with a clean cloth, the soap and

razor, sitting beside him again. "Be real still now, so I won't nick you," she said, gently applying soap to his chin with the brush.

Resting his head on the pillow, he studied her face while she shaved him. She smiled now and then, when she felt his gaze.

"I figure you'll be well enough to travel in a few weeks," she said. "Doc said it would take a couple of months for that leg to heal so you can ride. I suppose you'll be goin' back home to marry Elizabeth?"

He took his eyes off Sallie Mae for a moment. "Elizabeth stopped writing a long time ago. I reckon she got tired of waiting for me."

Sallie Mae halted her razor. "You was callin' out to her whilst you had the fever. Appears you still have feelins for her. Maybe her letters couldn't get through."

"Ain't likely," he sighed, pushing Elizabeth from his mind. "It's my guess Elizabeth made other plans. Can't say as I'd blame her much. I've been gone four years."

Sallie Mae's face grew serious. "You haven't forgotten about her, John. Sometimes, in your sleep, you call her name." The razor went back to work on his whiskers.

"I'm tryin' to forget her," he said softly, watching Sallie Mae's beautiful face until she put the razor down to wipe his neck and chin with the cloth.

"There," she said, smiling. "You're handsome as ever." Then she suddenly bent over him and kissed his mouth, being careful not to brush against his chest wound.

"That was the best part," John said. He raised one hand to touch her shoulder. Her kiss sent a tiny flutter through him and he wanted more. He pulled her slowly toward his face. "I'd like to do that again," he whispered.

She pressed her lips against his and allowed the kiss

to linger before she pulled away. She stared into his eyes a moment longer, then she placed her palm against his cheek. "Time I gave you that bath," she said quietly. "The water's hot by now."

She helped him out of his shirt, pulling it off his shoulders carefully. Then she tossed it on the floor. "Lie down, so I can get those britches off. I'll do it real slow, so it won't hurt your leg."

She unbuttoned the top of his pants, lifting the split pant leg away from his splints before she cupped her hand below his hips to pull his pants down. He felt no embarrassment when his genitals were exposed, not even when Sallie Mae's eyes lingered on his nakedness. The beginnings of an erection pulsed from his groin, bringing a quick smile to the girl's face.

"None of that now," she said playfully, picking up his soiled clothes before she left the bed. "You're hardly strong enough to lift a spoon. Maybe, when you're feelin' better . . ."

She crossed the room to boil his clothing, leaving him to wonder what she meant.

He hobbled out on the porch on a frosty morning in late January when he heard the dog barking at the bottom of the hill. Sallie Mae was at the shed milking the cow. Caleb Parsons was off running his trap lines and John wondered what might have alerted the dog.

Then he saw movement along the road that crossed the valley below the cabin. Sunlight glinted off the rifles carried by a platoon of marching infantrymen dressed in blue. Behind the foot soldiers, mules labored pulling a long line of artillery. Rattling harness chains and creaking caisson wheels echoed from the valley floor. John froze on the porch to watch the Yankees march south down the Waynesboro road, wondering if they would send a detail up the narrow lane to Caleb Parsons' cabin. And what they would do if they found him here.

Sallie Mae came running up the hill without her milk bucket. "Yankees!" she cried, pointing a finger toward the valley. "Get back in the house so they won't see you!"

He swung his crutch too quickly and almost fell, making the move toward the cabin door. His guns hung from pegs above his bed and he worried that he might be forced to use them. Of one thing he was certain . . . he would not allow them to capture him without a fight. During the weeks of his slow recovery he'd made himself a promise, that no matter what he wouldn't go quietly to a Union prison camp. His freedom was too precious and in his mind he wasn't a Confederate soldier anymore. He had stopped fighting this war at Franklin, if the Yankees would only allow him to ride back home peacefully to Texas.

He closed the cabin door with his heart pounding, forming a plan for his defense if Union soldiers came up the lane. His wounds would prevent him from making a run for it through the woods around the house, thus he was left with few choices. Fight, or go quietly to a prison camp.

Hobbling over to the wall, he took down his Sharps and pistol, quickly examining the loads. He heard Sallie Mae's footsteps as she crossed the porch.

"What are you doing?" she cried, bursting through the cabin door.

"I aim to put up a fight if they want one," he replied, sticking the pistol in the waistband of his pants. Balancing the rifle in his free hand, he crossed to a window.

"We'll hide you in the root cellar," the girl gasped, out of breath from her run up the hill. "There's too many of them. They'll kill you if you start shooting. Come with me, John, before they find the road to the

71

house. They won't think to look in the cellar behind the house. Hurry!"

He left the rifle on the bed and followed her out the door in his awkward gait, swinging his useless leg down the dog-run between the two rooms. Up the hillside behind the cabin was a door to a dugout where cream and other perishables were kept in summer. A thick layer of frost covered the grasses on the slope, making his climb to the cellar door slippery, using the crutch. Sallie Mae held the door open.

"There's an old milk stool where you can sit," she said, glancing over her shoulder, listening for the soldiers. "Don't make a sound 'til I tell you it's safe to come out."

Entering the tiny doorframe, he found himself in a small cavern lined with mossy stones. Without his coat, in bare feet, he was suddenly cold.

"There's candle on the shelf, and some sulfur sticks," she said, closing the door behind him. A shaft of sunlight beamed through a crack below the door, thus he decided against the candle.

He sat on the stool, resting the crutch against a wall, then his hand went to the butt of his revolver. In spite of the chill beads of sweat formed on his face as he listened for the first sounds of approaching soldiers.

The waiting seemed an eternity. Then the dog's barking came closer. John tensed every muscle, ignoring the dull pain from his wounds, listening for the footfalls of horses.

He heard voices and drew the gun from his waistband. The sounds of his breathing distracted him until he held his breath.

"How come a pretty lady like you is here all alone?" a voice asked. There were chuckles over the question from some others.

"My paw's just over the next hill runnin' our trap lines," Sallie Mae answered. "He'll be along shortly."

"Saw the smoke from your chimney," someone remarked. "You seen any rebel soldiers in these parts lately?"

"Lots of them," she answered. "Why, just yesterday a big army wearin' gray came down that same road you're travelin'. I 'spect you'll run into them down south a ways. They had lots of cannons too. If I was you I'd hightail it out of these hills before it gets dark."

John heard a dry laugh. "I say you're a damn liar, little lady. There aren't any tracks on that road, or we'd have found them. I say you're a damn southern sympathizer. We've got orders to burn every house we come to where help is being given to the Confederates. I've got my orders."

"My paw'll fill you with buckshot if you put a torch to this place," the girl answered quickly.

John picked up his crutch and stood, inching closer to the door to peer outside. He opened it a crack and saw five mounted men in front of the porch. One soldier wore a sergeant's stripes on his sleeve.

The Yankees were laughing. The sergeant swung down from his horse and John could see the grin on his face.

"We aren't scared of shotguns," the sergeant said. "This is the Fourth Artillery Brigade under General George Thomas. In case the news hasn't come this far south, we took Nashville last month and most of the rest of Tennessee. Can't find a rebel army that'll stop running long enough to stand and fight. You and your Confederate army have lost this here war, little lady. And we're claiming the spoils. Looks to me like you're one of the prettiest spoils we've found. What've you got under that dress, missy?"

The sergeant started for the porch steps and John

knew it was time to act. He simply couldn't hide in the root cellar while a detail of Yankees had their way with Sallie Mae. Cocking the gun in his left hand, he pushed the door open and hobbled out in the sunlight.

Chapter Eight

He heard the girl scream and worked the crutch as fast as he could, swinging his bad leg in a looping arc beside him until he rounded the front of the cabin. The soldiers weren't paying any attention to him, watching what the sergeant was doing to Sallie Mae just then. John knew the gunshots would bring more soldiers up the lane, but he was without choices. He couldn't stand by and let the Yankees harm the girl without doing everything he could to stop them.

John stopped at the corner of the house and raised his pistol. The sergeant held Sallie Mae by the arm. The front of her dress was torn.

"Let her go!" John shouted.

Surprised faces turned, and at the same time empty hands went toward holstered guns.

The .44 Navy exploded in John's fist. A blue-clad soldier cried out and toppled from his bolting horse.

John fired again, feeling the .44 slam into his palm as his second shot echoed from the hillside. A cavalryman was torn from his saddle, groping for the wound in his chest as John prepared to fire at a third target among the milling, frightened horses. He triggered the .44. A soldier was lifted by the lead ball's impact, flying across his horse's neck with arms outstretched. Then a gunshot sounded from the porch and John felt the whisper of a speeding bullet across his cheek. Flinging his crutch aside, John fired at the sergeant. The ball struck the sergeant's forehead with a dull crack, splintering bone.

One soldier remained aboard his lunging horse, trying to rein the animal around for better aim. It was all the time John needed. He squeezed off a shot and saw the soldier's tunic pucker, sending a shower of blood into the air that fell like crimson rain across the horse's withers. The Yankee slumped in the saddle and fell sideways with a hand pressed over his wound. His body fell under the horse's hooves with a soft thud. Suddenly, there was silence.

A wounded soldier groaned and tried to sit up as his horse galloped away from the cabin. Loose horses ran into the trees snorting and whickering to each other.

"Get me one of those horses!" John cried. A single load remained in his .44. "Bring it over here and help me get mounted. More of them will be coming. Please hurry!"

Sallie Mae ran from the porch, her eyes wide with fear, looking over her shoulder toward the road. A sorrel gelding with a U.S. brand on its shoulder had stopped to graze when the gunfire ended. Sallie Mae ran to the horse and grabbed its reins, leading it quickly back to John.

John seized the sorrel's mane and pulled as hard as he could.

"Push me," he cried, struggling higher with trembling limbs.

A sharp, stabbing pain went down his leg when the girl pushed him across the saddle, and his chest felt like it was on fire. He swung his splinted leg over the sorrel's rump and almost cried out involuntarily, until he caught himself. The girl handed him the reins.

"I'll lose them in the woods if they come after me. Get up behind me. You can't stay!"

He lifted the girl atop the gelding's rump and heeled the horse into the trees at a run. Tree branches slapped his face and his throbbing leg as the sorrel galloped through the forest. Behind them, they heard shouts coming from the valley, and the distant rumble of pounding hooves. Men were charging up the lane to the cabin, and it would be a matter of minutes before a squad of Union cavalry was on their trail.

"This way!" Sallie Mae cried, pointing over his shoulder. A trail wound its way up the hill behind the house. "I know a place where they'll never find us."

He sent the gelding up the trail at an all-out run, dodging pine branches and barren oak limbs along the way. Soon the horse was laboring for wind, slowing its gait to a steady lope.

"There's a canyon about two miles from here," the girl said, her arms around John's waist. "If we can get there first, there's a creek where we can hide our tracks. Nobody's following us yet. I'll show you the way."

Raw pain from his wounds drew tears to John's eyes as the sorrel galloped higher up the slope. Surrounded by trees, he was prevented from seeing any signs of pursuit along the trail behind them. When the throbbing in his leg became too great he reined the horse to a walk.

"Can't stand the jolting," he groaned. The wooden splint only worsened the banging his leg took when the horse was at a run. "Gettin' dizzy," he said weakly, gripping the pommel of the saddle with white-knuckled hands. "Need to rest a minute or two . . ."

He lost consciousness, trying desperately to keep his eyes focused on the trail until a dark curtain fell in front of him.

* * *

He awoke with a start and looked around. He was lying on his back. The scent of pine needles filled his nostrils. Green pine branches blotted out the sunlight overhead, making him wonder just where he was. He shivered in the cold and tried to sit up. A hand on his chest pushed him gently back to the ground.

"Rest easy. We're safe." He recognized Sallie Mae's voice.

"What happened? I remember getting dizzy."

"You blacked out," she said, in almost a whisper. "I held you in the saddle. It's safe here. Those Yanks won't ever find us in here, not even if they look forever. If you'd stayed in the cellar like I told you . . ."

"They were hurting you," he replied, remembering the scene in front of the cabin that had forced him from his hiding place. "I couldn't let them hurt you, Sallie Mae. Not after all you've done for me, you and your paw."

"Paw'll find us here, after he sees what happened at the house." Then tears suddenly flooded the girl's eyes. "If they burn us out I don't know what we'll do." Her hands balled into tiny fists.

John tried to shut out the ache in his leg to think clearly. "Maybe they'll keep marching to Waynesboro."

Sallie Mae was sobbing now, turning her face to hide her tears. "That little house is all we've got. If those damn Yankees burn it down . . ."

He reached for her hand. "There's a war going on, Sallie Mae, and lots of folks have lost their homes on account of it. Don't cry. Long as you're alive, you can start over. I reckon this whole thing is my fault. If you hadn't taken me in, you'd have been off with your paw this morning. I'm sorry I brought you all this trouble. I couldn't let those soldiers hurt you. I had to do something."

She turned to him and wiped away her tears with a

forearm. "It ain't your fault," she sniffled. "I wasn't cryin' for me anyway. I was cryin' for my paw, thinkin' what it would do to him if they burned our house down."

He squeezed her hand. "No sense worryin' about it now. If they find us, then we'll have plenty to worry about."

Sallie Mae grinned. "It'd take a mountain man to find this canyon. If a feller don't know these hills, he'll get lost in no time. That's why I brung you here, John, so they wouldn't find you. I've gotten sorta fond of you lately, John Cross. I wouldn't want to see you get killed or nothin' like that."

She bent over him and kissed his cheek, shivering from the cold. She had gone to the milking shed without her coat and shoes, though the temperature hovered near freezing.

John's gaze fell to the tear in her dress, glimpsing rounded breasts dimpled with gooseflesh and one perfect pink nipple. When the girl noticed his stare, she quickly closed the opening with her fingers.

"You wasn't supposed to see that," she said. Her cheeks filled with color, then she smiled.

In spite of his pain, he found himself stirred by her remarkable beauty. "I never dreamed a girl could be so pretty," he whispered.

Still clutching the front of her dress, her expression turned thoughtful. "What about Elizabeth? Is she pretty?"

He gazed up at the limbs above him. "I thought she was the most beautiful woman in the world. But that was four years ago, Sallie Mae, and Elizabeth is a rich man's daughter. She wouldn't wait for me, not four years, she wouldn't. I already told you she stopped writing letters. And besides, I've decided you're even prettier than Elizabeth. I swear it's true."

She leaned over him again, to kiss his mouth. "I like you a lot, Mr. John Cross," she said softly. "But I know what'll happen if I get to liking you too much. You'll ride off to Texas and I'll never see you again. You're still carryin' Elizabeth in your heart. Until you know if she's waitin' for you back home, you ain't got room for another girl inside your head."

He tried to think of the right words to deny feelings for Elizabeth, knowing they would be false. Down deep, he knew the girl was right about it . . . that he wouldn't be at peace with himself until he knew why Elizabeth stopped writing. It was plain fact that the little tintype of Elizabeth had carried him through the war. On countless nights, when he was alone on a darkened battlefield awaiting the killing that would start at dawn, her likeness had taken him closer to home, soothed away his desperate loneliness and calmed his fears. He could never give his heart to another until he understood why Elizabeth's letters stopped coming, even though he was sure he already knew the truth.

"You're still prettier," he said, reaching for her cheek, tracing a finger beside her nose. "Down in my gut I know Elizabeth isn't waiting for me. She found herself somebody else. But I reckon you're right . . . I'll have to find out for myself."

Sallie Mae shuddered, wrapping her arms around her. "Maybe you'll come back to Tennessee when you find out," she said, though she sounded doubtful. "I'd like it . . . if'n you did. Paw says a girl ain't supposed to make herself available to a man, that it's a man's duty to make his intentions real plain about a girl. I just wanted you to know that I'd like it if you came back. I'd be waitin', if I know'd you was comin' back."

"You're cold," he said, avoiding the subject of his return. "We can't build a fire or those Yankees will see the smoke."

"I'm okay," she replied. "Maybe I'll lie down beside you for a spell, if'n you don't mind. You could put your arm around me."

He motioned her down to the bed of pine needles. She snuggled into the crook of his arm gently, avoiding the bandage around his chest. Then she kissed his cheek. "I could love you, John," she whispered. "I could love you with all my heart if you'd allow it."

He kissed her lips lightly, looking deeply into her eyes. "I could love you too, Sallie Mae. I just know I could. But I've got to go back to Texas to see my family before I make any plans for myself."

"And to find out 'bout Elizabeth," she whispered. "I understand."

His senses keened and his muscles stiffened. Off in the distance he heard a horse splashing through the stream below the canyon. "Somebody's coming," he said. Sallie Mae sat up quickly, turning her face toward the sound as John drew his pistol from his pants.

"Maybe it's Paw," she whispered. "I'll run down and take a look."

She was gone before he could protest, trotting among the pines. He glanced down at the single unfired percussion cap remaining on the .44's cylinder. One shot would be all he had to fight a Yankee patrol, and he knew it wouldn't be enough to stop them. The sorrel was grazing in a grassy meadow at the back of the canyon, but without his crutch he couldn't get to the horse.

He pushed himself painfully to one elbow, watching the trees to the east, listening to the sounds grow louder. It was just one horse . . . he counted the footfalls in the water. With one load in the pistol it would be a short fight. Unless . . . unless there was just one soldier.

He saw movement in the pines, a dark shadow advancing along the forest floor. "Where's the girl?" he wondered, aiming his gunsights toward the shadow. The sun was directly overhead, making patches of light between the trees. He cocked the .44 and waited, listening to the beat of his heart.

Caleb Parsons rode his brown mule through an opening between two pines. Sallie Mae sat behind him on the mule's rump. John lowered his gun and let out a sigh.

The old man grinned through a faceful of gray whiskers when he saw John. "You're lookin' a mite peaked, son," he said, halting the mule a few yards away. "Glad to see you're both alive."

"You may not be so glad when you hear what happened back at the cabin," John said uneasily.

"Saw the whole thing," Caleb chuckled, helping his daughter from the mule. "Rode down there an' talked to them bluebellies after you an' Sallie Mae cleared out, so's they wouldn't rob me blind. That was some fancy shootin' you done, boy. Even crippled up the way you are, I'd say you're a damn decent shot with that pistol. Got five dead Yanks back there to prove it. The others was mad as a nest of hornets when they rode up, seein' what you done to their friends. I told 'em you was a deserter. Swore you'd kept a gun on us while you hid out from your own outfit. That bluebelly major believed every word, after I gave 'em four jugs of my best whiskey. They've been scourin' the hills all around the house, lookin' for you. Gave up 'bout an hour ago, they did, and headed down to Waynesboro. Eight or nine of 'em was damn near too drunk to sit a horse by the time they left."

"They didn't burn our house," Sallie Mae added. "Paw says they're gone now, so it's safe to go back."

Caleb hung his thumbs in his overalls. "Yessir," he said, his eyes twinkling with humor, "that was some mighty fine shootin' you done. Can't say as I ever saw none any better. Didn't know you was so handy with a gun. Never would have guessed it."

"I'll fetch the horse," Sallie Mae said.

It was then that Caleb noticed the front of his daughter's dress. "What happened to them buttons?" he asked, giving John a darkly suspicious look.

"Those Yankees done it, Paw," she said, gathering the opening in her fingers.

The old man's expression softened. "Jus' wanted to be sure wasn't nothin' betwixt the two of you," he said. "Proper woman oughta keep herself covered in front of strangers."

John eyed a clay jug hanging from Caleb's saddle horn. "I could sure use some of that corn," he said. "Leg's hurtin' something awful after that ride."

Caleb took down the jug and gave it to John, watching him pull the stopper and take the first swallow. "I'm obliged for what you done, savin' my daughter from them soldiers," he said when Sallie Mae was off in the woods. "They'd have used her, if you hadn't been there to stop 'em."

John took another mouthful. "I heard one of them say he wanted to see what was under her dress, an' when I heard Sallie May yell, they didn't leave me a choice. Had to stop them. Got lucky, I reckon."

Caleb shook his head. "Wasn't luck at all, son. Damn fancy shootin', was what it was."

Chapter Nine

By the end of February his pain had subsided enough that he could move about outside the cabin. Twice more they had seen Union patrols on the Waynesboro road, and Caleb learned from a storekeeper in town that Union armies occupied most of western Tennessee. Caleb brought a yellowed Memphis newspaper back that told of endless Confederate defeats across the south. Only Lee and Johnston still led sizable armies. Lee was surrounded in Pennsylvania along the Appomattox begging Jefferson Davis for reinforcements and supplies. The rest of the Confederate armies had been crushed by huge Union forces. John Bell Hood had resigned his command in January, abandoning his splintered army from Texas. John read the report with tears in his eyes. Thousands of brave men from Texas had lost their lives and it amounted to nothing.

Sallie Mae kept him well fed and saw to his wounds. Caleb made whiskey as fast as he could and sold it to the Yankees camped below Waynesboro. Only once had a Union squad ridden up to the cabin asking about Confederates in the hills, and this time Caleb had been at home while John was hidden in the root cellar. Cold winter days passed slowly, but John was healing. And his affection for Sallie Mae had grown as time passed.

When Caleb was away attending to his still, or in Waynesboro selling the finished product, John and Sallie Mae shared tender moments. Toward the end of February, John knew he was deeply in love with her. And he knew she loved him dearly.

On the first morning in March, while Caleb was on the road to Waynesboro with a wagonload of whiskey, John took Sallie Mae in his arms.

"I love you," he whispered, brushing her cheek with a kiss.

He unfastened the top button on her dress.

"I love you too," she sighed. She pressed her lips against his mouth hungrily and made no effort to stop him when he opened a second button, then a third. The cabin was warmed by a fire in the cookstove. John fingered the dress off Sallie Mae's shoulders. She let it fall to the floor around her ankles.

"We shouldn't be doing this," she protested. "It ain't proper for a man to see a girl naked."

"Come over to the bed," he said, leaning on the crutch.

He admired the perfection of her body as she walked beside him, the light scattering of freckles across her chest and down her thighs. Hard pink nipples jutted from her breasts . . . he touched one gently with his fingers before he lowered himself to the mattress.

She unfastened his pants and took them down, then she carefully went astraddle of him as he lay on his back. Eyes closed, she guided him inside her. Then she moaned softly and began slow, rhythmic thrusts, shivering with pleasant sensation. He placed his hands around her waist, rocking beneath her. For the first time in many years he lost himself in pure pleasure. Sallie Mae's soft skin and whispered cries made him forget about the war and the cause he'd risked his life for.

When they both were spent she lay in his arms, taking deep breaths that flared her tiny nostrils. He stared at her face in thoughtful silence for a time.

"I'll come back," he said, knowing she would understand.

"I'll be praying that you will," she sighed, stroking his cheek with her fingertips. "I love you with all my heart, John. I hope that'll be enough to bring you back to Tennessee."

He was seated on the chopping block behind the cabin one morning late in March when he made the decision to go. The weather was warming and his leg would support his weight when he did it carefully. Although there had been no news about the war, he knew it was going badly for the Confederacy. Caleb said the Yankee camp below Waynesboro had grown to twice its original size and found no resistance in the hills. Foodstuffs were in short supply in Waynesboro. Supply trains couldn't get through. Union forces had blown up the rail lines between major cities and seized any freight wagons they encountered. Store shelves were empty and Caleb claimed a sack of sugar would fetch ten dollars, when it could be found. John knew the war couldn't last much longer. It was time he started home.

Hardly a day passed that he didn't think about the three friends who'd ridden alongside him into the Yankee ambush, wondering if they had escaped with their lives. He'd seen them ride hard through the deadly cross fire and no one had fallen from his horse, though he vaguely remembered hearing a Yankee say that one had a bullet in his arm. Too, he remembered hearing the Yanks say they meant to go after the men who escaped the ambush. Had Billy Cole and the others gotten away? Even if they had, they faced a ride through hundreds of miles of dangerous country to reach Texas. He would learn their fate when he got back to Waco, if he made it himself without falling into Union hands. But his mind was made up to give it a try, for he'd grown restless at the cabin. It would be a sad parting to leave Sallie Mae, yet the time had come for him to go. The wound in his back was scabbed over and his leg no longer pained him.

He unfastened the bindings around the splints and tested the feel when he bent his leg, hurting only slightly. If he held the bay to a walk, he could make it. Still using the crutch, he got up and made his way around to the front of the cabin.

Sallie Mae saw him from the pole corral where she was feeding his horse and the mule. She waved and smiled brightly, making John feel worse about his decision to leave her. They had fallen in love quite by chance and he didn't want to hurt her any more than he had to. She'd known all along he would be leaving when he was well enough to travel, and he'd promised her that he would return when his affairs were settled back home. But the moment when he told her of his intentions loomed like a dark cloud. He tried to think of the right words to say, words that would hurt her less when he told her about his plans.

She came up the path looking more beautiful than ever, with her hair bouncing atop her shoulders. "Mornin', John," she said, smiling sweetly, a smile he knew he would remember across the miles to Texas.

Then she noticed his splints were gone.

"You took them off," she observed, frowning. "Doc said you oughta let him look at your leg before . . ."

Her expression changed suddenly. She gazed into his eyes and he knew she had guessed what he was about to tell her.

"You're goin', ain't you?" she asked. A tear crept into the corners of her eyes.

"It's time," he said quietly. "I've been a burden around here long enough. If you wouldn't mind stitchin' up my pants leg so I won't freeze . . ."

"Oh, John," she cried, rushing into his arms. Her body shook with silent sobs. "I've know'd this day had to come, an' I swore I wouldn't cry."

He held her against his chest, allowing a silence. "I'll come back, just like I promised," he said.

She looked up at him then, blue eyes sparkling when her tears caught morning sunlight. "I'll pray every night that you'll come back," she replied, her voice breaking. "If the Lord answers prayers, He'll bring you back to me."

"I said I'd come, soon as I'm able."

She nodded once and fingered away her tears. "I'll get the needle and thread."

The Mississippi yawned in front of him. A paddle wheeler sent a column of smoke above its lazy passage downstream. Smaller boats moved up and down the river's muddy surface. Up the river, a Union ironclad sat quietly, tied to a wharf with the stars and stripes fluttering from its mast. Approaching Memphis, he had learned what lay in store for him at the river. Union occupation forces held both sides of the Mississippi. A man dressed in Confederate gray would be shot on sight unless he surrendered. A temporary prison camp had been established east of Memphis. A traveler told him that the fenced enclosure held as many as five thousand men, and all of them were starving. Hundreds died of disease every week.

Keeping to back roads, he'd made the outskirts of Memphis and then swung south without encountering any Union patrols. A farmer confided that he could find refuge across the Mississippi line in Tate County, where it was rumored that remnants of an Alabama regiment were assembling. Crossing into Arkansas would be safer from Tate County, the farmer explained. Thus John reined his bay south, swinging wide of Memphis, keeping to the wooded hills wherever he could.

He had plenty of provisions and a jug of whiskey, a gift from Caleb before he rode away from the cabin. Not a day had passed that he didn't think about Sallie Mae's tender embraces and the feelings he had for her. The beautiful girl had captured his heart as surely as Elizabeth had so long ago. He carried her in his thoughts as he rode southwest across Tennessee, remembering the time they shared. He meant to keep his promise when the war was over. He would ride back to Waynesboro and ask Sallie Mae to marry him as soon as he could.

Keeping the Mississippi in sight, swinging wide of scattered farmhouses, he pushed on until dark at a steady trot. Sometime during the night he crossed over into Mississippi, walking his horse down wooded lanes beneath a sky full of stars.

The place was called Slater's Mill. The tiny outpost deep in the Arkansas woods had two stores and a blacksmith's shop. He rode cautiously down the single street, puzzling over the crowd of darkies gathered behind one of the stores. By their homespun clothing he knew they were slaves, more than fifty of them, men and women, a handful of children, and they all seemed to be talking at once. A few were singing, making John wonder about the occasion that brought them together.

He rode to a hitchrail in front of the store where an

old man sat whittling on a bench. His boots were covered with slivers of wood.

"What's the celebration about?" John asked.

The old man halted the motion of his knife, eyeing John's Confederate uniform. A plug of tobacco was balled in the old man's cheek. He spat. "War's over," he said. "Lee surrendered last week at a place called Appomattox. Newspaper came this morning from Memphis spreadin' the news. Them nigras is called freedmen now. A man caught with nigra slaves gets himself sent to a Yankee prison, 'cause it's agin the law." The old man spat again. "Lord knows what them nigras will do, now that they ain't slaves no more. Who's gonna feed 'em? They ain't got sense enough to feed themselves. Ol' Abraham Lincoln is to blame fer it. Them nigras will starve to death. Makes a man wonder what they're so all-fired happy about back there, singing like that and carrying on. Won't be a month 'til they're skin an' bones."

Hearing that the war was finally over, John's shoulders slumped. He was swept by powerful emotions, a mixture of relief and sorrow, sorrow for the thousands of dead who had laid down their lives for a failed cause. But the killing would stop now, and that thought brightened his mood. "Glad to hear it's over," John said in a tired voice.

The old man fixed him with a look. "Some ain't so glad," he said, shaking his head. "There's some in this neck of the woods who ain't happy to hear the news. Best you keep opinions like that to yourself, sonny, or you're liable to make a few enemies."

John bristled a little over the remark. "I did my share of the fighting," he snapped. "Got tired of watching young boys die before they were old enough to shave. Can't win a war without gunpowder and shot. Toward the last, we didn't have any."

The man returned to his whittling. "Like I said, I'd keep quiet about bein' glad the war is over 'til you get where you're goin'. Whereabouts you headed?"

"Texas," John replied, swinging down from his horse to stretch his legs.

The old man sighted along the western horizon. "That's a far piece from here, sonny. Take a month to git there ridin' a mule."

He tied off at the rail and climbed the steps to the store, meaning to have a look at the Memphis newspaper. His limp drew the old man's attention.

"Appears you took a ball," he said matter-of-factly.

"A couple of them," John answered, limping past the bench to the front door.

His nose was greeted by wonderful smells inside the musty old building. Rows of shelves held fragrant coffee beans and jars of hard candy smelling of peppermint and fruit. A barrel of pickles stood near the counter, making his mouth water, though he had no money.

A woman in a calico dress greeted him. "What's fer you today, soldier?" she asked.

"Got no money, ma'am," he said, limping over to the counter, "but I'd be obliged if I could read that Memphis paper tellin' about the war."

The woman smiled. "Wouldn't matter if you did have money, son. Likely be Confederate and it ain't no good now. Hard money is all that spends these days. If it don't jingle, it's worthless. Couldn't help but notice you had your eye on them sweet pickles when you walked in. Help yourself. You look like you could use somethin' in your belly."

"I'm grateful," he replied, reaching into the pickle keg for the biggest pickle he could find. "Would you mind if I took a look at that newspaper?"

She reached beneath the counter and handed him *The*

Memphis Sun. Emblazoned across the top of the page it read, LEE SURRENDERS AT APPOMATTOX.

He tasted the pickle and found it delicious. "Best pickle I ever had," he said, reading down the page. The account described the meeting between Grant and Lee. At the bottom of the story Grant was quoted. "Let the Confederates keep their sidearms and send them home. Let them have their mules, if they haven't already eaten them."

Another story told of the occupation armies being sent to restore order to the South. Northern judges would rule over all southern courtrooms to enforce the law of the land. Union troops had police powers in all Confederate states. State governments were suspended until appointed leaders arrived from the North.

The woman had been staring at him while he read the paper. "A drummer just came from Little Rock," she said, "and he claims he saw men wearin' fancy suits all over the place. Taking over everything, he said, at the capitol, and the banks. Folks call them carpetbaggers. Came down with those carpet suitcases full of official papers that give them the right to control everything."

John shook his head and pushed the paper across the counter. "Don't appear a southerner will have much say-so in the way things are done," he said. "I reckon times will be hard for a spell."

The woman made a face. "In case you ain't already noticed, times are hard right now. Can't buy sugar. Coffee's six dollars a pound, when you can find it. Buttons are as scarce as hen's teeth. Hasn't been much mending going on either. Can't buy any needles."

John ate the rest of his pickle and thanked her. "Much obliged for the hospitality, ma'am."

"Good luck, soldier," she replied. "Mind your backside for a spell, 'til everybody gets the news. Folks claim there's some who don't know the war is over yet. I'd keep a sharp eye if I was wearin' gray, until the word gets out about Lee."

Chapter Ten

The young darkie was powerfully built, standing over six feet without shoes. A group of bearded men in overalls surrounded the darkie beside the shell of a burned-out barn. On the ride across eastern Arkansas John had seen a number of scorched farms like this and he'd guessed it was the work of Union armies. Urging the bay to a trot, he approached the blackened walls of the barn where the men held the darkie at bay. Two of the men held shotguns. Another held a blacksnake whip. John saw bloody gashes across the darkie's chest and shoulders where the whip had torn through his tattered cotton shirt. A scrawny mule stood with its head lowered behind the group of men, wearing a harness bridle with blinders.

Some of the men turned when they heard John approach, and none of the bearded faces were friendly.

"What's happened here?" John asked, halting his horse a safe distance from the shotguns.

"Runaway slave," one man growled. "Stole a mule from old man Tompkins an' tried to run."

John eyed the darkie more closely. The boy's eyes bulged with fear of his captors. Blood trickled down his chest and arms. A deep gash in his calf puddled blood around his feet. "I don't reckon you men have heard the war's over. Lee surrendered two weeks back at Appomattox and slavery has been outlawed. A man can get sent to a northern prison for keeping slaves. The story was in the Memphis paper."

A barrel-chested man balancing a shotgun in his fist glowered at John. "Mind your own goddamn business, soldier. This here's between us an' the nigra. He stole Clarence Tompkins' mule and we're gonna hang him for it. Still a law against stealin' horses and mules in Arkansas . . . still a hangin' offense. Ain't none of your affair, so ride off!"

The darkie began to plead for his life. "I didn't steal no mule!" he cried. "It was gave to me! Master Tompkins said I could take that ol' mule 'cause he was so old he couldn't draw a plow no more!"

"Shut your lyin' mouth, blackie!" one man snarled, drawing back his whip. "You know you stole that mule from Clarence an' you're tryin' to lie your way out of bein' hung. One of you run fetch that rope on my saddle. We'll hang this lyin' black bastard and be done with it!"

John felt his mouth go dry. "Why don't you ask the man who owned the mule?" he said. He counted eight men in the group around the boy. It seemed fairness demanded that one of them should ask the mule's owner what happened.

The man with the shotgun jutted his jaw and took a step toward John. "I've done warned you to mind your own business, soldier. Keep your nose out of this or I'll shoot it off your face. Understood?"

John knew he could never allow it, not the hanging. If the darkie had stolen the mule he could be tried for his crime in the closest town. But not hung by a lynch mob like this without proof of his guilt. John's fingers curled around the butt of his .44, then he glanced at the darkie. "I'll take him to the next town and have him put in jail," John said, "but you ain't gonna hang him. I'm taking the darkie with me, and I'll kill any man who tries to stop me." He pulled the pistol from its holster and cocked the hammer, aiming for the big man carrying the shotgun. "You men back away from the barn. Do it real slow. I'd hate like hell to kill a feller who don't need killin', but if you push me, I'll damn sure oblige you."

Another man from the group turned around, slitting his eyes menacingly. "Never know'd they gave Confederate uniforms to nigger-lovin' bastards," he said, closing his hands into fists. "You're a disgrace to men wearin' gray."

John kept an eye on the two men carrying shotguns. "Call me anything you want, boys," he said, speaking almost casually as he leveled his gun in front of him. "But I want one thing made clear. I've spilled a lot of blood over the last four years on account of this uniform. Got nothin' to do with what's happening here. Back away from that darkie and let him get on that mule or I'll kill you right where you stand. I'll make believers out of the rest of you when the first man makes a move to stop that boy. Now drop those shotguns. And do it now!"

He saw indecision on the big man's face, thus he raised his gunsights to the man's chest. "Drop 'em!" he snapped. But no one moved.

"I say you ain't got the nerve," someone said, and in that same instant, both shotguns were moving.

John fired a ball into the big man's chest, then swung his sights, spooking the bay with the first explosion from his .44. The bay lunged sideways, but John was ready, gripping the pommel of his saddle as he fired at the second armed member of the group.

Men dove to the ground to escape flying lead as John tried to settle his horse. The big man staggered a few steps with a dark hole in the bib of his overalls, then his knees buckled.

John's second target collapsed on his back, slammed to the ground by the force of a shot at close range, discharging his shotgun when he fell. A spray of shotgun pellets whined into the charred boards on the side of the barn where the darkie stood, but John's attention was elsewhere. The first man he shot swayed drunkenly on his knees, trying to bring his shotgun to bear on John. Blood covered the dry grass below the wounded man's chest. Arms trembling, he brought the shotgun to his shoulder.

"Damn fool," John whispered savagely, then his .44 thundered in his fist. The bay jumped again, until John tightened the reins on the bit.

A groan accompanied the man's fall across his shotgun. In the following silence, no one moved. The others lay in the grass until John spoke to the darkie. "Get on that mule," he said.

The boy ran toward the rawboned mule, limping on his damaged leg until he hopped aboard the animal's withers. Gathering a long set of plow reins, the boy drummed his heels against the mule's ribs, hurrying away from the barn.

John followed at a trot, leaving two dead men in his wake that he would have preferred to leave alive. Once again, fate had given him poor choices, but his conscience wouldn't allow the hanging of the darkie until the truth could be learned about the old brown mule. He rode up beside the boy, noting that the mule trotted with a stiff gait that made for a jolting ride.

"I'm much obliged, mister," the boy said, clinging to the mule's withers with both hands. "I swear before God I didn't steal this here mule. Master Tompkins give it to me when he set all of us free. Master Tompkins, he know'd this war was over. He give us a piece of paper we could show, an' that paper say I'm a free man now. If'n you can read, I'll show you that paper. Can't read myself, but Master Tompkins tell us what it say."

John glanced over his shoulder. No one followed them away from the burned-out farm. Entering a spot where the road wound through a thick oak forest, he shook his head to the boy's question. "No need to show me your paper. I believe you, but we'll have to get at the truth about the mule. Where did you come from?"

"South," the darkie replied quickly. "The Tompkins farm is south, maybe five miles. You can ask Master Tompkins about his ol' mule. He'll tell you this mule got too old to pull a plow."

Judging from the mule's appearance, the boy could be telling the truth. The animal's muzzle was gray with age and John guessed it could easily be twenty years old, though it mattered little at the time. The mule wasn't worth a boy's life.

"What's your name?" John asked when they entered the woods. "And where were you headed when those men found you?"

The darkie shrugged. John noticed his cuts were bleeding through the tears in his shirt. "Name's Cal. Got no place to go 'cept away from here. Never been no place else 'cept Master Tompkins' farm, an' once I rode the wagon over to Silver Creek with a load of cotton. I was born'd right there on Master Tompkins' place. Don't rightly know where I'll go, now that I'm free."

"I'm headed for Texas," John explained. "Best you get as far away from here as you can, Cal. I killed two men back there, and the rest of them won't forget it. They'll come after you."

Cal studied the mule's ears a moment. "Can I ride with you part of the way, sir?" he asked. John heard the plea in his soft voice.

"I reckon. Isn't much left to eat in my saddlebags, but I suppose we'll get by."

Cal's hands disappeared into a pocket of his pants. "I got three whole dollars in silver the master give me," he said. "It'll buy some food, when we get to a store someplace. If you'll let me ride along with you, I'll buy us both some food with that three dollars."

John heard the coins tinkle in the darkie's palm. "No need of that," he answered. "You'll need that money."

They rode in silence for a time while John worried about the chances of pursuit behind them. The old mule couldn't run. If a posse came after them, it wouldn't be much of a race until the mule played out.

An hour later they encountered a broad, flat plain where tilled fields stretched to a range of distant hills. Last year's cotton stalks bristled from weed-choked rows of reddish clay soil. The road they followed crossed the cotton fields. They would be forced to travel out in the open, in plain sight, to reach the other side of the fields. To the north sat a flat-roofed house surrounded by boxlike slave quarters. White columns ran across the front of the big two-story home. The plantation bespoke its owner's wealth, though the fields lay untended now.

Glancing over his shoulder again, John decided to risk crossing the plain. He urged the horse down a gentle grade, following the road across the valley. Cal seemed edgy when he looked north. John supposed the house reminded him of his past, picking cotton as one of Tompkins' slaves.

The boy's cuts had stopped bleeding, but the old mule had begun to slow. Now and then, as they crossed the cotton fields, John turned back in the saddle to check their backtrail. He felt oddly naked riding across open land. Since he left Tennessee he'd been hiding, riding through the deepest woods he could find. Being out in the open seemed unnatural.

As the sun neared the western horizon they entered the hills, where the road turned south through a pine forest. John felt better when they rode into the first stands of trees. The road behind them was empty.

"We'll have to rest that mule," John said when they encountered a shallow stream coursing through the pines. "Good a place as any to make camp, where the animals will have water."

Cal shook his head, strangely silent since they rode past the plantation.

John selected a spot upstream to build a small fire, for as darkness came, so did an early spring chill. They tethered the horse and mule in the trees and built a circle of stones around a tiny blaze on the creekbank. John dug through his saddlebags for strips of smoked meat Sallie Mae had prepared for him, the last of the food he'd carried away from Waynesboro. Cal squatted across the flames, hungrily devouring the brittle meat in silence.

"You haven't talked much," John observed, watching the boy's face in the firelight. John sat with his bad leg extended to lessen the ache.

"Worryin' some," Cal explained, moving his eyes around the trees beyond the circle of firelight. "Ain't never been free 'til this mornin'. Don't seem natural. I 'spect I'll get used to it, bein' away from Master Tompkins' place."

John remembered what the old man at Slater's Mill predicted for freed slaves, wondering if Cal would be able to feed himself and find work on his own. Although he was big and strong, he reminded John of a frightened child. Perhaps it was only the brutal treatment he'd been given earlier in the day.

Soon the little fire died down to glowing embers.

100

John caught himself dozing fitfully, worn down by weeks of travel aboard the back of a horse. In a dark corner of his brain he worried that he and Cal should keep moving, to get as far away from the dead men at the old farm as quickly as they could travel. But the mule had gone footsore, and needed rest. John's concerns fell away behind a curtain of sleep, resting his head against his saddle.

"Somebody's comin'," a whispered voice warned. It was Cal's voice.

John sat up quickly, rubbing sleep from his eyes. Then he heard a twig snap in the darkness, and the sound was very close. His bay snorted a warning, sensing that some danger was close to the camp. John drew his .44, listening for the sound again.

"You're surrounded, soldier boy!" a voice barked from the trees. "Throw down that pistol or I'll cut you in half with this shotgun. I've got twenty men scattered in these trees. We'll kill you deader'n horseshit if you try to run!"

John's heart was pounding. Cal was crouched across the firepit, showing the whites of his eyes. John looked in the direction of the voice. "Don't want any trouble," he said. "Who's out there?"

He heard a dry chuckle. "Sheriff John Buford from Calhoun County. You're under arrest, soldier boy. An' so is that thievin' nigra. Lay down that gun and both of you put them hands where I can see 'em. Either one of you try anything funny and I'll blow your goddamn heads off. There's twenty guns trained on you and that runaway slave."

John tossed his .44 near the fire's embers, raising his hands. Cal stood up with his arms lifted skyward. John could hear Cal's teeth chattering.

Footsteps crunched across dry pine needles and twigs. Moving shadows filled the trees around them.

"Toss some wood on that fire," a voice commanded.

Someone John couldn't see placed pine cones on the coals. In seconds, flames sprung to life and then he could see the men circled around them.

"That's him," a harsh voice said. "That's the nigger-lovin' reb who kilt Amos and Carl."

John saw a face in the half-light. The man who spoke was the same man who had whipped Cal with the black-snake.

"Then we'll haul his ass to the Hampton jail." It was Sheriff Buford's voice.

The sheriff approached John, carrying a pair of iron manacles in one hand, his shotgun in the other. "Soldier boy, you've made one hell of a mistake. You committed two murders in Calhoun County, and that's my jurisdiction. Murdered two good men who was minding their own business. Dealin' with runaway slaves is a local matter, soldier boy. An' you stuck your nose in where it didn't belong. Rufus, put these irons on him. An' don't forget to chain up that nigra too."

A thick-set man in overalls fastened the manacles around John's wrists. A mirthless grin widened the man's mouth when John's arms were bound behind his neck. "Nigger-lovin' bastard," he hissed, then he shoved John toward Sheriff Buford.

The sheriff appraised John with a smug look. His lips parted, revealing yellowed, broken teeth. "We're gonna teach you a lesson, soldier boy," he said, his voice thick with menace. "You broke the law in Calhoun County. And I don't take lawbreakers lightly, even when they're wearin' Confederate uniforms. You killed two of Calhoun County's best citizens over a damned nigra thief. When Judge Warren gets through with you, you'll be dancin' a jig at the end of a hangman's noose." Then

Sheriff Buford turned to one of his deputies. "Put this gent on his hoss, an' tie that nigra on the mule. We'll take 'em back to Hampton to stand trial."

Chapter Eleven

The cramped cell smelled of urine and stale sweat. Hand-cut stone walls glistened with damp green mold, the same slime that made the floor slippery. Cockroaches skittered across the floor to dark corners where light from the single barred window didn't reveal their hiding places. In the cell beside John's, Cal sat on an iron bunk suspended from the wall on rusted chains, his head hidden between his knees, crying softly, shivering from the cold. John judged it was middle-morning. A shaft of sunlight beamed through the window above John's bunk, painting a barred shadow across the floor. Riding through most of the night, they had come to the little town of Hampton just before dawn, to be thrown roughly into these dank cells by Sheriff Buford and a surly deputy he called Rufus.

In the hours since, John was in the depths of despair. It seemed Lady Luck had turned her back on him. He had done the only thing his conscience would have allowed when he rescued the boy from a hanging. And now he faced a hanging himself over the men he'd been forced to shoot when he took Cal.

John stared at the floor, contemplating the unfortunate turn his life had taken. He had somehow survived four bloody years of war, a war where men on both sides died by the thousands until their number grew so large that nobody counted them. He had come through an ambush with life-threatening wounds, recovering with the help of Caleb Parsons and his daughter. And then, when the terrible war was finally over, fate handed him a cruel twist. He had the misfortune to come upon the hapless darkie, about to be hung by a vigilante mob without benefit of a trial. Had he not taken a side in it, he might well be in Texas by now. But it had always been John's nature to take a side when he believed it was right.

And now he awaited a hearing before a local magistrate, a man who would most certainly take a side against a darkie. The judge would rule that John provoked the shootings . . . there would be false witnesses, the dead men's friends. John would be convicted, and then, according to Sheriff Buford, quickly hung by the neck. It all seemed unbelievable, like in a bad dream. How could fate have dealt with him so cruelly?

The deputy named Rufus opened a door to the outer office, shuffling down a narrow hallway between the cells carrying two tin plates.

"Sheriff said to slop the hogs back here," he chuckled, sliding each plate through a small opening near the cell floor.

John examined the contents of his plate without getting up from the cot. A spoonful of black-eyed peas swam in watery broth, smelling suspiciously rotten. Decaying food was a subject John understood, having served with the Confederate army.

Rufus was watching him through the bars. "Ain't you hungry for some of this home-cookin', soldier boy?" He laughed. "I only cooked them peas back in March. Hell, they're better'n what you'd get most places. I bet that nigger'll eat 'em." He glanced over to the neighboring cell, scratching his uncut red beard while he stared at

105

Cal. "Maybe Judge Warren can fix it so we'll hang the both of you at the same time. Be fittin', since it appears you love that nigger enough to kill two white men for him. It'll be a double necktie party, hangin' you both at the same time. Folks would come for miles around jus' to see it."

Then Rufus gave John a blank, disinterested look, and went back down the hallway to the office. When the door closed behind him, John ground his teeth together and shook his head.

"I'm powerful sorry 'bout this," Cal whispered from his cell.

"Wasn't your fault," John replied evenly, still seething over the deputy's arrogance. "I knew we should have kept moving last night. I got careless, and this is the price to be paid."

"If Master Tompkins know'd they was gonna hang us on account of that ol' mule, he'd tell that sheriff the truth . . . that he done gave me that mule, and three whole dollars, when he set me free. If only that sheriff asked Master Tompkins . . ."

John stood up slowly, rubbing his sore wrists where the irons had been fastened too tightly. He limped to the window and stood on his toes to see what lay beyond it.

An alley ran past the back of the jail, reeking of rotting garbage. Broken wood crates and empty flour kegs were piled against a building across the alley. The bars across his window were embedded in solid rock and mortared in place. Even with a saw blade, it would take weeks to cut through the heavy iron.

He went back to his cot and sat upon it, overcome by a black mood. Sheriff John Buford meant to hang him. It would be a likely result. The trial would be a farce before a judge who owed his office to county voters. Killing Calhoun County citizens over a slave would be a crime the judge couldn't ignore.

Thus John sat in his jail cell to await the verdict he knew would be forthcoming. He didn't have a snowball's chance in hell of escaping a hangman's gallows. And the frightened darkie in the next cell would also swing, making John wonder about the nature of justice. He understood that his fate was certain, and that he was powerless to do anything to stop it. Telling his version of the story would be a waste of breath. But he would tell it just the same, and hope for some miracle that the truth might make a difference.

The morning passed slowly. The square of sunlight retreated across his cell floor, much to the delight of the cockroaches. Soon the bugs were swarming his untouched plate in a feeding frenzy. John watched them without feeling, for he too understood hunger.

He thought about Sallie Mae, as much to pass the time as anything. He remembered the first time he made love to her, and how wonderful it had been after so many years of forced abstinence with a fast-moving army. If he had stayed with Sallie Mae, as a part of him had wanted, he would be free of the bars around him. But he also understood there were many other kinds of bars, the kind that surrounded men's souls. His soul had yearned to see Texas, his family, and Elizabeth, to find out what fate had in store for him. Thus he'd known he couldn't stay in Tennessee until he knew why Elizabeth stopped writing, though an inner voice told him the reason. But until his eyes and ears learned the truth he would have remained restless. And so it was that he left Sallie Mae to ride back home, until he stopped to help a wayward darkie. Yet while he thought about it, he had no regrets. He would have done the same thing, given a second chance.

* * *

Sheriff Buford picked his broken teeth with a wood splinter, rocking back on his bootheels outside John's cell. A .36 caliber Colt pistol hung beside his right leg in an oiled holster. He gave John a bemused look. "That's a fanciful story, Cap'n Cross. It'd take a crazy man to believe it, an' I ain't crazy. Tell it to Judge Warren. Soon as he stops laughin', he'll order you bound for trial. Hearin' you talk like that convinces me you made a lousy soldier for the Confederacy. No wonder we couldn't win that war, Cap'n. With gents such as you leadin' our troops, we was whipped before we started. A man who won't hang a nigra for stealin' livestock ain't got no business fighting for the South. Didn't you understand what this war was all about? Didn't anybody ever explain it to you, that we was fightin' to keep our slaves?"

John struggled to keep his anger under control. "The boy says he didn't steal that mule. A man named Clarence Tompkins gave him the mule when he set the boy free. Cal's got a piece of paper in his pocket that grants him his freedom, signed by this Clarence Tompkins. It would be a simple matter to send someone to the Tompkins farm to find out the truth about the mule."

Sheriff Buford blinked, then he sauntered over to Cal's cell and leaned against the bars. "You got that piece of paper, boy?" he asked.

Cal nodded his head.

"Give it to me," Buford snapped.

Cal got up quickly and pulled a rumpled sheet of paper from his pants pocket, handing it through the bars.

Sheriff Buford scowled at the words. He shook his head and and sucked noisily through his teeth. "Says here you're free," he said. "Don't say nothin' 'bout no mule." Then the sheriff tore the paper in half, into quarters, and finally scraps. He opened his hand and let the pieces fall to the floor. A cruel grin lifted one corner of his mouth. "Now you're a slave again, boy. And you'll hang for stealin' a mule, soon as Judge Warren gets back from Little Rock."

John balled his trembling hands, fighting the urge to rush to the bars to grab the sheriff's throat. Until reason calmed him some and then his fists relaxed.

Sheriff Buford turned to John. "You got anything to say, Cap'n Cross. Got any objections?"

"None," John whispered, biting down around the word.

The sheriff chuckled. "You don't understand the way the law works in Arkansas. We don't cotton to outsiders who stick their noses into our affairs. We treat our nigras good, when they do like they're told. But when one of 'em gets high-minded notions, we get rid of him, so one bad nigra won't ruin the others. This boy is one of the rotten ones, Cap'n. He run off on a stolen mule. Now, if a man lets that sort of thing go unpunished, afore you know it, every nigra in this state will do the same. We aim to make an example out of this boy. Damn shame you had to come along an' stick your nose in it. You're a murderer, Cap'n, and we hang murderers in Calhoun County. To tell the truth, I'm gonna enjoy stretchin' your neck. A man who'd kill whites to save a nigra don't deserve to live."

The sheriff hooked his thumbs in his suspenders and walked to his office.

When John heard the door close, he whispered, "Damn him," angrily crushing a cockroach with his boot.

Four burly men preceded Rufus and Sheriff Buford down the hallway. Rufus carried a pair of leg irons and heavy wrist manacles to Cal's cell. Cal awoke with a start, lifting his head from the bunk when he heard rattling chains and footsteps. For a week they'd been given nothing but moldy bread and rancid peas, which Cal had eaten. The resulting sickness confined the boy to his bunk. John had only nibbled the bread.

Rufus unlocked Cal's cell. Cal's eyes rounded.

"Your time's up, blackie," Rufus chuckled.

John bolted off his bunk, fixing the sheriff with a look. "What are you aimin' to do with him?"

Sheriff Buford ignored John's question. Rufus and the other men entered Cal's cell. John recognized two of the men from the incident at the vacant farm.

Cal cowered against the cell wall, watching the men with a wary look. Weakened by food poisoning, Cal offered no resistance when his wrists and ankles were bound.

"Where are you taking him?" John asked, approaching the bars between the two cells.

Only then did Sheriff Buford acknowledge John's presence. He turned to John and hooded his eyes. "We're taking this boy to a tree, Cap'n Cross."

John gripped the bars. Bitter bile rose in his throat. "He hasn't been found guilty of anything!" John shouted. Cal's arms and legs had begun to tremble. "There has to be a trial! A judge has to hear the evidence against him!"

The sheriff swung toward John's cell. "You got it all wrong, Cap'n," Buford said in a hoarse, threatening voice. "Judges an' trials are for white men. A nigra ain't got no rights to such things, not when he's a thief. But you, Cap'n Cross, you'll have your say before Judge Warren, soon as the judge gets back. And then we'll swing you from the same tree, soldier boy. Thieves and murderers get hung in Calhoun County. It's the law. And I'll damn sure give you a trial before I put that rope around your neck."

"The boy didn't steal that mule!" John cried. The

110

men were pushing Cal toward the cell door. "Why don't you ask Clarence Tompkins? You can't just hang that boy without evidence?"

Sheriff Buford grinned. "Got all the evidence we need. Got a brown mule. A mule's property, and a nigra can't own no property in the state of Arkansas." Then the sheriff addressed his men. "Get that darkie outside!" he snapped.

Cal fell to his knees, looking up at the sheriff. "Please don't hang me," he whimpered, tears rolling down his face. "If you ask Master Tompkins . . ."

Before Cal could finish, Rufus kicked him in the ribs. The heavy blow sent Cal sprawling on his face, uttering a cry. "Shut up, blackie!" Rufus hissed.

John seized the bars with all his might, shaking with rage. "You can't do it!" he shouted. "You can't just take him out and hang him!"

Sheriff Buford seemed amused. "Like hell I can't," he said, watching Rufus jerk Cal to his feet with a fistful of his shirt. "I'm the lawfully elected sheriff of Calhoun County, an' when it comes to nigras, I can do anything that suits me."

"Can't you read?" John protested. His heart was breaking for the terrified boy. "The war's over. Owning slaves is against the law. That boy's a free man and you can't just up and hang him like this."

Cal was shoved roughly into the hallway. His leg irons made a dull, metallic sound on the stone floor. Sheriff Buford turned his back on John to follow the others toward the front office. A cry burst from Cal's throat when Rufus pushed him. "Please don't hang me. . . . Master Tompkins gave me that mule!"

"Shut up, you lyin' bastard," Rufus warned, pushing Cal through the doorframe.

John listened to the clanking chains around Cal's feet as the boy disappeared into the office. Limbs shaking,

111

he knotted his fists around the bars. "You can't do it!" he shouted. "He didn't steal that mule!"

The door banged closed and John was alone. "No," he said, a whisper of despair. "It ain't fair to just hang him. . . ."

Seething with blind rage, John whirled away from the bars. "I swear I'll make you pay for this, Buford," he snarled, gazing up at the window. "If I can find a way out of this cage . . ."

He slumped to the cot and bowed his head, swallowing a mouthful of bile. "Damn him," he hissed, grinding his teeth together, trying to calm the violent shaking in his limbs. "All he had to do was send someone to the Tompkins farm. That's all he had to do to get the truth."

A tear tumbled down John's cheek. He stared at the floor, swearing revenge against Sheriff John Buford. A roach darted across John's boot and he hardly noticed, for his mind was elsewhere, grieving for the boy. Hanging Cal was the most senseless act in John's lifetime of experience.

An hour passed, then two. He heard no sounds outside the jail or in the office. John sat on his bunk with his face to the floor, examining his feelings. He knew the boy was dead. Nothing could be changed, yet John's agony only deepened. Deeper still was the boiling rage inside him.

As his cell window darkened with nightfall, John left his cot to stare up at the first evening stars. The streets of Hampton were silent now, empty of wagon traffic and moving horses. John watched the sky in the silence of his cell, sorting through his thoughts until long after the window went from pale gray to black.

Later, still standing before the window, he whispered a promise to himself.

Chapter Twelve

The following Friday, three days after Cal had been taken from his cell, John's wrists were manacled by the sheriff and his deputy.

"Judge Warren wants to see you, Cap'n," the sheriff said.

He was taken from the jail to a brick building across the street, then up a flight of stairs. Bright sunlight hurt John's eyes when they crossed the road, having been so long in his dark quarters away from the sun.

He was guided through a door. Seated behind a desk was a man well past sixty with a flowing mane of silver hair hanging down past his stiff paper shirtcollar. The judge wore a threadbare black suit and vest. Rheumy eyes beheld John's approach toward the desk, darting nervously from John to Sheriff Buford.

"This is the reb who killed Amos Sikes and Carl Jackson," the sheriff began, standing at John's elbow. Rufus stood behind them, leaning against the judge's doorframe.

Judge Warren cleared phlegm from his throat. "I'm told you shot those men over a nigra," the judge said. His voice was flat, betraying no emotion.

"A bunch of men were whipping the darkie, claimin' he stole an old mule. Said they was gonna hang him.

The boy swore he got the mule from Clarence Tompkins. It was given to him."

The judge's face was still a blank. "There's witnesses who say otherwise. Those witnesses also say you pulled a gun and shot down Amos and Carl in cold blood."

"That's a lie," John replied evenly. "Two men aimed shotguns at me when I tried to take the darkie to the closest jail. Those men said they were gonna hang the boy. They had no evidence against him, except for the mule."

Judge Warren leaned back in his chair. A gentle breeze blew through an open window behind him, ruffling his silver hair. "I have a few things to say," the judge began. "Things you oughta hear. I'm a southerner, a Confederate. I swore allegiance to the same government you served in that uniform you're wearing. I gave money to the Confederate cause . . . did everything I could. I was too old to serve in the army. Can't hardly see past my nose, so I couldn't shoot anyway. But I firmly believe in our southern doctrines. And one of those doctrines allows the ownership of slaves. Some of this country's greatest Presidents owned slaves, Captain. George Washington, and a great many more. Slavery is an issue on which we're still divided. The war may be lost, but the issue remains. Our cotton can't be picked without slave labor in the fields. Those damn federals in Washin'ton haven't told us how we'll pick our cotton without nigras. It can't be done."

Judge Warren cleared his throat again. "You wear a gray uniform, Captain. I expected a Confederate soldier to have more sympathy for a southerner's position. If we allow freed nigras to steal our livestock before they head north, there won't be enough mules and horses left to plow the fields. Folks in this part of the state understand the dilemma. When you happened along that country road, you interfered with the efforts of sincere

114

men who were trying to put a stop to nigra thievery. It's been like a plague these last months of the war . . . nigras runnin' off on stolen horses, taking whatever they can find. To make matters worse, you shot and killed two innocent farmers . . . good citizens who pay taxes in this county. You mistook them for a lawless mob acting without legal authority. However, Sheriff Buford informs me that one of the men you killed was recently deputized by the sheriff himself, to help put a stop to these very acts of thievery in the south part of Calhoun County. You interfered with the official duties of a peace officer, Captain. You killed him, as he attempted to do his duty."

John turned to Sheriff Buford. A slow smile crossed the sheriff's face. "Amos Sikes was my deputy," he said. "Got the papers Amos signed right there in my desk."

John understood. Sheriff Buford was making sure John did not escape an appointment with the hangman, contriving a piece of false evidence that was sure to sway a jury. John simply shook his head and faced the judge again.

"I'm ordering that you be bound over for trial," Judge Warren remarked. "I'm charging you with two counts of murder. I've been informed that a Yankee judge is being sent down from Ohio to preside over this court as a part of our surrender terms. A military court officer is due to arrive here tomorrow, to make rulings until the judge arrives from Ohio at the end of the month. You'll face an old enemy, Captain Cross, a military officer in a blue uniform will decide your fate. With the evidence our sheriff has, and the witnesses, I suspect that Yankee officer will send you very quickly to the gallows." Then Judge Warren chuckled. "The war may be over, Captain, but old hatreds linger. When a Union officer metes out justice to an enemy who has cost him the lives of so many of his men, I expect justice will be swift and harsh. You'll hang, Captain Corss, as surely as I'm sitting here in front of you. Take him back to his cell, Sheriff."

John turned on his heel, certain that it would be a waste of words to argue with the judge. His fate would lie in the hands of a Union soldier, an officer, a man he'd been trying to kill for the last four years. A hangman's rope seemed certain now.

He was permitted to write two letters, one to his family in Texas, a brief note describing his arrest. The second letter he posted to Sallie Mae. He labored over it, seeking the right words to convey his feelings for her. On Monday, he was satisfied that he'd done the best he could with both letters, handing them to Rufus when his plate of black-eyed peas arrived.

That night be began to pace back and forth across his cell, preparing what he would say to the military court on the day of his trial. He was nagged by the thought that no matter what he said, he would be found guilty. But he prepared his remarks anyway, knowing it was his only chance to remain alive. Since his arrest he'd eaten only the moldy bread they gave him, and his strength had begun to fail. Walking the floor of his cell, he grew weaker, until his legs forced him to rest.

He stared out the window, overwhelmed by the sour turn of events that brought him to this moment in his life. It seemed he'd gained nothing by surviving all those harrowing battles, only to be faced with a hanging for trying to save a young darkie's neck from an unjust rope.

Later, he wondered aloud about his circumstances. "What the hell did I do wrong? Why did Lady Luck send me down that road when Cal was about to be hung? Didn't do any damn good to save him then. What happened to all that good luck that got me through the war?"

He found no answers that night, or the next, pacing back and forth across his cell. He wondered about the letters he'd written, wondered what Sallie Mae would think when she read the careful prose he sent her, to tell her good-bye.

When he slept, his dreams were frightening things. He saw Cal, shackled hand and foot, swinging from a tree limb at the end of a rope, still protesting his innocence in a strangled voice, his body swinging back and forth like the pendulum of a great clock. John often awoke with his body drenched in sweat when the dreams became too real.

Days passed slowly, and he grew weaker without food. No word came about the date of his trial. His despair deepened, as impossible as it seemed.

Then one morning, a week after being taken before Judge Warren, John heard a clamor in the sheriff's office. Muffled voices were angry, though John couldn't make out what was said. He went to the front of his cell, pressing his face to the bars.

The voices fell silent. A door closed. He heard footsteps leaving the jail and puzzled over what had happened. For the past few days Rufus had seemed edgy, without his usual haughty air. Something was afoot in Hampton that didn't suit Sheriff Buford and his deputy, making John wonder all the more about the disturbance in the office just now.

John went back to his bunk, noting with little satisfaction that his limp had almost disappeared. What did it matter if his leg was healed? When the military court ordered his hanging he could walk to the gallows without the limp.

He sat on the cot, idly rubbing fingers through two

weeks of beard, thinking dark thoughts. He had but one pleasant pastime, remembering Sallie Mae and those wonderful stolen moments when her father was away from the cabin. Now he wondered what she might feel when she read his letter. In his mind's eye he could see her pretty face when she read his last words. Would there be tears in her beautiful blue eyes?

The door opened suddenly. Two Union soldiers walked down the poorly lit hallway in polished cavalry boots. One wore a major's shoulder boards. A neatly trimmed waxed mustache adorned his face. Both men came to the front of John's cell. The major hooked his thumbs in his pistol belt, examining John's face.

"You're Captain John Cross," the major said. Then he wrinkled his nose. "This place stinks to high heaven." His gaze fell to the hole in one corner of the cell where prisoners rid themselves of excrement. "This jail isn't fit to hold men. Sergeant Bates, take this man outside. Allow him to bathe, and give him clean clothing. Let him use a razor if he wishes, then put him in an empty cell until this one can be cleaned properly."

"I'll get the key," the sergeant replied, turning on his heel.

The major's attention returned to John. "I'm Major Lionel Crook," he said. "I've been appointed the military governor of this district until Judge Parker arrives. I have a court order from the previous county judge charging you with two murders. I will hear your case tomorrow morning. After you've made yourself presentable, Sergeant Bates will get you something to eat. Myself, I wouldn't feed those peas we found in the front room to a dog. I'm surprised they haven't made you sick, Captain."

"I didn't eat them," John replied. "Just ate the bread that wasn't moldy."

The major shook his head. "You're damn lucky you

haven't come down with a bad case of dysentery." He watched a cockroach race across the cell floor. "My sergeant will see to your needs, and I'll warn you not to try to escape. Four hundred soldiers are camped outside this city. You won't get far."

John stood up, acutely aware of his filthy uniform in the presence of the well-dressed major. "I'm obliged. I've been here so long I'd almost gotten used to the smell."

The major turned to leave, then he hesitated. "Quite frankly, I'm surprised to find you in here, Captain. Unusual, I would think, that southerners would put one of their own in a jail cell."

John bowed his head, thinking how often he'd had the same thoughts. "The men I shot were trying to lynch a nigra boy. They accused the boy of stealing a mule. The mule wasn't stolen. I tried to explain it to Sheriff Buford. . . ."

"You'll have a hearing tomorrow, Captain. I'd rather not hear any more until then." The major hurried up the hallway as if he needed to escape the odors in John's cell quickly. Sergeant Bates appeared with the key to the cell door and a pair of wrist irons.

"You'll have to wear these bracelets," he said, unlocking the cell. "Another thing," he said, pausing before he swung the door open. "I'll take the irons off while you take a bath, but don't try to run when we get outside. Sure would hate to have to shoot you, Captain Cross. But I will, if you make a run for it."

"I understand," John said, extending his arms for the manacles. "Been so long since I had anything to eat besides green bread, I doubt I'd have the strength to run very far."

He was taken from the jail to the street, where he took a deep breath of wonderfully clean air, blinking when his eyes hurt in the bright sunlight.

"This way," the sergeant said, leading him down the quiet street.

A block away from the jail, John's legs became unsteady and a dizzy sickness made him stop to lean against the corner of a dry goods store to catch his breath. "Hold on a minute, Sergeant," he said. "Havin' trouble with my legs."

A carriage passed, dust spewing from its wheels. The town looked deserted. Most of the stores were closed.

"What day is it?" John asked.

"Sunday," Sergeant Bates replied. "How long have they kept you in that jail?"

He couldn't remember. "A few weeks. I don't know. . . ."

When he felt better they resumed their direction at a leisurely pace. The sergeant seemed to understand. "I'll send someone for some food while you clean up," he said. "You'll have to wear one of our uniforms, until yours can be boiled."

John was too weak to protest. Out in bright sunlight, he was keenly aware of how badly soiled his clothing was. He merely shook his head and continued down the street. Wearing a Yankee uniform seemed insignificant now.

He sat in a clean cell smelling of pine oil. Two soldiers had come with mop buckets to clean the jail. Dressed in a blue tunic with a private's stripe, and tight-fitting blue pants, he awaited the arrival of Sergeant Bates and a squad that would escort him to his hearing in Major Crook's tent at ten o'clock. Since dawn he'd been pacing back and forth until his strength played out, worrying about his defense, what he would say to the charges. At least the Yankees fed him well, he thought dully. He would hang with a full belly.

At last, he heard them coming for him, the regular thump of marching boots at the front of the jail. He took a last look at his cell and came to his feet. When he saw the insides of his cell again he would know his fate. John took a deep breath and turned toward the door.

Four infantrymen accompanied Sergeant Bates to the cell. All four were mere boys, even by Confederate standards. The sergeant unlocked the door. "Time to go, Captain," he said.

He was marched down the street past the Hampton courthouse where Judge Warren issued his charges. On porch benches along the way John saw handfuls of Confederate soldiers back from the war, some with missing limbs, the empty sleeves and pants legs rendered by the surgeons' bone saws. John saw the smoldering hatred in the Confederates' eyes as they marched past ... they couldn't know he was a Confederate himself, dressed in a Yankee uniform. The townspeople stopped in the streets to stare. Even the women made their dislike for Union soldiers as plain as they could. The occupation army would find little sympathy in Hampton. The fighting was over, but the deep division between northerners and southerners would be a long time healing here. It would be the same all across the occupied South.

The Union army was camped along the outskirts of town. Rows of white canvas tents fluttered in the soft morning breeze. Cooking fires sent columns of smoke into a clear blue sky. Soldiers moved about the camp. Cavalry details trotted sleek, grain-fed horses between the tents in columns of two. Seeing a Union army camp up close for the first time, John had a better understanding of the Confederate losses near the end of the war. The Yankees had better equipment, fresher horses, and plenty to eat. Men marched in good boots with gleaming new rifles. The armies of the South stood no chance of defeating forces such as this. Hungry, barefooted men with empty rifles had become little more than target practice for the Union.

He was shown to a tent with open sides. Major Lionel Crook sat behind a small table. A sheaf of papers fluttered in the wind beneath a paperweight in front him, papers that contained the charges against John Marshall Cross.

To one side of the tent, Sheriff Buford stood beside four men clad in overalls. All five would offer testimony against John in the forthcoming trial, testimony given without a word of truth about the incident that would cost John his life.

Chapter Thirteen

Major Crook read the charges aloud. John stood before the major's table to hear them, his hands manacled in front of him.

"To the charge of murder, taking the life of Amos Sikes, how do you plead?" the major asked.

John took a deep breath. "I shot him, Major. He aimed his shotgun at me. So did the other feller I'm accused of murdering. They raised their guns an' I figured they meant to kill me, so I did the only natural thing. I shot them, before they had a chance to shoot me."

"He's a lyin' bastard," one man shouted. A farmer who had been at the shooting incident complained loudly. "He shot ol' Amos down in cold blood. I was there."

Major Crook leveled an icy look at the farmer. "You'll have your chance to give testimony, Mr. Cullen. Until then, be silent or I'll have you removed from this tent."

"That ain't fair," Sheriff Buford protested angrily. "These men are witnesses who oughta be heard."

Major Crook's cheeks turned red. He calmly rose from his seat and came around the table. "Let's get one thing straight between us, Mr. Buford. I am the one conducting this trial. You have no more legal authority in this county, so don't arouse my ire by telling me who should be heard. If I want anything from you, I'll ask for it. If you open your mouth again without being asked, I'll have you put in that same jail cell where you kept Captain Cross, and I'll see that you're fed those same rancid peas. The treatment you gave this prisoner is a disgrace. Now hold your tongue or I'll make good on my promise to give you some of the same."

The major walked stiffly back to his chair. "Now tell me your side of the story, Captain Cross," he said, boring through John with piercing blue eyes.

Things hadn't gone well during the afternoon. John listened to the friends of Amos Sikes and Carl Jackson tell a fanciful version of events at the vacant farm. The major had listened attentively, asking pointed questions, making certain each story was the same. During the short break they took for lunch John felt momentarily hopeful. After lunch, his hopes vanished. The man named Cullen swore that John had gunned down two unarmed men. Three more identical versions of the tale followed Cullen's, then John Buford was allowed to speak his piece about John's arrest, adding the untruthful claim that John and Cal had tried to escape into the woods when they saw they were caught.

"The witnesses are excused," Major Crook said. "Sergeant Bates, escort them from the tent. Captain Cross, step forward and I'll pronounce sentence."

"Hang the turncoat bastard," Buford snarled. "He's a damn coward, shootin' unarmed men the way he done."

Major Crook glared at Buford. Sergeant Bates then ushered the five witnesses away.

The major appraised John with a lingering stare. "I've no choice, Captain. The weight of the evidence is against you. No one can corroborate your story. The black boy involved is dead and that leaves no other witnesses. I find you guilty of murder on both counts, Captain Cross."

John lowered his head, feeling the weight of his failure to convince the major of his innocence. "The farmer who gave Cal the mule might have told the truth. His name is Clarence Tompkins."

Major Crook sighed. "It would have no bearing on your guilt, Captain. Whether or not the mule was stolen, four men testified that you killed two unarmed men."

"They had shotguns," John whispered. "I reckoned they meant to kill me. I couldn't wait to find out."

The sounds of a trotting horse distracted the major. A Yankee officer rode up to the tent and snapped off a crisp salute.

"Major Crook, sir," the officer said. "I'd like a word with you about these proceedings. I know this man, although I don't know his name. Permission to speak, sir."

"Granted," Major Crook replied, frowning over the intrusion.

John looked up at the mounted officer. Captain's bars caught rays of sunlight. The soldier's sunburned face looked vaguely familiar . . . he wondered why he would recognize a Yankee officer.

"Last winter," the young captain began, "my men were engaged in a skirmish with this soldier and a force of Confederates in Tennessee. When I saw this man I recognized him, even without his Confederate uniform. I owe this soldier a debt, Major. In the heat of battle, he risked his life to pull one of my men from the battlefield, a man who was badly wounded, suffering greatly. The wounded man was also my cousin. I called for a truce, to see to my injured men. This Confederate captain returned the wounded prisoner, at my request. A moment ago I inquired with a Sergeant Bates about the reason this Confederate was brought to trial. I can't offer anything relating to the charges against him, but with your permission, Major, I'd like to ask for clemency in his case. We were at war with each other, this Confederate and I. His compassion for a wounded enemy was unusual. Begging your pardon for the interruption, Major, but this Confederate isn't a common criminal who would shoot two unarmed men, as your sergeant related the charges against him are filed."

At first, Major Crook seemed annoyed. "There were witnesses against Captain Cross," he said.

The young captain glanced sideways at John. "Perhaps the witnesses have a motive, sir. With your permission, I could make further inquiries into the facts in the case."

The major scowled. "What qualifies you to make inquiries in a legal matter, Captain?"

"I'm a lawyer, sir. Before the conscription order was given in Boston, I practiced law in the Commonwealth Lower Courts."

Major Crook chewed thoughtfully on his bottom lip, looking from John to the captain. "Very well. There is one bit of information that could stand a bit of looking into, Captain. A mule and a former slave were involved in this controversy. I'll allow Captain Cross to give you the details. If the mule wasn't stolen property, as the witnesses allege, perhaps I'll consider that when I pronounce sentence. Make your inquiries, Captain. I'll give you a week. Take the prisoner back to his cell."

The Yankee captain swung down from his horse. John felt a flood of relief wash through him when he shook the captain's hand.

"I never expected to see you again," John said. "I appreciate what you've offered to do."

The Yankee grinned. "I don't think either one of us ever expected to see the other. I'm Captain Robert

Smith, Second Massachusetts Cavalry. I heard the major say your name is Cross."

"John Cross," he replied quickly, remembering the snowy battlefield where he and Captain Smith had fought each other, the captain's tears when he draped his wounded cousin across the back of his horse, then their parting handshake, two enemies briefly at peace with each other in the midst of a war. John wondered about the odds against such a coincidence, that they would meet again.

"I'll accompany you back to the jail," the captain said as the four-man squad turned in formation to escort John away from the tent. "On the way you can tell me about the mule and the slave. Perhaps I can find something that will influence Major Crook's decision."

They started away from the tent. Once again, John found himself with a glimmer of hope, though he dared not trust the feeling. He started telling Captain Smith about Cal and the mule.

These had surely been the longest days of his life. He sat in his cell, staring vacantly at the floor in silent desperation, wondering why the Yankee captain had not returned. Finding Clarence Tompkins should not have been too difficult in the south part of Calhoun County. Had the farmer recanted? Telling a different story now? Or had Captain Smith discovered that Cal had indeed stolen the mule? John had believed Cal's story right from the start. Had it been an outright lie?

He sorted through a thousand jumbled thoughts and feelings, experiencing periods of hope, then despair. When the Yankee guards brought him his meals he begged them for news about Captain Robert Smith's whereabouts. None of them knew anything.

His gray uniform was returned, the tunic mended by

Sallie Mae where the ball was fired into his back, the patchwork trousers sewn up one leg where it was cut to accommodate the splints. He touched the faded yellow shoulder boards, their frayed edges, and his stripes. His flat brim cavalry hat was deeply soiled around the crown, its brim drooping low in front, darkened by sweat stains. He remembered the day he first donned a Confederate uniform, thinking himself a dashing figure, imagining the part he would play in magnificent victories for the South. He understood now that those had been the dreams of a boy not yet seasoned by the sights and sounds of dying. It had all seemed so glorious in the summer of '61. Before the year ended, the dreams of glory had been replaced by bloody realities.

He took off the Yankee uniform and folded it on his cot. He felt better when he was dressed in gray, perhaps only that he'd grown accustomed to it. When his pants were stuffed inside the tops of his knee-high cavalry boots, he began to pace the floor again, until fatigue forced him to rest.

Captain Smith strode down the row of empty cells in the company of a guard. John searched the captain's face for some clue that he bore good news.

"Unlock the door," the captain said sharply, impatiently.

John came to his feet as the key worked the lock. "Did you find Clarence Tompkins?" he asked, feeling a knot of fear in his belly.

Only then did Captain Smith change his expression. The corners of his mouth pulled. "I did. The man gave me a statement. I persuaded him of the importance of talking to Major Crook about the slave named Calvin Seven. It seems southerners don't bother with last names for slaves. They give them numbers instead. Cal was one of Tompkins' favorites . . . a houseboy. He insists he gave Cal his freedom papers, including a statement that the mule he was riding was given to him by Tompkins. Did Calvin Seven ever show you such a paper?"

John shook his head, gritting his teeth angrily. "He showed it to Sheriff Buford. I watched Buford tear it to shreds. Buford claimed the paper did not mention the mule. The boy Cal . . . he could not read, so he didn't know . . ."

"I guessed as much," the captain said. "The matter is in Major Crook's hands now. Come with me. The major wants to see you."

John put on his hat and followed Captain Smith to the front of the jail, wondering what Major Crook would do with him now. Had the story from Clarence Tompkins made any difference?

Captain Smith walked briskly toward the Union camp, down streets filled with wagon traffic and men on horses. Even more Confederates had come home to Hampton, a sad sight in their tattered uniforms along the boardwalks or loafing in small groups at street corners along the way.

Major Crook was in his sleeping quarters when they arrived at the Union camp. An orderly summoned him. John and Captain Smith waited outside.

The major's eyes clouded when he saw John. "I sent for you, Captain Cross, because of the new developments. I'm sure Captain Smith has told you about the statements made by Tompkins. While at first I felt this information failed to resolve the issue, I've had time to think about it. It would appear the slave told the truth about his mule and his freedom. He carried a piece of paper proving he was free and showing ownership of the mule. I still have some trouble with the killings, Captain Cross, but Captain Smith has convinced me of

Sheriff Buford's inhumanity. Records were kept by this sheriff, describing other hangings. On nothing more than his personal whim, he ordered the deaths of slaves who were said to be runaways. It boggles the mind, Captain, how little regard there was for human life around here. After all, these slaves are still human beings. I've ordered the arrest of John Buford and his deputy, Rufus Ballard. We can't find them, or their families. Their homes are abandoned." Then the major squared his shoulders. "In light of these new developments I'm setting you free, Captain Cross. It's been a long campaign and I'm sure you're eager to return home. I'm dismissing the charges against you. You are free to go any time you wish."

John was momentarily speechless. A curious ringing sounded in his ears. "Thank you, Major," he said. "I told you the truth, if it matters."

Major Crook pulled a humorless smile. "Thank Captain Smith for the clemency," he said quietly. "I'd already made up my mind to have you hanged."

The major disappeared inside his tent. John struggled to find the right words to thank the Yankee captain. "I'm sure you know I'm grateful," he said, turning, extending his hand. It seemed he had shaken hands with this Yankee more than he had his closest friends. "Don't know what else to say."

"I owed you a debt for the kindness you extended to David in Tennessee," he replied. "My cousin wasn't a very good soldier, I'm afraid, but he was family. I was with him when he died. You could have simply left him there in the snow."

"The debt's paid," John said hoarsely, remembering that final battle where he'd had this Yankee captain in his rifle sights.

Captain Smith nodded once. "I'm afraid you face a long walk home, Captain. I was told Sheriff Buford sold your horse after he arrested you. Your pistol is in a drawer at the jail. How far do you have to go?"

"Texas," John replied. "Don't suppose I'll mind walking. For a spell, until you came along, I figured I was gonna die here at the end of a rope. Walking home beats the hell out of hanging."

The captain accompanied him back to the jail. No words were spoken between them until John strapped on his gunbelt in the sheriff's office. Three percussion caps remained on the Dance Navy .44 unfired. It was all the ammunition he had.

He left Captain Smith in front of the jail as a noonday sun warmed the streets of Hampton. Walking southwest past the courthouse, he turned once to wave to the Yankee who had given him his freedom. And his life.

As strange as the feeling seemed, John felt like he was leaving a friend when he rounded the courthouse. Although he'd been a part of the effort to exterminate men who wore blue, he was glad a young lawyer from Boston managed to survive Confederate bullets to reach Arkansas in the spring of '65. His life had depended on it. Lady Luck hadn't entirely forgotten John Cross after all.

PART TWO

Chapter Fourteen

It was fate that the road he followed away from Hampton took him past the cemetery. When he saw the rusted wrought-iron fence encircling the grave markers his footsteps slowed, suddenly remembering Cal, the day of the hanging, and then the solemn promise he'd made that night in the darkness of his cell. He had sworn to avenge the boy's death if he ever gained his freedom. And now here he was, a free man at last, with his oath echoing through his mind to haunt him.

John stopped alongside the fence. Behind the fenced section stood another plot of graves, overgrown with weeds, untended. It was common practice that whites were buried separately. The graves in back of the fence would be where Cal was put to rest.

He tilted his face to the sky a moment, debating whether to simply keep walking toward Texas. Those weeks in the Hampton jail were a grim reminder of what would happen if he ran afoul of the law again. By incredible coincidence he had escaped a hanging. He understood that he wouldn't be that lucky again.

He remembered something Major Crook had said . . . that John Buford and Rufus Ballard had left town ahead of the warrants for their arrest. "I'd never be able to find Buford anyway," he muttered to himself. "He's cleared out for parts unknown."

He decided he owed it to the boy to pay his last respects at Cal's grave, thus he plodded around the cemetery fence to the weed-choked field where rows of little wooden markers stood in the sun. A pile of fresh earth took him to the right burial spot. Crudely carved letters read, "Cal Seven. Thief. 1865."

"He wasn't a thief," John whispered, holding his hat in his hands, remembering the boy's terrified expression when Rufus Ballard took him from the cell, the savage kick he gave the darkie's ribs when Cal was pleading for his life. "He was just a scared nigra boy, begging for someone to listen to the truth."

John wheeled away from the grave, socking his hat on his head as he hurried back to the road. He paused briefly beside the cemetery fence, glancing southwest, then he turned back toward Hampton with his mouth set in a hard line.

A woman hanging her laundry on a line directed him to John Buford's house. "He an' his missus left town last week," she said, fitting a clothespin to a shirtsleeve. "Shame them blasted Yankees ran a good man off his job the way they done. Lots of folks wished Sheriff Buford coulda stayed on to keep the peace."

John walked to the outskirts of Hampton, following a winding creek southward to a clapboard shack standing at the edge of a small cornfield. Last year's cornstalks rattled in the wind. No one had planted the field this spring.

The shack was empty. A shed behind the house evidenced old horse droppings. Across a tree-shaded lane stood a similar old house surrounded by a well-tended flower garden. An elderly man in faded overalls carried water from a well behind the shack to his flowers. John sauntered across the road.

"Sorry to hear ol' John Buford left town," he began. "I reckon those Yanks will ruin everybody before they're done around here."

The old man eyed John's Confederate uniform, then his wary expression softened. "Goddamn shame is what it is," the man spat angrily, tilting his watering can above his pansies. A cud of chewing tobacco filled the man's cheek. "Goddamn bluebellies have taken over the town like a plague of locusts. Everywhere you look you see Yankees. They run Sheriff Buford out of Hampton 'cause he done too good a job." Then the old man eyed John suspiciously again. "You a friend of the sheriff's? Never saw you round here before."

"Just passin' through," John replied, trying to sound casual. "Got a message about some of his kin. Talked to a man from First Arkansas Volunteers a while back. Promised I'd carry the sad news about Buford's dead cousin when I came through. Any idea where I can find John now?"

A stream of brown juice came from the old man's mouth. He adjusted his cud, looking thoughtful. "He didn't say where he aimed to go. Left in somethin' of a hurry." There was a pause. "But John's wife told my old woman that they was headed fer a relative's place in Texas. Gladewater, was what she said. I told the sheriff I'd keep track of that ol' mule 'til I could sell it fer him. But the mule's too damn old. Got no jaw teeth an' I 'spect it'll starve this winter when the grass gets short."

Across a split-rail fence John glimpsed a brown mule. He quickly recognized it. It had been Cal's. "I've been put afoot by those damn Yankees," John said quietly. "I'll be passing through Gladewater on my way to Waco. Wouldn't mind delivering that mule to John. I could ride instead of walk, if the mule can carry me."

The man gave John a toothless grin. "Be travelin' mighty damn slow." He looked across the fence at the mule. "Can't sell him anyways. Suits hell outa me if you take it to the Bufords. John left an old bridle hangin' in the shed out back. Tell John I tried to sell the mule fer him, like he asked. Couldn't get a single bid from nobody. Mule's too damn old. Liable to die afore you git to Texas."

John crossed the fence and quickly bridled the mule, worrying that the old man might change his mind. By traveling slowly, the mule could carry him across Arkansas, perhaps to Gladewater. Of far more importance, John knew John Buford's whereabouts.

He drummed his bootheels into the mule's ribs and rode away from the house, waving over his shoulder when the old man looked up from his flowers. John Buford's neighbor had unwittingly given John more than transportation. Now he had the scrap of information that would guide him toward his sworn revenge.

The nights were still cold. He had no blankets, and no food. Camping beside streams in the southern Arkansas woods, he made slow, steady progress aboard the mule.

There were days when he went hungry. At a farm he begged a piece of fishing line and a hook. The sympathetic farmer threw in some pieces of cornbread in a gunnysack, and a worn saddle blanket for the mule's withers that also served as a sleeping pallet when John made camp that night. Digging grub worms, he caught a few perch and smoked them on a stick above his campfire. Without a knife he couldn't prepare the fish and was forced to tear the meat off the bones with his fingers.

A week later he happened upon a sleepy village named Magnolia, where a wounded Confederate infantryman informed him he was in Columbia County. The Red River lay just fifty miles to the west. Beyond the river was Texas, a two-day journey away. Brightened by this bit of news, John hurried the mule through Magnolia without stopping to rest. As darkness fell he selected a campsite beside a clear stream, hobbling the mule in tall grass.

He climbed the opposite bank and stared westward. Beyond the treetops, another day's ride, was his home state. He looked wistfully in that direction for several minutes. Somewhere to the west, John Buford was probably enjoying a quiet supper. By now he would have forgotten the pleas of a frightened darkie he took from the Hampton jail to hang. But someone was coming to Gladewater to remind him of it before he died.

No fish would take the grubworm on his hook, no matter how hard he stared at the little stick tied to the line floating in the stream. At full dark he gave up and went to bed hungry, looking up at the stars. He thought about Sallie Mae for a time, then his mother and sister back home. He refused to allow any recollections of Elizabeth to enter his mind. Just before he drifted off to sleep he thought about Cal again, curling his fingers around the butt of the .44 he kept beside him while he slept.

Gladewater was like most other small east Texas towns, a collection of false-fronted stores along a single street, houses scattered around the business district along rutted dirt lanes. John rode the mule into town just after first light, carefully planning his arrival before most townspeople were about.

A blacksmith had begun working bellows at his forge. He gave John a friendly wave when the mule halted in front of his shop.

"That's a tenderfooted mule," the blacksmith said.

"Carried me all the way from Arkansas," John replied, watching the muscular smithy work his bellows. "I'm lookin' for a feller by the name of John Buford. Got word about some of his kin from the war."

The smithy nodded. "North about two miles, soldier. You'll come to a farm just after you cross Hog Creek. Can't miss it. Bufords moved in with the Feagin bunch. Claimed to be some kin of the Feagins. John Buford's helpin' clear trees from a new piece of ground behind the house. Been cussin' them dogwoods 'cause they're so hard to chop. Comes to town now and then, but he don't say much. Mostly just cusses them dogwoods while I sharpen his axes."

"Much obliged," John said, swinging aboard the mule. He reined north, allowing the mule to walk slowly away from town.

Following a narrow trail through the pine and hardwood forest, he let his anger build, remembering the day of Cal's hanging. His resolve remained firm since his release from the Hampton jail, but now he fueled his need for revenge with vivid memories of Cal's tearful pleas for mercy from Sheriff Buford and his deputy. The closer John came to the Feagin farm the more certain he became that he would commit murder in the name of vengeance. The three lead balls he carried against his hip would serve justice before he put his gun away to become a farmer.

He heard the distant sounds of an ax in the forest. Pulling the mule off the trail, he tied it in the trees and crept forward on foot. Soon he came to a creek wandering through the woods. He crossed it quietly and drew his pistol, for the sounds of the ax were very close now.

He saw John Buford standing at the edge of a clearing, already sweating profusely, sleeving perspiration from his forehead in the early morning sunlight. After a careful examination of the woods to be sure Buford was

140

alone, John crept forward again on the balls of his feet, keeping to the shadows below the trees at the edge of the clearing.

John was very close to Buford's back before Buford sensed someone else's presence. Halting the swing of his ax, he looked over his shoulder. A gun and holster lay near Buford's feet beside his folded jacket, the same .36 Colt he'd carried at Hampton. When Buford saw John standing behind him, he threw his ax aside and whirled around.

"Surprised me," he said, peering into the shadows of John's hat brim. "I know you from someplace, don't I?"

John stepped out of the trees, covering Buford with his .44. "I reckon you should remember," John said in a soft voice. "You tried to have me hung."

"It's you!" Buford growled. He glanced from John's gun to his own. "You was sentenced to hang. How did you find me, Cross?"

John gave Buford a crooked grin. "A helpful neighbor. I rode that old mule you took from the nigra boy you hung. That Yankee major let me go free when he found out the truth. The mule wasn't stolen. It said so on that piece of paper you tore up at the jail. You hung that boy, knowin' all along the mule was given to him by Clarence Tompkins."

"That's a lie!" Buford hissed, crouching slightly, balling his hands.

"It's the truth. Tompkins came to Hampton and told the major what he wrote on Cal's piece of paper. The Yanks set me free when they found out what you'd done to Cal. Now I'm here to settle things, to settle the score. You had me locked up and sentenced to hang with false testimony. You stole my horse and sold it. But that ain't the reason I'm here, Buford. I came here to kill you for what you did to that nigra boy."

Buford blinked. He swallowed and looked down at

141

his pistol. "You gonna gun me down whilst I'm un-armed, Cross?"

John let a silence pass. "I should. Be the same thing you did to Cal Seven."

John's hands had begun to shake with rage. He took another step toward Buford, then he slowly holstered his pistol. "Pick it up, Buford," he said in a hoarse whisper. "Pick up your gunbelt and strap it on."

Buford was suspicious. "You'll shoot me when I bend down," he said.

John grinned. "It's the only chance you've got. Pick it up, or I'll kill you where you stand."

Buford started to blink furiously. Sweat was trickling down into his eyes. He bent down slowly, carefully, his eyes glued to John's gun hand. "I knew I should have hung you myself," he said as his fingers opened above his pistol.

John tensed the muscles in his right arm, expecting Buford to trick him. Ten yards separated them. He knew he would not miss at this range.

Buford clawed for the butt of his revolver instead of picking up the belt. . . . John had guessed Buford's move and was ready for it. He drew the .44 with lightning speed and aimed for Buford's head.

A loud explosion rocked the silent woods. Buford's right hand tightened around his pistol grips, then relaxed, allowing the gun to fall to the ground. A groan sounded as Buford's feet shuffled backward. A few drops of blood splattered down on his boots.

John stood impassively as Buford struggled to remain on his feet. A dark hole below Buford's left eye dribbled blood down the front of his shirt, soaking his beard with crimson droplets that clung to the ends of each hair before they fell.

"That was for Cal," John said softly, seemingly without any emotion.

Buford's eyes focused. One hamlike hand went to the wound on his face as his gaze came to rest on John. "I'm shot," he groaned, sounding surprised. Then his knees buckled. . . . He caught himself with a booted foot and staggered forward, toward John.

John calmly cocked his .44 and fired again. Above the pistol's roar John heard shattering teeth as the ball entered Buford's open mouth. A strangled cry followed the echo of the gunshot. Blood and strands of Buford's hair flew from the back of his skull.

"That one was from me," John said, watching Buford topple over on his back, arms outstretched. Buford's head made a sodden, wet noise when he landed.

A thin wisp of blue gunsmoke floated away from John's gun barrel. He felt his emotions drain. Since the day Sheriff Buford and his deputy took Cal from his cell, John had planned this moment of revenge. Only now, as he looked down upon Buford's body twitching with death throes, could he put his anger to rest. The unjust hanging of a frightened boy had been avenged.

He picked up Buford's .36 Navy Colt and his gunbelt, hanging the belt from his shoulder before starting into the woods. Someone shouted from the trees north of the clearing. Buford's kinsmen would be coming, drawn by the shots.

He hurried through the dogwoods and pines to reach the mule. He meant to swing wide of Gladewater, traveling slowly through the woods where his tracks would be hard to find.

On a wooded ridge west of the clearing, John halted the mule to look over his shoulder. He smiled a satisfied smile and urged the mule onward, feeling better about Cal's memory. If there were such things as ghosts, Cal Seven's wouldn't haunt him now.

Chapter Fifteen

When he saw the Brazos River a lump came to his throat. For four years, he'd dreamed of this day. He remembered the words to a Confederate marching song and whispered them to himself as the heavy freight wagon lumbered downhill. "When Johnny comes marching home again, hurrah, hurrah." An unwanted tear moistened the corners of his eyes. Jolting over every bump in the road atop a load of pine planks, John Cross experienced his homecoming. The mule had taken its last step near a sawmill at Prairie Junction. A mule skinner at the mill promised him a ride to Waco at the end of the week. John had been too exhausted and hungry to attempt the walk of better than a hundred miles.

A huge Union army camp sprawled along the eastern riverbank near Waco. Approaching the city, John saw what he'd expected to see. Burned farms stood like black skeletons in cotton fields gone to seed. A few plantations whose owner's names he'd forgotten sat empty, windowless, fallen to sad states of disrepair, peeling paint at the end of tree-shaded lanes as if trying to hide their ugliness behind leafy branches. The magnificent home of Benjamin Fannin Johnson, one of McLennan County's most prosperous cotton plantations, was now only a smoke-blackened shell. Just two of the tall columns that graced the front of the mansion were still standing, shedding their paint inside a grove of towering pecan trees, almost hidden from view. John wondered then what he would find when he inquired about Elizabeth at the Lacy plantation south of town. It would be sad to see the once-beautiful lawns and gardens overgrown with grass and weeds, the big house fallen to ruin like the others.

Men were repairing the east-west railroad line near the river bridge where one of "Sherman's bowties" ended the rails. As the wagon rattled past the twisted iron he saw scores of hollow-eyed Confederates laboring to restore the track under the supervision of Union officers. "We're the slaves now," he told himself. An old Confederate waved to him when he saw John's gray uniforms as the wagon rolled toward the river bridge.

On the west side of the Brazos the road brought John to the most tragic sights of all. Hundreds of homeless Confederates were camped south of the railroad depot. Crude tents and tiny shelters fashioned from charred planks and other scraps of wood were crowded together in the abandoned cotton yard beside the gin. Before the war, bales of cotton filled the yard awaiting shipment. As a boy, John had played hide-and-seek among the giant bales. Gray-clad men now sat around smoldering cooking fires where John and his friends had hidden from each other, watching the wagon with blank stares. John had never imagined there could be so many gaunt-faced, hungry men. Most appeared to be starving. He saw sunken cheeks and bony arms. Men whose waists had shrunk held their pants in place with pieces of rope or binder twine.

"It don't appear there's much to eat in McLennan

County," John observed, deeply saddened by the soldiers' condition.

The mule skinner overheard his remark. "Them Yank bastards ain't none too thin," he said, rolling his cud to the other cheek.

John turned his face from the rebel camp to look at the city beyond the railroad depot. Most of the buildings he remembered were still standing. The Yankees had spared stores and shops, the hotels, and the saloons on Webster and Clay Streets. From the wagonbed John could see saddled horses at the hitchrails in front of the saloons, the Brazos Queen, the Cotton Palace, and Diamond Lil's where the whores would be plying their trade to Yankee soldiers. Beyond the saloons he could see the Planters Bank where Hiram Cross used to make fall payments on his farm mortgage.

He jumped off the wagon when they reached the depot, after thanking the driver for his kindness. Shouldering the gunnysack containing his few possessions and John Buford's gun, he watched the wagon roll away in a cloud of dust. The teamster had given John a piece of salt pork and a small sack of dry beans. It was enough food to nourish him for the seven-mile walk southward along the Brazos until he reached home.

He started south on stiffened legs with the sack swinging over his shoulder, ignoring the faces of hungry Confederates he passed at the edge of the camp below the cotton gin. For days he'd been wondering about Billy and Tommy Joe and Wild Henry. Had the three of them made it back to McLennan County alive? If Billy made it through, he would be at his little farmhouse not far from John's home place. John would pass it on the way.

Trudging down roads lined with older houses, he remembered so many things from his boyhood, things he'd forgotten while he was at war. Riding a bareback pony behind his father's wagon on the monthly trips to town to see the sights and buy a stick of hard candy, and once to see a circus parade and listen to a calliope. Swept away by a flood of old memories such as these, John made his way home.

When he came to the bend in the road where he should have been able to see Billy Cole's house, he found only a vacant field. Doubting his memory, he hurried toward the spot, ignoring the blisters on his feet. But the closer he came to the little grove of plum trees beyond the bend, the more certain he became that he was in the right spot. His footsteps slowed. What had happened to the house?

Then he saw remnants of the brick foundation, and charred lumber hidden in waist-high grass. Yankees had burned the house and the barn. Only a part of the corral fence remained where the barn had been.

"Yank bastards!" he cried. "This place was all Billy had!"

A covey of frightened quail darted from the tall grass near the foundation, fluttering west to a fencerow, then out of sight. John shook his head and started down the empty road again, now with proof that Billy Cole hadn't made it home. Billy would have come back to his farm if he had been able. With his spirits dampened John continued south, until he heard a voice behind him.

"I'd know that ugly face anywhere," someone said.

John whirled around, reaching for his gun.

"Don't shoot me, Johnny boy. Hate to get killed by a friend."

Billy Cole walked from the grove of plum trees, grinning through his whiskers. He hurried his strides to reach John. "We all had you figured for dead," he said, breaking into a trot. When Billy reached John he threw his arms around him, and now his voice was breaking.

147

"We couldn't go back, Johnny. Them bluebellies came after us hard and fast. We hid from 'em in the woods and tried to circle back to where they shot you, but they was so thick in them trees we couldn't. Damn! I've shed some tears over you, my friend. I just know'd you was dead. When they shot you off your horse . . ."

"I made it," John whispered, embracing Billy, not yet over the shock of seeing him there. "I saw what they did to the house. Where the hell were you just now?"

Billy jerked a thumb over his shoulder. "Been livin' in the root cellar. Got lots of things to tell you. Most of 'em ain't good either. When did you get back?"

"Just this morning," John said, stepping back to look Billy over. He seemed none the worse. Better than the starving men at the Confederate camp. "It's a long story," he added. Then he thought about his mother and sister. "Have you been down to our place?"

The look he saw on Billy's face prepared him for bad news.

"I'll need to tell you a few things," he said, his voice quieter than before. "Let's find us some shade where we can talk."

John followed Billy to the plum grove. Behind the trees he saw a trapdoor opened above the root cellar. Billy led them to a pile of old lumber. "Been pullin' the nails from the good stuff so I can build a shelter," Billy said, taking a seat on the pile of planks.

"Tell me about my maw," John insisted before he sat. "Mary too. Mary wrote that Maw was feelin' poorly. That was more'n a year ago."

Billy took a deep breath before he spoke. "Your maw died a few months back, Johnny. Some say she grieved herself to death after your paw died. Got to where she wouldn't eat. Just wasted away in her rocking chair 'til they found her one morning on the front porch. Sorry to be the one to tell you. They buried her beside your paw in back of the house."

John bowed his head. He'd known from Mary's letters that something was wrong. "What about Mary?" he asked softly.

"She moved to town. Took a job . . ." Billy didn't finish, avoiding John's eyes.

John shook his head, glancing south. "I'll visit my folks' graves and find Mary," he said.

Billy cleared his throat. "The place ain't yours no more. Got sold fer back taxes a couple of months ago. Planters Bank over in Waco owns it now. Got it rented out on shares to a gent from up north. There's land speculators all over the place now, buyin' up property fer taxes. Folks call 'em carpetbaggers. I figured you oughta know afore you got there."

"Sold?" John cried angrily. "For back taxes?"

"Mary told me," Billy replied. "Your place ain't the only one in this bottom. Land speculators bought up most of the good land fer back taxes. It's the law, Johnny. Union army and carpetbag judges are runnin' everything. They treat Confederates worse'n nigras. Some folks have tried to argue that it was their crops that paid the taxes, and when the war took all the menfolk away, wasn't nobody left to work the soil. Yanks don't pay no attention. Folks have been run off their farms at gunpoint. Evicted, they call it. Got ourselves a new sheriff in this county, a paid killer from Kansas Territory. Him an' his deputies serve the papers from that Waco bank. Folks that won't leave get dragged out of their houses. Some have been shot. Losin' that war has been a blight on this part of Texas. Damn Yankees will own everything before it's over."

John started to pace back and forth. "They can't do it," he growled, making a face. "They can't just up an' take a man's land like that! My paw paid off that mortgage at the Planters!"

"Like hell they can't," Billy answered. "They've done it already to lots of folks. I can't pay the taxes on this place, but the land's so damn worthless nobody took it over. Yankees burned the house. All I've got left is sorry land and no money to buy seed."

John looked down the road toward the Cross farm, another mile to the south. He halted his pacing. "I won't just lie down and take it, Billy. I'll do something. They won't just toss me off that farm without a fight. I'll go have a talk with the bank!"

"You're too late, Johnny. Papers have already been served while we was off in Tennessee. I talked to Mary."

John whirled around. "Where does my sister work? I'll go have a talk with her about it."

Billy couldn't look at him and he wondered why. "She went to work at Diamond Lil's," he whispered.

John was stunned to silence for a time. His mouth had gone too dry to speak. "Diamond Lil's?" he asked. The voice was not his own.

Billy nodded. "Took up with the Yankee colonel who bought the place. Mary's his woman. I saw it for myself when we got to town. I'm damn sure sorry to have to be the one to tell you all this, Johnny boy. If it makes you feel any better, wasn't nothin' but bad news for all of us when we got back home. Tommy Joe Booker got throw'd in jail fer stealin' two loaves of bread from Miller's Bakery. He was just plain too hungry to pass 'em by. Wild Henry found work as a gandy dancer at the railroad fer a spell, 'til he got crossways with that new sheriff from Kansas. Locked him up too. Cost him his job. Last I saw him, he was livin' in a dugout down by the river, catchin' fish to sell in town. Been hard times while you was away. Don't look like they'll get no better."

John wasn't really listening. Learning that his sister worked in the town's most infamous whorehouse ended his concentration on what Billy said after that. While Mary had always been pretty, she would never have sold her body for a price. Hiram and Cora Cross raised their children according to scripture. Hiram read from the Bible aloud every night after supper, filling the house with his sonorous voice, reciting passages until everyone knew them from memory. Mary would never have allowed herself to become a fallen woman. He was sure of it, no matter what Billy said. "I'll talk to Mary," he said after a thoughtful silence.

Billy stood up and dusted off the seat of his pants, then he clapped a hand on John's shoulder. "Don't take it too awful hard about Mary," he said. "Hard times can make people do things they wouldn't otherwise. Both of us know what it's like to be hungry."

"I'll talk to her," he said. "Best I went down to visit the graves, to pay my respects."

"Mind if I walk along?" Billy asked. "I could use the company."

John turned for the road. "Sure. We can talk."

He stood below the big elm tree with his hat in his hands. He shed no tears. Billy stood behind him. Below the hill where the graves had been dug, a man followed a team of mules gripping plow handles. It was late in the summer to be plowing, too late to plant a crop. For most of his life, John had plowed that same piece of land alongside his father, almost from the day he could walk. John couldn't look at the stranger plowing that field today. He kept his eyes glued to the simple markers above his mother and father, reading the inscriptions, remembering, trying to control his anger, struggling with his tangled thoughts. His bad luck seemed to have no end. The war, and its terrible aftermath, had destroyed everything he loved and valued in McLennan County. All that remained of the things he once cherished were his sister, and Elizabeth. He already knew what was in store when he visited Mary at Diamond Lil's, and for more than a year he'd prepared himself for the truth about Elizabeth Lacy.

A few minutes later he turned from the graves to Billy and pulled his hat brim over his eyes. "I reckon it's fair to say that the war cost me everything I had, Billy," he said. A hard edge had come to his voice. "I went off to kill Yankees, like they said we had to do, to keep what was ours. I believed them. I learned how to kill Yankees. Spent four years learning how." Then he hooked his thumbs in his gunbelt and looked up at the sky. "Got back today and found out I've got nothing left. No farm. No family, and my sister's a Yankee colonel's whore." John's hands began to tremble. Muscles tightened in his cheeks. "I got pretty good at killin' Yankees. Had plenty of practice, and I believe I'll try my hand at some more of it. They took this place for taxes, the bank did. Now I aim to collect a few taxes myself. That Planters Bank has got plenty of money in it. I'm tired of bein' broke and hungry. I'm gonna rob that bank, Billy. Then I'll be headed down to Mexico."

Billy stared at him. "You're joshin' me, ain't you?" he asked. "You're funnin' me, to see what I'd say."

John didn't answer for a long time, looking at the back of the house where he was born.

"I'm dead serious, Billy," he finally said. "I'll talk to Mary. But if what you say is true, I aim to take back what was mine. I'll ask the bank to give me back this land, and if they won't, I swear I'll empty that safe and ride to Mexico."

Billy rubbed his whiskered chin. "You ain't even got a horse," he said. "I still say you're only funnin' me."

John stalked away from the elm tree without a reply.

Chapter Sixteen

Diamond Lil's smelled of barley vapors and unwashed men. A film of cigar smoke hovered above the tables where drummers in vested suits and Yankee officers held fistfuls of cards or mugs of lukewarm beer. A few toyed with shotglasses of bad whiskey. The flow of good whiskey had been interrupted across the South by the war. John entered the batwing doors and was met by unfriendly stares. He was the only Confederate in the place. Union soldiers eyed his rumpled gray uniform and unshaven chin. John walked between the tables toward the bar, ignoring the looks they gave him.

A piano tinkled in a corner of the saloon. John approached a balding bartender. Lantern light from a brass fixture above the bar shone down on the man's gleaming skull.

"I'm looking for Mary Cross," he said, when he had the bartender's attention.

The barman chuckled. "Don't look like you can afford her, reb. She's upstairs in her room. Number twelve at the end of the hall."

He bristled at the remark, then let it drop and headed for the stairway to the second-floor rooms. Some of the Yankees were watching him when he took the stairs. He made his way down a poorly lit hallway until he came to number twelve.

His soft knock produced a muffled question. "Who's there?"

"It's John. Your brother. Open the door."

He heard scurrying feet and then the door swung wide. At first he didn't recognize the woman. Her hair was done in ringlets down to her shoulders. A red satin dress, cut low in front, revealed generous powdered bosoms. Then John looked closely at the woman's face. Mary smiled and rushed into his arms.

"Oh, Johnny, you're home!" she cried, smothering his face with kisses.

He gently put his hands around her waist. "Been a long time, Mary Nell," he said. He smelled sweet brandy on her breath.

Mary stepped back, sensing that something was wrong. John noticed a puffiness under her eyes. Her smiled faded. "I guess you already know about Maw," she said, her tone somber. "I can see it in your eyes, Johnny."

He nodded once. "I've been out to the place. Billy Cole told me about Maw, and where to find you."

"Then you know about that too," she whispered. "Come inside. I've got some things to tell you."

She closed the door gently behind him. The room was nothing more than a bed and a dresser with a washbasin. A dressing screen stood in one corner. The room was bathed in yellow light from a lantern beside the bed. Mary showed him to a chair near the window overlooking Webster Street. He took it, pulling off his hat. He could hear the piano playing through the wooden floor and the sounds of carriage traffic coming through the window as a soft night wind fluttered the lacy curtains beside the opening. John knew, before Mary started her story, that Billy had told him the truth about his sister.

"I know what you're thinking," she said, standing near his chair, silhouetted by the lantern behind her.

John fought the urge to cry. "I'm not thinkin' anything until I hear what you have to say."

"We needed the money, Johnny. Me and Maw almost starved that winter after Paw died. There weren't any jobs for women." She paused and took a shuddering breath, folding her hands into her skirt. "I did what I had to do. This was the only work there was."

"You're a whore," he said. The word stung him like the lash of a whip.

Crystal tears rolled down Mary's cheeks. Her lips had begun to quiver. "Call me anything you like, Johnny. We had to eat. Maw sold the mules to pay the doctor when Paw got kicked. Paw just lay there with his skullbone crushed, only he wouldn't die. He just kept layin' there for three whole months, needing medicine that cost a lot of money. We took charity from the neighbors until I couldn't stand it. I didn't have any choice. This was all there was."

Hearing Mary admit to her profession ended any hopes he had that there was some sort of a mistake. On the walk back to town he had argued with himself that Mary wouldn't sell herself in a whore's crib. But now he knew the truth. "It's wrong," he said, knowing how feeble it sounded. "It goes against Bible teaching. Decent women don't make whores, no matter what."

Mary's eyes slitted. "What do you know about it?" she cried, whirling away from his chair. She sobbed once, then gained control. "You weren't here, Johnny, to know what it was like. Maw just sat there in her rocking chair, wasting way to nothing, grieving over Paw. She wouldn't eat what little food we had, saying she wasn't hungry. We had to have some money. Wasn't no other way for us to survive."

She took a handkerchief from a pocket of her dress and wiped her eyes. She wouldn't look at John now, her face to the window.

"There just had to be another way," he said. "Bein' a whore is the worst thing there is."

Mary dabbed the last tear from her cheek. "You can think whatever you want," she said evenly. "I'm the one who has to live with myself. You went off to war and I didn't have anybody. I didn't know if you were ever coming back. The bank kept sending men out to the farm, claiming we had to pay our taxes. Then Maw passed away and I was all alone." She turned from the window and walked over to her dresser. She opened a drawer and removed a sheaf of currency. "Here's some money, Johnny. I saved fifty dollars for when you got back. It ain't Confederate. All I took was federal dollars."

John got up and shook his head. "I don't want your whorin' money," he said. "All I wanted was that farm. I reckon I'll be going now." He started for the door.

"What'll you do?" she asked, holding the money out to him.

"Don't rightly know just yet. I aim to have a talk with the bank, to see if they'll let me have the place back. I can pay those taxes out of next year's crop, if they'll allow it."

Mary dropped the money on top of the dresser. Tears filled her eyes again. "Take this money, Johnny. It'll help you make a new start," she said, pleading with him now.

He walked past the dresser and took the doorknob. "Good-bye, Mary. I don't reckon we'll see each other again, so long as you're working here. If you change your mind about stayin' in this whorin' business, you'll

157

be welcome back at the place any time, if I can make arrangements with the bank to get it back."

"It's too late for that," she said, reaching out to touch his arm. "The place is gone. Besides, it wasn't much of a farm anyways. Eighty acres is all."

"It was home," John whispered. He opened the door and went out in the hallway.

"Take this money, Johnny! Please!" Mary cried, offering him the bills again.

He shook his head and walked down the hall, listening to the hollow sounds of his boots moving across the floor. Piano music and laughter greeted him on the stairs. He wondered what it would be like to laugh again as he made his way out of the saloon.

Outside, he took a deep breath, ridding his lungs of cigar smoke, then he turned down the boardwalk, walking through squares of lantern light from the saloon windows. Soon the sounds from Webster Street were behind him.

Billy was boiling the beans the mule skinner gave him when he returned to the root cellar around midnight. The smells of cooked salt pork and beans filled the tiny dugout. A candle flickered in a corner, casting eerie shadows behind cobwebs netted from the wooden rafters.

"Did you find her?" Billy asked.

John sat down on a cornshuck mattress. Outside, a mesquite knot popped in Billy's cooking fire. "I talked to her. She ain't nothin' but a whore now, Billy. If Maw an' Paw know'd it, they'd rise up outa their graves."

Billy stared at the floor. "Hard times, Johnny boy. Don't be so quick to pass judgment on your sister. Maybe there was circumstances . . ."

John took the clay pipe Billy offered. A tiny twist of

sweet tobacco sat in the bowl. He lit the pipe with the candle and took a draw on the stem. "I'll talk to the bank tomorrow," he said thoughtfully. "If I can get the place back . . ."

"You're bein' a fool, Johnny. You ain't got no money. They won't listen."

"Maybe," John reflected, watching smoke curl from the pipe. "If they won't, I'll let 'em listen to the bark of this Dance .44 when I clean out that vault."

Billy's brow pinched. "I figured you'd give up on that fool notion. Those Yanks would catch up to you before you crossed the Leon River, if'n you didn't get your ass shot off whilst you was robbin' the bank in the first place."

"I'll come up with a plan," John replied.

Billy got up from the overturned water bucket where he'd been sitting, ducking to avoid cobwebs. "You're plannin' to get yourself shot or hung," he said. "Only a crazy man would try to rob the Planters Bank. It's the craziest notion you ever had."

Billy went out to spoon beans and salt pork onto tin plates blackened by the burning of his house. They ate the beans in silence. John was thinking about a plan to rob a bank. Billy was wishing he had a bottle of whiskey to go with his beans.

He introduced himself as Sheldon Blackwell when John entered the office. Blackwell wore a silky vest with a gold watch chain hanging across his ample stomach. He gave John's uniform a look of disdain, then he pointed to a vacant chair.

"What can I do for you, Mr. Cross?" he asked gruffly, impatient to get on with more important bank business. Walls of polished wood surrounded Blackwell's desk. A crystal brandy decanter stood on a shelf behind him. He did not offer John a drink.

"It's about the Hiram Cross farm," John began. "I'm told the bank took it for back taxes.

Blackwell hooded his eyelids. "There was a lot of land that owed taxes," he said. "We bought all we could for the bank. Good land makes a good investment."

"I want to get that farm back," John continued. "I could pay the back taxes out of next fall's crops."

Blackwell pursed his lips. "If I remember rightly, the bank has already rented that farm on shares. Perhaps the following year, Mr. Cross."

John stiffened in his seat. "It isn't fair. That place was owned by my family. The mortgage was paid. I was away fightin' the war and didn't know about the taxes. A feller oughta get a second chance to pay."

Blackwell arched one eyebrow. "Have you got any money, Mr. Cross?"

"Not just now. I'll find work, and there'll be crops next year."

Blackwell sighed. "You're telling me that you are broke, and still you want to own a farm."

"It was our farm," John persisted. "You took it away from my sister while I was gone with the army."

"The bank paid the taxes and owns the land," Blackwell said. "The law says that land can be claimed for unpaid taxes after a suit is filed. The county court ordered that farm sold for old taxes. The bank bought it, and that's the end of it. The same thing happened to plenty of Confederates, Mr. Cross. You do know that your side lost the war?"

"I hoped you'd listen," John countered, scuffing a boot on the white tile floor beneath his chair. Just outside the office door was the vault. John had examined it carefully before he went in Blackwell's office.

"If you'll excuse me," Blackwell said, pushing up

160

from his chair. "I have other matters to attend to." He checked his gold watch. "If the tenant arrangement doesn't work out, perhaps next year we might consider sharecropping that farm to you. But you'll have to have money, Mr. Cross, money for seed and a team of mules and so forth. I'm afraid that without any money, we won't be able to offer you anything at all."

John got up slowly, rubbing his chin. He had borrowed Billy's straight razor this morning to make a better appearance for his visit to the bank. "Is that your last word on it?" he asked.

The banker seemed put off by the question. "Of course it is," he replied quickly.

John turned for the door. "It's a decision you may come to regret. That land was mine, mine and my sister's. I don't give a damn what the law says, or what the county court did. You took something that was all I had to come back to when the war ended. Now you tell me it's gone on account of taxes. A man oughta get the chance to straighten things out."

Blackwell seemed mildly amused. "You're ignorant of the way law that works, Mr. Cross. It's out of my hands now. Good day to you, Mr. Cross. I simply must get back to work."

John walked through the bank lobby slowly with a hot flush burning in his cheeks. He glanced sideways, to the vault door behind a row of tellers cages. Stacks of currency lined shelves at the back of the vault. John looked at the money briefly, then he went to the glass-paned front doors and let himself out of the bank. "I'll be back," he said in a quiet voice, knowing no one else could hear him.

He was attending to the last bit of unfinished business when he walked up the lane to Elizabeth's house. It was

161

a sunny afternoon and he was sweating. Howard Lacy's cotton fields told the story of what had happened at the plantation long before John came in sight of the house. Last year's cotton still lay in the rows between the dry plant stalks. Here and there, new plants had sprung from fallen seed, creating scattered patchworks of green amidst the brown leaves. There had been no slaves to pick the cotton or hoe the weeds.

The lane was overgrown with summer grass. The lawn in front of the house stood waist-high where years before laughing couples danced to violins and guitars and banjos. Yet the house still stood as it always had, rising majestically from a flat plain, surrounded by a forest of pecans and elms. A lone magnolia tree stood near the front steps, something Howard Lacy shipped from Georgia during better times that would remind him of his ancestral home outside Savannah. John could smell the fragrant blossoms long before he neared the porch, adding another bittersweet memory to those he had of Elizabeth when they danced around the lawn before he went away.

He noticed that most of the windows were shuttered and he began to wonder if anyone still lived there, though he followed a worn footpath through the grass that showed signs of recent traffic. In places, he saw horse droppings along the path, thus he continued to the porch and climbed the steps.

He knocked several times on the heavy front door, hearing only silence inside. A curtain fluttered in an upstairs bedroom where the glass had been broken. There had been no burning at the Lacy plantation. Somehow the invading Yankees had missed it and it looked much as it always had. He knocked again, and got no answer.

A footpath led around to the back of the house. A marble birdbath and a stone lily pond were dry when John walked past them to the rear. Elizabeth's mother kept a rose garden at the back, he remembered. He found the roses blooming, pinks and reds and yellows. Fallen petals surrounded the bushes, curling at the edges, turning brown with age. No one was cutting the roses now.

Behind the house he saw horses in the stable. Howard kept good racers before the war, the best thoroughbreds money could buy. John knew someone still lived inside the house, someone who cared for the horses. He climbed the back steps and knocked again.

"Go away!" someone shouted. It was a man's voice.

"It's John Cross," he answered. "I've come to ask about Elizabeth. Please let me in."

He heard footsteps, and the tap of a cane on the floor. He pulled off his hat respectfully and prepared himself for news of Elizabeth.

Chapter Seventeen

The old man seemed to have some difficulty remembering him and John wondered if it could be failing eyesight. Howard Lacy leaned on his cane, squinting at John's face, bearing little resemblance to the man John remembered as Elizabeth's father.

"Who'd you say?" Howard asked again.

"John Cross. I came to ask about Elizabeth. Before I left with General Hood, your daughter and I planned to be married."

"Ah," he said, nodding. "Remember you now, Captain. Come inside. I'll open a bottle of my mulberry wine. Elizabeth isn't here, I'm afraid. I don't remember how long she's been away. . . ."

He followed Howard into the kitchen. The old man hobbled on his cane feebly, a mere shell of the man he was when John left. Dressed in torn riding pants and a yellowed linen shirt, he looked smaller, and frail. Snowy hair had thinned atop his head. His face hung in loose folds. "Sit," he said, offering a chair at a cluttered kitchen table. A pan of crumbling corn bread sat near a pitcher of molasses. An empty bottle of home-brewed wine stood beside the pan.

John took a seat. "Don't mean to bother you. Just got back from the war and wondered about Elizabeth."

Howard brought a bottle of wine from a cabinet. He pulled the cork and sniffed it, then he poured it into smudged glasses and set one in front of John.

"Elizabeth went with her mother to New Orleans," he began, taking a sip of wine. "Things got so bad around here . . ."

"I understand," John said. "I wrote to her. She stopped answering my letters."

Howard peered across the table. "My daughter married Charles Montgomery, Captain Cross. I suppose it was the loneliness. She didn't have the heart to write to you about it." He drank again. "Then Charles lost all his slaves. Took to drinking too much when conditions got worse. Elizabeth had his child, a son. Charles paid no attention to the boy. Went off on long business trips. One time he didn't come back. Elizabeth was despondent over it. When the Yankees closed Galveston Harbor I sent them by coach to New Orleans, with enough money to buy passage to England. I felt they would be safer there. That was last year. Or was it the year before? I don't remember now. My wife went with them. Not a word since. As you can see, I'm all alone here. Don't know what I'll do. I've had an offer to sell the land to a firm in Vermont. Damn Yankees will own it all, damn them!"

The old man was rambling. John drank his wine until Howard was finished. "I wanted to know why she stopped writing," he said.

"I'm sorry, Captain. She was only a girl when you left. I suppose we've all grown older. The damn war aged us. . . ."

"I loved her," John said. He thought about how many things had changed since he bade Elizabeth farewell in '61. At last he knew the truth. "I carried her tintype with me all through the war."

Howard poured more wine into their glasses.

"Women are unpredictable creatures," he said, as if to apologize for Elizabeth. "These have been terrible times. I worry that something may have happened to my wife and daughter on the road to New Orleans, or perhaps a ship's accident in the Atlantic. My grandson was sickly from birth. . . ." His voice trailed off. He gazed vacantly out a kitchen window.

"I wish she'd written to me about Charlie," John added. "It would have been easier if she had explained why she couldn't wait for me. I don't reckon it matters now." He downed the last of his wine.

"I spoiled her," Howard confessed in a tired voice. "She wasn't accustomed to waiting for things she wanted. You'd been gone hardly a year, Captain, when Elizabeth started to show an interest in Charles. He came calling, and she gave in to the loneliness, I suppose. They were married in July. It was a beautiful wedding and they were sure they would be happy together. Then news of the war made the slaves restless. Some were running off to the North. Charles became distraught. He couldn't keep his slaves in the fields. By the summer of '64 it became wholesale rebellion. Word had come that the Confederacy might fall at any moment. Confederate currency was almost worthless. I was losing a fortune and so was Charles. The blockade halted the shipment of our cotton. Warehouses were full and there were no buyers to be found. My slaves started to run away and my fields went fallow. I was ruined, as were many others. Charles couldn't handle it. He drank heavily and fought with Elizabeth over trivial matters. Then one day, Charles simply disappeared. I took what money I had and sent my wife and Elizabeth away. I didn't want them to see the bitter end of things. And there was my grandson to think about too. I wanted him in the care of the best doctors."

The old man's eyes were watering as he told the

story. He had been one of the county's wealthiest farmers. Some of the anger John felt toward Elizabeth began to dissipate. Hearing what had happened while he was away softened the pain of what she had done.

"I understand," John sighed. "I didn't have much to offer your daughter anyway. We were poor. Elizabeth was used to finer things. It likely worked out for the best."

John got up from the table and put on his hat. "I'm obliged for the mulberry wine. If you should happen to hear from Elizabeth, tell her I made it back. Tell her I came to pay her a call."

Howard struggled up from his seat using the cane. "What will you do, Captain, now that the war is over?"

John shrugged. "I was plannin' to farm my paw's place. I found out the Planters Bank took it for back taxes while I was gone. Don't rightly know what I'll do with myself. Got no place to go, an' no way to get there if I did. My horse was taken up in Arkansas. Lost my saddle and everything. Elizabeth's tintype too. I've done a lot of walking since I got home. Looks like I'll be doin' some more for a spell."

The old man's face brightened. "I'll sell you a horse, Captain. I've got six good colts at the stable. Good blooded stock, out of my Kentucky thoroughbred stud. I sold the old stud and the mares last winter. No grain to feed them, but I held on to the colts."

John shook his head from side to side. "I don't have any money, since hardly a man in the Confederate army got paid toward the end of the war. All I own is the clothes I'm wearin'. And this gun."

"Too bad," Howard said, downcast again. "Those two-year-olds are about to starve. As I told you, I have no more grain to feed them and the grass in the horse pasture is gone. A shame, Captain Cross, that you can't

167

buy one of my colts. They're runners, bred for speed and endurance. Not many horses can outdistance them."

Suddenly John's imagination put him on the back of a racing thoroughbred. He was headed toward the Mexican border ahead of a squad of Yankee cavalry. Tied behind his saddle were canvas bags filled with money from the Planters Bank. "I wish I could buy one," he said wistfully. "I need a good horse. I might find a way to get my hands on some money if I owned a distance runner."

Howard leaned on his cane and started for the back door. "I want to show them to you, son. Come with me. Perhaps we can arrive at an arrangement for one of the horses. You could pay me as soon as you made some money. There's a dappled gray colt I want to show you. Fastest colt I ever raised, and gentle too. Come along to the stable and feast your eyes on that gray. If you are a horseman, you'll know I'm telling you the truth as soon as I show you the gray."

John followed the old man down the back steps, then across the overgrown yard to the stable. In a corral behind the barn, he saw six long-muscled two-year-old geldings, two sorrels, and a black, a chestnut with a blaze face, and a high-withered roan. Off in one corner of the corral, John saw a tall dappled gray with powerful hindquarters and straight, fine-boned legs. It was indeed a most beautiful animal.

"Perfect horseflesh," John said, making no effort to conceal the admiration in his voice. "But like I told you, I don't have a cent to my name."

Howard nodded, as though he understood John's condition well. "I'm almost broke myself, Captain. This plantation is all I have left. Without slaves, the land is useless. I'll have to sell to the firm in Vermont. I kept these good colts, hoping I could turn them for a profit to a man who understood racehorses. But I fear the days of enjoying a gentleman's pleasures are over in the South. Most men are struggling just to eat since the occupation Yankees came." The old man paused, gazing at his horses. "So I'll tell you what I'll do, Captain. I'll make you an outright present of that gray colt. Consider it payment for having fought to save the South. You were trying to protect my land in that war, so I figure I owe you. Take the colt. There are bridles in the tack room, and an old Missouri flat saddle. Take it all."

John didn't quite trust his ears. "You'd give it to me?" he asked. Why would the old man be so generous?

"Give it to you outright, just like I said. It's broken to a saddle. A little green, perhaps, being just a two-year-old, but the colt is gentle. All I ask is your word that you'll give it good care. I never abused animals or slaves, like some of the other cotton growers in these parts. I want your word that you won't mistreat the colt and I'll be satisfied."

Still questioning his quick good fortune, John took his eyes off the colt to look at Howard Lacy. "Don't exactly know what to say. I'm mighty grateful, and I'll see that the gray is always fed and handled gently." John stuck out his hand.

Howard took the handshake, then he turned away from the fence. "Good luck to you, Captain. I'll tell Elizabeth about your visit. If only I hear from her again. I worry that some foul deed has befallen them. Texas is rife with desperate men who have no respect for womanhood. They were traveling alone when . . ."

Balancing with his cane, the old man started toward the house without finishing his remarks. His mind wandered when he talked about his wife and daughter and John supposed it was the weight of his concern.

"Thanks again," John said, watching Howard's feeble efforts to place his feet firmly while he walked. In the

169

four years John had been away, Elizabeth's father had become like his plantation. John wondered how things could have changed so quickly. Signs of age were everywhere he looked. It didn't seem possible that this was the same elegant mansion where Elizabeth's summer parties were the talk of the town.

He found the flat saddle and a bridle in the tack room. Cobwebs hung from the rafters, the blacksmith's anvil, dangling from empty saddle racks along the tack room wall. John took an old saddle blanket along with the rest of the gear, to spare the colt's withers below the saddle.

The gray came to him when he entered the corral, nuzzling his palm to catch John's scent. When the colt was bridled and saddled, he led it out of the barn, admiring the black dapples on the soft gray coat. Far better than the horse's color, its long-muscled rump would give it quick speed. He rubbed the colt's neck affectionately, unable to suppress a grin. "Didn't have the heart to tell the old man," he whispered to the colt. "But you're liable to be a bank robber's horse pretty soon. They'll never catch me if you can run as fast as the old man claims. You sure as hell look like a runner."

He stepped in a stirrup and swung aboard holding a tight rein in case the colt was factious, but the gray stood quietly until it felt John's heels. Thus John rode away from the Lacy plantation with a broad smile on his face, for he could feel the power in the gray colt's strides even at a trot.

When he was out of sight below the house, headed down a wooded country lane, he urged the gray to a run. No one lived along the lane to hear his joyous laughter as he galloped away from the Lacy farm. His laughter was purposeful, not mere enjoyment when he felt the speed of the horse beneath him. As the colt lengthened its strides John knew just how important the animal

170

would be if he made good on his attempt to rob the Planters Bank. Common horses stood no chance of catching the gray. The gift from Elizabeth's father could make the difference between success and failure, if he made it out of the bank alive. Up 'til now, the plan to rob the bank had no substance, something he thought about to cool his enmity and a focus for his anger. But with the dappled gray to carry him swiftly to the Mexican border, the plan began to take shape in his mind.

He slowed the colt to a trot with gentle pressure on the reins. For half a mile down the deserted road the horse had carried him faster than he'd ever traveled before. The colt hadn't broken a sweat and wanted to keep running. He patted the animal's neck. "You can damn sure cover ground," he said. The colt's ears turned back when he spoke.

He reined the horse to a walk and thought about the moment when he walked into the bank lobby and drew his gun. He would pick a time when there were fewer chances of encountering a Union patrol in the streets. And he would need to know the county sheriff's whereabouts before he pulled the robbery. John wondered about the new lawman from Kansas. Would he be a dangerous adversary?

Billy had said the sheriff was a paid killer. John's first order of business was to find out about the lawman, to learn his habits. How closely did he watch the bank? A thousand thoughts flooded John's mind at once.

A mile closer to town John began to hear a new voice inside his head, a voice demanding justification for the plans he was making to commit a crime. "I know it's wrong," he said aloud, to silence the voice, "but things are different now. That bank robbed me of my land, same as if they'd used a gun. Did it while I was gone, so I didn't have a chance to square things. I offered to take the place on shares. They said I needed money, and that they'd already rented it to somebody else. Wasn't fair, what that bank did. It damn sure wasn't fair."

Thus he debated his conscience on the ride back to Waco, at times arguing out loud that the robbery was justifiable, under the circumstances. The big gray colt plodded along, flicking its ears back and forth when its rider spoke.

Chapter Eighteen

Billy reminded John of a man caught staring at a beautiful woman. Billy walked around the gray colt, admiring the slope of its shoulder, then pausing to look at the bulge of its gaskin and the length of its croup.

"Damn, Johnny boy. That's one fine animal. Never saw one no better in my life. Any fool can see he's built to run."

"He can fly, Billy," John said, remembering the feeling when he'd asked the gray to gallop. "There ain't a horse in that Yank cavalry that can catch him."

Billy's face darkened. "You're still plannin' to rob that bank, ain't you?"

John shook his head. "I'm takin' back what's mine. I was robbed first. I'm only gettin' even for what they done to me."

Billy shoved his hands in his pockets. "If they don't kill you makin' the try," he said softly. "That's one hell of a fine horse, but it won't make no difference if you get gunned down in the bank, or whilst you're climbin' on this gray. And then there's the fact that the Planters Bank sits square in the middle of town. You'll have to ride plumb through Waco to get clear of Yankees and that lawman from up Kansas way. Lots of dangerous ground to cover to get out of town. Then there's maybe

173

four hundred miles more to the Rio Grande. Telegraph wires all the way. They could form a posse and cut you off, Johnny. You'd be riskin' everything."

"Got nothing left to risk except my life. All I own is this horse and my clothes."

Billy eyed him doubtfully. "You mean your life ain't worth nothin' to you?"

John shrugged. He'd thought it through and made up his mind. "It's no kind of life without a place to call home. That bank took my home. They owe me."

Billy toed the ground with his boot. "I still say it's a crazy idea. You can't pull it off by yourself."

"Then throw in with me, Billy. We can talk to Tommy Joe and Wild Henry. The four of us can take that bank easy as pie."

"I've been thinkin' on it," he replied. "Thinkin' about havin' all that money is a powerful temptation."

"Those Yankees owe you," John insisted. "They burned down your house. It sticks in my craw that they can do whatever they want. I say we make 'em pay for what they did to us. If you won't throw in with me I'll do the job myself. But there's one thing you can be sure of . . . that Planters Bank is gonna get robbed. I won't be cheated out of my land!"

Billy looked over at the remnants of his house. Fire-blackened brick was all but hidden by grass and thistles and sunflower stalks. He sighed. "Sorry sumbitches didn't have to burn it. Wasn't much of a house in the first place. They coulda left it alone."

"Then help me make 'em pay, Billy!" John cried. "Help me rob that bank and we'll hightail it to Mexico. We'll live like kings the rest of our days."

Billy seemed puzzled. "I can't quite figure the connection between the bank and the Yank bastards who burned my house. I don't get the connection. You say robbin' that bank is what we oughta do . . . ?"

174

John considered how he would explain it. "The bank is owned by northerners now. They took it over right after the war."

"You sure about that, Johnny?" Billy asked, sounding doubtful.

"I talked to a feller named Blackwell down at the bank. They told me he was the new president when I asked who I oughta see about my farm. This lady behind one of the tellers' windows said Blackwell was from New York. She said the first thing he done when he came to town was file papers against farmers who hadn't paid their taxes and mortgages."

"Sorry sumbitches," Billy muttered, kicking a rock with his worn boot toe. "I reckon I understand now. Robbin' a Yankee-owned bank makes sense."

John rubbed the gray colt's throatlatch, thinking ahead to the next part of his plan. "We need to scout that bank real careful for a spell. See how often a Yank squad passes it. And then there's that Kansas sheriff. Need to see where he spends most of his time, so we'll know the safest time to pull the robbery."

"I never said I was ready to throw in with you," Billy objected. "I said I was thinkin' about it, is all."

"Just thinkin' out loud," John replied quickly. "If you did happen to decide . . ."

"You'll need to talk to Tommy Joe. And Wild Henry. Ain't neither one of them got horses now. Sold 'em when they got back, so's they could eat. All I've got is that three-legged sorrel I rode home. Got ringbone real bad on account of the way I pushed him when we left Tennessee. You've got that fancy colt there, but the rest of us couldn't stay up. Best you do some thinkin' about fast horses for the rest of us, should we decide to throw in with you."

John had his answer ready. "Howard Lacy has got five more of these good thoroughbred colts he wants to sell. We could make an arrangement with him, to pay him for his horses after we got down to Mexico."

Billy chuckled, without intending any humor. "You aim to tell Lacy that we're gonna rob the Planters Bank so we can pay him for his colts?"

"Not exactly. I'll tell him we've got this business proposition down along the border. Soon as we get down there, we can send him his money. I figure he'll go along with us. We'll offer to sign a paper, promising him that we'll pay."

Billy was scowling. "Sounds mighty fishy. Why would a rich man like Howard Lacy go along with such an idea?"

"Because he ain't rich anymore. He can't afford the grain to feed his horses. Like the rest of us, those Yankees broke him. He said he'd have to sell his land before fall, to some Yankee outfit in Vermont. If we promise to pay him for those colts I think he'll do it. I just know he will, if the rest of you will throw in with me to pull the job."

Billy was gazing off at the horizon. "They'd brand us outlaws, Johnny. We'd be Wanted men for the rest of our lives."

John put a hand on Billy's shoulder. "We wouldn't be poor anymore. Bein' an outlaw don't sound so awful bad when you think about it. We'd be safe across the border in Mexico, and we'd never be hungry again. We could buy us a ranch down there. Maybe raise a few cattle. It'd be a good life, Billy. Think it over."

Billy nodded once, still staring at the horizon. "It's a powerful temptation. I've been givin' it some study." Then he aimed a thumb toward the root cellar. "I snared a rabbit whilst you was gone. Help me skin it while I get a fire started. Won't make much of a supper, but it's better'n nothing. There's a few plums left higher up in those trees. We can pick 'em before it gets dark."

They started for the cellar. Suddenly, Billy stopped. "If we made it all the way to Mexico," he said thoughtfully, "with all that money, we could sure have us a high old time."

They found Wild Henry Roberts at the river. When John saw him from a distance, working his trot lines clad in filthy rags, he knew how hard times had been for the old soldier. His bare arms were little more than skin and bones. A shaggy mane of matted hair and tangled beard made him resemble a circus lion. Billy said Wild Henry lived in a tiny cave dug from the riverbank. It saddened John to see a tough old fighter reduced to his present condition. No braver soldier had ever ridden into battle in John's company. Now he reminded John of a street beggar, and it seemed a terrible injustice that Wild Henry was given such a fate.

John and Billy halted their horses on the bluff above the river. Wild Henry turned around when he heard their hooves. For a time he stared at the two riders, then he waved and said, "Howdy, Billy."

It took a moment for him to recognize John. When he did, he blinked twice quickly and came to his feet. "Can that be you, Cap'n? We gave you up for dead in Tennessee."

John swung down from the gray. "It's me. Good to see you again, Wild Henry."

They met halfway down the bluff and shook hands. Wild Henry was grinning. "I'll be double damned, Cap'n Cross," he said. "I guess Billy told you we tried to go back to help you out. Too damn many of those Yank bastards, but we damn sure made the try."

"I understand," John replied, catching a scent of Wild Henry's unwashed body when a gust of wind blew downriver. "A whiskey peddler found me and brought a

177

doctor. A ball broke my leg and one more caught me in the back. Took a while to heal, but I made it. Soon as I got back, Billy told me where to find you. Came to look you up soon as I could."

Wild Henry's face fell. "You can see things ain't so awful good, Cap'n. Been catchin' a few catfish to get by. No work to be found around here. I've been thinkin' about movin' on."

"That's one reason I came to see you, Henry. I've got a proposition you oughta hear. I aim to make the same offer to Tommy Joe, when we find him."

Wild Henry grinned again. "If there's money in it, I'm ready to listen, Cap'n. You can find Tommy Joe down at the Baptist church around suppertime. Some of them church women make soup fer the soldiers who can't feed themselves. I go myself now an' then, when the fish don't bite. Been a mite rough around here lately. No work fer anybody."

John understood. The Confederate camp at the gin was a dismal place. Wild Henry had lost forty or fifty pounds since he last saw him. "My proposition stands to make some money. It's also dangerous. All I'm asking is that you hear me out."

There was a twinkle behind Wild Henry's sunken eyes. "You know damn well I ain't scared of nothin' on earth, Cap'n. Whatever that proposition is, you can count me in."

"Wait'll you hear what I have to say. Then you can decide."

Wild Henry looked at Billy, then down at his rumpled uniform pants with holes exposing both his knees. "You can see my situation, Cap'n. I'm damn near naked, livin' in a cave like some animal, eating the fish I can catch and sellin' the rest fer a few coins. I ain't gonna be very picky about what we're gonna do to make some money."

178

John thought about a question he wanted to ask. "Billy told me you'd been thrown in jail."

"Sure was," Wild Henry agreed. "Got in a fight over at the railroad camp. Broke this Yankee corporal's nose when he said Rebs didn't know how to fight a war. Cost me my job and two weeks in county jail, but I goddamn sure showed that Yank I know'd how to fight."

"What's the new sheriff like? The gent from Kansas?"

Wild Henry screwed his face into a frown. "Name's Buel Pope. Hard as nails, Cap'n. He was a bounty hunter in the territories. He'd kill a man for a pewter quarter. Got no scruples. Some claim he's a backshooter. Funny-colored gray eyes, like a wolf. Why'd you ask?"

"Just curious, for now. I'll explain later. Meet us at the Baptist church this evening. We'll find Tommy Joe and go have ourselves a talk." Then a thought occurred to John. "Have you still got your guns?"

Wild Henry shook his head. "Sold the rifle. All I've got is my pistol. No caps or lead. Sold my horse and saddle too, Cap'n. Couldn't buy feed for no horse. Can't hardly feed myself these days."

John turned up the bluff. "See you at the church. Make it around seven," he said, climbing the slope to board his horse.

They parted with a wave. When John and Billy were out of earshot, John spoke. "Wild Henry looks bad. Shame a proud man has to live like that."

Billy grunted. "The county's full of 'em, Johnny, proud men havin' to beg for bread crumbs. When a man gets hungry, he loses most of his pride."

"Some do, I suppose," John replied quietly. "There's some who won't bow down to another man, no matter what."

* * *

Two hours of waiting finally produced a result. John and Billy were slouched against an empty freight wagon down the street from the jail when Billy pointed.

"There he is, Johnny. There's Sheriff Buel Pope."

John saw a tall figure in a split-tail black coat coming from the jail. A black flatbrim hat shaded his face. Tied low on the man's left leg was a cutaway holster. A plated pistol with ivory grips rode high in its leather berth, catching rays of sunlight as the sheriff stepped off the boardwalk to the street. John made note of the man's gun hand, dangling beside his pistol. Buel Pope had ropelike arms and bowed legs. Each stride was purposeful as he crossed the road.

Another thing caught John's attention . . . the sheriff's head was constantly moving, looking in every direction, as though he expected to be surprised by someone close by. "He's a careful son of a bitch," John whispered to himself. "He's worried someone might get behind him."

"Wild Henry said Pope was a bounty hunter," Billy remarked, watching the sheriff walk past a group of idling Confederates at a street corner. "He'll be a tough bastard to throw off our trail if we rob the bank. He won't give up easy."

John kept his eyes on Buel Pope while he listened to Billy. "It figures he'll know how to read tracks," John agreed.

Billy was frowning. "Maybe we oughta find another bank to rob, Johnny. I'd hate to tangle with that sheriff."

John gave Billy an impatient look. "We're gonna rob the Planters Bank and none other. The Planters took my land. It's a Yankee bank, and they owe me. I'm not afraid of Buel Pope. If he follows our tracks, I'll kill him!"

Billy gave John's anger time to cool. "He's got a handful of deputies ridin' along when he serve the papers. Folks say a couple of 'em are gunslicks, just like Pope."

"Let them come," John hissed, clenching his teeth. "If they try to stop us I'll put a .44 ball in 'em for their trouble."

John pushed away from the wagonbed and started for their horses at a hitchrail down the street. Billy followed along, looking over his shoulder at Sheriff Pope's back before the Kansan disappeared around a corner.

They mounted and rode north, toward the Jefferson Street Baptist Church where they would meet Wild Henry. A supper line had already formed when they rode in sight of the churchyard. Men in gray uniforms stood patiently to await a bowl of soup from a big iron kettle boiling at the back of the church grounds. When John saw the soldiers his throat grew tight. The sight of so many hungry men dressed in rags was something he knew he would never forget.

"Hey, Billy!" a voice cried. "Where'd you find the captain?"

A scrawny boy left the soup line in a run, grinning through a faceful of whisker stubble. Tommy Joe Booker looked like a scarecrow. Baggy pants fluttered around his slender legs as he ran to greet his two friends.

John stepped down to shake the boy's hand.

"Good to see you again, Cap'n. We left you for dead. I reckon Billy already told you how we tried to ride back for you."

"He told me. So did Wild Henry. Soon as you get yourself that bowl of soup we'll find ourselves a shade tree where we can talk."

Tommy Joe's eyes darted from John to Billy. "The soup's free. Come stand in line and get some. Mostly just a little chicken broth and a few carrots throw'd in, but it tastes good if you're hungry. Sure am surprised to see you, Cap'n Cross. We jus' know'd you was dead from those bushwhackers back in Tennessee. Jus' now I thought I was seein' a real live ghost, when you rode up beside Billy. An' I'll swear that's the finest gray hoss I ever saw, better'n ol' Traveler owned by Gen'l Lee. I saw Traveler one time, but he weren't near as good a hoss as this one. I swear on my granpaw's grave he weren't as good as yours."

Chapter Nineteen

Tommy Joe was worried. "If ol' man Lacy won't sell us those horses on credit, then your idea won't work, Cap'n. Can't hold up a bank without horses. Fast horses!"

Wild Henry shook his head. "Good horses'll make it work. It's one hell of a long ride to the Rio Grande. I was down there once, back in '57. That's damn sure dry country. Hard on horses. But if a man stays off the main wagon roads, he won't see a livin' soul all the way to Laredo. Emptiest damn place I ever saw. Driest too. We'd have to carry water."

It surprised John to learn that Wild Henry knew the country. "It'll be a big help . . . that you know the lay of things," he said. "If we can find a surveyor's map and figure the distance between creeks and water holes . . ."

Wild Henry chuckled. "There ain't any, best I can recall. I damn sure don't remember there bein' any water below San Antone."

"First thing is the horses," Tommy Joe said. "If those colts can't be bought on credit, we can't pull the job. We'll need guns too. Leastways some ammunition for those we've got. I kept my saddle and pistol. Got no horse or powder so I'm in a hell of a fix.

Can't shoot or ride. Got just half enough to do one or the other."

"There's another way, Cap'n," Wild Henry said. "We could steal those horses if the old man won't sell. Don't seem no worse than robbin' a bank."

"That's different," John remarked. "I won't steal horses from Howard Lacy. He gave me the gray out of kindness. I figure he'll listen to a proposition for sellin' three more, but we damn sure won't steal from him."

Billy hadn't said a word until now. "We could all wind up getting killed, boys. I say this idea needs to be talked through, to decide if it's worth the risk. I ain't lookin' to get shot."

Wild Henry got up from the tree stump where he'd been sitting. "We could pull it off real careful," he began. "Two men could wait outside with the horses while two go inside. We pick a time when the streets will be empty. Early in the morning there ain't hardly anybody out and about. When the bank opens at ten o'clock, we ride up and get it done quick as we can. Maybe ride north to throw off the law, to make 'em think we're headed another direction. Outside of town we ride a big circle and go south across open country."

John had thought about a similar plan himself, riding west to the Bosque River, then south across rocky pastures he remembered below the river. The rocks would hide their horses' prints, making it harder for Sheriff Pope or the Yankee soldiers to find the direction they had taken. "West of the Bosque that ground gets mighty rough," he said. "Hard to read sign on solid rock. Ridin' good horses, we'll be hard to catch if they have to slow down to read our sign in rocky country."

"Once they see our tracks headed south, it won't take them long to figure we're aimed fer Mexico," Wild Henry said.

"They'll send wires to Austin and San Antone," Billy

warned, "to try to cut us off someplace before we get to the river."

"We could cut the telegraph wires afore we done the job," Tommy Joe suggested. "I could climb one of them poles and cut the wires goin' south. It'd take 'em a spell to find the cut and tie the wires back together. Maybe it'd buy us some time."

"Good idea," John said quickly, thinking out loud. "We could cut the line and tie it back together with binder twine so nobody'd see the cut from the ground."

Billy was shaking his head. He was the only one among them who still had doubts. "It's gettin' clear of that bank that bothers me," he said. "Once the shootin' starts, those soldiers will come runnin' and we'll be in a fight for our lives to get out of town. Have you boys forgotten what it's like to be duckin' a hail of lead balls?"

Everyone was silent a few moments, remembering.

"I damn sure ain't forgot," Wild Henry said. "If we pull it off real suddenlike, maybe there won't be any shootin'. Catch folks off their guard."

John was thinking, pacing back and forth as was his habit when his mind was at work. "We check the soldier patrols, to see what time they ride out every day. See if they keep a regular schedule. Then we do the same to Sheriff Pope, to see when he walks around town. Then we pick a time when there's the best chance of makin' a clean getaway to the north or west. If we plan this right, there won't be any shots fired."

"What if somebody inside the bank pulls a gun?" Billy asked.

John shrugged off Billy's concerns. "Nobody inside but two women and Sheldon Blackwell, when I was there."

"No guards?" Tommy Joe asked, like he couldn't believe it.

"Didn't see any. That's another thing we'll look for when we watch Sheriff Pope. Maybe he keeps a deputy close by . . . maybe in a back room. One of us can keep an eye on the bank, to see who goes in and out."

Billy walked to the edge of the trees where they held their meeting, watching the sky grow dark. "First off, you'll need to ask about the horses," he said. His tone told the others that he was worried. "Without fast horses, the plan won't work. No sense in talking anymore 'til we find out if Lacy will make us a proposition to buy the colts without any money." Then Billy turned to the others with his hands in his pockets. "It's a damn fool idea to try to rob that bank, but I reckon I'll go along with it if we can get our hands on those horses. If we make it to Mexico with all that money, our troubles will be over. Can't say as I've got much opportunity round here, things being the way they are. Without seed money, that forty acres won't grow much besides sunflowers."

"Count me in," Wild Henry said, eyeing John.

"Me too," Tommy Joe added. "I'd just as soon be called a bank robber as a Confederate soldier. Folks ain't got much regard for either one these days. I'm sick an' tired of standin' in that soup line waiting for a handout. Tired of sleepin' in an old tent with holes in the roof, worryin' that it might rain. I'd be just as well off dead, by most accounts. Folks run you off when they see you comin' . . . treat you like a stray dog nobody wants hangin' around. You get me a fast horse, Cap'n, and some ammunition for my pistol, and I'll damn sure help you rob that Planters Bank."

They left the trees in darkness, Tommy Joe to his tent at the Confederate camp ground, Wild Henry to his dugout above the river. John and Billy mounted their horses and rode away from the church at a walk.

Crossing town, John swung by the Planters Bank.

186

The road in front of the bank was empty. Behind the windows, in the faint light of a quarter moon, he could see the big vault door to the rear of the tellers' cages. He smiled.

Howard Lacy was decidedly drunk on mulberry wine. He had almost fallen off his cane when he answered John's knock at the kitchen door. Now he listened to John with one eye closed, trying to focus on John's face.

"We can send you the money. I'll sign a paper promising to pay, just like the paper my paw signed at the bank."

The old man remained silent.

"I'll only need three. You'll have two left that you can sell when you need some money. I swear we'll pay you for the colts as soon as we get where we're going."

"Where's that?"

John wondered if he was wasting his time. Would the old man remember anything tomorrow morning? "We're headed down to Laredo on the Mexican border. We need good horses to get us there."

Howard shook his head. He seemed to understand. "Those are race colts, Cap'n Cross. You won't find any better in the whole county. I raise good horses. Kentucky runners. The best money can buy. A little thin, maybe, but good runners."

"It's about the money, sir," John continued. "We can't pay you until we get where we're going. All I can do is sign a promise that you'll get your price when we get there."

"My price?" The old man seemed confused.

"We haven't agreed on the price yet. You set a fair price for three colts and we'll pay it. But I want you to understand that we can't pay until after we get there."

"You found work?"

"We found a way to get our hands on some money. Since the Planters Bank took over my paw's place I've got no way to make a living here. There's opportunity at the Mexican border. I can pay you for the colts as soon as I get there."

"Sounds strange," Howard said, frowning. "Always heard Mexico was poor."

John felt trapped. Howard had given him the gray colt out of the goodness of his heart. How could he explain his purpose without telling Howard the truth? "I reckon you could say we'd be in a horse race. With fast horses, we can get our hands on a sizable cash prize. You'll have to trust me, that I'll send you the money for those colts as soon as we get to Laredo."

Howard's puzzled expression only deepened. John sensed that his chances of buying the horses were slipping away unless he gave a better explanation.

"I'm asking a hundred dollars for my colts," Howard said. "Did I tell you they're Kentucky runners?"

"Yessir, you told me. And that gray colt is the fastest animal I ever rode. With three more, the four of us could ride down to Laredo and win those races. It'll be a distance race, to see whose horses have staying power and speed. I reckon it's hard to explain, but I swear you'll get your money. Three hundred dollars for three colts, and I'll put my name to a paper that says I'll pay your price."

"Never heard of such a race before, son," he said. "Are you right sure you understand what you'll be doing down there?"

Even drunk, Howard was suspicious. He wasn't fooled, guessing there was something about the proposition that didn't add up.

"I reckon I'll have to go by myself," John said. He got up and put on his hat. "Don't want you to think I'm not grateful for the gray colt. He's the finest animal I ever put a saddle on. I was only hoping you'd trust me to buy three more for some men from my company. They can't find work, same as me. We'd planned to go where there was opportunity. We needed fast horses."

"Don't make much sense," the old man said, shaking his head. "The dappled gray can win that race. He's the fastest colt. If you enter the gray he'll win the prize money. Can't figure why you need the other colts?"

John told himself that he should have known the lie wouldn't work. Howard sensed from the beginning that something was wrong. John let out a sigh and turned on his heel. "I'm a poor liar, Mr. Lacy. I owe you an apology. You gave me that good colt and just now I tried to lie to you about what we aimed to do. I'm sorry, sir. There isn't a horse race down at Laredo. Me and my friends would be runnin' from the law. I'll be going now. Give my best to Elizabeth if you happen to hear from her." John started for the kitchen door.

"Wait a minute, Cap'n Cross," Howard replied. "Are you in trouble with the law?"

John halted at the door. "No, sir. Not yet. I had this plan that would have given me a chance at a new start. I already told you the bank took our farm. That place was all I had an' they took it over for back taxes. Got no place to go now. No place to call home. With so many soldiers back from the war, there ain't any work to be found. I had this plan to start over down in Mexico with Billy Cole and a couple of others. We needed four fast horses."

"You said . . . you'd be running from the law."

John nodded and put his hand on the doorknob. "It was only an idea. Without those horses, it wouldn't work."

"What was it you planned to do?" Howard asked. There was no reproach in his voice, only curiosity.

189

"I'd rather not say. I reckon it was a dumb idea. I got all burned up when I found out what had happened to our farm. When a man gets mad, sometimes he gets foolish notions."

Howard was examining him closely. John saw a strange look in his eyes.

"Sit down, Captain. Bring another bottle of wine from the cabinet. Let's talk for a minute more."

The old man's request puzzled John, but he went to the cabinet and brought a bottle of wine to the table. Howard uncorked it and poured without saying a word. John pulled off his hat and took a chair.

"You said you'd rather not say what it was you planned to do," he began. He took a swallow of wine. "You also said the Planters Bank seized your father's farm. Now I'll admit to being a little drunk today, but I'm not so drunk that I can't draw conclusions."

John waited for the old man to say more, growing edgy. Howard was trying to guess the purpose behind John's request for three colts.

"A gambling man would lay odds that you are planning to rob that bank," Howard continued. A slow smile had begun at the corners of his mouth. "Being an ex-Confederate, you'd feel justified taking money from a bank run by federalists. After all, they did seize your farm, didn't they?"

John held his tongue, fearing the direction Howard's guesswork was moving. The old man knew why he wanted the horses and he was trying to dig a confession from him.

"You needed accomplices," Howard went on, enjoying himself. "The gray colt would get you to the Mexican border where the law couldn't reach you. But you needed help with the robbery. It would be suicide for one man to attempt it. You convinced three men to help you, but they needed swift horses too or they'd be caught. And so you've decided to promise me my price for three of the thoroughbred colts, because you knew they'd make it to the border ahead of the pursuit trying to recover the bank's money. My Kentucky thoroughbreds could almost guarantee your safety. That is why you didn't quibble over my price."

John swallowed uncomfortably. "I never said what it was we aimed to do."

Howard agreed. "No, you didn't, Captain Cross. I'll hand you that much. You didn't admit to a thing." He emptied his glass and poured another. John declined further drink, wanting more than anything else to escape Howard's accusations.

"I'd better be going," John said. "Forget about my proposition to buy the horses. I shouldn't have asked to buy colts when I didn't have any money."

The old man was smiling. "Money's a funny thing, son. It begins as a piece of paper. But it has been known to do curious things to men, even honest men. It has a certain lure, an attraction that defies rational explanation sometimes. It causes men to take unreasonable chances. It can bring a sudden end to a man's life."

John waited, knowing there was more.

"I understand your anger, Captain. You feel cheated, and you want revenge. You fought a terrible war, and we lost it. Now you return home, and your farm has been seized by carpetbaggers. You see this bank as yet another enemy. You want an eye for an eye."

John knew it was useless to deny that Howard had guessed. "I should have been given the chance to straighten things out before they took the land. It wasn't fair, what they did."

The old man's smile faded. "No, it wasn't fair. Fairness is being overlooked in this so-called Reconstruction. I'll be forced to sell my land because of it. I'll be homeless, just as you are now. I'll be forced to take less than half what my land is really worth. At least I'll have something to show for it. While you have nothing at all."

The old bitterness began to creep into John's thoughts. "I should have been given some time to pay those taxes."

"I agree," Howard sighed, gazing vacantly at the kitchen wall. A silence lingered. "Tell you what, Captain. You come back to see me tomorrow. I'm going to sleep on your offer to buy the colts. In the morning I'll be cold sober. If I should decide to sell them to you on a promisory note, I won't ask you what you intend to do with them. I make it a practice to mind my own business. Now and then, I indulge in some speculation, merely to satisfy my own curiosity. Should the Planters Bank happen to be robbed in the near future, I'll only be guessing who did it. Come back tomorrow and I'll give you my answer."

Chapter Twenty

He had gone over every detail of the plan a thousand times and couldn't find a flaw. He knew the soldiers' routine patrols like he knew the back of his hand. And he knew Buel Pope's daily habits so well that he could recite them from memory. The sheriff spent late nights in the saloon district on Webster and Clay, keeping a tight rein on revelers until the drinking parlors closed. Thus Pope never came to his office before eleven o'clock in the morning. The Planters Bank opened at ten.

He had discovered one unpleasant surprise. A heavily armed guard arrived at the bank every morning at ten sharp carrying a shotgun and two pistols. The guard stayed hidden in a room to the right of the vault, never showing himself during banking hours. A bank clerk was sent across the street to bring the guard his lunch. John and Wild Henry had talked about how they would handle the guard during the robbery ... one man slipping quietly through the door with a drawn pistol, counting on the element of surprise. It would work, if it was done quickly and silently.

The plan was made possible because of the horses. Howard Lacy understood John's need for vengeance. He had drawn up a paper for John to sign, and had given instructions on how the money was to be deposited in the bank in Laredo, Texas, under Howard Lacy's name. The old man would do the rest, he said. And then he'd given them bridles and saddle blankets and best of all, a box of horseshoes and hoof nails. A leather surcingle was fashioned to make a riding rig for Wild Henry, since he'd sold his saddle. Among the four, they had five pistols . . . John carried the Arkansas sheriff's .36 and his own .44. Billy still had his Sharps rifle and eight shells left over from the box they had bought in Tennessee. Tommy Joe had scrounged around for the caps and balls they needed for the sidearms, begging in the Confederate camp until he had what they needed for each of the guns. Wild Henry traded catfish for three battered wooden canteens from hungry soldiers. Tommy Joe had dyed a piece of binder twine with bootblack, to tie the telegraph wires in place so his cut couldn't be seen easily from the ground. Billy sold his lame sorrel to the rendering plant for six dollars, and with the money they bought food for the ride to Mexico. Everything was in a state of readiness, they all agreed. All that remained was to pick a morning for the robbery.

John planned one last visit with Mary, to beg her away from Diamond Lil's before he left town. He meant to tell her that he was headed to Laredo, without giving the reason. Then he would tell her good-bye, a last good-bye if she stayed. He would never be able to cross the border into Texas again.

"There's Pope," Wild Henry growled. The sheriff was walking down the street in front of the bank. John and Wild Henry stood in the shadow of a vacant building across the road, keeping an eye on comings and goings. The sheriff arrived at the bank at eleven o'clock, stepping inside briefly to inquire about things as he did every morning at eleven. Then he walked back out to the street and headed for his office, always moving his wolf gray eyes over the crowds along the way, always with his left hand near the butt of his gun.

"It's been the same all week," Wild Henry said. Pope ducked in the bank right on time, then came out again. His gaze passed briefly over John and Wild Henry. He continued on toward his office at the jail.

"We'll be long gone by this hour of the morning," John said quietly, watching the sheriff's back. "Those Yankees will have ridden out the old Gholsen road at ten. The only problem we'll have is taking care of that bank guard without shots being fired to alert the whole town that something's wrong. If one of us can knock him cold before he gets to a gun. . . ."

Wild Henry grunted. "I'm volunteerin' fer that job, Cap'n. They had me locked up in that jail fer two whole weeks on bread an' water. I'll swat that guard with my gun barrel. He'll snooze a while before he wakes up."

"We'll lay it all out again tonight," John said. All four had moved into Billy's root cellar. The horses were kept in the corral behind the plum grove, out of sight from travelers on the road. They had a surveyor's map Billy bought for a dime at the land office. They had studied the general route they would take to the border, aided by Wild Henry's recollections of the land.

This morning, Tommy Joe had ridden his sorrel colt down the south telegraph line, looking for a place to cut the wire where no one would see him climb the pole. A few miles southwest of Waco the line crossed empty rangeland. Tommy Joe said he knew just the right place to break the connection. With the black twine in place to hold the wire taut, it would take some careful looking to find the break.

Billy was off scouting their escape route west of town, looking for the easiest crossing at the Bosque River, a crossing they could make in a hurry. Then Billy's orders were to scout the way south toward Belton, riding to the Bell County line seeking the rockiest ground where they could hide their horses' tracks. It was a plan down to the last detail, if only they made it away from the bank with the sacks of money. The colts were shod with new iron. There was ammunition for every gun. All that was needed was putting the plan into action. Everything was ready.

"Let's ride the roads we'll take to get out of town again," John said. He insisted upon knowing every turn and alleyway in case there was trouble.

They mounted and rode away from the bank under a blistering summer sun. For two weeks they'd been conditioning the green colts, galloping them over longer stretches until they had their wind. The colts had grown fatter on the uncut grasses around Billy's forty acres. John decided things were about as ready as they ever would be. Tonight he would go over to see Mary, then there would be no unfinished business. It was Wednesday. If he made the decision to pull the job on Friday, they had just forty-eight hours to wait.

Riding up Columbus Road, they entered a quiet part of town where stately homes sat behind whitewashed picket fences. They passed an occasional carriage. Otherwise, the street was empty.

"We'll come spurring like hell through this part of town and nobody'll notice," Wild Henry said. "Some folks will remember seein' us, but there won't be nobody to shoot at us. When we get this far, we'll be safe."

John offered no opinion on the subject, examining alleys and side streets carefully, making mental note of each one. If, by some misfortune, they were cornered in this part of town, there were dozens of escape routes.

Soon they were in rolling hills west of Waco. Stands of post oak and elm and scrub cedar dotted the hills. A few miles farther west they would encounter the Bosque

River, where they would make the sharp turn toward the Mexican border. John reined in on a grassy hilltop to scan the horizon. "Open land," he said softly. "If we get this far, it'll come down to a horse race."

Wild Henry patted his roan colt's neck. The leggy roan was second only to the gray in speed. "We've got the race won, Cap'n. All we gotta do is get clear of town and stay off the main roads after that. Keepin' west of Austin and San Antone, we won't cross much settled country. Liable to be a few Comanches, but I don't figure we'll see any law or any Yankees."

John stood in his stirrups for a last look around, then he swung the gray off the hill and headed southeast. Everyone was to meet at Billy's place before dark. John had one thing more he meant to do, something that had been bothering him lately. More and more, he'd been thinking about Sallie Mae Parsons, wondering if he should write her before he left for Mexico. She probably thought him dead, for his last letter to her had been from the Calhoun County jail awaiting a hanging. Though he thought of her often, he hadn't written. Last night, staring up at the stars, he'd made up his mind to post a letter to her. When he made it to Mexico he would write her again, to tell her the truth about what he had done. And then, if she loved him, he would offer her a marriage proposal if she agreed to live below the border as his wife.

One thing he was sure of . . . he knew he loved Sallie Mae. He worried that she might not return his affections when she learned he had become an outlaw. A bank robber.

The call he paid on his sister had been a waste of time and he'd ridden away from Diamond Lil's in a black mood. Mary was in her room entertaining her

Yankee colonel and had only come to the door when he knocked to tell him he had to come back another time. He bade her good-bye and stalked out of the saloon, knowing he would never see his sister again. On the ride back to Billy's place he seethed over what the fates had done to his family. And to him. His resolve to rob the bank only deepened by the time he entered the plum grove around midnight. He saw himself as a man without choices. There had been times during the weeks of planning when he experienced periods of doubt. But now he knew what he must do. It was his nature to take sides, and on Friday morning he would take a side against the Planters Bank for what it had done to him.

He entered the cellar and found the others sitting around the pile of gear they would need for the robbery. By candlelight he checked over every item as the men watched in silence. The pistols were loaded and there were a few spare percussion caps for the .36's most of them carried, and a handful of balls. He had loads for his .44, though they were a precious few. The Sharps held a shell, and beside it, laid out in a neat row, were seven spares. Three army-issue wooden canteens, and saddlebags filled with brittle beef jerky and bags of dry beans and a hunk of salt pork to add seasoning. Very little would be eaten when the men were out of their saddles. It would be the hardest push of their lives, harder than anything during the war. They would sleep and eat in their saddles. Wild Henry would suffer most, for he had only the strip of leather and loops of rope for stirrups tied around a saddle blanket. Then John glanced at the folded map, the dyed twine, and a rusted piece of sawblade for the telegraph cutting, and finally their saddles and bridles. It was a paltry assortment of traveling gear for men who meant to cross over three hundred and fifty miles of rough terrain. It was all they had, the gear, and four speedy thoroughbred horses.

"It ain't much to look at," he said, squatting on his haunches.

"It'll do," Wild Henry replied in a hoarse whisper.

John read their faces in the light from the flickering candle. Wild Henry wore a look of eager anticipation. He would go inside the bank with John because of his limitless courage. No matter what happened once they got inside, nothing would rattle Wild Henry. He would perform his part in the robbery without hesitation. John knew he could trust him to think clearly and kill anyone who stood in their way.

Tommy Joe had a simpler nature. He followed orders and would never back away from a fight. The boy was a deadly shot at close range with a pistol and would do whatever he was told. As John looked into his eyes just now he saw no traces of doubt. Tommy Joe would stand guard outside the bank, holding the reins to Wild Henry's roan, keeping an eye on the street. If anything went wrong John knew he could count on Tommy Joe to keep a steady hand until he and Wild Henry made it out with the money.

Then John looked at his friend Billy, for he knew Billy was the weakest link in his plan. In battle, Billy was fearless and a skilled marksman with a rifle. During the war, he understood why he was fighting. But there was something about this robbery that didn't sit well with Billy's conscience. No matter how many times John explained it, Billy never completely understood why they were breaking the law to rob a bank. John could see it in his eyes when they talked about the plan. Billy had doubts about the right and the wrong of it. He would be holding John's gray during the robbery and keeping watch over the street. John worried about what Billy might do if any shooting started. Would his doubts make his hesitate? John's life might depend on Billy's actions. Could he trust him?

"We'll pull the job Friday morning," John said. He turned to Tommy Joe. "Did you find a spot where the wire can be cut without anybody seeing you?"

"Found just the right place, Cap'n. Them poles are mostly too slick to climb, but there's a place where the wire runs through the top of this tree. Got an insulator fixed to a limb. When I saw through it and tie it off, nobody'll ever find it. Could take days to locate the cut. By then, we'll be down in Mexico havin' a jug of tequila."

John looked at Billy. "What did you find on the way to Bell County?" he asked.

"Hard ground. Plenty of it. A horse don't hardly leave a track if we stay west of the Salado Stage road. Lots of cover too. Cedar trees so damn thick you can't ride through 'em. If we stay west of the stage road the damn blowflies won't be able to find us, much less a squad of cavalry. I broke some cedar limbs along the way, to mark our trail in case we're in a hurry. We'll be at Belton afore it gets dark. After we cross the Leon River we'll lose whoever is behind us. That's solid rock down there."

John looked down at the gear again. "That's it, then. Everything's set. We hit that bank at ten o'clock Friday morning. If every man does his job, we're about to be as rich as kings."

Chapter Twenty-one

They rode past the town square at a walk. It was a quarter to ten on Friday of the second week in August. No one paid them any notice. Men in Confederate uniforms were no cause for concern. At the close of the war the town had been overrun by them. There was hardly a doorstep in McLennan County where ex-Confederates did not beg for food.

A knowledgeable horseman might have noticed the difference in their horses, the long-legged thoroughbreds an experienced eye would know at once were bred to be runners. Four unshaven men in ragged gray uniforms might have seemed out of place on blooded racing animals worth a fortune compared to common cavalry horses and cow ponies. And a closer look would reveal that the men were carrying guns. If anyone in Waco was expecting trouble, they might have wondered about the four soldiers headed toward the bank that morning.

Few people noticed when the telegraph operator down at the railroad depot complained that his line to Austin was mysteriously dead since nine o'clock. The operator sent a boy to notify the Union army commander on the east side of the river.

The four men turned west on Columbus Road and

still no one seemed to notice them. Early morning traffic was limited to a few freight wagons and delivery hacks. It was a typical Friday in the middle of Texas during postwar Reconstruction. There was no reason to suspect that things were about to change.

The Confederates rode slowly past the Planters Bank as Sheldon Blackwell approached his office from the other direction in his shiny black Wooster carriage. Blackwell ignored the four horsemen as he drove past, his mind occupied with other matters. A barefoot mulatto boy waited for the carriage in front of the bank, to lead Blackwell's Standardbred trotter to the livery stable. A cloud of dust swept over the boy when the carriage came to a halt. The boy needed no instructions from the driver. Taking the horse and buggy away was his daily chore.

Sheldon Blackwell dug in his vest pocket for the key to the front door of the bank. At almost the same time, a bearded giant swaggered down the boardwalk with a double-barreled shotgun cradled in the crook of his arm. Claude Groves was on his way to work at the Planters Bank, to guard the vault full of money. A pair of .44 caliber Colt pistols hung from his waist. Claude hated all of Texas, particularly Waco, but he liked his job at the bank. He sat behind a locked door, peering through a tiny hole now and then, earning five dollars a week for doing nothing. And they fed him his lunch, whatever he wanted to eat from the café across the road. The food was better in Saint Louis, but the work was easier here.

"Morning, Claude," Blackwell muttered. He opened the door and stepped inside. Remembering the combination to the vault, he went across the lobby floor, then behind the tellers' cages. His fingers worked the dial. He listened to the faint sounds of the tumblers inside the lock, thinking about a mortgage payment that was past due on choice acres east of the river. The land would show a nice profit after foreclosure proceedings, maybe ten dollars an acre. Maybe more.

Claude Groves opened the door to his tiny room beside the vault and placed his shotgun on a table near one wall. He stretched and yawned. It had been a long night down at Diamond Lil's with a new whore fresh into town from Atlanta named Alice. Alice kept him up most of the night demanding more peach brandy. Claude hated peach brandy and all other forms of sweet liquor, but he had taken a liking to Alice. Fridays were always slow days at the bank anyway. He could doze behind the door and no one would notice.

Claude closed the door behind him, but forgot to lock it. It would soon prove to be a fatal mistake.

John nodded to his accomplices and urged his horse away from the alley. Not a word had been spoken between them. Wild Henry trotted his roan across the road, leaving the piece of shaded ground where he'd been waiting for John's signal. Two more horsemen came from different directions. All four arrived at the front of the Planters Bank at the same time. The street was empty.

John and Wild Henry stepped to the ground, checking their surroundings. They handed the other men their reins. Tommy Joe drew his revolver and rested it on the pommel of his saddle. Billy swung a look up and down the street, then he pulled his pistol and spit the plug of tobacco from his cheek, hiding his .36 beside his right leg.

John and Wild Henry entered the lobby. A teller looked up from counting the cash in her cash drawer. The vault door was open. The bank lobby was without patrons. Sheldon Blackwell was at his desk frowning down at a past-due mortgage.

Wild Henry made straight for the door near the vault. His right hand moved to the butt of his sidearm. The teller and Sheldon Blackwell noticed the holes in the knees of Wild Henry's gray pants. Blackwell pondered why a man like Wild Henry would come to a bank at all, so poorly dressed. He would probably be asking for a loan.

John circled the tellers' windows and drew his .44. The woman's eyes rounded and she opened her mouth to speak with her hands frozen above a stack of currency.

"This is a holdup," John said quietly, with a calm he didn't feel. "If you keep quiet, I won't have to shoot you."

"Lordy me!" the teller gasped. Her fingers began to tremble.

"Get some sacks for that money!" John snapped. His ears were ringing in spite of the silence in the lobby. "Put it all in bags and you won't be harmed."

Wild Henry opened the back door gently, and then he disappeared through the opening.

"What is it, Miss Meadows?" Blackwell asked from his office. "What do these men want?"

A muffled explosion came from the guard's door. John tensed and swung his gunsights toward the noise. Then he heard a soft cry and the fall of a heavy body on the floor. Sheldon Blackwell came racing around the corner from his office.

"Hold it right there!" John demanded, covering Blackwell with the .44. "Keep your hands where I can see 'em. Lie down on the floor or I'll kill you."

Wild Henry appeared suddenly around the doorframe, carrying a smoking pistol. He looked at John. "Had to shoot him, Cap'n. He went for his gun before I could thump him over the head."

John glanced toward the front windows, knowing the

gunshot would be heard all over that end of town. Now their time was running short. "Let's bag that money an' get the hell out of here!"

Wild Henry hurried to the vault. A pile of folded canvas bags rested on a shelf. Wild Henry tossed a handful of bags in John's direction, then he began stuffing stacks of currency into one of the sacks.

Blackwell was on his hands and knees. "You'll never get away with this," he warned.

John cocked his revolver and aimed down at the banker's head. "I told you to lie down!" he snapped.

Blackwell fell to the tile floor, covering his face with his hands. "Don't shoot!" he cried. A shiver ran down his arms.

Miss Meadows collapsed in a dead faint behind the counter, sprawling on her back with a whimper that ended abruptly when her head bounced on the tiles. A second teller cowered against the back wall pressing her palms over her mouth to suppress a scream.

John started pawing money into a bag from the stacks at the teller's windows. "Everybody heard that shot!" he yelled. "We're runnin' out of time!"

He filled three bulky bags with currency. Wild Henry had four sacks piled on the floor near his feet, glancing quickly over his shoulder to the window. "This safe's full of money," he said, tossing another bag to the floor. Bills of every denomination now littered the tiles, scattered by Wild Henry's haste. "We can't carry it all, Cap'n. I damn sure hate to leave anything behind, but we've got all we can carry."

John stuck the revolver in his belt and hoisted four bags. He caught a glimpse of movement beyond the window. Billy was waving to them. Something was happening outside the bank.

"Let's go!" he cried, keeping an eye on the window.

Billy had begun to beckon frantically, looking over his shoulder.

Wild Henry was tying the drawstrings together on two of the bags so they would hang from a horse's withers, reminding John that he had forgotten this important detail. He dropped two bags and fumbled with the drawstrings, making a hurried knot, still with an eye on the street. Billy's horse started to fidget and prance, fighting the pull of its reins. John quickly tied the last two bags together. Wild Henry had already started for the door balancing four overstuffed bags in his fists.

John was halfway across the bank lobby when he heard a noise behind him . . . it sounded like a groan. Glancing over his shoulder, he saw a sight that froze him in midstride and sent his right hand clawing for his pistol. The guard Wild Henry shot had only been wounded. With blood pumping down his chest the bearded giant staggered to the doorframe of the little room beside the vault, a heavy pistol clamped in his bloody fist. The dark round gun muzzle was aimed at John.

John whirled, swinging his .44 away from his belt. Time seemed briefly frozen. Bags of money fell to the floor with dreamlike slowness, bouncing on the white tiles. There was the click of a cocking gun, and then a deafening roar. A teller screamed behind the counter before the gun blast faded to silence.

The guard dropped his revolver and clutched his belly. The gun landed with a clatter beside his right boot. Then the guard's knees buckled. He made a choking sound and fell facedown a few feet from the vault. Blood splattered across the white tiles in the wake of the giant's fall. The woman behind the counter screamed again.

John quickly gathered the dropped bags. Someone was calling his name outside the bank and there was urgency in the voice. As he gave the bank lobby a final look, his eyes met those of Sheldon Blackwell.

"You shouldn't have taken my farm," John growled. "I warned you that you'd regret it." He turned on his heel and trotted to the front door.

"They're comin', Johnny!" Billy cried. John barely glimpsed the crowd that had begun to gather across the street as he ran to his horse, struggling to hoist a pair of sacks across the gray's withers. The bags spooked the young gelding and it jumped sideways to escape them, snorting through its muzzle, walling the whites of its eyes. Billy was reaching for the other pair of sacks, trying to steady his own mount in the confusion. John heard shouts from across the street. "They've robbed the bank!" someone cried.

He got the gray settled just enough to allow him to swing aboard its back without using a stirrup. Billy tossed him the gray's reins and swung his sorrel away from the hitchrail, adjusting his pair of money sacks atop the sorrel's withers. John glanced over his left shoulder. Wild Henry was aboard his roan with two bags in place, swinging his pistol in the air, reining the roan around to gallop west. Tommy Joe heeled his sorrel away from the bank with canvas sacks bouncing against the horse's shoulders.

"Watch out, Johnny!" It was Billy's voice he heard behind him as the gray lunged. At first, he was puzzled by Billy's warning. The road in front of them was clear.

The gray quickly gathered speed. Thundering hooves sounded all around him, echoing from the buildings on either side of Columbus Road. The four thoroughbreds pounded down the middle of the street in an all-out run, kicking dust and clods of dirt from their flying heels. They approached a street corner at blinding speed, leaving the bank farther and farther behind. Only then, as his horse galloped headlong toward the corner, did John find the reason for Billy's concerns.

Two men stood in the shadow of a porch roof, aiming pistols at John and his followers. One was dressed in a black frock coat and flat brim hat. Buel Pope and a deputy were waiting for them to ride into range. In the fleeting seconds before a gun was fired, John wondered how the sheriff had known to come to his office early on this particular morning.

There were three explosions in rapid succession as John heeled his gray past the porch. John leaned over the gelding's neck and tried to find muzzleflashes for targets as the slugs whistled around him. The gray's long mane whipped in John's face, blinding him at the moment he took aim. Then two more shots boomed to John's left and he heard the sickening crack of splintered bone.

He looked over his shoulder quickly. Billy's sorrel floundered as it still tried bravely to run with a ball in its shoulder, streaming blood along the wagon ruts down Columbus Road. The sorrel fell farther behind. Billy's horse was finished.

Suddenly the sorrel tumbled to the ground, spilling Billy from his saddle in an arc that lifted him safely above the gelding's flailing hooves. Billy fell on his chest and skidded through the dirt. The bags of money broke open and at once there was a great cloud of paper floating through the air. Currency tumbled and fluttered down Columbus, forming swirls in wind currents before it fell to the earth.

John jerked his gray to a halt and reined around. Billy was scrambling to his feet a few yards in front of the downed sorrel. John heeled the gray back toward Billy, riding through a fortune scattered by the wind along the road.

"Swing up behind me!" he cried, extending an arm to

Billy as the horse carried him closer. Billy swayed to keep his footing before John leaned out of the saddle to seize his free hand.

A gun thundered behind Billy. . . . John heard the shot and saw the bright yellow flash just as he reached his friend. Billy's eyes were locked on John's face when the ball struck Billy's back.

"No!" John shouted angrily. He saw Billy falter, then catch himself before he fell. John leaned farther out of his saddle and grabbed the front of Billy's tunic with both hands, dropping his .44 down the gray's withers to swing Billy across the gelding's rump.

"Hold on!" John cried, wheeling the gray down a side street as fast as it could run. He was separated from the others now, cut off by the move he made to rescue Billy. Two more shots banged in the distance, then the horse galloped out of pistol range to an alley running west behind Columbus Road.

"I'm hit, Johnny," Billy moaned, wrapping his arms around John's waist. "Hurt bad. I'm bleedin'."

"Don't let go," John shouted over his shoulder, guiding the gelding down the alley in a headlong charge between buildings. "We're not out of this yet. Got to find the boys and get out of town before Pope can mount a posse and send for the soldiers."

"Shot my horse," Billy said, gritting his teeth around the words. "Dropped all that beautiful money in the road . . ."

The gray raced to a cross street. John could hear shouts behind them. He swung the gelding back toward Columbus and heeled to a hard run. His mind was racing. The gray couldn't carry two men very far at a gallop, and his friend was wounded. He would need a doctor and there was no time to get help for Billy. Buel Pope and a posse would be coming as soon as their horses could be saddled.

He turned the gray down Columbus and saw Wild Henry and Tommy Joe galloping westward beneath a cloud of dust. Glancing over his shoulder, he saw people picking up money where the sorrel had fallen. But for the moment, there was no pursuit. He asked the colt for everything it had and tried to catch up to Wild Henry and Tommy Joe before they rode through the outskirts of town.

"I'm hurtin', Johnny," Billy groaned. His grip around John's waist had grown weaker.

John drew Sheriff Buford's .36 and tried to comfort his injured friend. "We'll be clear in a few minutes, Billy. Hang on with everything you're got 'til we're out of town. Don't give up on me, pardner. We've damn near made it now."

Wild Henry slowed his roan when he saw John. Soon the gray caught up with the other horses. They galloped through quiet rows of houses. Tommy Joe reined over and examined the wound in Billy's back, then he shook his head and looked at John, to say no words were needed. Billy's injury was bad.

"This colt can't go much more carryin' two," John said, after a glance over his shoulder. "When we get out of town we'll have to shift Billy to another horse for a spell, to rest my gray. If we keep changin' the double load we'll make better time."

Wild Henry showed his concern. "Can't go plumb to the border like this, Cap'n. What'll we do?"

John feared he knew the answer. Billy could never make a three-hundred-and-fifty-mile ride with a bullet in his back. "We'll think of something. Right now we've got to throw off a posse. Can't quite figure how that sheriff happened to show up when he did. Bad luck, I reckon."

Tommy Joe patted the bags across the pommel of his saddle. "We got the money," he said. "For a second or

210

two I thought about ridin' back for the rest of it, when I saw what happened to Billy."

"We got enough," John replied. They rode away from the last house at the edge of town at a gallop. The gray was tiring under Billy's added weight. They crossed the first grassy hills, and still found no one behind them.

John pointed to a stand of cedars on a distant hilltop. "We can make the switch in those trees." Billy's arms hung loosely around John's waist as the gray colt ran down a hillside.

Chapter Twenty-two

Billy was unconscious when John lifted him across Tommy Joe's saddle. Blood covered the front of John's tunic and the rump of the gray colt where Billy had been clinging to John's waist. John's heart was breaking. The hole in Billy's back dribbled blood to the ground below Tommy Joe's horse. John knew his friend was dying.

"Best we keep movin', Cap'n," Wild Henry said, keeping an eye on their backtrail. They wĕre hidden in a stand of cedars on a hilltop west of Waco. Billy had lost consciousness half a mile from the thicket, requiring that John hold him átop the galloping horse until they could find a safe place to make the exchange.

"He'll bleed to death," John said in a tight voice.

"The rest of us will hang if we don't get out of here," Wild Henry replied. "Billy know'd the risks. It was his bad luck to catch a ball."

"He didn't want any part of this. I talked him into going."

Wild Henry looked over at John. "Don't change a thing, Cap'n. It's done. If Billy could talk, he'd tell us to ride hard fer the border with this money."

John shook his head and turned for his horse, fighting

back tears. "I'd have rather lost an arm than Billy," he said.

They rode out of the trees, checking the eastern horizon.

"Nobody's comin'," Tommy Joe remarked.

They urged their horses to a trot, then a steady lope toward the Bosque River across open pastures. John tried not to think about Billy.

He was scarcely breathing now. His chest would rise and fall, then remain motionless for half a minute. The piece of shirttail John stuffed into his wound did little to stem the flow of blood. With the Bosque miles behind them John ordered a halt to attend to Billy's injury. Resting on a saddle blanket, Billy's face was a waxy white. Now and then his foot would twitch, or one hand would flutter. John understood that Billy was nearing his end.

"Can you hear me, Billy?" he asked, kneeling above him, peering down at his sleeping face.

Billy gave no sign that he was aware of John's voice.

"You were right. It was a crazy idea to rob that bank. If I could change things . . ."

Billy took a shuddering breath and went still. His lips parted in a ghostly smile, then his eyelids opened slightly. John saw urine running between Billy's legs as his bladder emptied. Billy was dead.

"May the Lord have mercy on him," Tommy Joe whispered. He took off his hat and bowed his head. "He's gone now, Cap'n. I reckon we'd better be moving on."

John stood up. His knees were trembling. He looked to the east and shook his head. "I owe that bastard Pope," he growled. "Billy was my friend. He didn't want no part of this robbery, but I talked him into it.

213

Damn the rotten luck that this had to happen to Billy 'stead of me."

Wild Henry swung down from his roan. He walked over to John and put a hand on his shoulder. "Can't nothin' be changed, Cap'n. Billy's dead. We'll all hang unless we get to the border in a hell of a hurry. Lots of miles left to travel. We'll have a drink to Billy soon as we get south of the Rio Grande. Let's go, afore they catch up to us."

John forced himself to look down at the body. "I can't just leave him layin' here. Help me pile some rocks over him, so the wolves don't scatter his bones."

"It'll cost us too much time," Wild Henry argued, glancing over his shoulder.

John whirled around. "I don't give a damn. Help me gather up some rocks," he said.

They rode wide of Belton in the dark, crossing the shallow Leon by moonlight. To a man they had been silent since Billy's hurried burial. John couldn't think of anything else across the miles, brooding over the loss of his friend. He hardly noticed the bulky moneybags in front of his saddle. The money seemed unimportant now.

He battled the guilt he carried on his shoulders, trying to explain the cruel twist of fates that struck down Billy Cole in his stead. The robbery had been his idea. Why had the bullet taken Billy's life instead of his own? It didn't seem fair that Billy had to die.

"These horses need a rest," Wild Henry said, awakening John from dark thoughts. "If we keep these colts fresh, we stand a better chance."

John's mood was too black to offer argument. "Find some trees where we'll be off the skyline. It still don't figure why there's nobody behind us. Makes me wonder what they're up to."

They found a thicket of slender mesquites on a ridge south of Belton. John and Tommy Joe uncinched their saddles. Wild Henry tied the colts to low limbs, allowing them to graze.

A piece of moon brightened the little clearing where the men rested. Tommy Joe had started counting the money by moonlight, until John stopped him.

"Put that money away," he said gruffly. "It don't seem right to count it right after we buried Billy."

Wild Henry passed around strips of jerky. The three ate in silence, listening to the call of distant coyotes from the dark hills around their camp. John rested his head against his saddle, still haunted by Billy's memory and the sound of that single gunshot on Columbus Road. Corporal Billy Cole had survived a thousand speeding Yankee balls through the bloodiest battles of the war, yet it took but one from a Kansas bounty hunter to end his life. The blame rested on John's shoulders, blame he would carry with him the rest of his life.

He closed his eyes, hoping to catch a few minutes of sleep as the horses filled their bellies, but sleep would not come. His thoughts kept drifting back to that terrible moment on Columbus Road when he leaned out of his saddle to grab Billy. He remembered the look in Billy's eyes. And then the fatal gunshot. Billy's face floated before him until he forced his eyes open to gaze up at the stars.

They crossed the Lampasas River before dawn. At first light, John studied the horizon behind them. "Nothing," he said softly.

They heeled their horses to a run. Mile after mile of empty rangeland passed under the horses' hooves. The men held an uneasy silence, wondering why there was no pursuit.

Just before noon they made the shallow crossing at the Colorado River, walking their colts for half an hour before John ordered a quickening of the pace. Late-summer heat started to build on the grassy prairies, sapping the young horses' strength. They were forced to rest the animals more often.

By midafternoon, Tommy Joe could stand it no longer. He had been secretly admiring the bundles of currency in the bags he carried in front of his saddle. "How much you reckon we got, Cap'n?"

"Hard to tell, Tommy Joe. Thousands, maybe fifteen or twenty, just takin' a guess. It'll be enough to last us the rest of our lives."

Tommy Joe reached into the neck of one bag and drew out a fifty-dollar note. "Sure is pretty, ain't it?"

Wild Henry joined the examination by taking out a crumpled twenty-dollar bill. He spread it out and held it up to the sun. "Most beautiful thing on earth," he said, grinning crookedly. "I say it's prettier than any woman I ever saw."

John remembered something Howard Lacy had said. "It's just pieces of paper. It cost Billy Cole his life."

Wild Henry put the note back in the bag. "We all risked our necks fer this money, Cap'n. I know you're takin' Billy's death mighty hard. Billy understood that we was takin' a chance. Plenty of good men from our outfit got killed in the war . . . dyin' so rich men could keep their slaves. Time'll take the edge off Billy's memory. Won't be so hard to think about him in a week or two."

John closed his eyes and ground his teeth together, then he urged the gray to a lope, scattering a herd of longhorns grazing in a shallow basin.

* * *

When they first saw the tiny specks on the horizon behind them, John couldn't be sure of their identity. He signaled a halt on a bluff and swung the gray around to study the specks. For half a minute they sat in silence to watch the northern hills.

"Those are horsemen," John said, "and they're gaining on us."

"Wonder how the hell they caught up?" Wild Henry groused, as his hand went reflexively to his pistol.

"Good horses, same as us," John replied. "Now it'll come down to a horse race."

They reined off the bluff and struck a lope. John began to ponder their dilemma. Fifteen riders, perhaps more, were coming along their tracks. Were they soldiers? Or possemen? In either case they had found what they were after quickly . . . the hoofprints of the bank robbers. Judging the distance between them in open country was guesswork, perhaps four or five miles. Somehow the men behind them had narrowed the gap. John knew the delay to bury Billy had cost them dearly.

Now they were faced with grim choices, to spend precious time riding down streambeds and rivers in an attempt to throw off the pursuit. Or, was the best choice to simply run hard for the Rio Grande in a test of horse-flesh? How could he be sure which choice presented the best chances of making their escape?

He reasoned that few men owned good thoroughbred horses bred for distance and speed. The best advantage John and his men had were Howard Lacy's horses. Thus it seemed best to use them to full advantage whenever they could.

Tommy Joe's face had gone pale. "I counted fourteen," he said, looking over his shoulder. Only when they crossed high ground were they able to see the men behind them.

"We don't stand a chance in an all-out fight," John answered. "Best we can do is try to outrun them . . . see if we can widen the gap between us. Whoever they are, they'll have to rest their mounts. We just have to make damn sure we ain't resting ourselves when they make their move."

Wild Henry grunted. "If we get any rest, we'd better do it in daylight, whilst we can see 'em. Wait 'til they get close and then ride off. It'll be a mite chancy, lettin' them ride up on us, but it's better'n gettin' caught someplace in the dark. If we push hard at night and rest durin' the day when we've got our eyes on 'em, we won't get caught off our guard so easy."

Wild Henry's idea made sense. "When we get to the tops of those hills, we'll let out horses blow," John said. "We can see them coming from those hills."

Galloping through ravines and dry steambeds to stay off the skyline, John led them toward the distant hills. The gray ran easily in spite of the heat, proving that the time they had spent conditioning the colts before the robbery paid off. Only Tommy Joe's sorrel showed any signs of tiring as they wound their way south . . . the colt had begun to flare its nostrils and gulp air as they started up the gentle slopes toward the highest hilltops.

They loped their mounts into a thicket of post oaks and swung around for a view of the riders. For a time they saw nothing but empty prairie. Then John pointed to a dust cloud lifting above the time of a ravine. "There they are," he declared quickly. "I can see their dust."

It appeared they had neither gained nor lost any ground to their pursuers. John waited until he saw the first rider in the distance. Frowning, he examined the second horse to come out of the draw. He couldn't see a rider on the animal's back. Then a cold realization numbed his senses ... the men following their hoof-prints were leading spare horses. If they made flying changes they would never have to stop and rest. They would keep coming on fresh mounts. It explained why the gap had been closed so suddenly.

"Trouble," John said in a hoarse voice. "They're leading a change of horses. There's just seven men down there. They're riding one horse and resting the other without a rider's weight. They aim to wear us down."

"Son of a bitch," Wild Henry whispered. "It'll work, won't it, Cap'n?"

John shook his head silently. He reined the gray around and started south again, gripped by a gnawing fear. In spite of his careful plan, he'd been outsmarted. Down in his gut he knew it was the bounty hunter's tactic. Buel Pope was the man behind them, using his experience tracking down Wanted men. John had been so sure of the thoroughbred colts against common horses that he hadn't considered another possibility. Two horses would easily wear down the best of animals in a contest of endurance.

Tommy Joe rode up beside John, his face pinched with worry. "They'll catch us, won't they?" he asked above the drumming of galloping hooves.

John's mind was racing. "Sooner or later," he agreed. "If we can find a place where we can throw them off our tracks, we can buy ourselves some time. Next stream we come to, we'll try to lose them by changing directions. It'll be dark soon. Our chances'll be better in the dark."

Wild Henry's face was grim. "It gets rocky west of Austin," he said. "Maybe we can lose 'em in those rocks...."

John sighted along the southern horizon. The sun was low in the west, lengthening shadows across the hilly country before them. Now their escape depended upon more than horseflesh. It would take cunning to outwit an experienced bounty hunter, cunning and a piece of luck. The land offered their best hope of escape, finding a spot where tracks would be harder to find.

Then John remembered how quickly a similar plan had failed in the rocks west of the Bosque. Pope and his deputies had found their tracks with ease. What could John and his men do to throw off the bounty hunter that they hadn't tried before?

Thinking desperate thoughts, John led his men across darkening hills at sunset. They had precious little ammunition for their guns. The Sharps rifle had been booted to Billy's saddle, thus they had only three .36 caliber pistols and a handful of shot to fight off Pope and his men. It presented a gloomy picture. For most of the war, John and his men were up against superior firepower. Lee's surrender at Appomattox hadn't changed anything.

And now they were forcing the colts to go without rest, holding a steady gallop that would soon wear them down to a walk. A bleak image floated before John's eyes, of three men on exhausted horses surrounded on a bald knob somewhere above the Mexican border, firing their last shots before tossing aside empty guns. He worried that he was seeing the future in his mind's eye, and then the bank robbery and Billy's death would have come to nothing at all.

Envisioning such gloomy possibilities, he listened to the gray colt puffing for wind as the sun went below the horizon. He knew time was running short.

Chapter Twenty-three

Pale moonlight illuminated the land around them. Pushing south at a trot, they swung wide of occasional ranch houses where lantern glow shone through distant windows. It was the emptiest country John had ever seen. They came upon scattered herds of longhorns bedded down for the night, but for the most part they saw no living things. Summer-dry grass whispered with the passage of their horses' hooves. Now and then they could hear the yipping cries of coyotes or the hoot of an owl. Otherwise, there was only an eerie quiet across the surrounding hills, putting John's nerves on edge.

He judged time by the stars. The hours passed slowly, the men keeping an uneasy silence, each with his own private thoughts now that the riders behind them were closing steadily along their hoofprints. John knew they had to do something to lose the trackers in the dark. The prairie grass showed their horses' tracks plainly in the moonlight. They were making it easy for Pope and his men to follow their quarry. John searched the hills for a rocky streambed running east or west that would allow them to change direction, with no result. Thus they continued south as rapidly as the young geldings could travel, turning anxious eyes behind them, watching for the relentless pursuit they knew was somewhere to the north.

"Wish we had some whiskey," Wild Henry said softly. They were crossing a moonlit ridge when he made the remark to John. It was the first word spoken between them for several hours. "This is hard on a man's nerves, Cap'n. We know they're back there someplace, only we can't see 'em."

John offered no reply, scanning the hills. He worried that they were a few short hours from a desperate situation when daylight came. If Pope and his men gained any more ground through the night, the chase would begin in earnest at dawn. The colts were tired, and Pope's men would have rifles. John and his companions would be sitting ducks for a marksman's bullets.

It was half an hour later, as they rode over a rise, that John found what he'd been looking for. A rocky draw snaked its way to the northwest across a shallow valley, continuing south and east. "There it is," John said, standing in his stirrups. "If we turn up that draw and keep our horses on the rocks, they'll have to wait for daylight to find our sign. When we get to the bottom of this slope, I want the two of you to swing northwest. I'll ride out on the other side and make some tracks where they'll be easy to find, then I'll double back and catch up to you. Keep movin' up that draw. I'll be along as quick as I can."

They struck a lope to the bottom of the hill, then slowed to ride down the bank of the dry wash. A bed of white limestone ran both directions down the draw.

"Perfect," John said, leaning out of his saddle to examine the rock. "Ride slow 'til you get up the draw a ways. I'll ride across and leave 'em some hoofprints."

Wild Henry swung his roan and started up the wash. Tommy Joe came right on his heels. John listened to the clatter of iron horseshoes until the sound faded, then he kicked the gray up the south bank and hit a lope through the dry prairie grass.

A hundred yards from the draw he drew rein and swung around, galloping back over the same prints, then down in the dry streambed again. This time, he trotted the gray southeast, marking his trail as plainly as he could in the pale moonlight. He rode a quarter mile before he heeled the colt up the southern bank again, crisscrossing the open stretches between cottonwood trees lining the creek, picking the hardest ground. In the dark, even a skillful tracker would have trouble chosing the right direction. It would take time to swing down off a horse to read the prints and sort them out.

He lost track of time, making false trails for Pope to follow, when he finally felt satisfied with the result. He rode the gray very carefully to the crossing again and broke off a cottonwood branch.

He led the gray northwest and tied it to a limb, then he crept back to the crossing and started sweeping the ground clear of any marks on the limestone, backing toward the spot where the colt was tied. He was sweating by the time the chore was done. He swung aboard the colt and struck a trot, looking over his shoulder in the direction Pope would come.

He worried that the wash took them the wrong way to make the border quickly, adding miles to their escape, though he knew their choices were few. Pope's tactics had thus far proven to be better than his. The sheriff was gaining. Unless John resorted to trickery and illusion, he and his companions were sure to be caught before they reached Mexico.

Two hours later, he caught up with Wild Henry and Tommy Joe. Judging time by the Big Dipper, it was a couple of hours past midnight.

"If it works, we bought ourselves five or six hours,"

he said, urging the gray to the front. "We'll stay in these rocks 'til dawn, then we'll swing south again."

"If we can make the Llano River," Wild Henry remarked, "we can follow it all the way to Junction. We'll be closer to Del Rio on the border from there."

John puzzled over the change in plans. "I promised to put the money for these colts in a Laredo bank," he said, thinking.

"We could ride down the Mexican side to Laredo," Wild Henry suggested. "Be safe as a newborn in his mother's arms that way."

Dawn put them in steep-walled canyons. Slabs of rock the color of rusted iron littered the canyon floors to the south and west. John picked a gentle climb and rode out of the wash at a trot, aiming due south across rough land dotted with cactus and mesquites.

"Mighty rough country," Wild Henry complained. "Never been this far west, Cap'n. We'll be ridin' blind 'til we get to the Llano. Map says it ain't far south of us."

"We'll follow the river west," John said, considering their chances. "Now that we know Sheriff Pope and his men can ride us down by changin' horses, we need to spend more time bein' careful where we leave tracks. When we come to that river, we'll ride up a few miles to wash out these hoofprints. It'll give these colts a rest, if nobody's pushin' us from behind."

"You reckon you threw 'em off our trail last night, Cap'n?" Tommy Joe asked, turning back in his saddle again.

"Ain't likely," John answered, taking his own careful look behind. "Somebody in that outfit can damn sure track a horse in rough country . . . figures to be Pope . . . learned it huntin' Wanted men in the territories. Best we can hope to do is slow 'em down some, and save these young horses for a hell-for-leather race when the time comes."

Wild Henry had been studying their backtrail. "No sign of them back there," he said cautiously, as though he wasn't quite sure of his remark.

They held the horses in an easy trot, entering the canyons along a deer trail winding through the mesquite and brush. They had seen no signs of civilization since midnight, nor any herds of cattle or recent cattle prints. The land had turned drier, offering only sparse grazing where thin topsoil appeared between stretches of orange-red rock. Cactus grew from tiny crags in the canyon floor, and in clusters below thorny mesquites. It was country too barren to support livestock, an explanation for the absence of ranch houses and traveled roads.

They found the river an hour before noon. The Llano was a shallow ribbon of clear water passing over gravel beds and long stretches of solid rock. John glanced over his shoulder and looked along the horizon, then he urged the gray into the river and reined west.

"We damn sure ain't leavin' no tracks," Wild Henry said, gazing down as the roan trotted through the shallows. "A bloodhound won't be able to follow us now, Cap'n. We can ride this river plumb to that place called Junction. Looks to be three or four days to the west of us, judin' by the map. Then we've got two choices, to ride fer Del Rio, or Eagle Pass."

John listened to the splash of horses' hooves, picking his way across gravel beds, turning often to examine the skyline. "It's early to be worrying about the direction we'll take," he said. "First thing is to make sure Pope and his men aren't ridin' our coattails. We've got ten days of hard country to travel yet an' I don't figure Pope's the kind to give up easy. We may have lost him for a spell, but I've got this feelin' down in my gut that we'll see him again before we set eyes on the Rio Grande."

They hadn't seen so much as a hoofprint for three days.

"This is the lonesomest place I ever saw," Tommy Joe said as they rode beside the river at a walk. The horses were rested and fresh after an hour of grazing beside the water's edge while John and his men ate a meal of jerky. John had been dozing in the saddle. He called a brief rest at dawn, too tired to continue without sleep. They'd spent three uneasy days traveling beside the river, stopping often to watch the skyline for the Waco posse and wonder about them.

The thoroughbreds had begun to show signs of hard use. Their flanks were drawn. Wild Henry's roan started to cough from the dust. John's colt walked with its head lowered. The sorrel had a saddle sore where the cinch rubbed its ribs. John worried that a hard run to escape a charge by Pope's men would finish the young horses. In spite of their toughness, they had been ridden too far without rest and grain. Breeding was no substitute for proper care.

Among the men, Wild Henry suffered most. Without a saddle, his pants had worn through, rubbing the insides of his legs raw until they bled. Though he offered no complaint, he rode with a pained expression on his face, rubbing fat from the piece of salt pork on his skin when they stopped to rest the horses.

John passed the time thinking about Sallie Mae, remembering their tender embraces when her father was away from the cabin. At times he allowed himself thoughts about Billy, until his throat grew tight with painful memories. He thought about the money too, when he needed to brighten his mood. There would be no more hungry days for John and his men when they reached the safety of Mexico. If Sallie Mae got his letter, there was a chance she would agree to marry him and live with him below the Rio Grande. He could buy her beautiful dresses. She would never have to wear floursacking again, if she would only come to the border to be his bride.

A recollection from the robbery lingered in his mind, of Sheldon Blackwell cowering on the floor of the bank with his hands over his face. It had been Blackwell's day of reckoning, for what he'd done to the son of Hiram Cross. But when John remembered the robbery, he couldn't escape the memory of Billy's face when Buel Pope's bullet brought an end to his life. Thus John hurried to put aside those thoughts, for they always reminded him of Billy.

John thought of other things ... of Mary, and how he wished for better chances for his sister. With the money they carried across their saddles, John could offer her a life outside a whore's crib. He sometimes debated whether he could forgive her for what she'd done, for selling her body to the conquering Yankees at Diamond Lil's. At times, he swore he couldn't. Until he remembered that he had become an outlaw, a bank robber. There really wasn't much difference, if you could measure right and wrong.

When he needed justification, he thought back to the eighty-acre farm on the banks of the Brazos. They had taken it from him, and done it while he was away at war. Robbing the same bank that took his farm squared things. Howard Lucy had called it an eye for an eye. John called it satisfaction.

"Yonder's a settlement," Wild Henry exclaimed, pointing to a tiny collection of buildings in the distance, as they rode around a bend in the river. "That'll be Junction, Cap'n. Sure would taste sweet to have a mouthful of whiskey. There'll be a trader's store where we could buy a jug. Shame to have all this money an' no place to spend it. I could use a saddle too. My ass is so sore I can't hardly tolerate sittin' on this colt's back."

John squinted in the sun's glare, examining the town carefully. "Too risky to ride in," he said. A row of telegraph poles ran beside a dusty wagon road leading north and south. A heavy freighter lumbered away from Junction, pulled northward by a team of oxen. "That'll be the road to Del Rio. By now, word of the robbery has been sent all over this part of the state. That telegraph line ends in Junction, so they'll be on the lookout for us. Best news is, I don't see a soldier camp. According to the map, there's nothing between here and the border. We should hit the Nueces River about halfway. Dry as this country is, I don't figure there'll be any water in between. We'll have to spare these horses all we can."

Wild Henry licked his lips. "Hate to pass up a place where we can buy whiskey, Cap'n." He let out a sigh and turned his colt away from the river.

They started due south around Junction, staying miles to the east to avoid being seen. Their canteens were full, and there was enough jerky. Below the town they would swing southwest to make Del Rio. John guessed they faced a hard four-day ride.

He glanced over his shoulder as they rode into the brush. It seemed they had managed to lose Pope and his posse, though John dared not trust the feeling. He was nagged by the certainty that Pope was still behind them, forced to trail them slowly across the rocky terrain and the places where John had purposefully led his men up the river's gravel bars to wash out their tracks. The plan had worked. Until now. But when Pope found their hoofprints turning toward Del Rio he would stop tracking and start running to make the border, changing horses on the move to make up for lost time. The most dangerous part of the journey lay before John and his men ... the race to the Rio Grande. Pope wouldn't be relying on guesswork from here on. He would know where the robbers were headed.

"You act like you're worried, Cap'n," Tommy Joe said, riding alongside John. "We ain't seen a sign of that bunch of lawmen for four whole days. I say we lost 'em in those canyons. Sheriff Pope weren't no smarter'n anybody else. Can't nobody track a horse in water. Not even an Injun."

"I'm not so sure," John replied in a quiet voice. "Got this crawlin' feeling down the back of my neck. This ain't the time to get careless. We keep our eyes open and stay off the Del Rio road wide as we can." Then John looked behind them. "Worst thing is this dust. A man can see dust sign for miles in this country. No way to travel without kickin' up a cloud of it. If Pope's back there someplace, he'll read our sign and come runnin' on our heels."

For a time the three watched the dust cloud above them. It rose in the still air like a giant beacon before settling slowly back to earth as powdery yellow snow.

Chapter Twenty-four

Two days of blistering heat wilted the horses first, and then the men. By the end of the second day they were leading their colts across the thorny brushland. Their canteens were empty, and the river promised on the map was nowhere in sight. The dry earth turned to chalky white powder that made the horses cough continually when it arose to fill their muzzles. Cactus and all manner of thorny plants obstructed their path, forcing the men and horses to walk around heavier undergrowth to keep from being cut to shreds by needles and spikes. Diamondback rattlers were a constant danger. The men's feet were soon blistered by walking. To the west was a roadway that would make for easier travel, the Del Rio road. But the road would be too dangerous for three Wanted men with bags of stolen money. Thus they were forced to walk through the tight brush and cactus a mile east of the road, staying hidden, and suffering as a result.

John's lips were cracked and bleeding. They had consumed the last of their water at sunrise, after a sleepless night on hard ground warding off rattlesnakes and scorpions. There was scant grazing for the colts beneath the brush, and always the risk that one would be bitten by a deadly night-feeding snake. Then two hours past dawn the heat started to build, sapping the strength of men and animals, draining them until each footfall was an effort.

"Need to rest a minute, Cap'n," Wild Henry panted as they faced a gentle rise in the desert floor. The sun had taken its toll on the older soldier first, weakening him so that each step he took became a stagger. "Feelin' a touch dizzy." He sat down in the shade of his horse and pulled off his hat, sleeving sweat from his forehead.

Tommy Joe squatted beside his sorrel to keep the sun off his face. "I'd give a hundred dollars from my share of this loot for just one big swallow of water," he said.

John looked behind them, shading his eyes. "No sign of that posse," he sighed, avoiding a further discussion of water. "Looks like we might make it after all. That river's gotta be ahead of us someplace. If we keep pushin', we'll be safe inside Mexico in a couple more days."

Wild Henry shook his head. "Don't know if I can make it. If I chew that damn salty jerky, I get thirsty. If I don't, I get so damn weak I can't walk. Never thought I'd see the day come when I admitted I couldn't keep up, but it looks like today's the day."

John glanced at the sun. Another hour of daylight remained. "It'll cool off in a couple of hours. We'll rest here until it gets dark."

Tommy Joe chuckled. "And then we'll be dodgin' snakes. A snake's got more sense than a man. Waits 'til it's cool to eat."

John patted the gray's neck. Their horses had been suffering too, existing on little hatfuls of water poured into the crown, until the canteens were empty. John wondered about the river on the map. Where was the Nueces? This country had no landmarks, no features, making it impossible to judge distance. They should have come to the river by now. "It could be just as tough to get from the Nueces to the Rio Grande," he said, gazing south, reflecting on the two arduous days they had traveled after leaving Junction. "Don't see how this country could be any drier below the Nueces. These colts are about played out. Soon as we find that river, we can rest a spell and give our horses a chance to get stronger. If there's any grass."

Wild Henry merely shook his head. Tommy Joe was dozing on his haunches.

They stumbled the last few steps down to the river, dragged to the water's edge by the pull of thirsty horses. John unbuckled his gunbelt and tossed it on the river-bank, then he waded into the shallows and let out a sigh. Moonlight gave the Nueces a silver sheen across its surface. John lowered himself into the cool water fully dressed, too tired to pull off his boots.

"Damn that feels good," Wild Henry exclaimed. He sat down in the river where the water reached his chin. Tommy Joe was kneeling on a flat rock, cupping water in his hands. Men and animals drank their fill in silence a few minutes more, then the sorrel moved up the riverbank and began to graze. Soon the gray and the roan joined the sorrel, nibbling shortgrass along the river's edge, trailing their reins.

John forced himself up, thinking of the horses. "Let's pull those saddles and bridles and hobble our colts," he said tiredly, wincing when he put weight on his blistered feet. "When the horses are tended to, we can catch a few hours of shut-eye."

All three men were limping when they left the river. Water squished inside their boots as they pulled the horses' gear and fashioned hobbles with their bridle reins. A narrow strip of green grass ran beside the river, enough grazing to last the horses until morning.

John was first to stretch out on the riverbank, resting his head against his saddle. Exhaustion quickly closed his eyes in a dreamless sleep.

He sat up when the first rays of sunlight fell on his face. Wild Henry snored beside him. Tommy Joe was standing downriver with the horses. He grinned and waved when he saw John was awake.

John got up to study their surroundings. The shallow Nueces twisted through the brushland, its surface sparkling with morning light. Upstream, a few stunted cottonwoods grew beside the river, drooping their leafy branches above the sluggish current. The trees would provide shade, a precious commodity in this unyielding heat. Then John wondered about the safety of remaining at the river during the heat of the day. It would be better to press on to the border . . . if the horses had the strength to make it the last two days' ride to reach Mexico. John pondered the best choice, to wait and let the animals rest, or push south at once. Was Buel Pope close behind them?

He gazed down at Wild Henry. The soldier's legs were raw where his pants had worn through. The soles of his boots had gaping holes in them. Dried blood had crusted on the bare bottoms of his feet. He'd grown so thin that his gray tunic hung from his shoulders in loose folds. He would be too badly weakened to walk much farther across this desert and the roan would have trouble carrying him for two days in the heat on an empty belly. "I reckon we'll wait here a day or so," John whispered, talking to himself. "Haven't got the heart to push this outfit any harder. If that posse shows up, we'll be in a fix. But it's a chance we'll have to take."

John went to his gear and took out the little sack of dry beans and the piece of salt pork. They carried a small tin pan in Tommy Joe's saddlebags. They could soak the beans and risk a fire to boil them beneath one of the cottonwoods. Wild Henry needed food and rest as badly as their horses.

He put beans in the pan and added water, placing them on a flat rock beside the river to soak. Then he set about to gather firewood, chewing a strip of jerky while he walked through the brush picking up mesquite twigs.

Later, Tommy Joe joined him. Soon they had two armloads of dry kindling. All the while, John kept an eye on the northern horizon, watching for telltale dust. For the moment, the sky above the brushland was clear.

"We'll stay here until sundown," John said, tossing the sticks beneath a cottonwood tree, "if we don't see any dust sign. One of us stays near the horses, just in case we need to saddle in a hurry. We'll take turns watching for dust to the north of us. The damn heat waves play tricks on a man's eyes . . . we'll have to stay awake, so that posse don't slip up on us."

"I figure we lost 'em," Tommy Joe offered. "Hadn't seen a thing for days now."

John shook his head. "I can feel them out there someplace. Never was superstitious, but there's some things a man can't explain. Now and then my skin starts to crawl and I just know they're out there. . . ."

They devoured the pan of beans and salt pork when the sun was directly overhead. The cottonwood diffused the smoke from their tiny fire and thus no column of smoke pointed to their camp. Wild Henry's strength returned after the meager lunch, and his mood improved as John stood guard while he and Tommy Joe opened the money sacks beneath the tree. John could hear them counting the stacks of currency. Tommy Joe's voice became filled with excitement as the tally rose higher. Wild Henry had only two years of schooling and could offer little help with large numbers, though he watched the counted pile of money grow with a satisfied smile.

John was content to watch the horizon and their horses. It mattered little how much money was in the bags just then. Unless they made it safely to the Mexican border, the money was added weight on the young horses' backs that would slow them down in a race for the river. John examined the colts closely, passing time, noting that their flanks had begun to fill on grass and water.

"If it wasn't for this miserable heat," he said aloud, "we'd be in pretty good shape to make a run for it." He glanced north again, squinting to keep out the glare. Heat waves danced above the distant brush, distorting the shapes of things, creating the illusion of movement where there was none. Beads of sweat ran into his eyes from his hatband. Sweat trickled down his back, plastering his shirt to his skin. Nothing in his experience could compare with the merciless sun in this part of Texas. They had ridden into a dry wasteland where neither man nor beast could survive the heat of the day. Only at night was it possible to move about at this time of year. He knew their horses would perish if they carried the weight of a rider for any distance.

The afternoon passed with monotonous slowness, broken by Tommy Joe's announcement that the bags contained more than eighteen thousand dollars in federal currency. "Imagine, Cap'n Cross!" he exclaimed. "That's six thousand dollars for each of us. I never dreamed there could be so much money in one place. We're rich! We won't never see another poor day the rest of our lives!"

John had been watching the horizon so intently that his eyes burned. "Hadn't got to a place where we can spend any of it yet, Tommy Joe. By my reckoning, there's still fifty or sixty hard miles in front of us."

Wild Henry grinned. "Won't nothin' stop us now, Cap'n. I got this close, and you've got my word that I won't let nobody keep us from crossin' that river. If I have to crawl, I aim to make it with that money to the border. Should that bastard Pope show his face around here, I'll whip him bare-handed to get to Mexico. I swear I will. I've been flat broke all my life . . . barely had enough to eat most times. But just now, I'm fifty miles from bein' rich, an' you can bet your ass I ain't gonna let a handful of lawmen stand in my way."

John chuckled and took his eyes off the brush. "I never heard so much speech-makin' before." Then his expression hardened. "I wish Billy was with us now. If that ball hadn't caught him . . ."

Wild Henry's face fell. "All of us wish Billy'd made it, Cap'n. He was a good soldier, an' a good friend to boot. Times, a man can't explain bad luck. Billy was in the wrong place, I reckon, when his luck ran out."

John nodded, studying the horizon again. "Wasn't his fault. He said robbin' that bank was a crazy idea." A dust devil swirled across the brush, but John's thoughts were elsewhere.

Every shadow in their path could be a hiding place for a rattler. They picked their way slowly through the dark, skirting the thickest brush, guided by a half moon above them and light from a skyful of stars. Their horses plodded single file on a twisting course, until John called a halt out of frustration.

"Can't ride a straight line south," he said. He took a deep breath and looked west. "We'll risk riding the road tonight. At sunup we'll go back to the brush to keep out of sight. These colts are about done-in. We need to save them every step we can."

He reined west and headed for the wagon road, being

careful to avoid snakes and thorns. Two miles through the brush, they hit a moonlit pair of wagon ruts running southwest. For a time they sat beside the road, listening to the night sounds.

"We'll trot these horses for a mile or two, then rest them at a walk," John said. An uneasy feeling grew larger in the pit of his stomach. "Keep your eyes and ears open, men."

He led them southwest at an easy trot. Though the air was cooler, beads of sweat formed on his skin. He couldn't shake the feeling that he was headed toward trouble. He made the choice to travel down the road to spare the horses, in spite of the gnawing worry that someone was waiting for them to make a fool's move.

Chapter Twenty-five

Empty miles passed beneath their horses' hooves, monotonous miles of sameness where only the sounds of rattling curb chains and the click of iron horseshoes broke the blanket of silence over the brushlands. Here and there, they passed the hulk of an abandoned wagon or donkey cart beside the road. In places, they found the bleached bones of horses and mules picked clean by the buzzards. This land they crossed bore the earmarks of death upon it, for the land itself was the enemy. Living things required water, and shade, in order to survive. Here, there was no water, and never enough rainfall to nurture even the hardiest tree. There were only the endless miles of thorny brush and cactus, awaiting the unsuspecting traveler to claim yet another victim. John listened to the water sloshing in the canteens as they rode deeper into the dry wasteland. Those canteens were their only hope of surviving this bleak desert and he meant to ration the water carefully.

By trotting their colts, then walking them for a brief rest, they made steady progress until the first gray streaks of dawn brightened the eastern sky. John signaled a halt and took his bearings. Without a landmark, he could only guess that they made a slow twenty miles through the night. Now their safety demanded that they leave the road again in daylight, to resume a much slower walk through the brush.

"Top of that next rise, we'll swing off the road," he said.

"Hell, Cap'n, we ain't seen a soul," Wild Henry complained. "I say we keep ridin' this wagon road fer a spell. It's easier on these horses, an' us to boot."

"Too dangerous," John replied quickly, swinging a look behind them. "We'd stick out like a wart on a hog's snout. Off in that brush, we can stay hidden. It's slower, but we'll be a hell of a lot harder to spot from a distance."

He urged the gray to a walk and rode toward a gentle crest where the road dipped out of sight.

"You worry too damn much," Wild Henry grumbled. "We ain't seen hide nor hair of that posse. We lost 'em in those canyons above the Llano and it don't make much sense to hide from somebody who ain't there."

Tommy Joe offered his opinion. "We're liable to get snake-bit off this road," he said. "Leastways out here, we can see 'em first."

John ignored their remarks, convinced that they hadn't ridden clear of danger. The Rio Grande would provide the only safety they could count on, thus he meant to move carefully toward it no matter what the others had to say. He still had the gnawing sensation that someone was very close to them now. . . . He could never have explained it, but the feeling was there just the same. As the first golden rays of sunlight appeared above the brush, he rode to the crest of a low hill, occupied with thoughts of leading their horses through the heat of the day, when suddenly he saw a plume of dust arise from the south. Hauling back on his reins, he came wide awake, focusing on the dust cloud. Every muscle in his body tensed.

"Something's coming!" he snapped. "Get down!

We'll lead our horses off the road until we know who it is."

He was down from his saddle quickly, still watching the spiral of caliche lift skyward in the distance.

"Prob'ly just a wagon, Cap'n," Tommy Joe said. "Comin' from the south, it can't be that posse from Waco."

John was leading the gray into the brush before he answered. "Don't much matter who it is. Can't let anybody see us. Now get those horses moving!"

They wound their way around clumps of cactus and bigger plants with dagger-shaped spikes, hurrying toward a shallow depression where the brush thickened, a hiding place for the horses. Broad cactus beds slowed their progress, forcing them wide of the depression, crossing waist-high stretches of thorns and spiney bushes to reach taller brush. John heard a rattlesnake issue its deadly warning off to his left. He kept moving past it, watching the skyline as the dust cloud grew larger, more distinct. Some inner sense told him that this dust was not coming from the wheels of a freighter. He could feel his skin crawling down his back, alerting him for trouble.

They reached the safety of the deeper brush mere seconds before dark shapes appeared against the southern sky. John could make out a line of horsemen below the swirling cloud of caliche. He tried to count them, peering through a tangle of thorny vines and limbs.

"Soldiers," Tommy Joe breathed. "Comin' mighty damn fast too. Wonder how the hell they got word about us?"

John could feel the jaws of a trap tightening around them. "I reckon there's a telegraph line runnin' up the border towns. No way anybody could have gotten to Del Rio ahead of us. There has to be a wire along the Rio Grande."

"Maybe it's only a patrol," Wild Henry suggested. "Maybe they ain't lookin' fer us at all."

John could see the soldiers plainly now, urging their horses down the road at a trot. He counted twenty, then thirty. Could Wild Henry be right? Was this only a routine patrol? It seemed an unlikely coincidence. Why would such a large force be moving through an arid wasteland?

Beads of sweat formed on John's forehead. If the soldiers found their tracks where they left the road, John and his men were in for a fight, a fight they couldn't win. Neither could they win a race against fresher horses, just two days from Del Rio, the direction from which the soldiers came.

"These colts can't outrun 'em," John said, "not after we pushed this hard better'n three hundred miles. Besides, this brush is too thick to gallop a horse. They'll get cut to pieces if we try to run from that patrol."

"What the hell are we gonna do if they come for us?" Tommy Joe's voice was a dry whisper.

John didn't have an answer that made any sense. "Have to wait an' see what they do. If they miss our tracks . . ."

Wild Henry drew his revolver. He swallowed and stared at the soldiers. "I aim to fight 'em fer this money, Cap'n," he said. "They'll hang us anyway, if they catch us."

The column moved closer. They would pass within half a mile of the spot where John and his men were hidden. Although the sun was only an hour above the horizon, the heat became oppressive in the thicket. Sand flies darted around the horses and men, making their harsh buzzing sounds. Off in the distance they could hear the rattle of armament and the click of horseshoes as the column advanced northward. John understood just how completely they were trapped if the soldiers followed their tracks to the thicket. It would be a bitter end to so many miles of hardship, to come up just short of their objective, less than fifty miles from freedom in Mexico.

"Seems like bad luck intends to follow us," he sighed. The patrol was nearing the spot where the tracks led into the brush. He watched the soldiers at the front of the column. Would they call a halt when they saw the hoofprints?

John held his breath when the first soldiers arrived at the spot where they left the road. For an agonizing moment he was sure the column would stop. He fingered sweat from his eyelids to be sure of what he saw. . . . The cavalrymen rode past the place without slowing their horses. Dust boiled from the horses' heels as the column continued north.

"They missed us," Wild Henry said quietly.

"Never saw our tracks," Tommy Joe added.

John watched the patrol ride to the crest of the hill, afraid to trust their apparent good fortune. Soon the last pair of horsemen went out of sight over the hilltop.

He glanced back to the south, toward Del Rio, forming a plan as quickly as he could. "They'll find our tracks sooner or later and they'll know they missed us. We've got just one chance to get to the border. We'll have to ride that road as hard as we can, before those soldiers realize their mistake. Let's get movin'."

John hurried away from the thicket, leading his gray, keeping a watchful eye on the horizon. He knew they would need a piece of luck in order for his plan to work, just a few hours, before the patrol discovered their hoofprints headed south.

They made the wagon road quickly and boarded their horses. The dust sign above the cavalry patrol had grown smaller, moving away. John heeled his gelding to a trot and focused his attention on the road ahead, stroking the dappled gray's neck. "Time to give me everything you've got," he whispered.

The gray's ears flicked backward when he spoke.

Heat waves created the illusion of water in the distance, adding to the misery of the men sweltering under a midday sun. Foamy white lather clung to the horses' necks as they trotted over each dusty mile. The roan was coughing more often now, forcing the others to rest until its lungs were clear. Three hundred grueling miles lay behind them, enough to test the endurance of the best seasoned horses. John worried that their colts would play out when they were needed most . . . the last dangerous stretch above the Rio Grande.

Trotting the geldings, then walking to cool them down, they rode through the worst heat of the day without sighting another traveler on the Del Rio road. Always glancing behind for the soldiers, John forced their pace until sundown. In the midst of a broad, level plain, he called a rest stop and gave each horse a few swallows of water, emptying one canteen. The men took sips from a second canteen and made ready to ride again when the colts had their wind.

As John swung in his saddle he glanced northward. Purple shadows lay across the brush. But on the horizon he saw the sight he dreaded most . . . a cloud of dust hovered above the road, turned a pale orange by the sunset. "Here they come!" he said in a hollow voice. "I can see their dust."

Wild Henry wheeled his roan. "Let the sumbitches come," he snarled, resting his palm on his pistol grips. "We come this far and we damn sure ain't gonna hand over the money without a fight."

Tommy Joe's face lost some of its color. "We're awful close to that river, Cap'n," he said.

243

John sent the gray forward, running through the possibilities in his mind. He judged they were a good twenty miles from the border, riding spent horses. If the soldiers had pushed their mounts all day, the contest would be roughly equal. Tactics would play a part in determining the winner, who made the right guess at the last with a fresher animal to carry them. With nothing but open road between them, they would be able to see each other's moves in the moonlight. It promised to be one hell of a test of judgment and horseflesh, to see who made the right choice.

They struck a steady trot into the deepening twilight, knowing their lives depended on their animals now. The land would not allow John another deception. There was only the arrow-straight road ahead of them and no place to hide from their pursurers.

Twilight became full dark. Cooler air lengthened the horses' strides for an hour, then two. The grim discovery of the dust cloud kept the men from conversation, eyes fixed on their backtrail for the first glimpse of a charge by the cavalry. It would be a waiting game, until the soldiers made their move. Then John and his men would find out if their colts had enough stamina to outlast the cavalry horses in the race to make the Rio Grande.

"Can't see 'em," Wild Henry said later, turned back in his latest effort to view the road behind them.

The colts were laboring. John called a brief halt to let the geldings blow, scanning the moonlit prairie. The wagon ruts made a pale slash across the darker brush behind them. "Looks like we're holding our own," he said finally.

Then he saw it . . . an inky shape moving along the wagon ruts at the top of a distant rise. More shapes appeared behind the first, coming soundlessly in their direction. "There they are," he whispered. "They're making their move right now. Some of 'em are strung out at the front. Riding the best horses, I reckon."

Wild Henry scowled. "Don't see how their horses can be no fresher'n ours, Cap'n. There's a couple of miles betwixt us just now. Let 'em get a little closer, then we'll stretch these colts out and ask 'em to run."

It was the only tactic left, to run and rest, keeping just enough distance to be out of rifle range. "It's our last hope," he said. "Let's give these colts the rest of the water."

Tommy Joe poured the contents of the canteens into the crown of his hat. Each gelding drank hungrily until the last drop was gone.

John was watching the mounted men draw closer, feeling his heartbeat quicken. When the distance between them was down to a mile he mounted the gray and turned the animal south.

The regular rhythm of pounding hooves filled his ears, mingled with the sounds of flared muzzles seeking more air with each difficult stride. Wind whistled through the gray's nostrils as it galloped down the road. Tommy Joe's sorrel was gasping, struggling to stay up with the others. John closed his mind to the cruelty of it, of using a horse beyond its limits. His life and the lives of his men depended on the toughness of the animals they rode. It could prove to be a fatal mistake to feel sorry for the colts at the moment when their lives hung in the balance, thus John closed his ears and drummed his heels into the gray's sides.

He glanced over his shoulder, counting six, then seven riders on their trail. He guessed that most of the cavalry horses had played out somewhere behind them. It seemed impossible that any of them could be gaining on the thoroughbreds. Yet there they were in the pale moonlight, galloping along the wagon ruts less than a quarter of a mile to the rear. No matter how briefly John rested the geldings, the men giving chase shortened the distance between them.

John led his men over a hill, sighting a strange grayness in the southern skies. Then he saw distant lights twinkling in a yawning valley below, and the silvery surface of the Rio Grande twisting and turning across the valley floor, brightened by the moon's glow.

"There she is!" Wild Henry cried. "Yonder's Mexico!"

Tommy Joe's horse was wheezing. John wondered if the horses had enough strength left to make the river.

Chapter Twenty-six

The first gunshot startled him. He heard the crack of a pistol and ducked his head reflexively. A bullet whined overhead. Wild Henry cursed softly. The rumble of galloping hooves continued as their horses sped down the gradual slope toward Del Rio.

Another gun banged behind them. John whirled in the saddle to check the range as a whistling lead slug sounded off to the right. He could see the dark horsemen racing along the moonlit wagon ruts. A gun popped, making a bright yellow muzzle flash in the dark. A speeding ball whacked into the brush beside the road. Firing with any accuracy aboard the back of a running horse was almost impossible at a distance. John knew the shooters were only trying to get lucky at this range, but the gap was steadily closing. In another half mile, the range would be deadly. But there were no alternatives . . . staying on the road was their only chance.

Wild Henry's roan began to cough. Tommy Joe's sorrel had difficulty staying up with the others, wheezing when it gasped for wind, its strides shortening. John tried frantically to think of a way to slow down the oncoming riders. There was but one choice, to stop and take aim at the first horsemen, making them think twice about a headlong charge toward a hail of bullets.

"I'm falling back!" he cried, trying to be heard above the drumming hooves. "Keep moving! I'll try to slow them down."

He hauled back on the gray and wheeled the gelding around in the road, drawing the Navy Colt from his belt as he chose his first target. Two riders galloped in front of the rest, shoulder to shoulder down the pale caliche ruts. John sighted the .36 across his forearm and waited.

Suddenly, guns started to pop in the distance. Bullets sped past him, whining above him, whispering through the air on either side. A slug plowed through the dirt in front of the gray. The colt began to prance, fighting the pull on its reins.

And still John waited precious seconds more, until he knew his ball would find its mark, risking death from the lead flying all around him, ricocheting into the brush on both sides of the road. He had to make sure his delaying tactic worked, giving Wild Henry and Tommy Joe a little more time on their faltering horses, for John knew the gray still had some reserve . . . he hoped it would be enough to carry him out of danger.

He could hear the pounding of the riders' horses now, between staccatos of gunfire. Steadying the revolver on his arm, he waited as long as he dared and squeezed off a careful shot at the inky shape of a man bent over his horse's neck.

The gunshot startled the gray colt and sent it whirling away to the right, ducking its head from the sharp report so near its ears. John pulled back on the reins and cocked the .36 again as a cry echoed from the darkness. A rider spilled from his saddle and rolled into the brush beside the road. John wasted no time aiming at the second horseman. . . . He fired again and felt the colt lunge underneath him, spooked by the explosion on its back. He heard something snap, like the crack of a dry twig, then the rider's horse collapsed on its chest, skidding through the caliche and brush at the edge of a wagon rut, legs flailing, groaning when the air left its lungs. The falling rider gave a muffled cry and fell out of sight.

Three answering shots came from the men higher up the slope. A spent slug careened off the road in front of the gray, frightening the colt into another desperate lunge that almost swayed John out of his saddle. He made sure of the downed riders, briefly puzzling over their appearance when they fell, then he turned the dappled gelding and heeled it to a flat-out run with bullets singing around him.

The gray quickly gathered speed, drumming its hooves down the hard-packed caliche, its mane flying in John's face. The guns behind him fell silent. He let the colt have its head to carry him out of range, momentarily satisfied that his plan worked. He regretted the misplaced ball that downed the horse, consoling himself with the knowledge that he'd aimed for the rider. Then he turned back in the saddle, trying to remember what he had glimpsed in the darkness that seemed out of place. One of the men who had fallen lost his hat, he recalled. Why had his attention been drawn to the rider's hat?

Five mounted men were halted in the road where the two had gone down from John's bullets. The delay was giving Wild Henry and Tommy Joe valuable time to get closer to the border. John wondered about the rest of the column, when it suddenly struck him why he had noticed the rider's hat. The man he shot was not a soldier! The men chasing them now were Buel Pope's men!

His mind was crowded with a thousand thoughts at once as the colt sped along the empty road. Where had the soldiers gone? And how had Pope caught up with them?

John listened to the rhythm of the gray's hooves,

249

sighting his two companions almost a mile ahead as they rode out on a flat plain above Del Rio. The town, and the river, was another mile away. John glanced down at the moneybags bouncing against the gray's shoulders. Just a few minutes more, if their luck held, and they would be safely across the border in Mexico.

Exploding guns roared behind him, awakening him from wishful thinking about the safety of the river. Glancing back, he saw horsemen bearing down on him with guns blazing. He knew now that the relentless pursuit was the handiwork of Sheriff Pope and his spare horses. The lawman had been too smart to be thrown off the tracks of his quarry for very long, and now he came to this final moment in the chase riding fresher mounts. His posse outnumbered John and his men two to one. The race to the Rio Grande had come down to the last two miles, with Pope holding every advantage.

John bent over the gray's neck and drummed his heels into its ribs. The colt responded with longer, quicker strides in spite of its exhaustion. The dappled gelding was running on heart, not just its legs. Flaring its nostrils, gasping for each breath, the horse drew from some reserve few animals possess, flying over dark prairie toward Mexico. With each powerful lunge of the colt's hindquarters the distance between John and the posse grew larger, until the guns stopped firing. Now John could see the lantern-lit windows in Del Rio clearly, and the silver river south of town. On the far side of the Rio Grande was the little village of Acuna. He could see the lights behind windows of scattered adobe huts on the south bank of the river. The moon bathed the brushland with soft white light, showing him the way to safety. The colt seemed to understand. . . . it ran harder, bobbing its head up and down with the rhythm of its run, racing closer and closer to the edge of town.

He caught up to Wild Henry and Tommy Joe at the outskirts of Del Rio. Their horses were covered with foamy lather, sucking wind through open muzzles and flared nostrils, struggling to hold a steady lope as they entered the deserted main street through town. Though it was well past midnight, a few lights burned behind windows the men galloped past, a brightly lit saloon on a street corner and a tiny café across the road. Their horses' hooves echoed off the storefronts as John led his men toward the river crossing beyond the sleepy business district. John could see the river's shimmering surface now, and the village beyond it where the chase would finally come to an end.

"We're gonna make it!" Tommy Joe shouted. He looked over his shoulder.

They raced their horses to a low bluff where the road dropped sharply to the river. Rows of tiny clapboard shacks stood on the cutbank, overlooking the Rio Grande. Wild Henry was first to send his gelding off the top of the bluff. The roan stumbled and almost fell, then caught itself and lumbered down the grade with wind whistling from its nostrils. Tommy Joe and John rode side by side over the rim of the cutbank at an all-out gallop. John could hear the thunder of hoofbeats behind them.

The roan splashed into the shallows, sending crystal spray into the night sky that caught moonlight, becoming glistening droplets around Wild Henry's dark outline as he leaned over the gelding's neck. Then the gray and the sorrel lunged into the water at full speed. A hundred yards of slow current separated the men and horses from Mexico.

John whirled in his saddle when he heard angry shouts behind them. The possemen swirled off the cutbank and came charging down to the river's edge. A gun banged, then another, as the riders drew rein on the last stretch of Texas soil.

One of the lawmen jumped down from his saddle . . . John saw him pull a rifle from his saddleboot.

"Watch out!" John cried, trying to be heard above the splashing hooves as the river deepened. "He's got a rifle. . . ."

Before the warning left John's mouth there was a tremendous roar, the explosion of a heavy bore gun. John heard the hiss of speeding lead, and then the sharp cry of a wounded man.

Tommy Joe pitched forward across his gelding's neck, his arms outstretched like a bird's wings. He landed precariously atop the sorrel's shoulders, where his hands made a frantic grab for the colt's throatlatch. He cried out again. "I'm hit, Cap'n!"

The sorrel lost its footing and started to swim. Water crept over John's knees, then the gray's front legs churned below the surface. John was swept from his saddle. He drew his revolver and aimed back at the bank where the rifleman stood, lifting his gun to keep the percussion caps dry until he could trigger off a hurried shot.

The rifle roared again, its sound trapped by the walls of the cutbank, magnifying the noise for the men caught in the river. A bullet skittered across the water, cutting a trail of glittering spray before it went out of sight harmlessly short.

John aimed and fired, knowing he'd done it too quickly. The ball whistled into the cutbank behind the lawmen, kicking up a puff of caliche dust.

From the corner of his eye, John saw Wild Henry lean off his roan to grab Tommy Joe before his body slipped into the river. Swimming horses blasted air from their muzzles in the brief moment of silence that followed, then two pistol shots popped from the riverbank.

John fired again, wide of the mark a second time, hoping to draw fire away from his injured companion until the horses could make the opposite bank. His shot was answered by a bellowing blast from the rifle. . . . The bullet whispered over John's head and whacked into a stand of cottonwoods on the Mexican side.

The sounds of swimming horses changed. The sorrel found its footing and rose up out of the murky water, then Wild Henry's roan hit solid ground, climbing toward dry land. John's colt ended its swim, hooves clawing for purchase in the river mud. Wild Henry held Tommy Joe across his horse's withers as the roan made the shallows, then the riverbank. A gunshot sounded in the distance, then all three horses entered the cottonwood trees where deep night shadows hid them from the guns on the Texas side.

The three colts lowered their heads, panting, too weak to take another step without rest. John slid out of the saddle and hurried over to Tommy Joe. "How bad is it?" he asked softly, helping the wounded boy to the ground.

"My shoulder," Tommy Joe groaned. In the darkness John couldn't see the bullethole . . . he touched it with a fingertip and winced when he felt the opening and the trickle of blood.

Wild Henry slipped off the roan and knelt beside John. "If there's a doctor on this side of the river, maybe . . ."

John glanced across the river, then back to the boy. "We'll lift him back on his horse and see if we can find a doctor. Help me get him up."

They hoisted Tommy Joe into his saddle.

"Let's lead these horses up the bank," John said. "One of us keeps an eye on the money while the other asks around in Acuna. It's a shoulder wound. He's gonna make it."

Wild Henry faced the Texas side of the river. "We all made it, Cap'n," he said proudly. "Tommy Joe'll heal up when he thinks about bein' rich. We've got ourselves six bags of wet money, an' the rest of our lives to get it spent. Tommy Joe won't want to miss the good times we're fixin' to have, now that we're safe in Mexico."

Tommy Joe nodded weakly, bent over his saddle with pain.

Then John heard a noise across the river. He turned toward it, and what he saw made his blood run cold. Four of the possemen had entered the river on horses, plodding slowly toward the Mexican side."

"They can't touch us over here," Wild Henry growled.

John still held the .36 in his right hand. Just two loads remained in the gun. "Maybe they ain't comin' as lawmen," John said softly. "Maybe they aim to rob us of our bank loot and leave us for dead. They know they've got no jurisdiction on this side of the river. Maybe Buel Pope has decided to turn outlaw himself, thinkin' he can gun us down and make off with our loot." John looked beyond the advancing riders. Two more of Pope's deputies covered the river with rifles to their shoulders.

Wild Henry clawed for his revolver. "Let the bastards come," he snarled. "If it's a fight they're after, we'll damn sure oblige them."

John whirled to Tommy Joe. "Hand me your pistol," he snapped, "and hope like hell those caps are dry."

Tommy Joe fumbled for his gun. John took it quickly and walked to the edge of the trees. The four riders urged their mounts into the deepest water. John could see their pistols lifted above the inky water as the horses started to swim toward Mexico.

Wild Henry arrived at John's shoulder. "I had this itch a long time ago to kill that bastard Pope," he said.

"Soon as those horses get close enough, I aim to empty a few of them saddles."

Silver moonlight shone down on the river, outlining the men as they rode closer to the cottonwoods. "I'll take the pair on the right," he whispered. "Wait 'til I shake my head, then take care of the other two."

Wild Henry nodded silently. An evil grin lifted the corners of his mouth when he raised his revolver to aim at the river.

Chapter Twenty-seven

John was sure he recognized the sheriff's flatbrim hat silhouetted against the river when the horses hit a trot through the shallows. He was immediately reminded of Billy, and of that fateful gunshot in front of the bank that ended Billy's life. As Buel Pope rode toward the cottonwoods, flanked by three deputies, John remembered the gunshot vividly. Wild rage erased John's earlier plan to down the pair of men to his right. With Sheriff Pope in his gunsights he was overpowered by the need for revenge.

John's arms were trembling with seething anger for the lead ball that robbed him of his friend. He could think of nothing else when his finger tightened around one of the triggers. The brazen sheriff rode straight for the trees, sure of himself and the larger force he brought with him for the chase to the border. But now he'd taken one step too many, come too far in pursuit of the money and ignored the boundary between Texas and Mexico. It was a mistake that John would make him pay dearly for, if he could only steady his hands for a well-placed shot.

He knew Wild Henry was growing impatient with the delay, for the four men were within pistol range now. But John meant to be sure of his target, dead sure, before he pulled the trigger.

The lawmen were thirty yards from the cottonwoods, leaving the shallows as four black silhouettes with moonlight glinting off their gun barrels. John steadied his revolvers, eyes fixed on the dark outline of Sheriff Pope, remembering Billy Cole. Once before he'd tasted sweet vengeance, when he fired a lead ball into John Buford's body. And now the fates dealt him a chance to square things for Billy. Thinking this, a surge of anger gripped John's chest. He thumbed back both hammers and took careful aim.

One pistol barked and spat orange flame, slamming the gun butt into his palm, rocking the cottonwood grove with noise. A horse reared, pawing its forefeet, whirling away from the explosion. John's gaze was focused on the sheriff and he saw nothing else in that fraction of time before the bullet struck its mark. For an instant John feared that his shot went wide ... Sheriff Pope sat his saddle ramrod straight as his horse took another step toward the trees.

Wild Henry's gun fired to John's left, spitting a flash of bright light aimed at the lawmen. But John's attention was on the sheriff; he was only dimly aware of a yell from one of the possemen. Slowly, Sheriff Pope's shoulders tented, then his free hand went to his chest. His horse bolted, rocking the lawman backward. Pope's body tilted. John stood transfixed, unable to think or act until the sheriff's body slumped off the rump of his horse. John watched it land hard on the river clay, bouncing with sudden impact, arms flopping beside it, one hand still clutching a pistol. John stared at the fallen man, seemingly unaware of the two deputies who should have been his targets, until a pair of gunshots rang out that sent molten shot hissing past his face.

John fired at one of the inky shapes. Both men were moving to his left, rattling spurs into their horses' flanks to escape the deadly fire from the trees. John's hasty shot was a miss. He could hear his bullet whistling across the river harmlessly.

Wild Henry fired again. A man screamed aboard one of the horses and toppled out of his saddle. In the ensuing brief silence, Wild Henry gave a satisfied grunt and fired again at the last mounted man galloping away from the fight along the riverbank. The slug plowed into the water, making a soft, sucking sound.

A rifle thundered across the river. In the cottonwood limbs above John's head a chunk of flying lead ripped through a cluster of leaves. Then one of the fallen deputies at the edge of the water groaned and tried to rise, pushing his torso off the ground with trembling arms. John heard Wild Henry cocking his pistol. A gun blast flipped the deputy over on his back like a rag doll with a strangled cry gurgling in his throat.

The hoofbeats of the departing rider faded. An eerie silence hung over the Rio Grande. John watched a filmy layer of blue gunsmoke swirl above the men who lay on the riverbank. His ears were ringing.

"I got Pope," he said softly, as though to reassure himself. The sheriff was sprawled on his back near the water's edge, his face bathed in pale moonlight.

Upriver, the surviving deputy splashed his horse into the shallows, headed back toward Texas. Loose horses milled about with their reins trailing, seeking an escape from the gunfire that emptied their saddles.

"Shouldn't have let that one get away," Wild Henry groused. "You told me to get the pair on the left, Cap'n. How come you got that first feller? He was mine?"

John let out a sigh. "When I saw Sheriff Pope, I forgot everything else. Wanted to get even for what he done to Billy."

Wild Henry nodded. "Let's make damn sure these gents are dead afore we see to Tommy Joe, Cap'n. Wouldn't want 'em to get up an' try that stunt again."

They walked cautiously from the cottonwoods, with an eye on the opposite bank where the riflemen stood, watching the men mount their horses. When the deputy swam his horse out of the river there was a hurried conference, then the lawmen turned back toward Del Rio and rode out of sight.

The first deputy they found was dead. John walked past the body to examine the sheriff's condition while Wild Henry walked upstream to check on the third. John came to the sheriff's form and looked down at his face. A pair of pale gray eyes stared back at John, eyes slitted with hatred. Pope's chest rose and fell.

"You . . . are a hard man . . . to catch, Cross," the sheriff croaked in a voice as dry as sand.

John shook his head. "That was my intention."

Pope's eyes closed briefly, fighting pain. A dark red stain covered the front of his shirt. When he opened his eyes again John was reminded of something Wild Henry said, that Buel Pope had the eyes of a wolf.

"Fooled me once," the sheriff whispered. "Lost . . . your tracks."

"It's over now," John replied in a quiet voice. "You're as good as dead, bounty hunter. If you hadn't crossed that river . . ."

Pope's mouth widened in a humorless grin. "Greed has ruined lots of men, Cross. I wanted . . . that money."

John heard a commotion behind him. He turned his face toward the Mexican village. Dozens of curious villagers had come to the river crossing carrying lanterns to see what all the shooting was about. Wild Henry noticed the crowd and motioned to the horses.

"I'll see to Tommy Joe, Cap'n," he said. "Ain't tellin' you how to mind your affairs, but I'd just shoot the son of a bitch an' be done with him. Talkin's a waste of time."

John worked his sweaty fingers around the pistol

grips before he turned back to Pope. It went against his grain to shoot a man who was defenseless. The sheriff would bleed to death in a matter of minutes, he guessed.

A slight movement near John's feet drew his attention. He turned, and saw a gun rising in Buel Pope's hand, the pistol he held when he fell. John heard the metallic click of the hammer and cursed his stupidity, whirling to bring his pistols to bear, cocking them in midswing.

John pulled a trigger and the hammer fell on a spent cylinder, making an ominous whack that stopped his heartbeat. He jerked the trigger on Tommy Joe's revolver as he fell to one knee, hoping to escape the sheriff's shot. A terrific roar engulfed John's ears in the instant both guns fired.

Wild Henry was running toward the spot, his boots making a soft patter across the river clay. "What the hell happened?" he cried.

Acrid gunsmoke rolled between the two men, forming a ball that circled lazily in the still air. A groan followed the shots.

John wavered on one knee, steadying himself, holding a smoking pistol in his left hand. Buel Pope's head was lifted off the ground, his wolf's eyes fixed on John. For a time the men stared at each other, then the sheriff's gun fell from his fingers. His right foot twitched, rattling the spur rowel tied to his boot, then his head dropped back and his gun hand fell limply beside him.

Wild Henry skidded to a halt above the body. His lips were twisted in a snarl. "I aim to make damn sure he don't get up off this ground, Cap'n." Wild Henry cocked his pistol and fired point-blank into Buel Pope's forehead. The sheriff's muscles convulsed once reflexively and went still. "He ain't goin' nowhere now," Wild Henry said.

The close brush with death put a tremor in John's

arms and legs. He turned away from the body, remembering Tommy Joe, and the money. "Let's find a doctor," he sighed heavily, trudging toward the trees with the pistols at his sides.

Tommy Joe was waiting in the trees holding the horses. His face was a mask of pain when John and Wild Henry reached him. A dark bloodstain ran down his right shoulder to his belt.

"We'll get you some help," John reassured the boy. He took the reins and led the gray and the sorrel with Tommy Joe swaying aboard its back to the road into Acuna. Dark-skinned men in white cotton homespun watched the three climb the cutbank from the river. Some held lanterns aloft to show the way.

"Is there a doctor in town?" John asked in a voice that could be heard by everyone, leading the horses toward the largest adobe building along the street.

No one seemed to understand John's question. Blank stares gazed back at him. John motioned to one of the older men, then he stopped and pointed to Tommy Joe's shoulder. "Doctor!" he cried, hoping someone knew what he meant.

A woman came toward John from the crowd. By now the number of curious villagers had grown to forty or fifty. "We have no doctor, señor," the woman said in broken English. "We have one who is called *Curandero.*"

"Go get him, and do it quick!" John snapped. He opened the drawstring on one of the moneybags and drew out a few bills. When he handed her the money, her eyes rounded. Then she nodded and bowed her head before she hurried away into the dark.

"Appears nobody speaks our language," Wild Henry grumbled. They stopped in front of the big building decorated by crudely lettered signs in Spanish. John guessed it was a store of some kind, for he could see baskets of vegetables and bags of flour behind one of the windows.

"They'll understand money," John said. He helped Tommy Joe down from his horse, grimacing when he noticed the amount of blood on the boy's shirt. Tommy Joe was too weak to stand without help.

"Señor!" a voice cried from across the street. John saw a balding man standing on a porch below a sign that read Cantina. The man was beckoning, holding a lantern aloft.

John lifted Tommy Joe's good arm around his shoulder and started for the cantina. "Bring the money," he said quietly when he came to Wild Henry. "And have somebody see to our horses. I want those colts fed and watered. We owe our lives to three good animals and I want them to get the best care there is."

"Done, Cap'n," Wild Henry said. He lifted the moneybags from his roan's withers, draping the tied drawstrings over his shoulder before he fisted the other pairs of bags.

John heard Wild Henry trying to explain what he wanted for the geldings. He helped Tommy Joe toward the cantina, where more lanterns were being lit inside. They crossed the threshold to find a young woman scurrying about, preparing a pile of blankets in a corner of the little adobe saloon.

"Aquí, aquí!" she said, pointing down to the makeshift bed.

John lowered the boy to the blankets.

"Thanks, Cap'n," Tommy Joe said. "I'm gonna make it. Don't worry none about me. Slug went clean through my shoulder. I reckon I was lucky. Hurts like hell, but I'll be okay."

Wild Henry entered the building with the moneybags. "I found an old man who speaks some English. He's takin' the colts to the livery. You keep an eye on these sacks and I'll make damn sure the horses are fed proper. I gave the old man five dollars an' his eyes plumb near fell out of his head."

Wild Henry placed the sacks near Tommy Joe's feet, then his gaze roamed to the rows of bottles on a shelf behind the long plank bar. "I could use a touch of whiskey, Cap'n. Been a spell since I wet my tongue on any of the good stuff."

John shook his head. Wild Henry took a few bank notes from a bag and motioned to the cantina owner. Moments later the old man hurried over with a pair of bottles filled with amber liquid.

Wild Henry wasted no time uncorking a jug. He took a big swallow and made a face. "It ain't whiskey, Cap'n," he said, grinning. "But whatever it is, it tastes mighty damn good just now."

John pulled the cork from the second bottle and sniffed its contents, then he tasted it.

"Tequila, señors," the bartender offered, smiling expectantly in the lantern light.

The tequila burned down John's throat like watery fire. He took another drink and handed the jug to Tommy Joe. "It'll help with the pain," he said quietly. "Burns like hell. It'll take some getting used to."

Tommy Joe sipped from the neck of the bottle. He grinned weakly and drank again.

"I'll see to the horses," Wild Henry said. He handed John his pistol and whispered, "Anybody tries to open one of them bags, there's two balls left in that gun."

John stuck the revolver in his belt, then Wild Henry hurried out the door and swung left down the dark street. A crowd of curious bystanders stood near the doorway, watching the strangers to Acuna from a distance.

John and Tommy Joe passed the bottle back and

263

forth, until the bartender stepped closer, still clutching the fistful of currency.

"Comida?" he asked, then he made a motion, eating with an imaginary spoon.

"Yeah. Bring food. Anything," John said. Suddenly he was overcome by exhaustion. He placed a hide-bottom chair near the moneybags and sat down with his back to the wall.

The bartender hurried off, disappearing into a back room. In a moment, John smelled woodsmoke. His stomach rumbled with hunger as he took another swallow of tequila.

An old woman in a shapeless cotton dress, faded by too many washings, appeared through the doorway, accompanied by the younger woman who left to find the *curandero.* The old woman smiled and came across the room to Tommy Joe, carrying a burlap bag that smelled faintly of horse liniment. She knelt beside the boy and frowned when she examined the bullet wound. "Take off shirt," she said in halting English, making a motion with her hand.

When the boy's shirt was removed, the woman began smearing a pungent salve over the opening. Tommy Joe's face pinched as her fingers touched the hole in his flesh.

John watched the treatment closely, wrinkling his nostrils at the scent, when a commotion beyond the front door drew his attention.

A swarthy figure moved through the crowd of onlookers, then to the doorway. A barrel-chested man in a dark blue uniform stepped into the cantina carrying a pistol beside his leg. He turned his bearded faced toward John. There was no friendliness in his eyes as he crossed the room.

Chapter Twenty-eight

"I am Comandante Ordunez. I hear much shooting. What is wrong here?" The *comandante*'s eyes strayed to the moneybags. He held his pistol loosely at his side.

"Some men tried to rob us," John replied uneasily, wondering what the Mexican soldier would do about the killings on his side of the river. John held Wild Henry's pistol on his lap. If the Mexican tried to use his gun, John meant to kill him.

The *comandante* frowned. "I see you men are soldiers in the gray army. Is it true that your side lost the war?"

John shook his head. "It's true. My friends and I came down to Mexico. Figured to do a little ranching, if we can find some land to buy, and some cattle. Made plans to live here. That war cost us our land over in Texas. Aimed to get a fresh start down south of the Rio Grande."

The *comandante* glanced at the money again. "You say some men tried to rob you?"

"Jumped us just north of Del Rio. Seven of them, claimin' to be lawmen from the east part of Texas, lookin' for outlaws. Had no choice but to fight our way out of it, *Comandante.*"

Ordunez stroked his chin thoughtfully. "These men

. . . did they show you any papers to prove you were the men they were after?"

John's mind was racing. He decided to gamble. The *comandante*'s attention always returned to the sacks of money. "Those men didn't have any papers on us. They were after the money we brought down to buy land and cattle. Had us figured for easy pickings, I reckon, seein' as there were seven of them and only three of us."

"Three?" The *comandante* was puzzled. He looked around the cantina for another Confederate soldier.

"One of my men is seeing to our horses at the stable," John said. He reached into one of the bags and withdrew a small stack of twenty-dollar notes. "It appears you're the law on this side of the river, *Comandante*. We'd like to offer you a little something extra, so we won't have any more trouble with men who'll try to rob us. All we're asking is that you keep an eye out for trouble, so we can go about our business down here and look for a cattle ranch." He offered Ordunez the money.

The *comandante*'s dark eyes lingered on the bundle of currency, then a slow smile parted his beard. He extended a fleshy hand and took the twenty-dollar notes, then he holstered his pistol and thumbed through the bills one at a time, counting silently as his grin broadened. "Four hundred dollars," he said. He stuck the money inside the front of his tunic and patted his stomach. "I will investigate this matter of the shooting in the morning," he remarked in an official tone. "If there are bodies down at the river, I'll be forced to make further inquiries." Then Ordunez fingered his beard. "However, if I find no bodies at the river crossing, there will be nothing further to investigate and the matter will be closed. My report to my superiors will say that shots were fired, yet there was no evidence requiring that I look any further." He gaze fell to Tommy Joe. "I see one of your friends was wounded. Señora Montoya knows the ways of a *curandero*. She will make him well again. Please accept the hospitality of our *pueblo*. Perhaps tomorrow morning, I will show you a few choice *hectares* of land that would make a fine *rancho* for raising cattle. If I can be of any assistance, my office is at the little *presidio* only a few *varas* to the south." The *comandante* turned on his heel, then he hesitated. "Your names," he said, as an afterthought. "For my report, the one I must make in the morning."

John stood up and extended a handshake. "I'm John Cross, and this is Tommy Joe Booker. Henry Roberts is down at the stable making arrangements for our horses."

"A pleasure, Señor John Cross," he said. Then he patted his stomach again and grinned. "You and your friends will be welcome in Ciudad Acuna. And while you are here, you will be under my protection. *Buenas tardes,* señor."

Ordunez assumed a stiff military posture and then walked to the cantina door. As soon as the *comandante* was out of sight, John planned what he would do when Wild Henry returned from the stable. Ordunez had said it plainly enough. If he didn't find any bodies tomorrow morning, the affair would be put to rest.

The old woman wound a bandage around Tommy Joe's shoulder and tied the cloth in place. "Tomorrow," she said, pointing to the tin of foul-smelling salve. *"Mañana. En la mañana,* señor."

She gathered up her medicines and rags and then bowed politely before she left Tommy Joe's side.

"I feel better already, Cap'n," the boy said. He grinned and took another swallow of tequila. "This stuff ain't so awful bad after you get used to the burn."

John returned to his chair and took the bottle. In spite of the bitter taste, the tequila was wonderfully warm in his belly. Moments later the bartender hurried from the back room with two platters of beefsteak and beans.

Seeing the food made John realize just how hungry he was.

He left Wild Henry guarding the money, eating beef and beans along with Tommy Joe. The walk down to the river was made in total darkness. The curious villagers had returned to their adobe huts and now he was alone.

He found one deputy's body west of the crossing, sprawled lifelessly in the river mud where Wild Henry's bullet had knocked him from his horse. Across the river in Del Rio, the town was dark and quiet. John bent down and seized the dead man's collar, pulling him slowly into the sluggish black current facedown.

He watched the corpse float away after he took the dead man's pistol. The river carried the deputy's remains out of sight when a swirling eddy pulled it down.

John walked east and hauled the second deputy's body through the shallows, until the river buoyed it and swept it downstream. When he was satisfied he returned to the bank and stood over Buel Pope, staring down at the sightless gray eyes fixed on the night sky. "You damn near had us at the last," he whispered. "You were smarter . . . bringing spare horses so you could ride us down. It almost worked, Sheriff. Wasn't nothin' personal 'til you shot Billy. He was my friend. We figured that Yankee bank owed us. If you'd stayed on the Texas side of this river . . ."

He felt a little foolish then, talking to a corpse. Lifting Pope by his shirtfront, John dragged him down to the river and towed him to waist-deep water where he let the current take him away.

Back on the riverbank, John looked up at the stars. "I reckon things are square as I can make 'em, Billy boy," he said. His voice carried across the surface of the Rio

Grande. "We made it down here with the money. Wish like hell you was here to spend it with us. Soon as I get back to that cantina, me and the boys will have a drink in your memory, ol' hoss. Best we can do, under the circumstances. Maybe later on we'll get us that ranch. I aim to ask that girl up in Tennessee if she'll marry me. Whatever happens, Billy boy, you can count on one thing. I'm sure as hell gonna miss you, my friend."

He turned slowly from the river and trudged back to the road leading to town, thinking about the letter he would write to Sallie Mae Parsons and how pretty she would look in an expensive wedding dress. The river flowed silently behind him, winding its way toward the Gulf of Mexico.

PART THREE

Chapter Twenty-nine

Resting his bootheels atop the porch rail of the little adobe hut they rented, John sipped tequila, passing the heat of the day while Tommy Joe rested inside on a cornshuck mattress. The boy's wound was healing nicely, proof that the *curandero*'s potions had some effect. For five quiet days, John and his men enjoyed the peace of the village, stuffing themselves with all manner of spicy food, washing it down with fiery tequila. It seemed Wild Henry had hardly drawn a sober breath since they arrived. Now, he strutted about in Acuna, dressed in the attire of a Mexican *caballero,* which they were told was worn by cowboys below the Rio Grande. John could see the river from their porch, the shallow crossing where the deadly duel was fought. In the room behind John were the sacks of money that had been the prize in their race for the border, although the bags contained much more than currency, in John's view. A terrible wrong in McLennan County had been righted by the bank robbery. Sheldon Blackwell's greed, his disregard for the families he displaced when he took over their land for back taxes, was balanced now by the holdup. John knew conditions back home would not change because of what they'd done, but it helped to think about the setback they had dealt to a ruthless carpetbag banker. John hoped the event was cause for a celebration among the landless farmers of the county. It made Billy's death seem more meaningful too, when John thought about it this way.

A gust of hot wind swept past the porch, swirling dust down the road toward the crossing, reminding John of other things, the bit of bad news they were given this morning. Comandante Ordunez stopped by to inform them that a traveler coming from Texas was told that a five-thousand dollar reward had been posted for the capture of John Cross and his band of outlaws, dead or alive. Five thousand was a tremendous sum, enough to encourage some men to take risks. Hearing about the reward ended John's brief feeling of contentment. And there had also been something about the *comandante*'s manner when he gave John the news, some intangible thing that suddenly made John wary. Was the *comandante* plotting to earn a share of the reward? John knew he was not imagining the subtle change in Ordunez today. It would pay to keep an eye on his comings and goings, until Tommy Joe was well enough to ride.

The day before, he'd sent Sallie Mae his carefully penned letter by way of a small Mexican boy, to the Texas side of the river. He told her everything, the dark truth that he'd become an outlaw, and then he tried to explain his reasons. Much harder to write, he had asked her to come to Nuevo Laredo to be his wife. He knew his prose was awkward, though he tried his best to convey what was in his heart. The letter would take months to reach Sallie Mae, with the railroads all but destroyed across the south. By then, he and his men would be in Nuevo Laredo, to make the promised deposit in the name of Howard Lacy, payment for the good young horses that brought them so swiftly to the safety of Mexico. Today, as John stared at the river crossing into Del Rio, he fully understood that he could never ride north of the Rio Grande again. The five-thousand-dollar reward made it too dangerous to set foot on Texas soil. His choice, to become an outlaw, would keep him in Mexico for the rest of his life.

Such a prospect didn't seem so bad, not if Sallie Mae Parsons were at his side. He couldn't remember just when it was that his feelings for her deepened. Perhaps it began when he learned what had happened to Elizabeth, when his heart knew why she stopped answering his letters during those long, lonely years of war.

"I hope she'll come," he muttered, remembering Sallie Mae's pretty face.

A stirring in the room behind him ended his reverie. Tommy Joe came out on the little porch in his stocking feet with a half grin widening his face.

"You talkin' to yourself out here, Cap'n?" he asked, fingering the bandage around his sore shoulder.

John nodded, giving Tommy Joe the tequila. "Rememberin' that girl up in Tennessee. Asked her to marry me in that letter I wrote. Sure as hell hope she'll agree to come down."

Tommy Joe took a long swallow of tequila, then he drew his shirt sleeve across his mouth and gazed at the river. "You sure can't go over yonder to do your courtin'," he said thoughtfully, squinting to see the buildings of Del Rio in the afternoon heat haze. "Now that our hides are worth five thousand dollars over there, we'd be fools to go back. Hell, there wasn't nothin' back in Texas fer us 'cept hard times anyway. I won't miss a damn thing 'bout McLennan County. Not one damn thing." He smiled and aimed a thumb over his shoulder. "With all that loot to spend, I sure wouldn't trade what we done fer the best job there is in Waco. I ain't never goin' back. Not never."

John thought about Sallie Mae again. "Only reason I'd go is to bring that girl down here, if she agrees to it.

For her, I'd chance it just once. Let some time pass and folks'll forget about that bank robbery."

Tommy Joe was frowning. "It'd be a mistake to go, Cap'n," he said earnestly. "If that girl loves you, she'll come on her own. For that five-thousand-dollar reward, some gents will have long memories about what we done. Five thousand's a hell of a lot of money."

John took the tequila and sipped from it, watching Wild Henry emerge from the little cantina down the road. Dressed in his Mexican outfit, sporting a freshly shaved chin, he hardly resembled the man John found beside the Brazos River that day. With his pants stuffed into the tops of new stovepipe boots, Wild Henry now looked like a gentleman of some wealth. John chuckled when he saw him. "Right at first, I thought there was a stranger in town," he added softly.

Wild Henry came up to the porch, a bottle in each fist. When he reached the shade below the thatched roof, he glanced over his shoulder at the river, scowling. "Might be trouble comin', Cap'n," he said darkly. "Just a while ago, some owlhoot wearin' a derby hat was askin' questions about us over at the mercantile. Said he only wanted to know if we was still in town. I saw him leave the store and mount up on his mule. There was a bunch of guns hangin' off his saddle, a rifle an' a scattergun, and a blind man coulda seen the bulge of that gun he was hidin' under his coat."

"Where is he now?" John asked, taking his boots off the rail to look more closely at the center of town.

"Rode back across to Del Rio," Wild Henry answered. "I only got a glimpse of him, but I damn sure didn't like what I saw. Could be he's a bounty hunter lookin' fer a chance to earn that big reward. I say we'd best keep our eyes peeled from now on. Maybe we oughta get the hell out of here . . . start ridin' down the river for Laredo. Our horses look rested. We can take it slow, on account of Tommy Joe's arm."

John was thinking out loud. "Maybe it is time we cleared out. I didn't like the way Comandante Ordunez acted when he told me about the reward. Could be it's time we made tracks away from here, so we can put our money in a Mexican bank down at Nuevo Laredo." He looked up at Tommy Joe. "Can you ride?" he asked gently.

Tommy Joe nodded. "You give the order, Cap'n, an' I'll ride plumb 'til doomsday. Most of the soreness is gone. If we take along some of that Mexican whiskey, I can make it."

John pondered their choices. If the man wearing the derby hat was a bounty hunter, he'd be looking for the chance to jump them when the odds were in his favor. And there was Ordunez to worry about now, if John was any judge of men. For a share of the reward, the *comandante* might look the other way while bounty hunters came across the Rio Grande. "I reckon it's time," he said later, after a moment of thought. "We can take it easy, ridin' that river. I wrote Sallie Mae that I'd be in Nuevo Laredo in a couple of months. Won't do any harm to strike out in that direction now."

Wild Henry searched John's face. "That kid you sent with the letter yesterday done a funny thing before he went across the river. I was sittin' in the cantina when he ran across the road to show your letter to the *comandante*. Ordunez seemed mighty interested in that envelope, Cap'n, like he wanted to know what was inside."

John stiffened a little in his chair. "Did you see the kid take the letter across?"

Wild Henry scratched his clean-shaven chin. "After a bit, I saw him ridin' over on a donkey. To tell the truth, I wasn't payin' much attention right then. Had a fresh bottle an' a bowl of them little limes to go with it, so I was otherwise occupied. But I saw the kid go across, so I figure your letter got sent. Only thing is, maybe Ordunez knows what you wrote to that Tennessee gal. I couldn't say fer sure. . . ."

"That settles it," John said with a sigh, as he came slowly to his feet. "We're clearing out of this place. I'll head down to the store an' buy us some provisions. Some extra guns too, and plenty of ammunition. We're liable to find ourselves in a shootout, carryin' all this money. I won't sleep too good until we get our loot inside a Mexican bank down in Nuevo Laredo. You men can start packin' your gear so we can leave tonight, when it's cooler. We'll need an extra saddle for Wild Henry's roan and a small sack of grain for the colts. I'll see to the provisions while you boys bring our horses around to the back."

John sauntered off the porch, heading down to the mercantile. "One of you keep an eye on that money," he said over his shoulder, as though he'd forgotten all about it until now.

Dusk paled the desert flats below Acuna as they saddled their horses and readied their gear. Added to their armament was a pair of .52 caliber Sharps & Hankins breechloaders and enough powder and shot for their handguns. Wild Henry had purchased a Mexican stock saddle from the liveryman. When their gear was tied in place to saddle strings, John and Wild Henry began securing the sacks of money to each horse.

When the chore was finished, John handed one of the rifles to Wild Henry. "Tommy Joe's arm won't let him use a long gun," he said. "Let's load our pistols before we ride out of town, just in case somebody tries to jump us when it gets dark."

Each of them made short work with the balls, wadding, and caps. Tommy Joe was first to pull himself slowly to the seat of his saddle, wincing when it pained his arm. John gave the horses a final inspection, then he picked up the remaining Sharps and boarded the gray. Their departure had drawn the attention of some of the townspeople who watched from darkened doorways and windows across the village. John swung his colt away from the hut, when he spotted Comandante Ordunez hurrying down the road in their direction.

"He'll want to know where we're headed," John muttered under his breath. "I don't aim to tell him much. . . ."

The *comandante* waved and quickened his strides, until he arrived at a spot in front of the horses. "Are you leaving us so soon, señors?" he asked as he gave John a weak smile.

"For a spell, *Comandante,*" John replied, "but maybe we'll be back before too long."

Ordunez pinched his brow. "It is a very long ride to Nuevo Laredo," he said quickly, sounding doubtful. "Will you be traveling close to the river?"

The question ended John's surprise that Ordunez knew their destination. "We'll keep it in sight," he answered guardedly, wondering why the Mexican wanted to know their route. John couldn't remember telling the *comandante* about their plans to ride down to Laredo. How had he known?

Ordunez smiled now. "Then I wish you a safe journey, señors," he said, his gaze briefly flickering over the bags of money. "The people of my pueblo will look forward to your return. You will always be welcome here in Ciudad Acuna, my friends." At that, Ordunez bowed slightly and stepped out of the horses' path.

John gave the *comandante* a lazy salute and heeled the gray to a walk, more puzzled than ever by the Mexican's interest in the route they would take. Had

Ordunez already plotted an ambush for them at an out of the way place along the river? Perhaps hatched a plan with bounty hunters so he could share in the big reward?

Wild Henry and Tommy Joe rode up beside him as they left the outskirts of the village. "I don't trust that bastard," Wild Henry said, glancing over his shoulder.

John was only half listening, thinking back to the *comandante*'s question. Why had he asked about the route they would take? And how had he known about their destination? John wondered if he was becoming too suspicious of Ordunez. Or was he simply putting things together now, the high stakes in a dangerous game. Five thousand dollars was a powerful temptation for men in the bounty hunter's trade, and there was the much larger lure of the stolen bank money they carried. Until their money was safely locked away in a Nuevo Laredo bank vault, their troubles were far from over. The man in the derby hat asking questions about them in Acuna was evidence enough that a river could not guarantee their safety.

"The gent you saw in the derby hat has got me worried," John said as they left the village behind to enter a narrow goat herder's trail through the brush along the riverbank. Darkness had begun to blanket the land, adding to the edge on his nerves. "Asking if we were still in town only adds up to one thing . . . he's after that reward they put out on us. Maybe even this money we're carryin'. There's a bunch of empty land between here and Nuevo Laredo. Lots of places to try an ambush. The *comandante* wanted to know which way we aimed to ride. I don't figure he was just bein' sociable."

Off to John's right, Wild Henry grunted, scowling at the trail ahead. "Let 'em come, Cap'n," he growled, resting the barrel of his Sharps across the pommel of his saddle. "We took care of that bastard Pope when he got too close. Same's gonna happen to any fool who makes a try fer this here money, or tries to claim that reward. We've got plenty of guns and powder this time. The owlhoot wearin' that derby don't scare me. I'll fill his ribs with enough lead to sink him plumb to the bottom of that river yonder."

John heeled the gray to a trot as he scanned the brush on both sides of the trail. Soon it would be full dark, offering bushwhackers more places to hide. He decided upon a change of plans, despite the punishment it would mean for their horses. It was too risky traveling through this tight brush at night, thus the need to ride during the heat of the day, when they could see what awaited them. "We'll ride for a couple of hours," he said, thinking out loud, "then we'll find us a spot to make camp. We're riding' blind along this trail and I don't aim to chance it. Come sunup, we'll be able to see what's out there."

John settled back against the cantle to watch the brush with a hand wrapped around the stock of his Sharps. Off to his left, the river flowed sluggishly beneath a night sky sprinkled with stars.

Chapter Thirty

The village was named Piedras Negras. On the opposite bank of the Rio Grande lay the Texas town of Eagle Pass. A two-day ride along the river passed uneventfully. As John led his men into Piedras Negras just before sundown, he stayed wide of the business district, hoping to attract less attention to the arrival of three Texans. Across the river in Eagle Pass, lanterns brightened store windows along the main street through town. John wondered if word of the reward had reached Eagle Pass. He saw no telegraph line into the city, but found no comfort in the discovery. News was carried by travelers and mule skinners to remote outposts like this. Were he a betting man, he would have given long odds that word of the Waco bank robbery and the generous reward had reached Eagle Pass ahead of them. Piedras Negras on the Mexican side looked no larger than Acuna and it seemed a safe enough place to purchase more supplies for the much longer ride to Nuevo Laredo. Wild Henry had been told that it was a six-day journey beyond Piedras Negras. The food John bought was running short and they needed more grain for their horses. The land they traveled along the Rio Grande had been empty. They'd seen no one until they were within a few miles of the village, where they encountered a few goat herders and an occasional donkey cart loaded with baskets and sacks of corn.

"Ain't much of a town," Tommy Joe remarked as they slowed the horses to a walk to enter a collection of widely scattered adobe huts west of a plaza in the heart of Piedras Negras.

Dust rolled away from the horses' heels, swept eastward by a gentle breeze blowing at their backs. John gave the village a careful inspection as they drew closer to the cantinas and stores. "We'll buy the things we need at that little market south of the plaza. Won't be so noticeable that way. Keep our horses around at the back while I buy the provisions. I won't be long."

They swung around to the rear of the tiny adobe market as a blazing crimson sunset painted the western horizon. John dropped off the gray and handed his rifle to Tommy Joe, then he hurried around a corner and made for the front of the store.

Several curious villagers stared at him when he entered the building. Suddenly, the chatter of Spanish stopped and there was an uneasy silence. John went quickly to the shelves for tins of peaches and a bag of flour. When he placed money on the counter, the Mexican storekeeper eyed him with suspicion, paying close attention to John's Confederate tunic and his flat brim cavalry hat, despite its layer of sweat-caked dust.

"How much?" John asked.

The storekeeper answered him in Spanish, then he took a few of the silver coins and waited expectantly for John to say more. John pointed to a barrel of dry field corn and said, "Some of that." He could feel the stares of the other patrons while he waited for the corn to be sacked. He had been wrong to think they could escape being noticed in the Mexican village. Word would spread quickly about the men who came to this market, word that might reach a bounty hunter on the other side of the river, someone who was shadowing the men wanted for the Waco bank robbery until the opportunity came to make his move.

With his purchases under both arms, he strode quickly through the front door and turned for the horses, glancing at the middle of Piedras Negras once before he rounded a corner of the store. His gaze flickered over a saddled brown mule, resting hipshot in front of a cantina near the plaza. John halted to examine the mule more closely, remembering the man Wild Henry had seen in Acuna. Even in the half dark, he could make out the butt of a rifle booted below a stirrup leather against the mule's ribs. Then his eyes wandered to the dark porch across the front of the cantina, coming to rest on the figure of a man, leaning against the dried mud wall. The outline of a derby hat atop the man's head was easy to see. The distance was too great to be certain of it, but John had the uneasy feeling that the man was watching him.

"Damn," he whispered, wheeling away to hurry for the horses. He knew he wasn't imagining what he had seen. When he reached Wild Henry and Tommy Joe he was almost out of breath from running.

"What's wrong, Cap'n?" Wild Henry asked, raising the barrel of his Sharps.

"That feller you saw wearin' a derby hat is just down the road a piece," John answered, handing the bags of provisions to each of them before he swung up on the gray. "His mule is tied in front of a cantina. He was watchin' me when I came out of the store. It isn't just coincidence that he's here. Can't quite figure how he got here ahead of us. Must be one hell of a fast travelin' mule he's got."

Wild Henry urged his roan alongside John's gray. "Then I say we ride around there an' kill the son of a bitch," he snapped angrily.

John shook his head. "Right now we don't need any troubles with Mexican lawmen," he warned, reining the gelding south. "Until we get this money to a safe place, we swing wide of trouble. Let's make tracks outa here, maybe throw that feller off by heading south, like we aim to ride for the middle of Mexico."

They heeled their horses to a lope and rode away from Piedras Negras toward a hilly desert landscape purpling with nightfall. A winding wagon road coursed into the brush-choked hills. John kept looking over his shoulder to see if anyone followed, but the pale caliche wagon ruts remained empty until they rode out of sight over a hilltop.

Now John understood that he was forced to consider the prospects of a bounty hunter following them into Mexico. The safety they sought below the Rio Grande merely halted pursuit by duly sworn peace officers. The man in the derby felt no such restraints, crossing over whenever it suited his purposes. To collect the reward, or perhaps get his hands on the stolen money himself, he could enter Mexico and wait until his chance came. "He's just one man," John mumbled, guiding the colt down the darkening road. "Maybe Wild Henry's right . . . maybe we oughta just kill him and be done with it."

Another mile to the south, they encountered a shallow ravine that would take them back to the river. When John turned back in the saddle, no one was behind them. Swinging southeast down the draw, they slowed their horses to a walk and rode into the darkening night. A diamondback rattled angrily in the brush over the horses' intrusion. Later, there was only the steady click of iron horseshoes over rock to mark their passage through the inky shadows at the bottom of the ravine. For a time, John was alone with his thoughts while the men rode in silence behind him. Sighting the man in the derby left John seriously shaken, but as they left Piedras Negras behind to follow the river again he began to relax. By the time they reached the banks of the Rio Grande, he had collected himself.

Once again, they were alone traveling the starlit brush. But with the ever-present danger of an ambush in the dark, John selected a campsite near the water's edge and ordered a halt to wait for sunrise. When the colts were unsaddled, John offered to take the first watch while the others slept. They spread their bedrolls around the pile of canvas moneybags, and shortly thereafter, Wild Henry and Tommy Joe were snoring. John listened to the night sounds with his rifle across his lap while he thought about the fortune he was guarding. Just a few more days of constant vigilance were needed until they reached a Mexican bank. Only then could they truthfully say that the money belonged to them. The way things were now, the twenty thousand dollars could be claimed by anyone who had the cunning and toughness to take it. The brief rest John and his men had enjoyed in Acuna served only to prepare them for the last leg of their journey. Until the money was inside a bank vault, it was there for the taking.

The three gaunt-flanked horses bearing trail-weary men attracted little notice in Nuevo Laredo. All three riders were slumped in their saddles from the six-day ordeal. Beard-stubbled faces examined every alleyway and cross street while nervous hands gripped rifle stocks and pistol butts. John searched the storefronts they passed for a sign that read BANCO. A perilous journey that had begun in the middle of Texas was almost at an end.

"Yonder's a bank," Wild Henry said quietly, riding alongside John toward a tree-shaded plaza near the center of town. He turned to look behind them and found only donkey carts and a few pedestrians.

"Looks as good as any," John replied, urging the gray colt to a faster trot.

They rode three abreast to the front of Banco Del Norte and halted their horses to step down. John removed the pair of moneybags from the gray's withers and slung them over his shoulder to tie his horse to the hitchrail. "Tommy Joe," he said, "you stay outside with our horses and rifles. Me an' Wild Henry will carry the money inside."

Tommy Joe took the rifles while Wild Henry shouldered two pairs of canvas sacks. "Looks like we made it," he said softly, casting a cautious glance around the plaza. "Now we're gonna be as rich as kings."

John led the way to the front door of the bank. A Mexican dressed in a business suit opened the door to admit them, though the expression on his face turned wary when he saw the condition of John's uniform and a week's worth of beard growth darkening his cheeks.

"*Passe,*" the man said quietly, motioning them inside with the wave of a hand.

John halted near the door. "We don't speak any Spanish, but we want to make a deposit in your safe," he said, hoping the man understood.

The Mexican's eyes moved to the moneybags, then back to John's face "I speak some *Ingles,*" he replied. "How much money do you wish to leave with us, señor?"

John looked across the bank lobby, at the door of a big iron safe. "About twenty thousand dollars, give or take. It needs to be counted."

The man's face changed suddenly. He smiled broadly and pointed to an office behind a pair of tellers' windows. "Please come this way," he said brightly. "I am

Adolfo Garcia, *presidente* of Banco Del Norte. I have brandy and good cigars in my office, Señor ... ?"

"I'm John Cross, and this is Henry Roberts. We've ridden a long way ... brandy and a cigar sounds mighty good about now. Soon as this money's counted, you can direct us to your best hotel. We could use a hot bath an' a soft bed."

They were shown to the office, where the moneybags were placed atop a polished mahogany desk. John settled into an upholstered leather chair to accept a glass of sweet-smelling brandy and a cigar. The banker summoned a woman from one of the cages, and then together they began to count the money and place it in neat stacks across the desktop while John and Wild Henry looked on. Later, when the counting was only half finished, John turned to Wild Henry.

"Go out and tell Tommy Joe to stable our horses. We can pick up our gear on the way to a hotel. Right now, I want those colts to get the best of care."

Wild Henry downed the rest of his brandy and stood up, glancing one last time at the piles of currency as he spoke around the stump of his cigar. "We'll see to the horses and meet you back here, Cap'n" Then he smiled and pointed to the money. "That's the prettiest sight I ever saw. Prettier'n any woman. I'm gonna like it down here in Mexico." He wheeled and walked out of the office.

Adolfo Garcia stopped counting to look at John. "Perhaps in the days ahead, we can discuss making some investments here?"

"Maybe," John replied, blowing cigar smoke toward the ceiling thoughtfully. "First thing you can do for us is take four hundred dollars an' deposit it in the name of Howard Lacy of McLennan County, Texas. I'll need to have a letter sent, advising Mr. Lacy that the deposit has been made."

"Of course, Señor Cross," Garcia answered. "I will see to the matter personally . . . the deposit, and the letter."

An hour later, John walked out of the bank with a receipt for eighteen thousand four hundred and thirty dollars tucked inside his tunic. For a moment, he stood on the front steps for a closer look at the city. Nuevo Laredo was teeming with activity, its streets clogged with mule-drawn wagons and donkey carts. A pall of yellow dust arose from the wheels of so many conveyances. Pedestrians of every description walked in front of the stores and shops amid the chatter of rapid Spanish and occasional laughter. When he looked to the north, beyond the central plaza, he could see the Texas city of Laredo on the far side of the Rio Grande. "We made it," John said softly. "Damned if we didn't make it all the way. Wish you was here, Billy boy, to enjoy the sights. Hell of a fine place if you've got money to spend."

He went down the steps to gaze in a store window, where a fine suit of clothes was displayed on a wooden coat tree. John halted in front of the glass to stare at the split-tail frock coat and the silky blue vest underneath it. "Fancy outfit," he said to himself, thinking about how he would look in such fine attire. "Sallie Mae will marry me for sure when she sees me dressed like that."

His thoughts drifted to Sallie Mae and the wonderful moments they shared at her mountain cabin in Tennessee. "Wish a letter didn't take so long to get there," he complained, dreading the months it would take for her answer to come. All during the ride to reach Laredo he'd been thinking about her. Were it not so dangerous, he might have risked the ride back to Tennessee to ask for her hand. He was sure of one thing now . . . that he loved her deeply. The months until he saw her again would pass slowly.

Off in the distance, a church bell started to ring. It was late in the afternoon and the wind carried the sound of the bell along with the dust across the beehive of activity in the business district. John allowed himself a feeling of contentment now. The money was safe inside the bank. A bright future awaited the three Confederate veterans who made off with Sheldon Blackwell's Yankee currency, money that couldn't be used to buy more McLennan County land for unpaid taxes. Thinking about it now, the robbery seemed a just cause, though it had branded John Cross and his men for the rest of their lives. John took a deep breath and turned away from the store window. It didn't seem so bad just then, thinking of himself as an outlaw. He'd taken money from a greedy man who came south to exploit the defeated Confederacy. Weighing things, the robbery was a small victory for the men in gray from McLennan County. He remembered those hundreds of starving soldiers living in the camp beside the cotton gin. If there were only some way, John would have taken great delight in buying a month's supply of food for every soldier in the camp, and enough whiskey so that they could all drink a toast to the empty bank vault belonging to Sheldon Blackwell. It was a fanciful notion, to be sure, but as John gazed north toward Texas he found himself grinning at the thought of it.

Wild Henry and Tommy Joe came toward him down a side street. John aimed a finger at the El Palacio Hotel. "Fanciest place in town," he said when the men arrived. "The banker said we'd like it there. Let's buy ourselves some good whiskey and the biggest beefsteak they've got. Time we started some serious celebratin', gentlemen. And I aim to become a gentleman now . . . hope you'll both do the same. All it takes is money and a suit of fancy clothes to make a gentleman. Come tomorrow, we'll buy the clothes and start acting like gentlemen of proper breeding, tippin' our hats to the ladies an' such." Then John smiled and swept a hand across the city. "We made it to the end of the line!" he cried happily. "We've seen our last poor day! Let's head for the El Palacio! First round of drinks is on me!"

They walked three abreast toward the hotel with their backs turned to the river crossing into Texas. Near the crossing, a powerfully built man wearing a dusty derby hat opened his suitcoat to reach an inside pocket. He removed a folded piece of paper and opened it slowly to read down the print. The brown mule he rode stamped impatiently at a fly while the man frowned at the contents of the page. Booted to his saddle was a Remington Rolling Block Rifle, a .50-.70 caliber centerfire. Tied to the pommel by a leather shoulder strap was a Whitmore twelve-gauge shotgun. Hidden inside his coat, a Walker Colt .44 was holstered around his waist. The big man grunted and looked up to watch the three men enter the hotel, then he pocketed the piece of paper and reined his mule back toward the shallow crossing to Texas.

Chapter Thirty-one

The dappled gray colt had grown sleek and fat as late summer days slipped away with the coming of fall. John had taken to riding the colt every afternoon to view new sections of the Mexican countryside. At the suggestion of Adolfo Garcia, John inspected a few nearby ranches which could be purchased, should the offer be made. A plan had taken shape among the three former Confederates to enter a cattle raising enterprise. What John also sought was a place to settle down with Sallie Mae as his bride, for as the weeks passed, his loneliness only worsened. He'd received no answer to his letter as yet. Passing time, he had ridden out to view a few of the ranches below Nuevo Laredo, always with the hope that one day soon, one of them might become a home for the John Cross family.

As the third week of September ended, John sat on the veranda of his upstairs room at the El Palacio, considering some sort of action that would unite him with Sallie Mae. Her long silence had begun to worry him. Had his letter reached her? How could he be sure? Sharing a bottle of good brandy with Wild Henry as the cool of evening settled over the city, he talked about his concerns.

"She'd have answered me, if she got that letter," he

said, toying with his half empty glass. "I wrote her while I was in jail over in Arkansas, an' then I wrote her just before we robbed the Planters Bank, tellin' her I was out of that Calhoun jail and plannin' to head down to Mexico. I don't figure she got the last letter I sent from Acuna. Something went wrong . . . maybe that boy done something with it and it never got sent."

"He showed it to the *comandante*," Wild Henry remembered. "I wasn't payin' much attention, but I saw him hand it to Ordunez."

"It's been long enough," John sighed, staring blankly at the rooftops of Nuevo Laredo. "I've been thinkin' real strong about ridin' up to Tennessee. . . ."

"If they catch you, you'll hang," Wild Henry insisted. "There ain't no woman worth that, Cap'n. Every bounty hunter and lawman north of the Rio Grande will be on the lookout for a man of your description, tryin' to earn that big reward."

"It'd be risky," John agreed. "If I traveled the back roads, I could slip through. I'd stay wide of Waco. Soon as I crossed the Red into Arkansas I'd be all right. Nobody's lookin' for me that far east."

Wild Henry adjusted the lapel of his tailored suitcoat absently while he thought about the plan. Like John and Tommy Joe, he wore the best clothing Nuevo Laredo merchants had to offer. "I sure as hell wouldn't go," he said earnestly. "You could send that gal another letter, but I damn sure wouldn't set foot across that river yonder. You're liable to dance a jig at the end of a rope if'n you do. Five thousand is enough to keep folks watchful. If that Tennessee gal has feelings for you, she'll come down here soon as she can. If you remember, it's a hell of a long way from Tennessee to Texas. Takes time fer a letter to get there. I'd wait, Cap'n, if it was me."

John downed the rest of his brandy, then filled his glass again. "If I stayed off the main roads, I could make it," he said, which brought a scowl to Wild Henry's face.

A slender Mexican boy tapped on his door in the second week of October. John had been pacing the floor of his room when the knock came. For days he'd been unable to sleep without the aid of tequila and brandy, worrying that some harsh fate had befallen Sallie Mae Parsons on her way to the Mexican border. Or that she had not gotten his letters. Or that like Elizabeth, she had married someone else when she learned he had become an outlaw.

The boy withdrew a yellowed envelope from the waistband of his baggy cotton pants. "For you, Señor Cross," he said in halting English.

John took the envelope quickly and handed the boy a coin. "I thank you," he said as a tiny tremor shook his fingertips when the letter was in his hands. He closed the door and hurried over to the veranda so there was enough light to read what was on the paper he took from the badly soiled envelope. When he read the first line, a dark frown crossed his face.

"My dearest John, I have reached Waco, where I had the misfortune to fall ill. I secured the services of a doctor here, though he tells me I am much too weak to travel further. I hired a room at Carothers boardinghouse on Franklin Road. My treatments and medicines have used up the small amount of money I had. Please come, if you can. I know it may be dangerous, so come at night, after midnight, to the third door at the top of the stairs. Knock twice, so I will know it is you, and we will talk about our future together. I love you dearly, my beloved John. Please come quickly, so I might hold you in my arms just once until this illness passes."

He stared at Sallie Mae's signature for a moment, admiring the careful artistry of a woman's hand. His heart leapt with joy as his brow furrowed with worry. What sort of illness has stricken her? he wondered. Was her condition so grave that a doctor put her to bed?

He read the letter again carefully, his heartbeat quickened by her words and the knowledge that Sallie Mae had written him at last. Here was proof that she loved him. Despite the crime he had committed. She had been on her way to him when illness halted her. It was added misfortune that fate forced her to stop in McLennan County, the most dangerous possible place for John Marshall Cross. But with Sallie Mae's plea still echoing in his ears when he read the letter a third time, he knew what he must do. He had to return to Waco, the scene of his crime, to assist her from her sickbed and escort her across the southern half of Texas to become his wife. There was no choice in the matter. Sallie Mae had once risked her life to nurse him back to health when her father's farm was surrounded by Union patrols. He knew he must go to her and do it quickly, in spite of the dangers he would face returning to the scene of the bank robbery.

"I love you, Sallie Mae," he whispered, looking beyond the balcony at a cloudless blue sky. "I'll come. Life without you has been lonely. I miss you, sweet Sallie Mae. I'll be there as soon as I can."

He placed the letter on a washstand beside his bed and hurried around the room to pack his gear. Only once did he seriously consider the risks of making a return to Waco, then he withdrew his gunbelt from the bottom of a dresser drawer. The pistol had been his instrument of death when he shot Buel Pope on the south bank of the Rio Grande. In the months since, he hadn't carried a gun. In the peaceful surrounds of Nuevo Laredo, there had been no need for a gun. But as he thought about the prospects of making a return to the place where he'd become a Wanted man, he felt the first stirrings of fear in the pit of his stomach. There was, however, a more important consideration. The beautiful young woman who had risked her life to save his was now asking that he come to her bedside. From the moment he read her letter there was never any doubt about what he would do. He meant to go to her in her hour of need, regardless of the risks. He could do no less for the woman who had so unselfishly taken the same chance for a dying Confederate soldier in the middle of Tennessee.

"Don't go, Cap'n," Tommy Joe implored. "They'll string you up if they catch you."

John's cheeks hardened. "My mind's made up," he said evenly. "That girl and her paw risked their lives to hide me at their cabin 'til I was well enough to travel. I owe her a debt."

Wild Henry shook his head. "Somethin' smells like dead fish. How come that girl went to Waco? You said you wrote her that we was headed to Mexico. Figures she'd stop most anyplace else, if'n you told her we robbed that bank. It don't add up, Cap'n. I've got this feelin' there's somethin' wrong."

John was silent long enough to consider Wild Henry's concerns. "She sent the letter here. She knew I'd be in Nuevo Laredo. I reckon it's just bad luck that she fell sick where she did, but I've got no choice. . . . I've got to go to her."

Tommy Joe looked deeply into John's eyes. "They'll hang you sure as hell, Cap'n Cross," he said softly. "You could send her a letter, explainin' why you can't come across the river. Maybe she don't know about that big reward. You could put a little money in the envelope, enough so's she can pay the doctor. . . ."

"I have to go," John replied, ending Tommy Joe's argument. "I can't turn my back on her, not after what she did for me."

Wild Henry stood up and walked to the balcony overlooking a courtyard below his room. For a time, he said nothing. Then he turned to John, wearing a grave expression. "I reckon I'll go along, if you can't be talked into stayin'. Two pairs of eyes are better'n one. I can watch your backside."

"I'll go too," Tommy Joe said in a faraway voice. "Can't let you ride up there to face 'em alone. We've been through a lot together, the three of us. If you're dead set on goin', I'm goin' with you."

"You're both stayin' here," John said with a note of finality in his voice. "I'm grateful for the offers, but this is my affair. Besides, they'll be lookin' for the three men who robbed the bank. A man traveling alone won't draw so much attention. Nobody'll recognize me until I get to McLennan County. I'll ride in at night an' go straight to that boardinghouse where she's stayin'. If she's able to travel, we'll be out of town before daylight. Dressed in a business suit, not showin' a gun, I can slip in and out before anybody knows I'm there. In the dark, nobody'll see my face."

Wild Henry was scowling. "I still say there's somethin' wrong with that letter, Cap'n. It don't hardly seem sensible that she'd come to Waco, not after she knowed about the robbery."

John sighed, rounding his shoulders. "It was my home before the war. Maybe that explains why she came that way, rememberin' what I told her about growing up in McLennan County. All that matters now is that I do everything I can to help her. I owe her that. Truth is, I love her. Took me a while to come to my senses, but I reckon she's the finest woman I've ever known. I aim to marry her, if she'll agree to it." He turned and started for the door, looking back at his two friends. "I'll be back as quick as I can," he added. "I may be gone several weeks. Depends on Sallie Mae and how she's feelin' when I get there." Touching the brim of his hat, he gave them a half-hearted salute and then walked out of the room into the hallway to pick up his valise and his bedroll, listening to the hollow echo of his boots when he started for the stairs.

Much of the country had changed. Fall rains greened the pastures with a final surge of growth before the first frost. The dappled gray traveled easily, strengthened by months of good grain and rest. Since leaving the Mexican border, he stayed away from heavily traveled roads to ride cross-country. But as he neared McLennan County at the end of the second week of his journey, he was forced to use wagon roads due to the number of fences he encountered. Wearing a black broadcloth suit and a new flatbrim hat of the same color, he was sure he passed as a traveling drummer and prepared a story to match his appearance, should anyone ask. On those rare occasions when he used a name, he called himself Robert Smith. Remembering the boyish Yankee captain who had saved him from a gallows, John found it fitting to use his name to elude another warrant for his arrest. Now, as he crossed the Falls County line into McLennan County, John remembered what it was like to be in a jail cell, awaiting certain death. In Waco, there would be no Robert Smith to save him from a hangman's noose. He would have nothing more than his wits and a fast horse to help him stay alive.

Passing occasional travelers along the road, he often tipped his hat and spoke a greeting. A visiting drummer would have nothing to hide, riding the main roads toward his destination without fear of being recognized. As the afternoon wore away, John sighted the distant rooftops of Waco, and when he did, his heart began to hammer beneath his ribs.

To calm himself for the task at hand, he thought about pretty Sallie Mae and her moment of distress. He knew he must find her quickly and then make good their escape before sunrise. It was a bold undertaking to be sure, but something he owed her. If she was well enough to travel, they could flee the city and later find a safer place where she could rest and regain her strength. Everything depended upon getting Sallie Mae away from Waco in the dark of the night, a dangerous plan even if everything went well. Just one mistake could expose him and then his fate was certain. Reminded of the risks, he reached inside his split-tail coat to touch the butt of his hidden pistol. Six lead balls would have to be enough in the event his identity was discovered.

He let the gray strike an easy trot, as though its rider felt no need to hurry. Traffic had begun to thicken along the road, increasing the chances that someone might recognize him. He pulled his hat brim low over his eyes and continued toward town as a cold sweat formed on his skin.

Chapter Thirty-two

Following a familiar road along the Brazos River bottom, John came toward Waco from the south. He purposefully avoided riding the route they had taken to make their escape, not wanting to view the grave where they buried Billy, fearing the memories it would evoke. The road running beside the Brazos would take him past the Lacy plantation, thus to accomplish a bit of unfinished business. Howard Lacy had never answered the letter from Banco Del Norte, nor had he collected the payment for his colts. John carried Howard's four hundred dollars with him now, to fulfill his promise. Some unforseen difficulty kept Howard from calling upon the Mexican bank, and John meant to discover what it was.

At the lane leading up to the Lacy mansion, John halted the gray to examine the grounds before he rode in. Cotton fields around the house lay untended, weed-choked, and now uncut grass grew waist-high across the lawns. The look of neglect was far worse than he remembered and he wondered if the old man had simply given up all attempts to keep the yards and the gardens. The gray seemed to know it had come back home, prancing, fighting the pull of the bit to begin the short trip up the tree-shaded lane.

John let the horse have its head. Trotting along the

overgrown ruts leading to the house, there was no evidence that the road had been traveled. Drawing near the front porch, John saw the same glassless windows as before, some curtained with lengths of faded cloth, others standing open as empty black squares in the blotchy white walls that were shedding layers of paint.

"Nobody's here," he said to himself, reining the gray around to the back. "Something happened to Howard. . . ."

He rode past the untended rose gardens to the back door of the mansion, remembering the cluttered kitchen where their deal had been struck for the thoroughbred colts. He stopped the gray and cupped his hands around his mouth. "Mr. Lacy! Mr. Lacy! Are you there?"

A noise behind him startled the colt. John was reaching inside his coat to draw his gun as he whirled toward the sound. His right hand relaxed and came away from the gun butt when he saw an elderly black man coming from the barns. The gray settled underneath him while John waited for the old man to arrive.

"Masta Lacy is gone," the old man said, halting a few yards from the horse.

"Gone where?" John asked, briefly examining the man's tattered clothing and runover riding boots.

The old man looked up at the sky. "Gone to sing with the angels, suh," he replied softly. "His body lie round back of the barn."

Hearing of Howard's death shocked John to silence for a moment. "How did it happen? When?" he asked when he had his wits about him.

"Las' month, when word come 'bout his wife an' girl child. The boat they was on went down someplace. Terrible storm come up an' that boat sunk to the bottom of the sea. When Masta Lacy got the word, he put a gun in his mouth an' killed hisself. Folks who knowed him was mighty grieved about it."

John bowed his head and closed his eyes briefly. Hearing that Howard had taken his own life was bitter news. Without the kindness he had shown John, there would never have been a robbery at the Planters Bank, or much of a future for three homeless Confederate soldiers. "That's terrible news," John said later, his voice tight, strained. "I owed him a debt. He was a fine gentleman, a friend."

The old Negro nodded sadly. "He was a good man. I worked for him mos' my life, 'til they freed us. He treated us kindly, them that worked here. Was a sad day when we left this place. Like leavin' home, it was. I come out to see 'bout his hosses when I heared the news. Them hosses was near 'bout starved to death. Now they's sold to the renderin' plant to make soap. Shame, what them Yankees done to good hosses. They was runners. . . ."

"I know," John said quietly. "Good racing stock." He looked into the old man's eyes. "Why are you still here?"

The man shrugged. "Got no place to go, suh. Been sleepin' in the barn since las' week, rememberin' times when things was better. S'pose I'll be goin' now." Then the old man tried to peer into the shadow below John's hat brim. "Beggin' your pardon, suh, but you look mighty familiar. You been to this place afore? Maybe a long time back?"

John shook his head, perhaps a bit too quickly. "I'm new around here. I just wanted to inquire about Mr. Lacy." He lifted his reins and swung the gray around. "I'm obliged for the information," he said as the gelding started off. "Sorry to hear about it." He heeled the colt to a lope and galloped around the house, trying to shut out the memories of Elizabeth and Howard and happier times. Another part of his past was gone forever, like the kinship he felt with Billy Cole. A war that had united the South in dreams of glory had taken more than the thousands of soldiers' lives it exacted as its price. The bitter aftermath of the struggle continued to take its toll, and it seemed to have no end. As John rode away from the Lacy plantation he found he was unable to look over his shoulder, as if seeing the place empty and in ruins might somehow worsen the discovery that Howard had ended his own life. Hurrying the gray down the road between cotton fields gone to fallow, he turned his thoughts to Sallie Mae. In a rundown board-inghouse he remembered on Franklin Road there was a woman who loved him. All that mattered now was the success of his plan to get her out of the city. And then, safely to the Mexican border where they could begin their lives anew.

Dusky dark blanketed the abandoned cotton gin and the camp ground near the railroad depot. Smoldering fires twinkled across the city of tents and crude shelters erected by the homeless soldiers. John had been waiting in a canebrake beside the river for darkness to come before he risked riding into town. He had been content to watch the activity from his hiding place among the cane stalks, though it saddened him to see the pitiful lot of the starving soldiers. Conditions had not improved since he last saw the campground. Men who were little more than gaunt skeletons shuffling about in tattered uniforms, begging for food. Later, he remembered something Billy said when they carried a wounded boy to one of the wagons during the fall of Franklin. "You can't save them all, Johnny boy," he had said, and his words bore a terrible ring of truth. Neither could he help the hundreds of homeless soldiers here, thus he closed his mind to it and waited for full dark.

Another hour and the night had deepened. He intended to ride past the boardinghouse to get the lay of things, scouting for a place to tie the gray colt at midnight before he climbed the stairs to the third door. If Sallie Mae could be moved, he meant to carry her in front of him aboard the gray until they were safely out of town and then somewhere farther south, purchase a horse and saddle for her. Or a small buggy, if he found her too sick to ride. Until he knew the nature of her illness, he'd gone as far as he could with plans for their journey to the border.

Moving quietly, he led the colt out of the canebrake and mounted. Before him, dozens of campfires glowed, providing warmth for the early fall chill that had come with the dark. He urged the gray to a walk and swung away from the light from the fires. To the north and west, lantern-lit windows brightened the city. He would choose the darkest roads to make his approach to the boardinghouse. No one would question a lone horseman, his face covered by his hat, riding slowly along the back streets of Waco. He was sure of his plan as he skirted the tents and shanties near the depot, aiming for a dark street corner to the west. The gray's hooves made soft grinding sounds over the hardpan around the cotton gin as John proceeded to move away from the campground. As he neared an abandoned cotton wagon, its rear wheels cast aside with broken spokes, the gray colt snorted softly and pricked its ears forward. John paid no heed and urged the horse onward, his attention focused on the street corner ahead, when with lightning suddenness, a shadowy figure came from behind the wagon to block the colt's path.

John was reaching for his gun when the figure spoke.

"You're John Cross. I'd know that dappled horse anywhere."

John's fingers curled around the pistol grips, ready for a swift pull. "You're mistaken," he replied in a hoarse whisper as his heart leapt into his throat. "My name is Robert Smith. I've never met anyone by the name of Cross. Please step out of my way, or there'll be consequences. I'm armed."

"It's you!" the figure insisted, moving closer, almost within reach of the colt's bridle. "I watched you ride that dappled horse away from the bank that day! This is the same animal. I'd stake my life on the proposition!"

John drew his gun from his coat and swung the barrel toward the man blocking his path. "It's your life you are wagering, stranger, by standing in front of my horse. Now move aside, or I'll claim the bet you've made and put a ball through your chest!"

Still, the figure did not move. "You and your friends made us all happy that day, Captain John Cross! When news of what you done reached 'em down here, there was rebel yells all over the place. It was like that charge at First Bull Run, when we sent them damn Yanks to full retreat, yellin' our fool heads off like the war was already won. It was like that right here the day you boys robbed that bank. We was all sorry to see that your friend got shot, but it was one hell of a slick job you pulled. You gave a bunch of hungry men somethin' to cheer about that day!"

"You are badly mistaken," John replied slowly. "My name is Robert Smith and I'm here on business. I've never heard of this Captain John Cross. Perhaps we resemble each other, and both ride gray horses, but I am not the man you think I am, so please step aside and I'll be on my way . . . no harm will be done."

The man was silent for a time, looking up at John in the pale light from the stars. "You're worried that I'll point a finger at you so I can claim that handsome reward," he said, lowering his voice. "You have nothing to fear from me. I lost my land to the Planters Bank, same as most of the boys who live down here. You won't find many men in this camp with sympathies for a Union bank. We're outcasts, livin' on the fish we can catch and bread crumbs we beg from rich folks. Your secret is safe with me, Captain Cross. I give you my word as another Confederate soldier."

"I'm not John Cross," John said flatly. "It's dark. Tomorrow morning, I'll come back so you can see my face and then you'll admit your mistake. Now stand aside. I have business in another part of town."

The man chuckled softly. "We can settle it tonight. Climb down from your horse and we'll walk over to one of the fires. If your name isn't John Cross, you'll have no objection. . . ."

"I'm in a hurry," John snapped, tightening his fingers around the gun. "There's nothing to settle. My name is Robert Smith and that's the end of it. Move out of the way and let me pass," he said coldly, clamping his heels against the colt's ribs.

An arm snaked out to seize the gray's bridle. John raised his pistol and thumbed the hammer back.

'Release my horse or I'll kill you!" John ordered, trying to keep his voice low so he wouldn't be heard at the campfires.

"You won't shoot me," the man said confidently, still gripping the colt's headstall. "You can't afford to make a ruckus. A gunshot would bring half the men in the camp over here and then you'd be recognized!"

Despite the chill, John's palms were sweating. The success of his plan to escape with Sallie Mae hung in the balance. "What do you want from me?" he demanded as the colt fidgeted in the stranger's grasp.

"Merely a moment of your time, Captain," he replied. "I won't do you any harm. You're a brave man, to return to the scene of your crime and I'm simply curious. Why have you come back?"

John took a deep breath, torn by terrible choices.

Killing the man who held the colt's bridle would set off a manhunt that would prevent him from going to Carothers boardinghouse. But an admission of his true identity was no less dangerous, should this stranger decide to sound an alarm that John Cross had returned to Waco. "If I humor you and admit that I'm this Captain John Cross, will you be satisfied?"

"I suppose it would be enough," he answered after a pause. "I won't tell anyone your secret. I've already given you my word."

John lowered the hammer on his pistol. "I'm John Cross," he whispered. "Release my horse. A sick friend needs my help. In the name of Confederate honor, say nothing about my presence here. The blow I struck at the Planters Bank was for every man, woman, and child who lost their homes to Union greed."

The stranger shook his head and let go of the colt's bridle. "It grows worse, Captain," he said softly. "They use our tax records at the courthouse to evict us. No one can pay those back taxes, the way things are now. There isn't any money, and no work for men who lost their farms."

John heard the pain in the man's voice . . . it was pain he understood. "Someone should burn those records," he said thickly, remembering his first visit to Sheldon Blackwell's office. "Without proof the taxes have not been paid, men like Sheldon Blackwell can't profit from another man's misfortune."

John saw the stranger stiffen.

"Of course!" the man cried much too loudly. "That's it! Why didn't someone think of that before? Burn the records! A fire would destroy everything they use against us!"

Hurriedly, John looked over his shoulder. "Keep your voice down," he whispered, watching the campfires. "There are men in those tents who would have me hung for the price on my head. I trusted you when you gave me your word."

Now the man stepped closer to John's stirrup. "I can be trusted," he whispered. He stuck out his hand. "My name is Oscar Freemont. I served in Hood's Twelfth Infantry. I have a small group of trusted friends, men who can be counted on. The seed you just planted has given me a splendid idea. We can enter the courthouse at night and burn those tax records. You have my gratitude, Captain Cross."

He shook hands with Oscar Freemont, and saw his face for the first time by starlight. "It will be dangerous, but it may save others from losing their farms," he remarked, releasing Oscar's hand. "If the records are destroyed, there is no evidence that taxes are owed. Under different circumstances, I'd go with you on such a raid. While it's too late for some, you'll be saving others from the fate we both shared."

Oscar pointed to the abandoned wagon. "I've been living under that wagonbed since I came home from the war. I lost my place to back taxes, same as lots of others. We're treated worse than criminals in this county. When you and your friends robbed the bank, some of us felt like it evened the score." Now he backed away from the gray colt and swept a hand toward the street corner where John was headed. "Be on your way, Captain Cross," he said, grinning. "Godspeed. I will carry your secret to my grave. And if you hear of a courthouse fire in the days to come, grant yourself a part of the credit. My friends and I will plan things carefully. If we fail, it can be no worse than living under the bed of a crumbling wagon."

John heeled his horse forward, returning the pistol to his coat. The gray struck a lazy trot to the darkened street corner. Just once, before the old cotton wagon was out of sight, John turned around in the saddle. Oscar

Freemont was running toward one of the campfires, a fleeting shadow moving among the irregular rows of tents.

Chapter Thirty-three

He tied the colt to the lowest limb of an elm tree in the alley behind the boardinghouse. This part of the city was dark, no lights burning behind windows in houses on either side of Franklin Road as the hour approached midnight. He left the cinch pulled tight around the gray's heartgirth, knowing how precious time might seem if anyone discovered them as they made good their escape. He crept away from the horse on the balls of his feet, keeping to the deepest shadows as he left the alley. Silver starlight brightened a pathway to the front of the boardinghouse, illuminating a crudely lettered sign hanging crookedly above the door reading CAROTHERS.

He mounted sagging wooden steps and tested the doorknob quietly. The door swung inward on creaking hinges that made John wince when he heard the sound. A dark hallway ran between boarders' rooms, then to a set of stairs leading to the second floor. When the hinges quieted, the big house was silent. Feeling his heart race, John entered the hall soundlessly and tiptoed toward the stairs while his eyes adjusted slowly to the absence of light. At the bottom of the staircase, he paused to listen. Somewhere, a man snored loudly behind one of the closed doors.

He removed the pistol from his coat and started up the stairs as softly as he could. Here and there, a board would creak under his weight. A slow step at a time, he advanced up the staircase toward his beloved Sallie Mae, barely breathing now, his heart hammering wildly.

At the top of the stairs he paused again to get his bearings in the darkness. Outlined faintly by coats of brighter paint, he counted the doors leading into the hallway. He found the third door and took a deep, shuddering breath, then he started forward on the balls of his feet, covering his progress with the gun. Loose floorboards protested under his boots, making a dry sound. Creeping closer to the third door, each sound made by his boots seemed magnified. Sweating in spite of a slight chill in the old house, he came to the door to Sallie Mae's room and rapped twice softly, glancing both ways up and down the hall.

"Who's there?" a woman's voice inquired in a breathless whisper.

"It's me, John," he answered as quietly as he could.

Shuffling feet sounded on the other side of the door and John almost forgot about the danger, waiting to take pretty Sallie Mae into his arms. A floorboard creaked in the room as light footsteps approached the door. John lowered his pistol. A key clattered in the lock and then the door was pulled inward slowly.

"Come in quickly," Sallie Mae whispered, her voice curiously hoarse. John supposed it was a symptom of her illness.

He entered a room that was pitch dark, smelling faintly of rosewater. "Where are you, my darling?" he asked, wondering why Sallie Mae had not rushed into his arms.

"Over here," she replied from the velvety curtain of black before his eyes. "Come to me, darling John."

He took a step toward the voice, puzzled by some

vague feeling that something was wrong. Another step brought a crack from the floor underneath him and a similar sound just to the rear. In total darkness, his ears gave him the only warning he had that something was moving swiftly behind him.

A crushing blow struck the back of his head, knocking him forward through the inky blackness. Flashing pinpoints of light appeared in front of him as he felt himself falling to the floor helplessly. A gray fog swirled around the flashing lights. He landed heavily on his face and chest, too stunned by the blow to break his fall with his arms. His mind began to whirl, spinning like a child's top. What was happening? Who delivered the blow to his head?

He knew he was losing consciousness and he struggled against it with every ounce of his will. Now he heard muffled voices close by, though he couldn't identify them or the words. Through the hazy mists surrounding his eyes, he saw a flicker of golden light just beyond his reach. Dark shapes moved between him and the strange light. The voices spoke again.

"That's him," a deep voice said, the only words he recognized.

A woman's laugh, like the cackle of a laying hen. Why was Sallie Mae laughing? he wondered. He tried to focus his eyes on the shapes moving about the room, fighting to remain conscious. A dark blur came closer, and he recognized it as that of a man, a man with thick, muscular shoulders.

John's last conscious thought was one of despair. Someone had tricked him, but now his mind was too fuzzy to consider who might have done this to him. He slipped slowly into the swirling mist around him and closed his eyes, wondering who had betrayed him.

* * *

He awoke in a damp jail cell and thought he might be dreaming of his confinement in Hampton. But as his mind cleared, he knew with a dull certainty that this was no dream. He was lying on an iron cot in a barred jail cell. Striped sunlight cast a pattern on the floor below his bunk. He raised his head and was rewarded by a stab of knifing pain at the back of his skull. Tenderly, he ran a fingertip over an egg-sized knot on the back of his head, and when he looked at his finger it was red with blood.

"Damn," he groaned, slowly pushing himself up until he sat on the edge of the cot. The odor of dampness filled his nostrils. He remembered his trip up the boardinghouse stairs, then his careful entrance into Sallie Mae's room. And that's when someone hit him from behind. . . . He remembered that much.

"Someone knew I was coming and set a trap to claim the reward," he mumbled to himself, touching his wound again gingerly. A dull ache throbbed inside his head. "Wild Henry and Tommy Joe were right. They'll hang me now for sure."

A stirring in an adjoining cell startled him. In the half dark, he thought he was alone. Looking through a wall of clammy iron bars coated with rust, he saw a man sitting on a bunk in the next cell.

"So you're the famous John Cross," a voice said. The man on the cot was grinning crookedly when he spoke.

John's mind raced to form a denial. "I'm Robert Smith. There must be some mistake," he replied.

The man chuckled. "There's no mistake," he said. "They've brought half a dozen witnesses in here who identified you while you were out cold. That fat banker came. He said he'd never forget your face. When you robbed him, he got a good look at you."

John wagged his head from side to side, though it

313

pained him. "It's a case of mistaken identity," he protested. "I must look like the man they're after."

The man got up and shuffled over to the bars between them. "It won't work," he said quietly, "claiming you're the wrong man. They know who you are. You're quite a famous feller in these parts, Mr. Cross. Most of the soldiers around here say you're a hero. I've been havin' a hard time figurin' why you came back to Waco. Accordin' to what was in the newspapers, you an' your bunch made it all the way to Mexico, so why the hell 'd you come back?"

"My name isn't Cross," John insisted, irritated by the man's assumption. "They've jailed the wrong man this time."

"My name's Willie Sutton," he said. "I've been charged with stealin' a cow, only I wasn't stealin' it. I found it grazin' beside the road and was leadin' it to a neighbor's house when the law rode up. I'm an innocent man, only I can't prove it. The word of a Confederate soldier ain't worth spit in this county, or the next. Damn Yank judges won't listen to a word from a Reb's mouth. So you can save your breath, Mr. John Cross, or Mr. Robert Smith, if that's who you lay claim to be. They think you robbed that bank an' by God, you'll swing by your neck for it after a bluebelly judge hears your case. You've been identified by that overstuffed banker. And what's worse, you was caught by that detective they hired to trace the money. He's been bringin' witnesses in here all mornin' while you were asleep, and to a man, they say you're John Cross."

"A detective?" John asked, searching Sutton's face, alerted by this scrap of new information.

Sutton nodded. "Big feller, near 'bout as famous as you, according to the stories floatin' around the county. I heard him tell the banker that he followed you to Mexico. Claimed he'd been waitin' for months for you to show up around here again."

John quickly sorted through the possibilities. Some of Buel Pope's men escaped the shootout at the river that night. One of them had to be the detective Sutton was talking about. But why had anyone suspected that John would return? Only Sallie Mae Parsons knew of his plans. Had she betrayed him to collect the reward? It didn't seem possible. "They're all wrong about me," he said, although his voice lacked conviction now. "I'm not the man they're after. It's all a terrible mistake."

"Nobody's gonna listen," Sutton said. "You'll hang, even if you ain't John Cross. They've got witnesses."

John sighed and cupped his chin in one hand, staring at the floor vacantly, for now his thoughts went to Sallie Mae. Someone had been waiting in her room, someone who had known he was coming. Willie Sutton said he'd been caught by a detective who was hired to trace the stolen money. Why had Sallie Mae lured him into her room when she knew she was leading him into a trap? Why hadn't she warned him that someone else was there? Had the detective forced her to help him? None of it made any sense. "Tell me about this detective," John said without taking his eyes from the floor.

"Sam Kincaid," Sutton began. "Came from Natchez, somebody said. Word is, he was Union spy during the war. He happened to be in Waco when the robbery was pulled. Soon as the bank offered that five-thousand-dollar reward, he headed down to the Mexican border. He came back emptyhanded an' that looked like the end of it. You made it easy for him, comin' back the way you did."

"He arrested the wrong man," John said again, his mind elsewhere. Sam Kincaid had been hiding in Sallie Mae's room last night. How had he known John was coming? Sallie Mae's letter contained her instructions for the moment he arrived. Kincaid had to have known what was in her letter, but it still did not explain why Sallie Mae helped the detective by luring John into her room.

"You can protest your innocence all the way to the gallows, my friend," Sutton remarked. "Either way, you'll hang."

Overwhelmed by despair, John stood up slowly and glanced at the window above his cot. Heavy iron bars filled the opening, admitting shafts of slanted sunlight. He remembered the stinking jail cell at Hampton, which only deepened his misery. He wondered how long he'd be pacing back and forth in this jail cell before he met his appointment with the hangman.

"Those bars are solid," Sutton said when he saw John looking up at the window. "Unless you've got a friend with a mighty big powder charge, you won't escape through that window."

John turned away from the opening when the throbbing worsened inside his head. "I've got no friends here," he said, settling back on his bunk to contemplate his gloomy fate. He closed his eyes and rested his head against the cool masonry wall, being careful to avoid touching the bump on his head. He heard Willie Sutton return to his cot. Again, John's thoughts turned to Sallie Mae. Why had she betrayed him?

Heavy boots clumped toward his cell. He opened his eyes. In a dark corridor leading to the cells, he saw a shape moving, and then another. He sat up and rubbed his eyes. A man and a woman came to the door of his cell and stopped. John looked at the woman briefly, for it was the man who commanded his attention. He recognized the bulky figure staring back at him through the bars. The man in the derby hat he'd seen at Piedras

Negras stood at the doorway to his cell. John caught his breath, for now he understood a part of what had happened to him. This was Sam Kincaid, and John had foolishly walked into the detective's clutches.

"Good afternoon, Captain Cross," Kincaid said. His tone was almost pleasant, although his square-jawed face and hooded eyes belied the gentleness in his voice. "You have been a difficult man to capture, a worthy adversary. I apologize for the bump on your head, however I felt I had no choice in the dark. I was sure you would be carrying a gun. I wanted to avoid gunplay at all costs. I took your gun and your money belt. Mr. Blackwell was keenly disappointed when we discovered less than a thousand dollars of his money in your keep. I'm sure you understand that he hoped to recover the rest of it. I'm sure your two friends will enjoy spending a larger share when they learn of your execution."

John blinked, putting aside so many other questions to ask the most important one. "What have you done to the girl?" he asked, for it was pointless now to deny his identity.

"Ah, you must mean Miss Parsons of Tennessee," Kincaid began, with a false note of surprise that John detected easily. "I've never met her. I suppose she is still in Tennessee. The letter you received was not written by Miss Parsons. A *comandante* of the Mexican *federales* intercepted the letter you wrote to Miss Parsons and had it delivered to me in Del Rio. I followed you and your men to Nuevo Laredo and then waited an appropriate length of time. I devised the letter you were sent and had it written in a woman's hand, so you would believe it came from Miss Parsons. All I had to do was wait, Captain Cross. Affairs of the heart have ruined any number of stalwart men. Your affection for Miss Parsons and your desire to come to her aid was all I needed to collect the bank's reward. A generous fee will be paid to Comandante Ordunez. Without his cooperation, I was faced with a much more demanding task, getting you out of Mexico."

For a moment, John was speechless, learning that he had been so easily tricked. He remembered Wild Henry's expression of concern that something wasn't quite right with Sallie Mae's letter. Now the cold realization that he'd been fooled by Kincaid struck him to the bone. He recalled feeling that something was amiss just as he stepped into the dark room at the boardinghouse. "It would seem I've played right into your hands," he said softly.

Kincaid gave him a satisfied smile. "You'll have to admit it was a clever ploy, Captain Cross. But such is the nature of the detective profession. I must be able to outwit the men I'm after. Otherwise, it becomes a business of guns and bloodshed, which I dislike. Had you remained in Mexico, you'd have given me no choice but to resort to more violent means of capturing you. I doubt you'll agree under your present circumstances, but it worked out better this way."

John lowered his chin to his chest, staring at the floor, at the square of striped sun light cast by the bars. "You outwitted me, Kincaid," he said in a hoarse whisper, succumbing to feelings of hopelessness and defeat. "How soon will I be hanged?"

Kincaid shrugged and turned away from the bars. "That is none of my affair," he replied, taking the woman's hand.

Until now, John had paid no attention to the woman. "Are you the one who spoke to me last night?" he asked, watching the woman's face.

She smiled, wrinkling her heavily rouged cheeks. "I also wrote the letter," she replied in a coarse, hard voice. "I'm acquainted with your sister, Mary. Until I met Sam, I worked at Diamond Lil's. I wouldn't want

Mary to know that I helped Sam catch you. She'd be furious." Then she looked up at Kincaid. "Sam and I will be leaving town, as soon as he collects the reward money. Let's get out of here, honey. This place has a terrible smell."

Kincaid and the woman walked down the corridor and disappeared through a door. For the first time since the bank robbery, John let his thoughts drift to Mary. There would be plenty of time to think about his sister and a thousand other things, awaiting his date with the hangman.

Chapter Thirty-four

A man with a metal star pinned to his shirt came slowly down the corridor, balancing two tin plates on his palms. He stopped in front of Willie Sutton's cell and pushed a plate through the opening at the bottom of the bars. Then he approached John's cell and shoved the last plate inside. When he straightened, he looked through the bars. The hour was late, a gray evening sky filling the window above John's bunk. For a while, the lawman simply stared at John, saying nothing.

"You don't look so all-fired tough," he said a moment later, mocking John with a leer. "Fact is, I'd say you're a coward, Cross. I watched you gun down Buel when he rode out of that river. You ambushed him the way a yellowbelly coward would." He laughed dryly. "Without a gun, I don't figure you amount to much. When they fit a rope around your neck, I'll be there. They named me sheriff after you killed Buel. I'll be the one to escort you to the platform, an' I'll damn sure be enjoyin' myself. There'll be a big crowd. *The Tribune* is printin' a special edition with the story about how ol' Sam Kincaid arrested you. Yessir, I figure there's gonna be one hell of a big crowd to watch you swing." He looked down at the plate of food. "Enjoy them taters, Cross. You ain't got much time left to enjoy anything."

The sheriff turned and swaggered back up the corridor. Hunger rumbled in John's belly despite the anger hardening his cheeks after being called a coward. He got up and picked up the plate. A handful of boiled potatoes was surrounded by soggy crackers.

"It don't taste too bad," Sutton offered from his cell, spooning potatoes into his mouth. "Same every day . . . boiled spuds. Don't let Sheriff Hogan get your goat. He talks real brave when those bars are in front of him."

John carried his food to the cot and sat. His first bite of potato was tasteless. His anger cooled while he consumed his supper. Hogan had been one of the men who stayed on the Texas side of the Rio Grande when Buel Pope crossed over, John reasoned. Not much bravery demonstrated that night, he told himself.

When his plate was empty he lay back on the cot, watching darkness blacken the cell window. All afternoon he had battled the hopelessness of his plight. For the sake of a woman, he had given up his freedom and a share of the fortune they had taken to Mexico. He knew now that he had played the part of a fool, riding off on his own to help a lady in distress. Only there had been no lady, merely a very clever plot to capture him. And it had worked perfectly.

Later, he closed his eyes to dream about those wonderful weeks with Sallie Mae in Tennessee. Had he known what lay in store for him when he returned home, he would have stayed in those mountains and tried to make something of himself for Sallie Mae's sake. Yet the lure of another beautiful woman kept calling to him, beckoning him homeward. Sweet remembrances of Elizabeth had simply been too much to ignore. Thus he found himself in yet another prison, awaiting his final hour. He had escaped a death sentence once, by sheer luck and happenstance. In his heart, he

321

knew Lady Luck would not smile on him twice. This time, he would surely hang.

"You've got a visitor," Sheriff Hogan said, glowering at John through the bars. "I've already searched her, makin' damn sure she don't bring you no gun."

A woman in a flowing red dress came down the corridor. At first he did not recognize her. When she came near the slanted morning light from the cell window, John saw Mary's face.

"She claims she's your sister," the sheriff added, starting back toward his office. "You got five minutes, lady," he said over his shoulder, passing through the door.

John got up and walked to the bars. Tears glistened in Mary's eyes as she spoke to him.

"Why did you come back?" she stammered, her chin quivering. She dabbed at her eyes with a handkerchief. "The newspaper said you came back to see a woman ... ?"

He reached between the bars and took Mary's hand. "I was tricked by a detective named Sam Kincaid. I got a letter from a woman I met while I was in Tennessee. The woman helped me when I was wounded in a Yank ambush. I felt it was my duty to offer to help her, but the letter was a forgery. I walked right into Kincaid's trap, and now I will pay for my mistake."

"Oh, John," Mary cried. More tears streamed down her face. "Why didn't you take the money I offered you? You'd be free now. You wouldn't have robbed the bank!"

John shook his head. "I didn't want ... that kind of money. You could have found another line of work."

Mary stiffened. "You don't know what it was like," she whispered, her voice thick with anguish. "There wasn't any work. Everyone was so poor those last years of the war!"

He released her hand. "There had to be another way," he said quietly. "Bein' a whore is the worst thing there is."

"Is it any worse than becoming a bank robber?" she cried, her shoulders shaking with tiny sobs.

He found he couldn't look at her any longer. "I suppose it's just as bad. They took our farm, Mary. I just couldn't let them do it. Paw paid off that mortgage with years of sweat and toil. It was wrong that they were allowed to take our place. I wanted revenge for what they did. It was the only thing I could think of that would make 'em pay for what they done."

Mary reached between the bars to touch his cheek with her fingertips. "You'll be executed," she said hoarsely. "It was in the newspaper yesterday. I came as soon as I could . . . as soon as I could get away."

He wouldn't allow himself to ask what delayed her, for he knew she had been with her Yankee colonel at Diamond Lil's. Talking about it would only worsen the way he felt about the choice she had made, though he had also made a poor choice, one that was certain to end his life. "No need to come back," he told her, backing away from her touch. "We've both changed. Things won't ever be like they were when we were growing up. They'll hang me and I will have paid for my mistake. I hope you'll give up the whorin' profession real soon. You can start over someplace else, like I'd aimed to do down in Mexico. If you take the notion to start a new life, take a coach down to Nuevo Laredo in Mexico. Ask for Henry Roberts or Tommy Joe Booker at the El Palacio Hotel. Tell them you're my sister. I can give you a letter asking that you get a part of my share of the money."

"It's stolen money," Mary replied evenly, fixing John

with a look. "It's no better than the money I offered you when you came back from the war."

"It don't seem the same," he argued, a weak argument and he knew it now.

She stepped back and turned to leave. "I don't want your money. Good-bye, John. I'll do as you ask ... I won't come back to visit you again." Lifting the hem of her dress, she strode up the corridor and left by the door.

John sighed and returned to his bunk.

"You've got a pretty sister," Sutton remarked from his cell.

John glared at him, then looked away, silencing Sutton. A wave of regret swept over John for all the bitter changes a war had wrought upon his family and friends. Almost nothing was the same as it had been before the shelling at Fort Sumpter. Tens of thousands of decaying corpses marked the battlefields, engagements hardly any of the soldiers understood. But in many ways, the survivors who fought for the Confederacy were no better off than the dead. Starving, homeless soldiers had little to be grateful for when they returned home.

He stared at the floor until his eyelids grew heavy, for he had slept little during the night. Haunted by visions of what might have been had he not returned to Waco, he tossed and turned, wishing things had turned out differently. Later he rested his head against the wall and dozed, though it was a fitful sleep.

Toward the middle of the afternoon, as John was dozing, a pair of uniformed militiamen followed Sheriff Hogan to John's cell. Both men were darkies and the uniforms they wore were not Union issue. One carried a set of manacles and leg irons. Sheriff Hogan was grinning when he unlocked the cell door.

"These state policemen are gonna take you to see the

magistrate, Cross," Hogan said. "He'll set a date to hear your case. Put out your hands so they can chain you. You try anything funny and I'll kill you ... Save the county some expense, havin' a trial."

John extended his wrists. One policeman fitted the manacles while the other bound his leg chains. John knew the effect black policemen would have on the soldiers at the campground. The newly appointed Texas governor was adding insult to injury, employing freed slaves to police the state so soon after the war.

One policeman drew his revolver. "Move to the door," he said, waving his gun barrel menacingly.

John started out of his cell, his strides shortened by lengths of heavy chain that rattled across the floor. Marching stiffly in front of the gun, John moved up the corridor, then through a boxlike office to a boardwalk outside the sheriff's door.

"That way, Cross," Hogan muttered, pointing down the street. Up and down the boardwalks, townspeople stopped to stare at the chained prisoner and his armed escort.

Walking soon became painful, when the leg bands slid down his boots. "Keep movin'," one of the guards said gruffly, then John felt the muzzle of a gun against his spine.

He was forced to trudge past three intersections to reach the McLennan County courthouse. Along the way, people halted to watch him go by. Several soldiers were gathered near the courthouse steps when John approached, but the former Confederates were not looking at him, for it was the black policemen they stared at without hiding their contempt.

"Give 'em hell in there, Captain Cross!" a soldier cried as he started up the steps. "Don't bow down to the Yankee bastards! You give 'em Billy hell when you git the chance!"

Again, the gun was shoved into John's back when he hesitated to listen to the soldier. "Move, Cross!" a policeman snapped, pushing John higher up the stone steps.

Amid the clatter of John's leg irons, they entered an office and went to a desk in front of an open window. A balding man in his fifties seated behind the desk watched John approach.

"This here's John Cross, Judge," Hogan said when John's chains ceased their rattling.

The judge looked John up and down, as though he were appraising the value of a horse. "I'm Judge Montgomery," he said tonelessly. "You've been charged with bank robbery and murder, Mr. Cross. I have signed statements from witnesses that identify you as one of the men who robbed the Planters Bank. Sheriff Hogan signed a statement that said he saw you kill McLennan County Sheriff Buel Pope at Del Rio. The state of Texas seeks the death penalty in your case. You will be tried two weeks from today. This will give the state's attorney time to prepare his case against you. If you have money, you may retain a lawyer. Otherwise, you can act in your own defense." He glanced down at a piece of paper on his desk. "John Marshall Cross, how do you plead to the charge of bank robbery?"

John drew in a breath. "I'm guilty," he replied softly.

"And to the charge of murder?" the judge continued.

John lowered his face to the floor. "I killed him. He was shooting at me, so I fired an' knocked him off his horse."

Judge Montgomery seemed to be contemplating something. He stared at John for a time, saying nothing. "You will be executed," he said a moment later. "I'll order that you be hanged by the neck from a public gallows. I intend to make an example of you in front of the rest of these surly Confederates here. It will keep them from any similar notions, Mr. Cross, when they see the trapdoor fall below your feet. This city is on the brink of having to deal with a disorderly mob amongst those Rebels. I'll make an example out of you that will keep mob violence from developing." He looked at Sheriff Hogan. "Return this man to his cell. If there are any other prisoners in your jail, I want them removed. Mr. Cross is to be kept in solitary confinement until his trial. Allow no visitors."

"Yessir," Hogan replied, seizing John by the arm to swing him toward the office door. "I'll let that Sutton feller go. He claims he wasn't stealing that cow. I figure he's learned his lesson by now, so I'll turn him loose."

John was pushed out of the office at gunpoint, to begin the long march back to the jail. When he came out on the courthouse steps, a crowd of Confederate soldiers had gathered on the lawn.

"Give 'em hell, Cap'n," someone shouted. A half-starved soldier shook his fist at the guards.

"Hope you spent every last cent of that money!" another cried.

As John started slowly down the steps, a cheer went up from the group of soldiers. So many voices shouted at once that the sound muted the rattle of John's chains. Even as he was paraded away from the courthouse lawn, the cheering continued, growing softer as he plodded toward the sheriff's office.

"They won't have so much to cheer about when that rope stretches your neck," Hogan said, looking back once at the gathering of soldiers. "Let the fools have their fun 'til judgment day. They'll be singing a different tune when that trapdoor falls. Step lively, Cross. I ain't got all day."

He was returned to his cell and then unchained by the black policemen. When Willie Sutton learned that he was being released, he hurried out of his cell and looked over his shoulder at John. "I wasn't stealin' that cow," he said, as though he had to explain his release, then he trotted through the office door.

John's cell was locked. He sat on the cot to rub his sore ankles as the three lawmen entered the office and closed the door. Later, he gazed up at the window, remembering Judge Montgomery's stern warning that he would most certainly hang. Then he thought about the men who cheered him outside the courthouse, a slow smile crossing his face. "They know why we did it," he whispered, wondering if Billy Cole had heard the soldiers' shouts when John was marched down the courthouse steps.

Chapter Thirty-five

Each day became more grueling than the last, waiting in the deep silence of his cell for his trial. As before, he passed long hours pacing back and forth, yet this time he was without hope that a wrongful charge might be discovered which would set him free. His guilt had been acknowledged, for it was inescapable, witnessed by too many to offer any hope that he might somehow be discharged. Facing certain execution, he passed each lonely hour in bottomless despair. Twice daily, in the morning and just before dark, Sheriff Hogan brought him a plate of boiled potatoes. As the days went by, the sheriff stopped taunting him, hardly saying a word when he brought the food and water. John measured time by watching the square of sunlight move slowly across the floor of his cell. He imagined that he could judge the hour by the position of the square, although he had no timepiece by which to gauge his accuracy. His beard thickened as days stretched into a week, for he was denied shaving materials and bathwater. At times, he stood on his cot to listen to the sounds outside his window, imagining sights to accompany the sounds. Horses and wagons rolled back and forth along the street in front of the jail, and sometimes he heard bits and pieces of conversations when the wind came from the right direction.

When he heard a woman's voice, he was always reminded of Sallie Mae. In moments of quiet desperation, he jumped high enough to grab the bars across his window, thus to pull himself up for a glimpse of the world outside. But the window overlooked an alley that gave him precious little to see, a garbage dump and the rear door to a harness maker's shop that was never opened.

As the days crawled by, he began to fear that he was edging close to madness. More and more, he talked to himself while pacing back and forth. At first, hearing his own voice was a comfort. But he began to wonder if his mind might be going when he discovered himself mumbling imagined conversations with Billy as if his friend's ghost shared the cell. Then for a time he paced silently, or stared at the floor, until he caught himself mumbling again.

The evening of his eleventh day of confinement passed like all the others. At dark, he slumped on his bunk and closed his eyes to doze. Sometime later, he heard a horse in the alley outside his window and the sound jolted him awake. Looking up at the velvety square of night sky sprinkled with stars beyond the bars, he listened to the slow hoofbeats until they stopped below his window. A heavy silence passed until a whispered voice cried, "John Cross! Can you hear me?"

He scrambled to plant his feet on the cot, then he jumped to grab the bars. Straining, he pulled himself higher with trembling arms until he had a view of the alley below. A rider seated on a dark horse was looking up at him. "I'm John Cross," he answered quietly. He did not recognize the man, though the light was poor in the alley. "What do you want with me?"

"You may not remember me," the voice replied. "My name is Oscar Freemont. We met when you rode past my wagon."

"I remember," John said, summoning all his strength

to keep clinging to the bars, his arms aching with fatigue. "Why have you come?"

Freemont's head turned both ways quickly, making sure they were alone. "My friends and I intend to help you," he said, lowering his voice so that John barely heard him. "Be ready. Tomorrow night, if things go well, you will hear a firehouse bell. When you hear the bell, you will know we were successful. When the fire is discovered at the courthouse, everyone will answer the call of the bell to help fight the fire with a bucket brigade. With the fire as a distraction, we'll try to break you out of jail, so stay watchful. We found the livery where they are keeping your horse. If we succeed, your horse will be hidden in this alley. The rest . . . making your escape, will be up to you. Remember, listen for the bell."

Before John could utter a word, Freemont heeled his horse down the alley and rode out of sight. John freed his grip on the bars and landed atop his bunk, exhausted, yet filled with a sudden breath of wild hope. There was a chance that he might escape a death sentence a second time! Just the thought of it made him feel like shouting. To be free again, to have his life handed to him by a man he only met once, seemed like an impossible dream come true. He jumped to the floor of his cell and began pacing back and forth rapidly, his mind suddenly alive with possibilities of an escape. He saw himself aboard the dappled gray colt, wind streaming through the horse's mane as it galloped away from Waco. In his vision, the colt's strides were much longer, carrying him swiftly away from all pursuit.

"Listen for the bell," he said aloud, a reminder of Freemont's last words. "They plan to burn the courthouse tax records, to keep men like Sheldon Blackwell from using them."

He halted his pacing below the window, staring up at

the star-filled sky beyond. "The fire bell will bring everyone running to the fire," he whispered, excitement surging through him. He knew someone guarded him at night, hearing sounds from the little office at the front now and then. He wondered how Freemont intended to handle the guard during the jailbreak. If Freemont and some of his friends were armed . . . ?

Resuming his strides back and forth, he began considering the risks. The night guard would be armed and Freemont's plan might fail. There was also a chance that someone might see the attempt and summon help before he could be freed. He knew there were a thousand things that could go wrong, but at last there was hope. The shadowy figure he encountered at the abandoned cotton wagon now seemed like the workings of fate.

He paced until well past midnight, thinking things through while in a state of wild anticipation. Until tomorrow night, he promised himself that he would not explore the chances of failure. For the first time since his capture at Carothers boardinghouse, he could look forward to the possibility of freedom. Now, as exhaustion forced him to rest, he sat on the edge of his cot filled with hope. If Oscar Freemont and his friends managed to unlock the door to his cell, it would be the last time iron bars imprisoned him. He would fight and die, if necessary, but John Cross would never see the inside of another jail. With a good horse underneath him, and a gun, he would never be caught again. He swore this oath while staring up at his cell window, remembering a similar oath he'd taken in Arkansas to avenge the death of a frightened, innocent boy.

The man in the vested suit stood near the cell doorway. A noonday sun brightened the window, shedding light on the man's narrow face and close-set eyes. He watched John for a moment without uttering a word, then he cleared his throat and spoke. "I'm Nathan Hayward, the state's attorney for your prosecution, Mr. Cross. Have you employed an attorney for your defense?"

"No," John whispered. "I'm told I have no money to hire a lawyer. Sheriff Hogan claims the money I had belongs to the Planters Bank, so I'm penniless."

Hayward wore a satisfied expression. "Then you'll defend yourself," he said. "Judge Montgomery and I have selected a jury. Your trial will begin in three days." Now his look turned smug. "It has been difficult to find jurymen without prejudice in your case," he added. "Among the poor in this county, you have become something of a folk hero with your exploits. However, I can promise you a swift trial, Mr. Cross, and a speedy verdict of guilty. You will hang for your crimes. I can assure you of that, and it will be justice well served. You are nothing but a common criminal, a thief and a murderer. All men of your ilk should be hung. The South is full of Confederate rabble-rousers like you, men who refuse to accept their defeat. It will be a service to the state of Texas when you are executed. You have entered pleas of guilty to both charges and there should be few deliberations by the jury. I bid you good afternoon, Mr. Cross. The next time we meet, it will be to secure your death sentence."

Hayward turned on his heel and walked briskly down the corridor to the sheriff's office. When the door slammed shut, John permitted himself the beginnings of a smile. "Maybe not, Mr. Hayward," he said in a quiet voice. "If you hear the firehouse bell tonight, it may mean that our next meeting has been postponed."

He resumed his steady march across the floor of his cell, his thoughts focused on the coming night. His life depended on the actions of a man he hardly knew, mak-

333

ing it a difficult loyalty to explain. A casual remark, that the courthouse records should be burned, had apparently been enough to win the help of Freemont and his followers. But John knew it ran deeper than that. It was a kinship among veterans of a terrible war, where men were bonded to each other by death and incredible hardships. In the hearts and minds of southern soldiers, the Confederacy was more than an army and a loose-knit government of slave-owning states, since few soldiers owned slaves. It was an idea centered around brotherhood among men who were neighbors and friends. A challenge to the way of life across the South was an attack on their freedom that could not be ignored by honorable men. It had seemed a just cause, until the wounded and dying lay like a carpet of grass across the battlefields. Perhaps only then was any thought given to the price of honor, when it was too late to halt the carnage until one side or the other was humbled by total defeat. Through it all, men came to know each other through adversity in a way that would not have been possible in quieter times. Shared hardship made brothers of strangers. Oscar Freemont had not forgotten the lessons of war. The offer to help John escape the McLennan County jail could only have come from a fellow southern soldier.

The afternoon wore away slowly. John paced and then rested, his thoughts occupied with a hundred details. When his cell door was opened, his first objective would be to get his hands on a gun. The first place to look was the sheriff's office, perhaps take the night guard's weapon, or whatever else he could find. Then he had to make it around the corner of the building to the alley, and his horse. Without his hat or his coat, he knew he would be easily recognized, even in the dark. Thus he would have to ride alleyways and empty streets to get out of the city.

To save the gray colt extra miles, he planned to head due south down the road to Falls County by which he had come. As soon as his escape was discovered, telegraph lines would spread the alarm. He would have to avoid larger towns served by a telegraph, where posses of lawmen would be the first to try to hunt him down. There would also be dogged pursuit from the rear, Sheriff Hogan and his deputies, and far more dangerous, the clever detective, Sam Kincaid. It would be a horse race, and a game of cat and mouse all the way to the border. Everyone would know Mexico was his destination, making it that much more difficult to reach the Rio Grande. Lawmen from larger towns to the south would try to intercept him, warned of his approach by the telegraph lines. He would be one man against hundreds of peace officers seeking to claim the reward for his capture. The odds against him would be unthinkable, yet it was the only chance he had to escape a rope. His survival would depend on his wits, and the stamina of a gray colt.

For a time, he stood below the window, listening to the sounds outside. Tonight, he would be listening for just one sound that would spell the beginning of his attempt at freedom. When the fire bell echoed across the city, it would be the most welcome sound he ever hoped to hear.

Chapter Thirty-six

It had been dark for several hours. Every nerve in John's body tingled with a mixture of excitement and fear. Cold sweat dampened his shirt and his forehead as he strode the width of his cell, his face turned to the barred window, his mind filled with doubt. No bell had sounded. Had Freemont's attempt failed?

He paused now and then to listen closely, fearing that the grinding of his boots across the floor might have kept him from hearing the distant ringing of a bell. Fear knotted his stomach. What had happened to Freemont and his fire?

Near exhaustion from his day-long pacing and a night without sleep, he sat on the edge of his cot, fighting feelings of despair. It was early, he reasoned, trying to convince himself that nothing had gone wrong. Freemont would wait until the city was asleep to break into the courthouse, to avoid being seen. John stared at the square of starlight on the floor of his cell, forcing himself to wait patiently. The trembling in his hands lessened and he relaxed against the wall, breathing deeply, slowly. Earlier, he had heard the scrape of a chair in the sheriff's office. The night guard was in place, the man Freemont must disarm before John's cell could be unlocked. Outside the window, traffic noises from the street fell to an occasional creak of a buggy wheel. Less often, he heard distant hoofbeats, until finally, there was only a heavy silence. Somewhere in the alley, a cricket began to chirp. Much farther away, a dog barked briefly, then stopped.

"Any time now," he whispered, listening to the beating of his heart. He ground his teeth together and closed his eyes, filled with a sense of foreboding. Something had gone wrong with Freemont's plan, he was sure of it. Minutes passed, then half an hour more, accompanied by silence. A part of him felt like weeping for the chance at freedom that would never come. He tried to push his sorrow aside, summoning one last desperate hope that a fire bell would ring sharp and clear in the next few minutes. But as the minutes passed, his hopes fell. The city of Waco was wrapped in a blanket of total silence.

He did not realize that he'd been dozing, when a noise awakened him with a start. He shook his head to clear away the cobwebs of sleep, when he heard the noise again . . . the clang of a faraway bell. He sprang to his feet in the darkness of his cell and turned toward the window, cocking an ear. There it was, the ringing of a fire bell, as plain and distinct as if it were ringing inside his own heart.

"At last," he whispered, as every muscle in his body tensed. He glanced toward the office door at the end of the dark corridor. Now, the most difficult part of Freemont's plan had to be accomplished, overpowering the guard. If it could be done quietly, John would have more time to reach his horse and ride across town before his escape was discovered.

The bell continued to ring, yet there was only silence from the sheriff's office. Beyond the window, faint and indistinct, men's voices cried. Moments later, a horse galloped down the street in front of the jail at full speed, hoofbeats echoing off the storefronts. Gradually, the sound faded, while the bell kept up its distant clanging.

John crept to the door of his cell, gripping the bars with sweat-soaked hands, straining to hear the slightest sound from the front of the building. For half a minute more, he heard nothing at all.

Suddenly, very close to the jail, someone cried, "Fire! Fire! The courthouse is on fire!"

Something scraped across the floor of the sheriff's office, as though someone was dragging a very heavy object. Then a muffled voice said something John couldn't hear, followed by a thud. John's hands tightened around the cold iron bars. What was happening?

He heard the door open, and saw a figure rush down the corridor toward his cell. The man arrived out of breath, jangling a ring of noisy keys.

"Hurry, Cap'n Cross," a voice said as a key turned the lock with a clatter. "Your horse is at the end of the alley. Sergeant Freemont is waitin' for you there."

John bolted through the cell door as soon as it opened. "I need a gun," he said quickly, staring up the hall at a run.

"There's a pistol in your saddlebags," the man replied as he trotted close at John's heels. "Ain't got but four loads an' the cylinder is loose. It's all we had. You'll have to hold the cylinder in place so it'll fire. Best of luck, Cap'n. Turn left when you get outside. Your horse'll be in the alley."

They ran through the sheriff's office. The front door was standing ajar. To one side of the door, a body was sprawled on the office floor, and beside it, John saw the faint gleam of gun oil on the barrel of a shotgun. He skidded to a halt and picked up the heavy weapon. "I'll take this along," he said, forgetting to look for extra shells in his haste to leave the office.

Outside, he wheeled around to the man who had

338

opened his cell. "Thanks," he whispered, watching the street, finding it dark and empty. "I won't forget what you've done for me." Then he was off without waiting for a reply, racing down the boardwalk, his boots thumping out a rhythm atop the boards.

He rounded the corner and made a dash for the alley, only dimly aware that the fire bell still tolled. Gasping for breath, he aimed for a black shadow at the mouth of the alleyway, clutching the shotgun to his chest.

Just a few feet into the alley, he almost stumbled into the hindquarters of his gray colt. A man on a dark bay horse held the gray's reins. John made a lunge for his saddle and swung quickly over the seat, balancing the shotgun in one hand. Then he looked at the grinning face of the man aboard the bay.

"She's burnin' like dry tinder," Oscar Freemont said proudly, handing John his reins. "Won't be no records left by the time they get it put out. 'Twas your idea, Cap'n Cross. There'll be a bunch of grateful folks in this county tomorrow mornin'. Now ride, Cap'n! Outrun them sons of bitches to the border! An' remember Freemont's raid when you get where you're goin'. There's a pistol in your saddlebags if you get in a scrape. It's plumb wore out, but it'll still shoot if there's a need."

John swung the colt so it faced the street, looking over his shoulder at Freemont. "I'm in your debt, my friend. Come to Nuevo Laredo when you can and I'll repay you." He dug his heels into the gray's ribs and felt its powerful lunge carry him out of the alley in a single bound. Reining south, he let the horse have its head to reach full stride as ironclad hooves clattered over the wagon ruts. The colt gathered speed, racing across the first dark intersection with its mane flying in the wind. Soon the gray's pounding gait became a drone in John's ears, blotting out the sound of the fire bell still tolling in the heart of the city. Galloping down a shadowy side street, John felt the colt give him a new burst of speed when it felt the pressure of his heels. Dashing past darkened buildings and storefronts, John urged the gelding to give him everything it had. With the shotgun clenched in his right fist, he rode away from the business district to silent rows of houses. Here and there, a dog barked, alarmed by the rapid approach of a horse. Half a mile from the jail, the homes became more widely scattered as he neared the outskirts of town.

"I'll make it," he told himself, the sound of his voice lost to the rattle of flying hooves. In the distance, he could see the silvery surface of the Brazos. When he looked over his shoulder, he saw an orange glow brighten the sky above the rooftops in the business district. Freemont's fire was growing.

The gray galloped the length of the dark street and responded to a pull on the reins when John made the turn toward the cotton gin at full speed. The gelding's hooves beat out a staccato, running effortlessly, carrying him farther and farther from the jail. Crossing the empty wagon yard below the gin, John chanced a look at the camp and found no fires. The hour was late and everyone was asleep when the fire bell sounded.

The colt charged past Oscar Freemont's wagon, then past the canebrake where John had waited for darkness the day he arrived. Before him now lay the river road that would take him to Falls County. A sliver of moon hung low in the night sky, revealing the road's empty ruts. Just once more before he rode out of the city he glanced over his shoulder. The orange-yellow light was even brighter than before, evidence that the fire was burning out of control. The fire would occupy most every available citizen, giving John more precious time to outdistance the pursuit that would certainly come. Yet he dared not celebrate his early advantage, for a telegraph message outran the most fleet-footed horse. Very soon, John could expect to encounter his enemies from all sides as a network of telegraph lines spread the news of his escape.

Racing down the dark road, the colt's ears bobbed up and down with the power of its long strides. The gray was beginning to breathe hard as the miles fell away behind it. John gave a gentle tug on the reins, slowing the horse slightly to save its wind. He checked again and saw no one behind, then he remembered the gun in his saddlebags. Resting the shotgun across the pommel, he opened one of the leather pockets to remove the pistol.

He felt keen disappointment when he examined the gun by starlight, an early model Remington .44 caliber revolver. The cylinder rattled loosely in the frame, warning of the danger of a misfire or an explosion that could mangle the user's hand. Although the gun was a much-needed gift from the impoverished Confederates who had so little to spare, it was a weapon that could not be trusted. John stuck the .44 in the waistband of his pants, awakening to another grim discovery which had escaped him in the haste of his departure from the jail. He had just one round for the shotgun, the load it carried now. If he was pressed into a close-quarters fight, he had but one chance to slay an enemy with the scattergun, and only four balls for his revolver. He had no money to purchase more ammunition, and no money for food. He would be reduced to begging for a meal here and there to stay alive until he reached the border. And he would have to use caution wherever he asked for food or shelter, avoiding anyone who might have learned about his escape.

Heading south as fast as his horse could travel, the bright prospects of his freedom had begun to take on a darker side. He was free, to be sure, but his freedom would only last until he made a mistake. The countryside would be crawling with lawmen. Citizens would be on the alert for a chance to earn the reward. Only by exercising the greatest of caution was there any hope that he might make it back to Mexico.

Later, he slowed the colt to a trot so it could rest and gather wind. Glancing back, the road behind him was empty. He patted the gray's neck and spoke softly. "Save your strength. You're liable to need it tomorrow."

Many hours south of Waco, he crossed the Falls County line without having seen another traveler or ridden close to a farmhouse along the road. Thus far, his escape route would go undetected since no one had seen him. At daybreak, things would change. Anyone who spotted a lone rider on a dappled gray horse would remember it. Before dawn, he would be forced off the main roads to travel unnoticed. A plan started to take shape in his mind as he hurried the colt through the darkness. During daylight, he had to remain hidden and move south through forests or down streambeds, a tactic which would greatly slow his pace. Above all else, he had to keep from being seen and identified during his travels. Only at night would it be safe to hurry his horse. Poorly armed and alone, facing a direction that would be bristling with guns lying in wait for him, he felt he had no choice. He was sure of one thing . . . he would not allow himself to be captured again. He would lay down his life to remain free, but he would never go back to jail.

In the gray light of false dawn, he spotted a distant campfire and smelled woodsmoke. Riding the Brazos River bottom had taken him well west of Marlin. Thick stands of tall pecan trees hid him from view until he came upon this unexpected campsite far from the main road leading south. He halted the colt at the edge of a pecan thicket to survey the camp from a distance. As the eastern sky paled with the coming sunrise, he could make out the shape of a wagon below a towering oak tree. Someone tended the fire, the mere silhouette of a man in the shadow beneath the oak. A team of mules grazed on picket ropes not far from the wagon. The wagon was of a type used by peddlers and medicine men, a square-roofed affair completely enclosed by wood. It was an unusual place to find a drummer or a healing practitioner, so far from a road where travel by wagon was easier.

John's stomach demanded food while he considered the risks of approaching the wagon. Whoever the traveler was, he wouldn't know about the jailbreak yet. But in the next town, or the next, he would be able to identify the man who came to his fire and worse, it also revealed the route John had taken away from Waco. Weighing things, he waited for sunrise at the edge of the thicket while the colt grazed on lush grasses below the trees. Hunger drew him ever closer to a decision.

Half an hour later, the first rays of sunlight beamed across the side of the wagon, revealing a sign painted on the surface. In ornate block letters it read DR. BARNABY HILL, and below, HILL'S MAGIC ELIXIR. ROOT REMEDIES AND HEALING POTIONS.

"A medicine man," John muttered, watching the figure near the fire. A short, stocky man with deeply bowed legs busied himself with a coffeepot. John's stomach growled. By his own rough guess, he had come more than forty miles since his escape. He hardly touched his supper yesterday, too concerned with details of the plan to eat. Now hunger and fatigue sapped his strength. Resting a few moments at the peddler's fire, perhaps granted a bite to eat, became too inviting to ignore. "I'll chance it," he told himself as he mounted the colt and rode slowly out of the trees, keeping the shotgun out of sight beside his leg.

The peddler heard John's horse and hurried to one of the wagon wheels, then a gun appeared in his hands. He stood at the corner of the wagon to watch John ride in, cradling his weapon loosely in the crook of an arm.

John halted his horse a short distance away, wondering what made the man so jumpy. "Hello the fire!" he shouted. "I'm a traveler, seeking a bit of warmth from the morning chill. A cup of coffee if you have any to spare."

The peddler still seemed suspicious. "What takes you off the main road?" he asked sharply.

John decided it was best to answer with a dash of truth. "I had some minor difficulties with some gentlemen in another town. Our disagreement has forced me to use caution in my travels. These men would do me harm if they found me. They feel I bested them in a horse trade, but it was an honest business proposition."

For a moment more, the peddler appeared uncertain. "Might those men be from the city of Marlin?" he asked.

John wagged his head. "I did not come by way of Marlin. My difficulties occured farther north."

The man seemed satisfied now. "Ride in," he said, lowering the barrel of the shotgun he held. "Warm yourself and have a cup of my coffee, if you wish. I'm Barnaby Hill, and you're welcome at my fire, so long as your intentions are honorable."

Chapter Thirty-seven

He dismounted and shook hands with Barnaby, after a quick glance over his shoulder to make sure his back-trail was clear. "I am Robert Smith," he said, sounding casual about the introduction. "I've ridden all night to put some distance behind me."

Barnaby nodded and pointed to the fire. "The coffee is ready. I understand what it is like to be hounded by scoundrels, Mr. Smith. Just two days ago, I ran afoul of the authorities in Marlin, when a handful of scalawags falsely claimed that my elixir contained nothing more than distilled spirits and flavoring. It seems one of the town's leading matrons became drunk after she took my stomach remedy. She complained to the local magistrate and I was forced to flee just ahead of a warrant for my arrest. Tie your horse to my wagon and I'll share what I have with you, for it would appear we have a common bond, you and I."

John tied the gray to a rear wagon wheel and rested his shotgun against the hub, then he started toward the fire. Barnaby cast a wary eye at the pistol in John's waistband, his shotgun dangling beside his leg when he followed John to the coffeepot.

"I keep a spare cup in that chuck box," Barnaby remarked, making a motion toward a small wooden crate near the flames.

John poured himself a cup of weak coffee. "I'm grateful," he said, blowing steam from the rim. Barnaby was giving him a thorough examination, still a bit suspicious of an unshaven stranger who showed up unexpectedly so far from traveled roads. "I see by the sign on your wagon that you're a doctor," John continued, hoping to ease the man's fears.

Barnaby shook his head. "I'm not a surgeon," he replied as he placed his gun on the ground near his feet to pour coffee. "I suppose I am best described as a purveyor of medicines. I received training in the compounding of natural remedies. Since the war, my profession has fallen on hard times. No one has any money these days. I make a meager living traveling from town to town, selling curatives to those who have hard coin. But alas, there isn't much of it. On some occasions, there have been unfortunate incidents like the one in Marlin. A shame. I was doing rather well. Now I'm headed south, to seek my fortune elsewhere, hounded by an unjust warrant."

John was only half listening, studying the trees to the north through which he had come. "I've had a problem or two with the law," he said absently, wondering just how closely pursuit might be nipping at his heels. "Union rule can be heavy-handed when it comes to a southerner. I'm headed south myself, to get away from hard times and the misunderstanding I told you about."

Barnaby was eyeing the gray colt. "You ride a magnificent animal, Mr. Smith," he offered. "I'm an experienced judge of horseflesh. The dappled gray is a blooded horse, so I'm not surprised to hear that his previous owner wants him back."

It was a story that fit John's circumstances and he decided to stick with it. "A good horse," he agreed, sipping coffee. Barnaby had not picked up his shotgun again. "I acquired the colt in an honest transaction. I won't surrender it to men who suffer remorse. I aim to keep the gray, no matter what."

Barnaby turned for his chuck box. "I have some fatback," he said, walking to the fire in a curious, bowlegged gait. "You are welcome to some of it, Mr. Smith."

"I'd be obliged," John replied, noticing a goodly amount of patchwork on Barnaby's trousers. Learning that Barnaby hoped to elude lawmen from Marlin was a stroke of good luck, making him less likely to talk about the stranger who rode up to his camp. For the first time in many hours, John began to relax. He watched Barnaby place an iron skillet beside the flames. "Do you know the back roads in this part of the country?" he asked.

Barnaby looked up from cutting strips of salt pork. He gave John a knowing grin. "I'm familiar with the secret slave routes," he confided. "Runaway slaves used them for years. We are not far from one of the trails right now. I'd planned to travel it today, to stay out of sight until I'm well away from Marlin. When I'm convinced of your integrity, Mr. Smith, I might be persuaded to show you the way. But I must know that you don't intend to rob me at some out-of-the-way spot. I have very little money, so it would hardly be worth your time."

Mention of the runaway slave routes caught John's attention at once. "Where do these trails lead?" he asked quickly.

Barnaby went back to his cooking. "They run all over the state in places. Some are well marked. Others have not been used for many years. The one I plan to follow ends just to the east of San Antonio. I'm told there were

347

hardly any slaves south of there. Too dry for cotton, suppose."

John went closer to the fire, reading Barnaby's face. "If I can convince you of my honesty, I'd like to be shown that trail. I have reason to believe that the men who are after this gray horse will follow me to the ends of the earth."

Barnaby frowned, stirring strips of fatback with the point of his knife. "We could travel together as far as San Antonio," he said, although his tone hinted of doubt. "For our mutual defense, should we be beset by scoundrels. Let me think on it, Mr. Smith. We both face a long and perilous journey alone, hounded by misguided men seeking recompense. If I felt you could be trusted . . ."

John wondered if traveling along with the wagon would be too slow. Far more important than speed, however, was the need to make the trip undetected. Lands to the south would be thick with armed men sworn to hunt him down. If the secret slave roads offered any hope of slipping past them, John needed Barnaby's help desperately. "What can I do to satisfy you?" he asked.

He was given no answer for several silent minutes, while Barnaby occupied himself with the meat. The delicious smell of frying pork set John's mouth to watering. Sipping coffee, he waited for Barnaby to speak.

"You talk like a straightforward fellow," Barnaby said, removing strips of meat from the skillet, "so I'll ask you a straightforward question. Did you steal that dappled horse?"

John shook his head quickly. "The gray is mine. I'm not a horse thief."

"I wondered," Barnaby replied. "You keep looking over your shoulder, as though you suspect someone is following you. You told me it was a misunderstanding over the horse. I wanted to be sure you aren't running from a lynching party. . . . I might be hanged as your accomplice before I had time to explain." He sighed and picked up a tin plate loaded with meat. "Our breakfast is ready, Mr. Smith. No harm will be done if we travel together, I suppose. As soon as we've eaten I'll harness my mules and we'll be on our way."

John gratefully accepted some of the food. An accidental meeting with Barnaby Hill showed promise of providing solutions to some of John's most pressing problems—an escape route and a few meals. "Thanks," he said around a mouthful of salt pork. "You have nothing to fear from me. Like yourself, I'm only looking for a way out of this part of the country. Traveling together, we stand a better chance of making it."

Barnaby looked up from his plate, and although he said nothing, John was sure he saw doubt in his eyes.

They finished their meal in silence, as the sun warmed away last night's chill. John began to worry about the telltale column of smoke drifting skyward from the cooking fire, for it could serve as a beacon to a posse of lawmen from Waco who were scouring possible escape routes to the south.

"Mind if I douse that fire?" he asked when his nerves grew raw-edged, from the spiral of smoke.

Barnaby shrugged. "Suit yourself. It's time we started moving anyway." He chuckled softly, reading John's expression. "Two men on the dodge shouldn't advertise their position. While you smother the fire, I'll go fetch the mules."

The harnessing took little time. Barnaby's mules were an old, experienced team, somewhat thin to be pulling a load over long distances in John's view. When the wagon was packed, Barnaby climbed to the driver's seat and shook the reins. "Gee-up, Maude, you lazy wench," he cried. "Gee-up, Brutus."

John mounted and fell in behind the wagon. Barnaby aimed south across a grass-thick stretch of bottomland. The heavy wagon jolted and bumped over uneven ground, moving at a snail's pace. John kept looking over his shoulder. The medicine wagon could only sustain a crawl traveling overland, giving John's enemies plenty of time to catch up as soon as they learned the direction he had taken. But with so many miles to cover through hostile territory, John had few choices. The gray could never outrun so many men on horseback when the alarm was spread along telegraph lines. Thus he reasoned that extreme caution was a far better plan than an all-out race toward the Rio Grande. As in the child's game of hide-and-seek, he would be better off avoiding discovery, for now, saving the colt's strength and stamina. Down deep, John knew a time would come when he would need every ounce of reserve his horse could muster.

The opening in the forest of post oaks led them to a tunnel-like trail between the tree trunks. Hidden by thick grass and weeds, two wagon ruts softened the progress for the iron-rimmed wheels. In places, oak branches brushed the sides of the wagon. It was evident that the road had not been used for some time. As the afternoon wore away, the mules began to tire, requiring that Barnaby resort to the use of a whip he carried under the seat. They had not passed a farmhouse or a settlement all day. The trail wound through deep forests. Here and there, they encountered tiny meadows where grass had started to yellow with the first signs of fall.

When the sun fell below the tops of the trees, the forest shadows changed. Now the mules were down to a crawl. All day, John kept an eye on the road behind hem, examining every shadow. And each time, he found them alone.

As dusk approached, Barnaby drove down a gentle grade to a tiny stream surrounded by oaks. The mules halted to drink their fill. John rode the gray to the creekbank where the horse could drink, then he turned to Barnaby.

"There aren't any towns, not so much as a single farmhouse," he remarked.

Barnaby nodded. "Runaway slaves needed to avoid being seen by anyone. We won't strike a settlement until we reach a little place called Westphalia. It's a German community. They mind their own business, so it was a safe place for slaves to buy a few supplies. The road continues south to another German village named Buckholtz. From there, it takes us to Bastrop. The men who are looking for you won't find us here. I'm sure you're safe now, Mr. Smith."

John glanced over his shoulder. "They won't give up easily, I'm afraid," he said quietly, as nightfall darkened the road. When he looked toward the wagon, he found Barnaby staring at him.

"You are running from the law, aren't you, Mr. Smith?" he asked, and by the tone of his voice, he was certain of it.

John swallowed. "This horse isn't stolen. I've told you that," he protested.

"Perhaps it isn't the horse causing your difficulties," he said thoughtfully, as if he were talking to himself. "Something else I suppose, if I missed with my first guess. It would appear we are both men on the run from the law. I'm quite sure I'm right about it. I'm a pretty good judge of men's behavior. In any event, it does not matter, so long as you are not plotting some misdeed against me. As I told you once before, I have very little money. My wagon, and these worn-out mules, represent the sum total of my worth."

"I won't harm you," John protested, resting the shotgun across his lap. "What can I do to convince you, Dr. Hill?"

Barnaby seemed to be contemplating something. "I suppose I'd have fewer concerns if you kept your guns in my wagon until we reach our destination. I won't worry that I'll be murdered in my sleep."

The suggestion took John by surprise. "I'd be defenseless if the men who are after me jumped us along the road. My word that I won't harm you should be enough."

Barnaby had his answer ready. "Carry them during the day, then, but grant me my peaceful slumber by keeping your guns in my wagon at night. A man with honorable intentions could find no flaw with such an arrangement."

The idea held too many risks, making John easy prey for a surprise attack in the dark. "My word will have to be enough," he said flatly, meeting Barnaby's gaze. "I won't disarm myself."

"As you wish, Mr. Smith," Barnaby sighed. "I suppose I can learn to sleep with one eye open. Gee-up, Maude, Brutus!" He slapped the reins over the mules' rumps and drove his wagon across the stream.

John crossed behind the wagon, remembering the oath he'd sworn in the McLennan County jail. No one would ever take him alive to await another date with the executioner. So long as he had a gun, he could fight his way to freedom.

The wagon rolled noisily through the forest twilight, drawn by trail-weary mules. John fell farther back, looking behind himself, for it seemed as though the trees were closing in around him like a pack of hungry hounds.

Chapter Thirty-eight

By lantern light, Barnaby showed John the interior of his wagon. Shelves on both sides held crocks and jars of ginger root, wintergreen, and dozens of other mysterious powders and oils. Paper cartons filled with half-pint bottles bearing various labels for Dr. Hill's remedies occupied the rest of the space. A sleeping pallet was rolled in one corner. The wagon contained so many smells that each one lost its identity.

"That is a genuine Persian rug," Barnaby said, pointing to the floor where John stood.

John had noticed a curious elevation to the floor of the wagon as soon as they entered. "The rug covers something, doesn't it?" he asked.

Barnaby gave him a weak smile. "There is a false floor," he confided. "Step back to the door."

Barnaby pulled the rug back, revealing several loose boards. When he lifted a board, John saw a two-foot space packed with bedding straw, and masonry jugs in neat rows on both sides.

"My basic ingredient," Barnaby said. He removed a jug and pulled the stopper. "Good corn whiskey," he added, offering it to John. "I recommend it highly for whatever ails you."

John took a cautious swallow, then another, enjoying

the delicious burn traveling down his throat to his stomach. "It's good stuff," he said when his breath returned.

Barnaby poured two tin cups and returned the jug to its hiding place. There were a large number of empty spots where the floorboards had been removed, evidencing that the supply was running low. Barnaby carried his lantern down the rear steps. They brought their cups to the tiny firepit encircled by stones where Barnaby had prepared their supper of fry bread and dried sausages. John seated himself across the glowing coals from Barnaby to drink his whiskey. A chill had come with the dark, making the contents of the cup and the fire's embers equally welcome.

"I sleep in the wagon," Barnaby said. "I see that you are without a bedroll. I have a blanket you can toss beside the fire. You are traveling without a coat, Mr. Smith, and I have none to spare. I would guess you began your journey in something of a hurry. . . ." His voice trailed off.

"I won't deny that I pulled out quickly," John admitted. "The circumstances left me no choice."

Barnaby was frowning at the contents of his cup thoughtfully. "These are difficult times," he said softly, as though he was remembering something. "I've left a few towns with my shirttail flying in the wind. This Reconstruction government has made Texas a poor place to make a living. I've given some thought to heading west into the territories. I've been told there is opportunity out there."

John offered no opinion on the subject, looking into the darkness. A faint noise caught his attention while Barnaby spoke, a distant sound coming from the north. "I heard something," he said quietly. "I'm sure I heard it just now. . . ."

Both men were silent. From the corner of his eye, John saw the gray colt lift its head, pricking its ears forward. Then the horse gave a low nicker through its muzzle, which brought John scrambling to his feet.

"Someone's coming!" he whispered, trying to pierce the night shadows for a glimpse of the source of the sounds. The soft thump of hoofbeats came from the road they had traveled. "They've found me," John added bitterly, wheeling toward his saddle where the shotgun lay.

The sounds grew louder. There wasn't time to saddle his horse. Crouching, he readied the twelve-gauge, thumbing back the hammer with his gaze fixed on the trail. Then he heard Barnaby's footsteps behind him.

"Hide in the wagon," Barnaby whispered, taking his shotgun from its resting place against a wagon wheel. "If they are the men following you, I'll tell them that I traded a sorrel mare for your dappled gray and then you rode off in a hurry. If it's a posse from Marlin seeking to serve a warrant on me, I'll be counting on your help. We'll have them covered with two shotguns. Hurry! Hide in the wagon until we know who they are!"

Filled with misgivings that he would be cornered in Dr. Hill's wagon, he had few choices. A running gunfight in the dark put him at a disadvantage without a saddle and spare ammunition for his guns. He raced up the steps and pulled the door closed just as the drum of hoofbeats announced the arrival of several riders. John knelt near the door with his heart pounding, listening for the first voice that would tell him who they were.

The horses halted. . . . John judged they were less than thirty yards from the back of the wagon. He caught his breath, clamping sweaty hands around the stock of the shotgun.

"Who's the owner of the wagon?" a deep voice shouted. "Come out where we can see you! This is an official visit! We are deputies from McLennan County with a lawful warrant for the arrest of an escaped criminal!"

John's stomach knotted. The men were Sheriff Hogan's deputies. He was trapped in the wagon and there was no escape, with just one charge in his shotgun and four balls in the chambers of the old Remington stuck in his waistband. A tremor raced down his arms. This was the fight he had so desperately hoped to avoid, a fight he stood little chance to win.

"There are no criminals here," he heard Barnaby shout from one side of the wagon. "I am a practitioner of the healing arts traveling alone. Perhaps you've heard of my Magic Elixir? I am Dr. Barnaby Hill."

"Come out where we can see you!" the voice demanded. "If you're who you claim to be, you have nothing to fear."

John heard Barnaby's feet scuffle through the dry grass.

"I'll light this lantern," Barnaby said, "so you will plainly see that I'm not the man you're after."

John's mouth had gone dry. When Barnaby learned John's real identity from the possemen, he could simply point to the wagon and a share of the reward would be his. John would be returned to the Waco jail and all would be lost. Unless he was killed making a dash to reach the dark forest.

"Now, gentlemen," Barnaby said. "Look at my face in the light. I'm a traveling doctor, selling cures from town to town. I am not a Wanted man as you can clearly see. I was preparing for bed when you arrived."

A lingering silence followed. Then another voice spoke. "That's his gray hoss over yonder. That's the hoss got stole from Collins Livery!"

The first voice spoke again. "Where's the owner of that dappled gray?" he cried. A gun was cocked, then another.

Barnaby cleared his throat. "I traded for the good gray early this morning, gentlemen. It had developed a limp, and the man who rode it said he was in a hurry to reach a sick friend. I traded a fine-boned pacing mare for that gelding, although I must admit freely that the mare was a stump sucker, most troublesome to keep in good flesh because of it. But a trade's a trade among grown men. Should that fellow return asking for recompense, he'll be barking up an empty tree, for the dappled horse is mine now."

Another silence came, lasting much too long. A horse stamped a hoof impatiently, then the deputy spoke again. "All the same, Dr. Hill, we'll search that wagon of yours. John Cross is a dangerous man, a fugitive, wanted for murder and bank robbery. There's a five-thousand-dollar reward paid to anyone who finds him. Roy Lee, you an' Ward climb down an' go have a look in the wagon. Keep your guns handy, just in case this here snake oil peddler is lyin' to us."

Hearing this, John's mind raced. He remembered the space below the false floor. Out of sheer desperation, he wheeled around and crept hurriedly to the opening, feeling his way in the dark. Two loose planks had been put aside. John pushed his shotgun into the hole and lowered his body onto the bed of straw. Replacing the boards would take too much time and there was a risk of noise that would give him away. Squirming into the tight space, he reached for the Persian rug and quickly covered himself the best he could, hoping that darkness would keep the men from discovering his hiding place. His hand closed over the butt of the Remington as footsteps approached the wagon. Would Barnaby give him away? Now that he knew about the reward?

"Hold on there, gentlemen," Barnaby said, speaking in a very loud voice. "There are medicines in there ... very valuable potions in glass vials that are easily broken. I'll permit you a look from the doorway, but no one can go inside. I won't have my crockery kicked all over the floor. You can see that the wagon is empty as soon as I open the padlock. Stand back, gentlemen, while I search my pockets for the key."

John took a deep breath. Barnaby was stalling for time to give John the chance to hide below the floor. If Barnaby meant to betray him, he wouldn't have told the story about the key.

"Hurry it up, Doc," someone said. "If Cross ain't here, it means he's getting' away on that stump suckin' mare you swapped him. Ward, you hold that lantern up high so I can see when the doc opens the door."'

"Hell, he ain't here," another voice said. "Let's get mounted. We're wastin' time."

John heard the rattle of metal. Barnaby was pretending to open the padlock. Then hinges creaked.

"Have a look, gentlemen," Barnaby said. "As you can see, my wagon contains nothing but medicines."

A boot scuffed close by. "It's empty," a voice said. "Let's hit our saddles. Cross is likely halfway to the Meskin border by now. Kincaid was right about the direction he took. That dappled hoss is the proof."

The door closed with a bang. John let out the breath he'd been holding and relaxed his grip on the gun. He could hear the men moving away and the sounds filled him with relief, until he heard a sharp command from the leader of the posse that made his blood run cold.

"That gray horse is evidence in a bank robbery trial, Doc," he said. "Witnesses identified it. The judge ordered it held until the trial is over. We're takin' it back with us. You can file a claim with the state's attorney, if you've got a bill of sale that proves it's yours. But the judge ain't gonna let nobody touch that horse until John Cross stands trial for bank robbery and murder. Ward, tie your lariat around that gray's neck and bring it along.

Ve got proof that Cross is headed down to Mexico gain."

"But it's my animal now!" Barnaby protested.

"Like I said, you can file a claim after the trial, Doc. Jntil then, the gray stays in McLennan County, by order f the judge."

John's heart sank to the pit of his stomach. Without a orse, he stood no chance at all of making his escape to he Mexican border. A close brush with death had been voided, but now he was afoot, still hundreds of miles rom the Rio Grande.

He lay motionless on the bed of straw until the ounds of horses moved off into the night. Sighing, he hrew the rug aside and pushed upward, wriggling free f the cramped space. When he opened the door a crack o peer out, he found Barnaby looking up at him with he wick turned low in the lantern.

"You heard them," Barnaby said quietly. "They took our dappled steed. It would seem you haven't been :ompletely honest with me, Mr. John Cross. I'm told ou are a murderer and a bank robber, with a five-housand-dollar reward posted on your head. Robert 5mith indeed! Now I learn that my traveling companion s a killer and thief!"

John started down the steps, then he slumped to a sit-ing position and rounded his shoulders. "It's a long story," he began, his voice heavy with fatigue and hope-essness, now that he had no horse. "I thank you for not ;iving me away. It was a kindness I don't deserve, un-ess you can see my side of things. Since the war began, :vents have conspired against me. I lost everything to :hat war except my life, or so it seemed." Now he looked deeply into Barnaby's eyes. "You gave me back my life tonight, and I'm grateful. If I can make it to the Mexican border, I'll see, that you are well paid. I have some money in a Mexican bank, but the chances look slim that I'll make it now. Without a horse, I'll be easily caught."

Barnaby chewed thoughtfully on his bottom lip without taking his gaze from John's face. "Hand down one of the jugs of whiskey," he said a moment later. "We could both use strong spirits after our brush with the law. And we might discuss a business arrangement, you and I. You said I'd be well paid if you could reach Mexico. Perchance, for the right price, my humble wagon offers you the best chance of reaching the border. We can talk about it, over a drink or two. The hidden compartment beneath the floor might be just the right trick to see you safely across the Rio Grande. But first, we must agree on a price. A business deal must be struck between us, so pass down a jug and tell me the story of your crimes. If we are to become partners in this endeavor, I want to know what sort of fellow you are under the skin. And of course, the price you will pay for my services if I agree to help you."

John got up slowly, his fallen spirits renewed by a fresh flicker of hope, to get one of the whiskey jugs. When he reached into the space beneath the floorboards, a wry grin crossed his face briefly. Could this tiny compartment see him safely to Nuevo Laredo, he wondered. It had already saved his life once. Did he dare to hope that a passageway to freedom might be accomplished in this wagon?

John came down the steps with the whiskey. Barnaby extinguished his lantern. When drinks were poured, John settled on the bottom step to begin telling the story of his misfortunes. He took a sip of corn liquor, glancing around them once. "Hope that posse doesn't come back," he said as an afterthought. "I reckon they believed your story about the sorrel mare."

"They left in a hurry," Barnaby remembered. "Seeking to earn the reward, I suppose. It's been my experi-

360

ence that greedy men get in a hurry and often make mistakes."

"They found my trail . . . they knew about this road."

"One of them was a darkie," Barnaby remarked. "It would seem Governor Davis intends to make lawmen out of every freed slave in the state. Most Texans won't take a kindly view of the practice so soon after the war. So tell me now, Mr. John Cross, how is it that you're a man wanted for robbery and murder?"

John closed his eyes. He decided to begin at the beginning of his sad homeward journey, when he disbanded his company rather than face another hopeless battle where more lives would certainly be lost. He looked up at the stars, then words began tumbling from his mouth.

Chapter Thirty-nine

The wagon rattled noisily up a steep grade. The dry hills east of San Antonio were rocky, making for hard work when the team encountered a climb. The road they followed would take them to a tiny outpost called Sutherland Springs, where Barnaby meant to buy a few badly needed supplies. John rode on the wagon seat beside Barnaby most of the time, but when they saw any travelers, John hurried to the back of the wagon to prepare his hiding place. After eleven days of slow travel, they were within a few miles of San Antonio. The back roads they followed had slowed them down, yet they made it through heavily populated country without incident in this manner. There had been no more visits by possemen and John had begun to relax. The hidden compartment beneath the wagon floor would allow him to escape all but the closest scrutiny. Barnaby had agreed to make the long, dangerous drive to the Mexican border for a fee of one thousand dollars. At first, John had worried that the size of the reward being offered for him might tempt Barnaby toward a betrayal. But as the days passed, he and Barnaby had gotten to know each other, and for reasons hard to explain, John had begun to trust him. The story of Barnaby's life after the war was a string of failures and missed opportunities not unlike his own. John felt that a bond had developed between them as the miles passed beneath the wagon wheels.

At the top of the grade, Barnaby sawed back on the reins and brought the wagon to a stop. Below the rocky knob where the wagon sat, a small cluster of clapboard buildings were arranged inside a grove of tall cottonwood trees.

"Sutherland Springs," Barnaby remarked. "I came through here a long time ago, when it was just a building or two. There is a spring where we can water the mules. I have a few dollars left. I'll buy some jerky and a small bag of flour. Perchance I can trade a few bottles of elixir for the things we need."

"I'll hide in the back," John said, climbing down from the wagon seat. He gazed down at the quiet village. A dusty street ran the length of the settlement. Here and there, a saddled horse was tied in the shade of a cottonwood. Sutherland Springs seemed to be asleep.

He got in the back of the wagon and felt the jolt when Barnaby urged the mules forward. Kneeling, he removed the rug and lifted the loose boards out of the way. There, lying in the bed of straw which kept the jugs from breaking on rough roads, was John's shotgun. He lowered himself to the straw as the wagon bumped and rattled down the hill. Spreading the rug over the opening, he lay back in the darkness as he had more than a dozen times before when they neared a town or a group of travelers along the road. Hiding in the secret compartment had become so routine that he gave little thought to it now. Resting atop the straw, he closed his eyes and thought about Sallie Mae again. The knowledge that his letter to her was never sent filled his thoughts. He would write to her again when they reached Nuevo Laredo, begging her to come.

The wagon creaked and bumped to a halt. John listened for the sounds Barnaby made when he left the wagon seat. Instead, he heard a voice very close to the wagon, and suddenly his limbs went numb with unreasoning fear.

"Open the back of that wagon. Keep your hands where I can see them while you're about it."

John recognized the voice at once. His right hand fumbled for the shotgun beside him. He drew the stock of the twelve-gauge to his shoulder and pulled the hammer back. The voice outside the wagon belonged to the detective, Sam Kincaid.

"By what authority do you demand a search of my wagon?" Barnaby asked.

John's finger closed around the trigger. He heard Kincaid grunt.

"By the authority of this warrant in my coat pocket," Kincaid replied. "I've been searching for this wagon all over creation, Dr. Hill. Now climb down and open the door. I know you're hiding John Cross in there. Open it quickly and get out of the way. My warrant for Cross grants me the right to take him dead or alive. I'll kill him this time if he offers any resistance, so stay out of my line of fire."

"There's no one inside," Barnaby protested as the springs below the wagon seat creaked. "There is no need to point that gun at me, kind sir. My wagon is empty. I've never heard of this John Cross."

"Open it!" Kincaid snapped.

John heard footsteps move down the side of the wagon. Clutching the shotgun with sweat-dampened hands, he caught his breath and tried to still the tiny tremors racing down his limbs.

The door opened with a crack. A small shaft of sunlight came from one corner of the rug. Time seemed frozen while John held his breath, awaiting the detective's next move.

"As you can plainly see, the wagon is empty," Barnaby said with a note of irritation in his voice. "Step aside and I'll close the door. You've delayed me with your false accusations long enough!"

"That rug," Kincaid said in a rasping whisper. "I'll have a look underneath that piece of carpet. . . ."

A wooden step squeaked with the weight of Kincaid's foot, and now John knew there was no escape. The muscles in his arms and legs tightened. Barnaby's warning that Kincaid had a gun in his hands told John that time would be measured by fractions of a second when the detective discovered John's hiding place. The man who fired first would survive their deadly meeting. At this close range, no one could miss. Steeling himself for the moment when the rug was thrown aside, John forced his limbs to still. The hammering of his heart was like the beat of a drum.

"There's something under this floor," Kincaid growled. "It's too high. There's a space under there. . . ."

John's lungs ached for a breath of fresh air. Sweat trickled down his forehead, cold, like icy raindrops. The moment of death was at hand. Waiting only added to the risks.

He jerked the muzzle of the shotgun upward, forming a tent with the Persian rug above him. Without taking aim, he pulled the trigger and felt the stock slam into his shoulder as a deafening roar filled his ears.

The concussion was trapped inside the wagon, adding to its fury, magnifying the sound. The wooden sides convulsed with the power of the explosion, sending the startled mules into a frenzied lunge away from the noise. The wagon jolted forward as John was scrambling to his feet. Above the din of exploding gunpowder and the rattle of harness chains, the crack of a pistol sounded and there was a wet, garbled scream. A boiling cloud of blue gunsmoke prevented John from seeing what was before him. Bits and pieces of shredded carpet swirled about, when something thudded into John's ribs, driving him backward with the force of a mule's kick, sending him sprawling on his back in the bedding straw.

Someone cried, "Whoa!" to the mules, though John barely heard the voice through the ringing in his ears. A wave of pain spread across his chest and suddenly, he could not breathe. The wagon came to a lurching halt, and for a moment there was silence. Despite the white-hot pain knifing through him, he forced himself up on his elbows with the acrid sting of gunpowder burning his eyes. His right hand pawed through the straw, seeking the Remington .44 blindly. He knew he had to be sure that his first shot struck Kincaid . . . make certain that the hulking detective was dead, and that he was alone when he found Barnaby's wagon.

His fingers closed around the Remington's pistol grips. Blinking tears from his eyes, he sat up and was rewarded by renewed stabs of pain in his chest. He had been wounded . . . he knew that now, but it was only a dull awareness as he struggled to his feet gripping the .44.

His vision cleared. Below the threshold of the door-way into the wagon, less than a dozen yards away, a man knelt in a pool of blood with his hands pressed to his face, rocking back and forth as though keeping time to a melody no one else could hear. His suitcoat and vest were torn to shreds, tiny rivulets of blood trickling down from the tears to his trousers. Blood poured between his fingers, coloring his forearms a glistening red. As the ringing left John's ears, he heard moaning. A pair of pulpy, misshapen lips tried to form words between the hands covering Kincaid's face, amid a stream of blood flowing from countless buckshot wounds.

A wave of nausea almost took John off his feet. With

his free hand, he steadied himself against a shelf lined with jars of Barnaby's potions. He took an uncertain step toward the rear of the wagon with the .44 aimed down at Kincaid, fighting the pain slicing across his rib cage.

Barnaby hurried around to the back of the wagon, looking up when he saw John standing in the doorway.

"My God, you've been shot!" he exclaimed. He glanced over his shoulder at Kincaid, then he started up the steps to reach John.

Only then did John notice the flow of blood from a hole in the front of his shirt. A dark crimson stain had spread to the waistband of his pants. "Are there any more?" he asked as Barnaby climbed the steps, his face pinched with worry.

"He was alone," Barnaby replied, taking John by the arm. "Lie down, so I can see how bad it is."

John shook his head, peering over Barnaby's shoulder at Kincaid. "Got to make sure he's . . ."

It was as if a black curtain had fallen in front of his eyes, rendering him blind. He was vaguely aware that he was falling toward the floor of the wagon, then there was nothing but velvety darkness.

It was dark when he awakened. Bright stars filled a cloudless night sky above him. A coal oil lantern burned beside him, and in the lantern's glow he saw Barnaby's face hovering over him. A scowl deepened the wrinkles around Barnaby's eyes. A sharp pain awakened John's senses and he flinched.

"Hold still," Barnaby whispered, his attention fixed on John's chest. "I'm stitching you up with a needle and thread. I'm almost finished. . . ."

John remembered his wound. "How bad is it?" he asked, his voice rattling with phlegm.

367

"You were lucky. The ball grazed your left side. It opened a nasty gash along your ribs, but I don't think the damage is permanent. I can see by these old scars that this isn't your first bullet wound. You'll live, Mr. Cross, but there will be some festering and probably a touch of fever."

John winced when the needle pierced his skin again. "What about Sam Kincaid?" he asked feebly as his mind cleared.

Barnaby pulled a length of bloody thread until it was taut before he answered. "He died a few minutes after you lost consciousness. He bled to death. Your shotgun made a mess of his face."

"Where are we now?" John wondered aloud, staring up at the stars to rid himself of a vivid recollection floating before his eyes, that of Kincaid on his knees in a pool of blood.

"We're about five miles south of Sutherland Springs. Some of the townspeople started asking questions. I told them a fanciful story, that the man you shot tried to rob us. I removed the warrant for your arrest from his coat pocket, and some money he carried. I thought it wise to take the saddlebags off the mule he rode, to keep anyone from being able to identify him. To the people of Sutherland Springs, he's a nameless robber. The settlement is too small to have a sheriff, so I expect the matter will be dropped. A blacksmith agreed to bury the body in a pauper's grave in exchange for the mule and saddle." Barnaby began tying a knot in the thread. "Tomorrow morning, we'll swing southwest. I got directions to a place called Legarto. From there, it's almost a straight shot across the desert to Nuevo Laredo." Then he looked up from his stitching. "I'm afraid you face eight more days of travel, my friend, before we reach the Mexican border. Some of it will be painful as your wound begins to swell. I've done about all I can for you now. I have a small vial of laudanum that will help with the pain. And of course, there is still plenty of corn whiskey."

Slowly, an inch at a time, John pulled himself up on his elbows to look at the scar across his ribs. His skin was bound together by green thread. Blood still oozed from the wound, dribbling down his side to the blanket where he lay. "Once again, I'm in your debt," he said quietly, lifting his gaze to Barnaby. "You could have surrendered me to that detective for a piece of the reward. You didn't, and I suppose I'll always wonder why."

Barnaby turned down the lantern wick, until there was only a faint glow from the globe. "Contrary to what you may think of me, I'm an honorable man," he began, pouring two tin cups of whiskey. "When I give my word, I always keep it, often at my own expense. Some may feel that I make a dishonest living selling curatives which have no effect. Others claim I'm selling nothing more than flavored whiskey to gullible patrons. The medical value of potions I concoct may be subject to some debate, but no man who speaks the truth can say that I've broken my word. We agreed upon an arrangement that would see you safely to Mexico. I intend to see that you get there, so I may earn my fee." He handed John a cup and rocked back on his heels to sip whiskey.

"I'm grateful," John replied, lifting the cup to his lips with a trembling arm. "Your fee will be paid, and you have my word on that."

Barnaby chuckled softly. "Not many men would value the word of a bank robber, Mr. Cross. But after hearing the story of your long string of difficulties, I'm inclined to accept your word. The war took a terrible toll on many southerners. Hard circumstances can force good men to make hard choices. I've made a few, when

369

times were seemingly at their worst. It is a dilemma I understand."

John savored the fiery warmth of the whiskey. He shivered once. "I'm cold," he said, then he drank again.

"I'll help you to the wagon," Barnaby offered. "I had a terrible time getting you out of there by myself."

With Barnaby's assistance, John climbed slowly to his feet. A dizzy sickness washed through his skull, requiring that he steady himself against Barnaby's shoulder for the short walk to the wagon.

He lay down on the bed of straw and closed his eyes, after taking a swallow of bitter laudanum from a tiny purple bottle Barnaby kept on a high shelf of the wagon. He heard Barnaby go down the steps.

It was inescapable, thinking about how close he had come to death back at Sutherland Springs. He had been just a fraction faster than Sam Kincaid. If his luck held, he stood a chance of making one last crossing of the Rio Grande. Luck, and the services of Barnaby Hill, were needed to see him safely to the river. In his present condition, he was almost helpless, not unlike his circumstances the day he was found by Caleb Parsons on a Tennessee back road, having been left for dead by a Union patrol.

The laudanum was making his thoughts fuzzy, but not before he had begun a tally of the people to whom he owed his life . . . a Yankee cavalry captain, Caleb Parsons and Sallie Mae, then a complete strange named Oscar Freemont. And now there was Barnaby Hill, upon whom his fate rested now.

He slept.

Chapter Forty

He had no sense of time. Days and nights came and went, marked only by Barnaby's announcements when he brought John food, or changed his bandage. The monotonous bumping and rattling of the wagon lulled him to fitful slumber, aided by sips of laudanum and generous amounts of whiskey. The jolt of the wagon wheels continually brought him pain. The swelling had worsened around his wound, and now a yellow substance oozed from between the stitches, smelling of decay.

On two occasions, Barnaby had halted the team to hurry into the back of the wagon. In John's fevered state, he had been only dimly aware that something was wrong. Barnaby covered him with the rug and the wagon would resume its travel. Only later, during moments when the laudanum had worn off, was John able to understand that a sizable posse of lawmen had been encountered on the road below Legarto, and a day later, a patrol of Governor E.J. Davis's State Police. Each time, Barnaby had been instructed to open his wagon for a search. And each time, the hidden compartment went undetected. John's woozy sickness while in the grips of a fever prevented him from being aware of the danger until it had passed. Once, he'd been alert enough to fully understand how worried Barnaby had become.

"They're looking for you everywhere," he told John in an anxious voice, as he changed the dressing on John's wound. "They know where you're headed, my friend. It won't be easy, getting across that river. I've got no choice but to use a shallow crossing, because of the wagon. They'll be waiting for you at Laredo. I'll have to think of something. . . ."

In his weakened condition, John could only lie atop the straw helplessly, passing in and out of consciousness, until the day came when his fever broke.

He awoke to find himself bathed in sweat, more aware of his surroundings than ever since Kincaid's bullet struck him down. He sat up and touched his side, blinking sleepily, discovering that the pain was less around his injury. The wagon rattled and banged over a rough road. Through a crack below the door, John saw sunlight.

Still weak, arms trembling, he pushed himself slowly to his feet in the swaying wagon bed, steadying himself between the shelves. One uncertain step at a time, he made his way to the door and opened it.

A stretch of empty caliche road touched the horizon behind the wagon. Desert brush and cactus grew in scattered clumps as far as the eye could see. He knew they were close to the border when he saw the land. But how much farther was the river? For now, he could only wonder.

He lowered himself to the floor and slumped against the side of the wagon, drained by the effort to stand and walk. Some time later he dozed off again with one hand pressed over the bandage.

He awakened to a strange sound, and found that he was lying on the floor. He listened to the sound closely . . . water was splashing underneath the wagon. Could it be the Rio Grande?

He tried to get up, and fell in the attempt, losing consciousness when his head struck the hardwood floor. His final thought was a desperate question . . . had they finally reached the Mexican border?

Someone spoke to him, and he opened his eyes. A face hovered above his. For a fleeting moment he did not recognize the face, for his attention was drawn to the silence around him. Why had the wagon stopped?

"John," a gentle voice whispered. "Can you hear me?"

He examined the face more closely now. A woman with golden braids of hair and a lightly freckled complexion watched him expectantly. He tried to clear his mind of worry over the absence of wagon sounds to study the woman. Something in his sleep-fogged brain told him that he knew her.

A cool, damp rag passed over his face. Then the woman smiled and his heart started to flutter with excitement. "Sallie Mae," he whispered. "Can it be you?"

"I'm here," she replied, and when he heard her voice a second time, he was overcome with joy.

"Where am I?" he asked quickly, glancing at his surroundings. He was in a room with thick beams across the roof, and he was lying in a bed atop a linen sheet.

"You're in Mexico. You're safe now," Sallie Mae answered, her warm smile filling him with reassurance. She cooled his cheeks with the cloth, then she bent over and kissed him lightly on the mouth.

"How did I get here?" he asked as his mind filled with a hundred questions. "And how did you get here? How did you know . . . ?"

Her eyes beheld him lovingly. "Your second letter said you were headed to Nuevo Laredo. You wrote me that things hadn't worked out between you and Elizabeth. I asked Paw if I could go. I told him I loved you

373

with all my heart, an' he gave his blessing. I rode that ol' red mule plumb across three states to find you. Got lost along the way a time or two. A girl travelin' alone can get in a fix now an' then, on account of there's so many soldiers. But Paw gave me his pistol. I got by."

Across the room, someone stirred. John looked past Sallie Mae to see who were there. Wild Henry grinned at John from a chair in one corner of the room.

"Glad to see you're okay, Cap'n," he said, standing up with a bottle of tequila in his fist. "Tommy Joe's helpin' the doc with his mules an' wagon. They'll be along directly." He sauntered over to the foot of the bed. "We started out to find you, Cap'n, when you was so long gettin' back. Just south of San Antone, Tommy Joe looked at a newspaper when we stopped at this little tradin' post. Good thing he did . . . you already know I can't read nary a word. But that newspaper said you'd escaped from the Waco jail, so we figured we'd never find you. Started back, dodgin' lawmen most of the way. When we got here, this pretty gal was askin' all over town about you. So we made the introduction. Missy Parsons has been real fretful, waitin' fer word to come about what had happened to you. Fact is, we was all mighty worried fer a spell. 'Til that doctor showed up here at the hotel with you in the back of his wagon."

"Barnaby," John sighed. "I owe him my life." He looked at Sallie Mae again. "He took care of me when I caught this bullet, just the way you did up in Tennessee."

Sallie Mae shook her head. "Your wound's healed over some. Time them stitches came out. Dr. Hill said he'd see to it tonight."

Relief lifted John's spirits despite the dull ache in his side. When he looked at Sallie Mae now, things seemed complete. "I wrote you another letter, askin' you to marry me," he said softly. "A man who was after the reward offered for me got the letter, instead of you. I'm sure glad you came. I've got some things to tell you, and some of 'em I'm not too proud of."

"I know about the holdup," she replied. "Henry and Tommy Joe told me why you done it. I'll be your wife, John Cross, if you've still got the notion. There's some who'll call you an outlaw for what you done. When I think about it, I tell myself it was just a part of the war. Yankees took your land, an' you took some of their money. Won't shame me at all to marry a man who took money from a Union bank. . . ."

He reached for her hand, then he squeezed it gently. "We can be happy here, Sallie Mae. I've got enough money so we can start a new life. There's a little ranch south of town. A big adobe house with lots of trees and a pretty garden. You'd like it there. We can raise some cattle. Maybe a few good horses too."

She bent over and kissed his forehead. "You can show it to me, soon as you feel better."

He heard footsteps in the hall, and the door opened. Barnaby and Tommy Joe walked in the room. Tommy Joe waved a greeting when he saw John awake. Barnaby came toward the bed with a yellowed newspaper under his arm.

"It would appear you're recovering," Barnaby said. "I'll cut your stitches out tonight, but first I intend to have a plate of decent food and a hot bath." He glanced down at the paper and opened it to show John the headline spread across the front page. OUTLAW JOHN CROSS ESCAPES WACO JAIL, it read. And below it was a caption that caught John's attention. COURTHOUSE FIRE DESTROYS TAX RECORDS IN COUNTY. FREEMONT RAIDERS BLAMED.

John took the newspaper. A trace of a smile widened his lips when he read about the courthouse fire. It was being called "Freemont's Raid" by the *San Antonio Crier.* The story related that a brigand by the name of

Oscar Freemont was seen breaking into the courthouse late at night, and that Freemont's whereabouts were unknown, having fled the city of Waco shortly after the fire.

"Freemont broke me out of jail," John said. "I owe him, same as I owe you, Dr. Hill. I've got a lot of debts to pay. And I'll pay them. Because I'm a man of my word."

Tommy Joe came to the foot of the bed. "You gave us a scare, Cap'n," he said, a dark seriousness in his eyes. "We never know'd you was thrown in jail, 'til we happened to see a newspaper on the ride toward Waco. Me an' Wild Henry decided you was in trouble, on account of you was gone so long. We'd made up our minds to try an' find out what happened to you. Soon as we crossed the river a few miles from town, we started runnin' into army patrols and bunches of lawmen. Right then, we didn't know they was lookin' for you."

"Good thing Tommy Joe can read," Wild Henry added. "Otherwise, we'd have ridden right into a hornet's nest."

John remembered Wild Henry's concerns about the forged letter. "I was tricked by the gent we saw in the derby hat. That letter I got wasn't from Sallie Mae. Sam Kincaid had it written, so he could fool me into thinking Sallie Mae was in trouble. That *comandante* in Acuna intercepted the letter I wrote and sent it over to Kincaid. I was played for a fool . . . walked right into Kincaid's trap. I was jailed and a judge promised me a swift execution. A handful of Confederates led by Oscar Freemont broke me out of jail."

Wild Henry adopted a satisfied look. "I know'd there was somethin' rotten about that letter you got. I could feel it in my bones."

John looked at Sallie Mae. "It's over now. There's no reason for any of us to cross back into Texas again. Everything we'd ever want is right here." He squeezed her hand again. "Soon as I can sit a horse, we'll ride south, down the road to Monterey. We'll look that cattle ranch over real close. Make an offer for it, if we're all in agreement."

Barnaby folded the newspaper and cleared his throat. "There is the small matter of my fee. . . ."

John turned his attention to Barnaby. "You've earned your money, my friend. Without your help, I'd be at the bottom of a six-foot hole right now, or waiting for a rope to be fitted around my neck. Soon as I'm able to walk, we'll go down to Banco Del Norte. Our money's locked up in their safe."

"No hurry," Barnaby replied. "I plan to stay awhile, until my mules are rested."

Wild Henry offered John the bottle of tequila. "You look like you could use a drink," he remarked. "This Mexican whiskey ain't half bad. Take a while to get used to the taste."

John raised himself on an elbow. He took the bottle, then he gazed around the room at the faces of his friends. He was alive and safe below the Mexican border. Despite the pain from his wound, he had never been happier. What had begun as a bleak trek homeward from Nashville was finally coming to a promising conclusion. There was just one dark memory he knew he would never escape. "Here's to Billy Cole," he said quietly, raising the tequila aloft.

A breath of warm wind fluttered the curtains where a balcony overlooked the main street through Nuevo Laredo, carrying the musical chatter of Spanish into the room. Off in the distance, a church bell tolled, announcing the evening mass. John listened to the bell as he took a swallow of tequila, hoping Billy could hear it too.

Epilogue

Seated in the shade beneath the *ramada* running across the front of the *hacienda,* he watched the boy play, chasing a baby goat around the sunlit yard surrounded by an adobe wall. The boy's yellow hair caught sunlight, turning it golden, like that of his mother. Watching Billy play was one of his favorite pastimes, as soon as he finished ranch chores. He counted the child as his greatest blessing. And now, Sallie Mae's abdomen was swollen with another baby, promising that soon, his blessings would be twofold.

Across the yard, sitting in the shade of a giant live oak tree, Mary watched the child attentively, smiling when Billy caught the goat's tail, only to lose it again when the animal bleated and fled to another part of the yard. Mary's presence was another bit of happiness he enjoyed now, acting as governess at her own insistence after she arrived in Nuevo Laredo. Until then, John hadn't known what a governess was. Having Mary to look after Billy Cole Cross gave John a feeling of completeness. He found it easy to forget about her past, in much the same way he'd forgotten about his own. Life at the ranch was good, filled with contentment. He knew Sallie Mae was the biggest part of it. With Sallie Mae as his wife, he found more joy than he ever thought possible. Then Little Billy came along, and soon there would be another child.

A pair of horsemen galloped toward the *hacienda* from a hilltop to the west. John watched the dust arise from the horses' heels. It would be Oscar and Tommy Joe, he told himself, coming in from a check of the summer pastures. It was an added touch of satisfaction that Oscar Freemont had ridden up to the ranch last spring, giving John the chance to repay Oscar's bravery with a job working cattle, and safe refuge from the McLennan County warrants for his arrest. When he thought about it, it pleasured him greatly that the ranch provided a livelihood and shelter for his family and friends. He seldom ever thought back to those black days after the war ended. There was too much to look forward to now. Remembering the past was a waste of time.

Wild Henry came out of the barn below the house, leading a big chestnut colt toward one of the corrals. He spotted the approaching riders and waved a hand above his head. Wild Henry had chosen to work with the horse herd, when responsibilities were first decided. Now he had a pretty young Mexican wife who shared the cooking duties with Sallie Mae.

Billy caught the kid goat's tail again and giggled with delight when the animal bounded from his grasp. The child's laughter was like sweet music to John's ears, a sound he would never tire of. Billy's voice brought Sallie Mae from the kitchen. When she walked out on the veranda, John took his gaze from the boy to watch her. The rounding of her stomach beneath her soft white cotton dress made her seem more beautiful than ever. In his heart, John knew that Elizabeth Lacy had never been as beautiful as Sallie Mae. He had been a mere boy when he was stricken by Elizabeth's charms, a boy from one of the poorest families in the Brazos River bottom who briefly caught the attention of a rich plantation owner's daughter, an infatuation that was never meant to be.

"I heard Billy laughing," she said, squinting when she looked across the sunlit yard.

John got up from his bullhide chair without taking his eyes off Sallie Mae. She had never looked more beautiful. He walked over to her and bent down to plant a kiss on her cheek. "He's learning the cowboying profession," he said, grinning. "Pretty soon he'll be swinging that lariat Wild Henry made for him."

Sallie Mae looked into John's eyes. "We'll have another cowboy to feed very soon," she said gently, placing a dainty palm over her stomach. "I can feel him moving now. I just know it's a boy."

He laughed at her seriousness, and was set to protest her calm assurance that their next child would be a son, when the pair of riders galloped up to the low adobe wall in a cloud of dust. Tommy Joe swung down first. Oscar dismounted more slowly.

"Counted thirty-four head west of the creek," Tommy Joe said, looking across the wall at John. "The calves are fat as ticks on a barnyard dog. They'll bring a good price in the fall."

John nodded without offering a reply, for his attention was drawn to the brand on the flank of Tommy Joe's horse. All their cattle and horses bore the Four Star brand . . . it was something John had insisted on, almost from the beginning.

He remembered the cool summer night when he gazed up at the sky, considering the brand they would use to identify their livestock on the open range around the *hacienda*. He saw the stars above him and remembered the stars and bars of the Confederate flag, a banner they had all risked their lives for during the war. Four stars was a number he demanded when he told

Wild Henry and Tommy Joe about his decision the following morning at breakfast. Three of the stars represented each partner in the ranching enterprise. The final star belonged to Billy Cole. No matter where his body lay, he would always be a partner to the three friends who escaped the bullets fired at them on that fateful day when circumstance turned each of them into an outlaw.

FOLLOW THE SEVENTH CARRIER

TRIAL OF THE SEVENTH CARRIER   (3213, $3.95)
The enemies of freedom are on the verge of dominating the world
with oil blackmail and the threat of poison gas attack. *Yonaga*'s
officers lay desperate plans to strike back. Leading a ragtag fleet
of revamped destroyers and a single antique WWII submarine,
the great carrier must charge into a sea of blood and death in
what becomes the greatest trial of the Seventh Carrier.

REVENGE OF THE SEVENTH CARRIER   (3631, $3.99)
With the help of an American carrier, *Yonaga* sails vast distances
to launch a desperate surprise attack on the enemy's poison gas
works. But a spy is at work. The enemy seems to know too much
and a bloody battle is fought. Filled with murderous rage, *Yonaga*'s officers exact a terrible revenge.

ORDEAL OF THE SEVENTH CARRIER   (3932, $3.99)
Even as the Libyan madman calls for peaceful negotiations, an
Arab battle group steams toward the shores of Japan. With good
men from all over the world flocking to her colors, *Yonaga* prepares to give battle. The two forces clash off the island of Iwo
Jima where it is carrier against carrier in a duel to the death—and
Yonaga, sustaining severe damage, endures its bloodiest ordeal in
the fight for freedom's cause.

*

Other Zebra Books by Peter Albano

THE YOUNG DRAGONS   (3904, $4.99)
It is June 25, 1944. American forces attack the island of Saipan.
Two young fighting men on opposite sides, Michael Carpelli and
Takeo Nakamura, meet in the flaming hell of battle that will inevitably bring them face-to-face in a final fight to the death. Here is
the epic battle that decided the war against Japan as told by a
man who was there.

*Available wherever paperbacks are sold, or order direct from the
Publisher. Send cover price plus 50¢ per copy for mailing and
handling to Zebra Books, Dept. 4160, 475 Park Avenue South,
New York, N.Y. 10016. Residents of New York and Tennessee
must include sales tax. DO NOT SEND CASH. For a free Zebra/
Pinnacle catalog please write to the above address.*

THE SURVIVALIST SERIES
by Jerry Ahern

Available wherever paperbacks are sold, or order direct from the Publisher. Send cover price plus 50¢ per copy for mailing and handling to Zebra Books, Dept. 4160, 475 Park Avenue South, New York, N.Y. 10016. Residents of New York and Tennessee must include sales tax. DO NOT SEND CASH. For a free Zeb Pinnacle catalog please write to the above address.

BENEATH THE CALM OF THE DEEP,
BLUE SEA, HEART-POUNDING DANGER AWAITS

DEPTH FORCE

THE ACTION SERIES BY

IRVING A. GREENFIELD

#4: BATTLE STATIONS   (1627-1, $2.50/$3.50)

#5: TORPEDO TOMB   (1769-3, $2.50/$3.50)

#9: DEATH CRUISE   (2459-2, $2.50/$3.50)

#10: ICE ISLAND   (2535-1, $2.95/$3.95)

#11: HARBOR OF DOOM   (2628-5, $2.95/$3.95)

#12: WARMONGER   (2737-0, $2.95/$3.95)

#13: DEEP RESCUE   (3239-0, $3.50/$4.50)

#14: TORPEDO TREASURE   (3422-9, $3.50/$4.50)

*Available wherever paperbacks are sold, or order direct from the
publisher. Send cover price plus 50¢ per copy for mailing and
handling to Zebra Books, Dept. 4160, 475 Park Avenue South,
New York, N.Y. 10016. Residents of New York and Tennessee
must include sales tax. DO NOT SEND CASH. For a free Zebra/
Pinnacle catalog please write to the above address.*